Iron and Gold

S.J.A. Turney is an author of Roman and medieval historical fiction, gritty historical fantasy and rollicking Roman children's books. He lives with his family and extended menagerie of pets in rural North Yorkshire.

Also by S.J.A. Turney

Tales of the Empire

Interregnum
Ironroot
Dark Empress
Insurgency
Invasion
Jade Empire
Emperor's Bane

The Ottoman Cycle

The Thief's Tale
The Priest's Tale
The Assassin's Tale
The Pasha's Tale

The Knights Templar

Daughter of War
The Last Emir
City of God
The Winter Knight
The Crescent and the Cross
The Last Crusade

Wolves of Odin

Blood Feud
The Bear of Byzantium
Iron and Gold

IRON
AND
GOLD
S.J.A. TURNEY

CANELO

First published in the United Kingdom in 2022 by

Canelo
Unit 9, 5th Floor
Cargo Works, 1-2 Hatfields
London SE1 9PG
United Kingdom

Print ISBN 978 1 80032 132 8
Ebook ISBN 978 1 80032 131 1

Cover design by Tom Sanderson

Cover images © ArcAngel, Shutterstock

Look for more great books at www.canelo.co

Printed and bound in Great Britain by Clays Ltd, Elcograf S.p.A.

1

For Ken

A note on pronunciation

Wherever possible within this tale, I have adhered to the Old Norse spellings and pronunciations of Viking names, concepts and words. There is a certain closeness to be gained from speaking these names as they would have been spoken a thousand years ago. For example, I have used Valhöll rather than Valhalla, which is more ubiquitous now, but they refer to the same thing. There is a glossary of Norse terms at the back of the book.

Two letters in particular may be unfamiliar to readers. The letter ð (eth) is pronounced in Old Norse as 'th', as you would pronounce it in 'the' or 'then', but in many cases over the centuries has been anglicised as a 'd'. So, for example, you will find Harald Hardrada's name written in the text as Harðráði (pronounced Har-th-rar-thi) but it can be read as Hardradi for ease. Similarly, Seiðr can be read as seithr or seidr. The letter æ (ash) is pronounced 'a' as in cat, or bat.

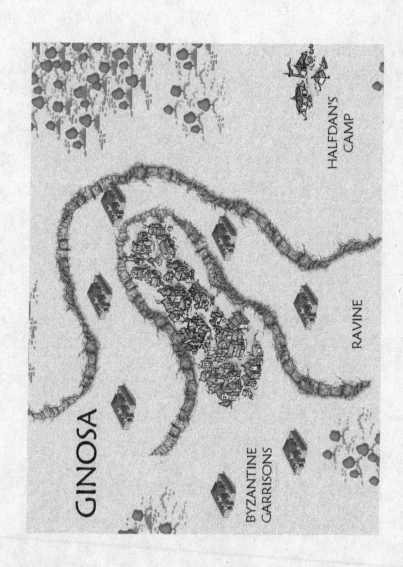

GINOSA

BYZANTINE
GARRISONS

RAVINE

HALFDAN'S
CAMP

Part One

ᚹᛟᛚᚠᛖᛋ ᛟᚠ ᛟᛞᛁᚾ

The Northman of Apulia

Chapter 1

'Hold steady!' the officer called.

Tyche's Arrow was the ninth ship to beach, crunching up into the soft, giving sand of the shore. Halfdan fought the urge to give commands. This was not his ship, not his crew, not his world by any means. He was a simple mercenary now, leading a handful of friends among a huge force of Byzantine soldiers moving to retake lost lands in Italy. His gaze darted to Ketil, who had been growing more and more quiet during the journey west from Constantinople – *Miklagarðr*. Occasionally Halfdan had caught Ketil staring at him, sullen, resentful. It seemed clear the Icelander blamed him for their predicament, believing Halfdan's decisions had dragged their band ever deeper into trouble.

'I love the sea, but it'll be good to feel solid ground beneath the boots, eh?' he pondered, eyes sliding to Ketil, who ignored him as usual.

His decision *had* led them to this, of course.

Oh, they had gold; they had more gold now than they'd ever had. With the remnants of the haul in bags organised by their former companion Harðráði, they were very wealthy men. But they'd kept the bulk of the gold concealed in their kit through the journey. For an unknown crewman to disclose his fortune was a sure way to be tipped over the side and left to drown. So, they had kept hidden the riches they carried and lived as poor mercenaries.

And despite their wealth, they had lost much.

Their fame, as champions of the empress of Byzantium and members of the *Varangoi*.

Their ship, for the *Sea Wolf* was likely heading north even now, somewhere in *Rus* lands, captained by the mad and dangerous Harðráði.

Most of their crew, all dead or lost.

For all they were rich, the seven of them were alone, ship-less and at the mercy of their travelling companions. Halfdan glanced at Ketil again, the rangy Icelander's black cloak snapping in the breeze. With every mile of sea, it seemed all the rapport and trust Halfdan had built up with the Icelander since the day he had taken *Sea Wolf* from the man was ebbing away. Perhaps, now that they were arriving in the war zone, something would change.

'Ketil may have strayed from your trust,' a stoic voice murmured at his shoulder, 'but he will come back, and the others remain your *karls*, Halfdan.'

Gunnhild was right. At least the others still seemed to trust him. She had been somewhat coy about what had happened prior to their departure from Miklagarðr, but from what Halfdan had gleaned it seemed that she had put herself at odds with the gods and risked everything she was for him and the crew, which was no small matter for anyone, let alone a *völva* who walked with *Freyja*. Bjorn, of course, was ever at his side, and Ulfr was determined to stick with him until they could retake the ship he had lovingly built with his own hands. Leif and Anna, perhaps, were a little less tied to him, with her connections to the city they had just left and Leif's eastern Rus origins, yet even they had made no complaint. In truth, there had been no *complaint* from Ketil, though Halfdan could sense the growing distance between them, regardless. He clenched his teeth. They were rich, no matter the conditions, and he would reclaim what was theirs. They had tales to tell in the mead halls of the North, and they would have many more yet. Here, in this crucible of war they called Apulia, he would make a new name for them and Ketil would cleave to him once more. For all the trouble he could be, after all they had been through together, Halfdan could not imagine a world without his friend.

His eyes drifted back to the land before them. Dry, hot and mostly brown, the countryside lay spread in a wide arc before the landing fleet. It was almost uniformly occupied, the Byzantine army of Apulia waiting in blocks and columns for the fresh manpower arriving from the east.

Halfdan had learned a little of the situation in the region during their journey, from men who had already fought out here. Once, long ago, the Byzantine empire had owned these lands, and now they fought to reclaim them from the Northmen – Normans, as they were known here – and other local warlords. Every small state seemed to have its own lord and government, and so the war was a complex beast with many faces, each of them baring sharp teeth. The Byzantines had been faring well until the changes of emperor back in the capital, which had led to failures of command and logistics, leaving the army hesitant, uncertain and poorly supplied. They had all but lost control of a huge island called Sicily to the south these past few years, and their control on the mainland had now devolved to strips of coastline on the south and east of the peninsula. The west was held by Italian nobles, with the hilly inland under Norman control. It was a mess.

But, when it came to war, a mess was a useful thing for a mercenary. It meant there was money to be made and, for those with no national loyalty, changing sides when it was most profitable was always an attractive proposition. Yes, Halfdan could lead his friends to success here.

The first ship to beach had been the flagship, commanded by the officer who had led this relief force from Miklagarðr – a smarmy and unpleasant man by the name of Pardos. Unlike a northern army, which would beach as fast as possible and move on, everything Byzantine was slow and regimented. The troops began to assemble at the prows of the ships, ready to disembark on the word of Pardos, who even now was striding down the ramp, followed by bannermen and musicians and colourful courtiers, making his way to meet the great figure awaiting him on the beach.

Halfdan remembered Georgios Maniakes from that dreadful day of the revolution in Miklagarðr, and the sight of the giant brought back hair-raising memories. But Maniakes was a warrior born and bred, as much as any Northman, and if there was one person who could perhaps lead an army to recover the empire's lost lands here, it was him.

It came as something of a surprise when Pardos's hand went up, signalling the disembarkation of the relief force before he had even reached the enormous *katepan* on the beach. Halfdan had been warned by one of the officers that they would be unlikely to set foot on land for at least an hour. The commander would have to report to Maniakes and await the katepan's instructions for the distribution and settling of forces.

Halfdan turned, brow raised in question, to Gunnhild. She had an uncertain look in her eyes – increasingly common these days and something that Halfdan had never expected to see. Still, she shook her head. 'Something is wrong.'

'The goddess whispers to you again?'

She clenched her hands on the rail, her fingers busily finding a substitute for the stout ash of her staff, lost in the east. 'No. But I have eyes and ears. This is not how this is supposed to go.'

'Hardly a surprise with Halfdan *Loki*-cursed steering our ship,' grumbled Ketil behind them, earning a glare from both Halfdan and Gunnhild.

'Watch the two leaders,' she advised, as the officers on the ship began ordering the army to disembark and drop to the sand. Halfdan and the others landed lightly, among the first of the newcomers to feel the ground of Apulia beneath their feet. Gesturing for the others to follow, he ignored any further orders issued behind them, shouldering the bag containing his gold and the rest of his meagre kit and grunting under the weight. Something was definitely amiss, he could feel it. The Loki serpent mark on his forearm was itching. There was duplicity here somewhere, and it could only involve those two men on the beach. They were nominally two officers of the same nation, and should be bowing in respect and relief, yet the way they were standing, the way they gathered their guards close as they moved, they looked more and more like two enemies warily approaching a parlay.

'Why does Maniakes have his hand on his sword pommel?' Leif murmured.

The two commanders met at the edge of the beach, where the sand gave way to dry, hard grass. Maniakes was already a huge, imposing figure, but standing on the slightly higher ground, he looked truly massive, towering over the oily courtier.

'A thousand men? I expected more,' he announced with no preamble. 'How does the imperial ignoramus expect me to reclaim his domain with this handful of soldiers? I expected twice as many ships, or more.'

Pardos drew himself up as best he could, a mouse standing off against a wolf. His men moved a touch closer, and Halfdan noted that most hands had now strayed to sword pommels. Both Maniakes and Pardos were anticipating trouble.

'Georgios Maniakes, it is my unpleasant duty to remove you from command as katepan of Italy.'

As these words, loud and officious, drifted across the sand, the entire army stopped moving – eyes widened across the beach; soldiers held their breath as one. Even the officers with Pardos appeared surprised by this turn of events.

'Don't be a fool,' the giant snapped.

'This is no joke, Maniakes,' the new arrival replied, his lip curling. 'I am but the messenger. The message comes from the throne itself. You are no longer katepan.'

'You, Pardos?' scoffed the big man. 'You could not reclaim your undergarments after a difficult shit.'

7

The courtier recoiled, face paling. 'You misunderstand, Maniakes. I am not your replacement. The office of katepan has been reassigned. Even now a ship docks to the north, granting your position to our former opponent, Argyrus. He is to be your replacement. I am merely here to oversee the transition of command and to ensure that you are on board one of these ships by sunset and sailing for Constantinople, where your presence is requested by the emperor.'

Halfdan flinched. He remembered the horrible, foolish new emperor, Constantine Monomachos, well, and he knew precisely how much love and respect there was between the fat arse that filled the throne and the great Maniakes. The general would be lucky to leave the imperial presence merely blinded. Execution likely awaited. Still, Halfdan found that he was expecting Maniakes to bow his head and step down. It was the Byzantine way. Everything was rigid, ordered and carried out according to law and tradition. It therefore came as a surprise when Maniakes snorted and straightened.

'Get out of my sight,' he snapped, raising a hand in warning, as though to slap the newcomer. 'I have a campaign to plan.'

The smaller man balked. Facing off against Maniakes would panic most men, but Pardos knew that if he returned to the emperor having failed in his mission, he would likely take Maniakes's place at the execution. He had little choice but to press his orders. He straightened, his expression hardening.

'You no longer command here, Maniakes. You have no authority.'

'Fuck off, imbecile,' the general sneered, and this time, the hand came down, delivering a stinging slap across Pardos's cheek. The courtier fell back, and his men's swords slid halfway from their scabbards.

'This is your last warning,' hissed Pardos. 'You know the officers and men will obey the emperor's word. They will see me, a scion of an ancient house from the great city, bearing the imperial insignia and commanding in the emperor's name, and they will obey me. *Me*, not some provincial general who rose to power through brute force and who still reeks of farms and horse shit.'

Maniakes stopped in the middle of turning to his men. Halfdan saw it: the moment the general had decided enough was enough. The young *jarl*'s eyes went to the soldiers behind the katepan, and then slid back to those still disembarking. Pardos had miscalculated dreadfully. He believed the men here would fold beneath an imperial command. He was wrong. Most of the troops were *Varangians* or provincial, local levies, or men who had been fighting in Italy for so long that now their main allegiance was to survival, which was clearly better offered by Maniakes than this new katepan Argyrus. Pardos was walking into a trap he had set himself.

'You smell shit, do you, Pardos?' the katepan barked. 'So do I, for your words reek of it as always.' He glanced to the men around them. 'Seize him.'

The courtier stared in disbelief as a score of battle-hardened Varangians swarmed past Maniakes and grabbed Pardos unceremoniously. His guards drew their swords but before they could come to their commander's aid, they were surrounded by grizzled soldiers from the katepan's army on the beach.

'You think I would walk back to that idiot's court and debase myself? I have seen a slew of feeble men on that throne these past years, but Constantine Monomachos is by far the weakest. No, he shall have neither my loyalty, nor my head.'

'Listen—' began Pardos, a hint of desperation now in his voice.

'No,' Maniakes cut him off. 'Hold him,' he said to the soldiers gripping the courtier. As they did so, the katepan pulled on his great leather gauntlets and turned to a Varangian standing close by, holding his horse by the reins. Rounding the beast, he crouched and collected a double handful of fresh, steaming dung. In moments, he was bearing down on Pardos, whose already wide eyes were now bulging in panic.

'Wait!'

It was the last thing he said, as before he could close his mouth again, Maniakes had rammed a sizeable handful of manure into it. Pardos gagged, trying to spit it out, but one great leather gauntlet closed over his lips, holding them shut. The man gasped and vomited into his own full mouth. Even as the giant held him, his other hand, still gripping more manure, came up.

'Now at least there's a good reason for his terrible breath,' Maniakes said, raising a chuckle from the men around him. As his victim choked, drowning in damp horse dung, the huge katepan pushed more into his ears, filling them both. Then, as Pardos bucked and thrashed, he smeared the last into his nostrils.

The courtier's eyes were filled with tears as the reality of his fate was driven home. He was struggling, his lungs burning, unable to catch even a half breath of air, dung filling his mouth and nose. He lurched and shook, held tight by the Varangians.

Halfdan watched, carefully impassive.

Pardos died slowly, in extreme pain; Maniakes holding his mouth and nose shut, sealing the horse shit in. Only when he gave one last jerk and sagged, dead, in the hands of the soldiers, did the big man let go of him. He tumbled to the ground, dung dribbling from his face as his glassy eyes stared up at heaven in supplication.

'You realise what this means?' murmured a senior Varangian at his commander's shoulder.

Maniakes nodded. 'I have cut my ties with the throne.'

'You could be a great warlord,' another man suggested quietly. 'Apulia is ripe for conquest, and it need not be for the eagle of the empire.'

Maniakes shook his head slowly. 'No. I am no traitor. I am a loyal son of Rome. I have not abandoned the empire, Alexios. I have abandoned a weak emperor. We need a new man on that throne.'

Halfdan kept carefully still. He could see where this was going, and a glance at the others made it clear they were equally aware. Sure enough, moments later a voice cried out the katepan's name. In a handful of heartbeats, the cry had become a chant. Maniakes's name echoed out across the shore of Apulia, as the army proclaimed him emperor. The giant waited long enough for the chant to fade, and then climbed onto his mount.

'This land will wait,' he announced in a powerful tone that echoed across the beach. 'We have garrisons to hold what we can, but there is a more important prize to be had.'

A roar rolled across the beach from the assembled troops. Maniakes waited, face stony, for silence once more. 'These ships will join our main fleet at Bari. There we shall put to sea and make for Bulgaria. Nothing will stand in our way. Constantine is dull-witted and selfish and should never have been given the throne. He has squandered the best of the empire and has little strength to put in our way. The best and hardest men in all Byzantium are here on this beach. We shall march on the capital and take the throne from the fool. Let there be a new empire. A *strong* empire.'

This last was shouted and was answered with a roar across the beach.

Halfdan looked around. The vast majority of the army was cheering and swarming toward the rebel emperor, but small pockets of men remained standing with their officers, less certain, less enthusiastic. It came as no surprise that the majority of those not flocking to Maniakes's banner were Varangians or local levies. The latter had no interest in the internal politics of the empire; they were only here because they had been called up for this war. And the former? Halfdan could understand well their reticence.

'Why do they not join him?' Anna said quietly. 'Even the Varangoi know of Constantine's failings and must prefer Maniakes.'

Halfdan turned to the former maid, who clung to Leif's arm. No wilting flower these days, still Anna was wary around so many warriors.

'The Guard gave their oath to the emperor. A Varangian's word is important and they do not break it easily. They may hate the emperor, but they swore their lives to him.'

Maniakes was moving now, wheeling his horse and making for the distant walled city of Taranto, the nearest Byzantine power base and likely the katepan's current residence. The army moved after him, cheering their commander. Units freshly arrived from the ships joined those that had waited on the beach and followed in the wake of the rebel emperor.

'What are we waiting for?' Ketil demanded, pointing after the departing general.

'We are not going with him,' Halfdan answered quietly.

'What?'

'Another imperial civil war is not for us, Ketil. We have other business.'

The Icelander blinked. 'Are you mad, Halfdan Loki-born? You *know* Maniakes and you know Monomachos. The giant can't lose. He will be the next emperor of Miklagarðr, Halfdan, a city that overflows with gold.'

'It is not for us,' Halfdan said again. He glanced at Gunnhild, half-expecting uncertainty, but her eyes were set, and her expression more so. She agreed with him with a silent look. And yet still she seemed passive, unassertive. Before whatever happened in the great city, she would have stepped in with some goddess-given wisdom. Now, he felt it was her resolve alone that she displayed. That worried him a little.

Ketil threw out his arms in exasperation. 'But we know Miklagarðr. We know how it works and how to squeeze it for gold. And if we help put Maniakes on the throne, he will be grateful. He will be our pet emperor, Halfdan. Think of what awaits.'

'I am,' the young jarl replied quietly. 'Our path is not back to the corruption of that great city. North is where we are bound. Somewhere in the North, in the lands of our ancestors, lie all those things we vowed to find. Hjalmvigi, the death-priest. Harðráði, who owes us all. The *Sea Wolf*. Our time with

12

the empire is done, Ketil. Apulia will give us what we need, and then we make for home.'

'No,' Ketil snapped. 'No, you're being foolish. We can go north from Miklagarðr, too, but pick up everything we need on the way and depart with the thanks of an emperor. You are being stubborn.'

Halfdan turned to Gunnhild, a silent request passed to her. She *must* intervene.

She straightened and turned to Ketil. 'Our path runs onwards from here, not back to where we were. Freyja wills it. The *Norns*—' she stuttered for a moment, a sign of nerves or uncertainty Halfdan was hardly expecting, but she recovered in an instant. 'The Norns weave us a path through Apulia, and that will take us home to find all that we have lost.'

Ketil fixed the woman with a flat look. 'You no longer walk with Freyja. I've seen it. You've not cast the bones in a month. Your staff is gone. Something you did in the city has changed you. You're not a völva anymore, Gunnhild of Hedeby, and I know it even if you won't admit it. You cling to Halfdan even though it's wrong, because you won't go back. You won't face the empress who abandoned you, and you can't look upon the city where you drooled like a lusty girl over Harald Fairhair.'

Gunnhild hissed as the gaze of the Wolves, shocked and stunned, turned uniformly on her. 'You will regret that, Ketil the long-legged,' she whispered.

'It is the truth,' Ketil snapped, turning back to Halfdan. 'She cannot guide you now, young jarl. She cannot even guide herself. She is lost. You are walking into the unknown. Not me. I am for Miklagarðr and the gratitude of an emperor. When I am dripping with gold, you will hear of me, for I shall have a new ship and a new crew, while you lie rotting on some Italian wasteland.'

Now, Bjorn took a step forward. 'You do not speak to your jarl like that,' he growled menacingly.

'He is not my jarl,' Ketil answered in a neutral tone.

While the others stared in shock, Gunnhild's face remained carefully impassive – though it had escaped no one that even Bjorn had stepped in to defend Halfdan and not the former völva. Ketil continued, his tone harsh.

'His Loki cunning allowed him to steal from me my ship and my crew. I have followed you, Halfdan, through some glory and some terror, but you are making a foolish choice now, based on your own desire for revenge and on the word of a woman who no longer has the goddess's ear. You *have* to see that I'm right, Halfdan. For the sake of us all.'

'No,' Halfdan replied, glancing at Gunnhild as he spoke, looking for reassurance in her eyes. He *almost* found it. 'No, Ketil. We go north.'

'I will not. Our journey ends here then, Loki-born, for we must part ways. I believe only death and disaster lie in your path, while glory and riches await me back in Miklagarðr.'

Halfdan realised that Bjorn was at his shoulder now, Gunnhild at the other. The pair had ever been his closest allies, the strength and wisdom upon which he had relied time and time again. His gaze strayed to Ulfr and Leif, and Anna, standing slightly apart.

'What say you?'

Ulfr looked distinctly uncomfortable at this sudden division, and well he might. He had crafted a ship for Ketil but had signed on with Halfdan. His loyalty at such a split could easily be called into question. Halfdan would have hated to admit how relieved he was when the stocky, red-bearded *Svear* stepped to his side.

'Somewhere north, Halfdan says we'll find the *Sea Wolf*. I want to see her again, not these shaky, flat-bottomed sows the Greeks sail. I am with my jarl.'

'Then you, too, are short-sighted,' Ketil said sadly. He looked to Leif. 'What of you, little Rus?'

Leif was clearly even more uncomfortable, suddenly having Ketil and Halfdan both looking at him expectantly. He looked back and forth between them, and then to Anna. Whatever he saw in her face resolved the matter for him. He turned back to them with a sad expression.

'My Anna is a daughter of the empire. I owe it to her. If there is a chance we can have a grand future in Miklagarðr, then I have to try. I am sorry, Halfdan. I really am. You understand?'

Anna pulled herself closer to Leif. Her expression offered an apology, but she nodded nonetheless. 'My heart lies in the east, Halfdan. You know that.' Her gaze slid to Gunnhild. 'I'm sorry. I really am.'

Halfdan sagged a little. To be without the fractious Icelander was one thing. To be without Leif the Teeth was entirely another. The diminutive Rus had been their translator, their teacher, and their knowledge throughout their time in the east. He would be sorely missed. But Halfdan had seen Leif and Anna growing ever closer since their time in the city and he knew now that they would never be parted. The Rus would climb *Yggdrasil* and conquer the nine worlds for her. Certainly he would follow Ketil back to her homeland. Halfdan sighed and nodded.

'I do understand, Leif. And Anna. I do. I shall miss you both, but I do understand.'

Ketil took a deep breath and fixed him with a look. 'I do not wish to part on poor terms. We have been through much together and I have respect for you, Loki-born. Perhaps one day the weaving of the Norns will bring our threads back together. That day I will be grateful.'

Halfdan met his gaze. 'As will I, Ketil. I do not want you to go, and you will be sorely missed, but if you must, then I wish you good fortune. May the Allfather ever shield you and guide you.'

Ketil bowed his head. 'Good luck, Halfdan Loki-born. Do not let these Normans and Italians ruin you.'

The four remaining Wolves of Odin stood clustered on the beach for some time, watching their friends march away, sacks of gold and belongings weighing them down as they trudged off through the sand in pursuit of the giant Maniakes and his rebel army.

'Do you think he's right?' Ulfr said at last, quietly, as their three friends disappeared into the distance.

'No,' Gunnhild said. 'Nothing good lies within the empire now. They will find only poverty and death. This I saw when I still had my staff, and I said so even then – disaster was all Byzantium had to offer us. If Odin is forgiving, perhaps they will survive and make their own way, but they will never see Miklagarðr again. On that I would lay my life as a wager.'

This seemed to satisfy Ulfr, and it certainly did Bjorn, who rumbled quietly and then turned to look about the beach. Groups of disconcerted, confused and worried warriors were gathered here and there. 'We will not get far with just four of us, my young jarl. There are others here. Good Northmen, but led by weak Greeks.'

Halfdan, one eyebrow rising as he turned, realised that Bjorn was correct. They had lost a crew and a ship in the great city. They might not be able to take a ship now, but there were certainly men. Svears, Geats, Danes, Norse and Rus, all here with their Varangian kit, abandoned by the army, unwilling to follow a usurper against their emperor. One such bunch, in particular, were seemingly engaged in a heated debate with the Byzantine officer commanding them.

'Shall we?'

Determined, with the others at his back, Halfdan stomped across the sand toward the Varangian unit. Seeing their approach, the northerners fell silent, frowning, and finally the Byzantine did the same, turning in surprise.

'What is it?'

Halfdan smiled. 'It seems the empire has left you to your own devices. My friends and I are heading inland. Emperors and usurpers be damned, there is gold to be made in this land, and we will find it. I have space in my *hirð* for any warrior with a strong arm, a sharp eye and a thirst for gold and glory.'

Uncertainty painted their faces, but he could also see interest, intrigue and even hunger here and there among them. The Byzantine officer, however, wrinkled his lip in distaste.

'Begone, mercenary. These men are oath-bound to the emperor. We will not follow the general, but we must maintain our garrisons and control the imperial interest in this land until the new katepan finds us.'

One of the Varangians behind him cleared his throat. 'I do not want to serve under Argyrus. He is not to be trusted. He has been our enemy these past ten years.'

'And now he is our katepan,' snapped the officer, and, turning to Halfdan, 'You will not take my men.'

'They have their own minds,' Halfdan said quietly.

The officer drew a short blade from his belt. Bjorn made to grab him, but Halfdan held him back. 'If you intend to use that, be sure to make a kill with your first blow, for you won't get a second.'

'You will not suborn the forces of the empire to your base plans,' the officer snapped, and stepped forward, bringing up his hand, holding the blade horizontally in front of Halfdan's throat. 'Step away lest I use this.'

Halfdan was growing tired of this day and of men changing his plans for him. He moved so fast that even Bjorn blinked in surprise. His hand shot out, grabbing the officer's fist over his grip on the hilt, and twisting. In the blink of an eye, the blade was now pointing at the Byzantine. The man gave a shocked squawk, but said no more. The sharp blade slammed into its owner's neck and drove deep, slicing through windpipe and throat, lodging in the spine. The young jarl let go, and the Byzantine spent a few gasping moments trying to pull his own knife back out of his neck before he collapsed, shuddering, to the sand.

Halfdan looked up into the faces of the gathered Varangians and frowned at the collection of expressions he saw there. Some were approving, some grinning, but many were shocked and had turned pale. He wondered at such womanish ideals for a moment, until they began to mark out the Christian cross over their chest with two fingers. He realised then that his arm was still up where it had grabbed the knife, and that his sleeve had slid back. The entwined serpents of Loki – a blessing or curse since the day of his birth, perhaps both – were on open display. He usually kept them safely concealed.

'Diabolos,' one of the Varangians hissed, wide, fearful eyes darting back and forth between Halfdan and the fallen officer. There was another flurry of crossing and many of the guardsmen began to back away.

'Devil spawn.'

'Cursed ones.'

'Pagans!'

Halfdan stood, impassive, arm still raised, watching them back away. Good. If they could not accept him, then they certainly were not men he could rely upon. As the majority of the Varangians moved off to join another unit along the beach, the young jarl eyed those who remained. As he did so, one by one, they reached up to the heavy, silver crosses at their necks and deftly flipped the pendants over, where they now hung as *Mjǫllnir*, the hammer of *Thor*.

Halfdan nodded. Twelve new men to add to his own. Sixteen was a small crew, but it was a start.

Chapter 2

'Tell me more about this Fuck,' Halfdan said, looking around the prospective camp site.

'*Fulk*,' replied the former Varangian with patience. 'Fulk de Courvaudon.'

Halfdan nodded. Of the dozen men who had joined him on the beach, Farlof was the only one who hadn't arrived on the fleet. He had fought in the area and, consequently, he had a passing knowledge of the region and its people. In an effort to work out some sort of plan, Halfdan had quizzed the man relentlessly on their slow journey from the beach near Taranto.

'He calls himself Lord of Ginosa, but that's pushing it really. He's more trapped in it than lord of it.'

'But who is he?' Halfdan persisted, as he dumped the two heavy bags with relief.

'Nobody special. Just another Norman warlord. You have to understand, Halfdan, they don't have the same sort of rules here as we did at home. Here you can be a jarl if you can seize and hold a town for more than a week.'

'But the big lords are further north?'

'Yes. The most powerful is William Iron Arm, at Melfi.'

Halfdan rolled his shoulders and started to rifle through the bags. 'Then we must stay on the good side of this Iron Arm. Gold can be had here, I'm sure of it, but first we need to jam a foot in the door. The Byzantines are of no use to us now. We need to find a way in with these Normans, and a minor lord is a good start.'

He looked around the camp again. Bjorn was busy arguing with Ulfr over a nice spot under a tree, while Gunnhild stood and glared at both of them. The others were generally settling for the night and sorting through their new acquisitions. They were, at least, well stocked now, which was a relief.

They'd departed Byzantium in such a hurry that they had left half their belongings there. On the journey west the ships had occasionally docked at ports and the friends had managed to replace some of their missing gear, but it was only now that they were fully supplied. They'd been careful to avoid the city of Taranto, where Maniakes would be making his first move to gather and supply his army for his coup, but had managed to find everything they needed from three small settlements heading north-west as they moved inland. Halfdan's prime goal had been to resupply and move away from the Byzantine-controlled coast. Then, he needed to find an ally. That was where this Fulk de Courvaudon could come in useful.

'What do you know of the numbers at this Ginosa place?'

Farlof shrugged. 'Not much. There won't be many, though, on either side. It's not a rich town, nor really important, just usefully placed. I've heard the Norman defenders referred to in reports as "a handful".'

'Probably not more than a dozen or a score, then.'

'I imagine not. The Byzantine forces around Ginosa will be more than that, enough to contain the town within a picket line, but the katepan has not bothered devoting a lot of men to shifting the Norman garrison. It has been a low priority.'

'Take a guess,' Halfdan urged, as he pulled out his sleeping blankets.

'A hundred or so.'

'Shite. Even with the Norman lord alongside us, a hundred would be too many. There has to be a way, though.'

Farlof glanced at the entwined serpent mark on Halfdan's arm. 'You'll find it.'

'There will be a difference between the two forces there,' Halfdan said. 'This Norman Fuck—'

'Fulk.'

'*Fulk*, is fighting for his life and his property. If he claims Ginosa, and he's trapped, he will be like a cornered wolf. And if it is true that these Normans really carry the same blood as Harðráði, then they will fight like us and stand like us.'

A nod from Farlof; clearly he believed so.

'But the Byzantines are just a garrison sent to pen them in, a small part of a very large army, with a small officer on his own, far from their leaders. They will be complacent and not inclined to push for a fight, I think. In such a situation, two of them are not worth one Northman.'

'That still does not even the odds.'

Halfdan sucked in warm evening air through his teeth. 'True. I will find another way.'

Crouching, he pinned a curse brooch to the mouth of his bag, warning others not to go through his things. There was still a lot of gold in the bag, and though these new friends might suspect that Halfdan's party was well off, they could have no idea just *how* well off. Gunnhild had fashioned a little curse brooch for each of them to prevent people rifling in their belongings. And just in case the new additions were not put off by the threat of divine trouble, Gunnhild had dabbed a spot of poison on each brooch, too. An unsuspecting thief would suffer for some time – and be rather obvious.

Across the camp, Bjorn was busy arm-wrestling with one of the newcomers, while two others swiftly built a campfire from the twigs and logs they found in the undergrowth. The wood was dry and old, this region having seen no rain for some time, and as Ulfr chipped his flint and steel together, the sparks took quickly and soon a roaring fire filled the centre of the camp.

As Bjorn and his friend finished their bout, the great albino winning as expected, the men produced the deer they had brought down a few miles back and began to skin and prepare it for roasting. Halfdan watched half-heartedly and almost jumped when Ulfr suddenly spoke, right next to him. He'd not heard the shipwright approach.

'Have you given thought to a plan? These seem like good men, but from what I understand we are likely to be facing odds of seven or eight to one if we go to help this Norman lord.'

Halfdan puffed out his lip and shrugged. In other times he would have consulted Gunnhild, asked her to walk with the goddess, but now things were different. Had she done something to distance herself from Freyja, or was it perhaps that Freyja just couldn't hear her in this parched southern world? Whatever it was, she had lost something that had been an essential part of her, and until she regained it he was going to have to be twice as clever and twice as lucky. He straightened. 'A plan will present itself in time, of that I'm confident. For now I'm going to watch back down the trail we took. Will you take a place on the path ahead? We need guards. This is an unfriendly land.'

Ulfr nodded, clapped his hand on Halfdan's shoulder and strode off. Moving back to his bag, Halfdan picked up his shield, freshly painted with his three wolves during the sea voyage, and a chunk of flatbread, and waved to the others before striding out to take a watch position.

They had chosen high ground for their camp. A considerably easier route had followed the flat farmlands up from the coast, but this land was still held by the Byzantines and there would be questions at best if they bumped into the empire's military. Thus they had climbed the low hills to the north of the road, following a minor track instead. In the last of the evening light, Halfdan could see the sea in the distance, a shimmering whale road, almost as flat as the glass windows of Miklagarðr. He could see Taranto in the distance, and the mass that would be Maniakes's army. Closer to, the trees hid much, and he could see barely two hundred paces down the slope before the path turned from view.

He sat on a rock and tore at the bread, shield resting at his side. Stuffing the hard but nourishing morsels into his mouth, he tried to remember the names of all his new men and assign to each a trait. In any planning it was useful to know what everyone was good at, so that assignment to a task could be swift and decisive.

He had no idea how long he'd been sitting there before he heard the noise.

At first he thought it some wild animal, scurrying about in the undergrowth nearby, but then a shape moved between the trees off to the north side of the path; a shape the size of a human. The bread tumbled from his hands as he swept up the shield, his hand going to the hilt of his sword. He turned, feet planted apart, and peered into the darkness beneath the trees.

'Be thankful I'm not an archer,' Gunnhild said with a strange smile as she emerged from the darkness. 'With a literal forest for cover, you choose to face a threat standing in the wide open.'

He relaxed as she stepped into the light. Even walking without the goddess, she was impressive.

'At least I was alert.'

'You need to be more so.' Her smile was gone. In her hand she held a straight branch, perhaps four feet long, hefty and with fronds still hanging from it. She used the overgrown stick to point back where she'd come from. Was she making a new staff? What did that mean? 'There is company here somewhere,' she said.

He frowned. 'Oh?'

'I found a ruined building just a few hundred paces down the slope. It's been used as a base by a small group of armed men very recently. The ashes of their fire were barely cold, and I found a broken whetstone.'

'Byzantines?'

Gunnhild shook her head. 'I don't think so. Byzantines like camps and forts and move in units. Bandits, I suspect.'

'Perhaps they were passing through and moved on?'

'Again, I don't think so. The building has been well used.'

'Let's warn the others.'

The two paced back up the track toward the clearing, identified easily by the flickering orange beacon of their campfire. 'Maybe we should put that out,' he suggested, pointing.

'It's too late for that. They're coming.'

Halfdan turned, frowning, hopeful. 'The goddess speaks?'

'No. The wildlife does.'

As she lapsed into silence, Halfdan realised he could hear birds scattering in the treetops and the crackling of undergrowth. The fauna of the area was being disturbed by something in the woods. Damn, but she was sharp even. They picked up to a jog.

Emerging into the camp at speed and breathing heavily, Halfdan threw out an arm. 'Swords!' he called. All eyes turned to him in surprise, but before anyone could question the call, one of the new men let out a cry as an arrow thudded into his upper arm.

Men dived for the ground and grabbed shields desperately as arrows began to thrum through the gloom from the darkened woods around them. The shots were sporadic, the work of just two or three men, and loosed at will, unlike a military unit's volley. And now, aware, Halfdan's men were getting to cover and defending themselves. Halfdan glanced across the clearing. All the arrows had come from one side. At least it seemed they weren't surrounded, but he needed to be sure.

'Ulfr and Sveinn, take the far side and search for men. Make sure we're not flanked.' The two Northmen nodded at him and ran for the edge of the forest, axes out. As Halfdan sized up the situation, someone called a warning and he turned to see an arrow coming straight for him. With a jerk of his arm, he pulled his shield up and the missile struck the boss, hurtling off harmlessly into the woods. His men were now mostly in cover, shields up. Only Halfdan, Gunnhild and Bjorn stood in the open. Halfdan turned to tell them to get down, but as he did so he realised the arrows had stopped.

There was only one reason for that.

24

'Here they come!' he shouted. He and Gunnhild ran toward the shadowy eaves from which the arrows had come, and as they closed, the others all rose, weapons and shields gripped ready.

The first bandit emerged from the woodland and ran straight at Halfdan, having identified him as the man shouting the orders. He was armoured with a shirt of thick leather over simple hose and poor-quality boots. He wore a cap of green felt and bore a straight, short blade pitted with rust marks. As he ran, he gripped the sword in a double-handed grip and tried to swipe at Halfdan's side.

The attack was poor, the move of a low brigand used to fighting unarmed merchants or farmers. Halfdan simply leaned away from the blow and stuck out a leg, catching the man on his shins and sending him flying to the dirt, where he landed hard. Before he could roll over or rise, Gunnhild took one step toward him and brought her branch down, end-first, on the back of the bandit's head.

By the time the two turned back, more men were bursting from the treeline. They were not skilled, but there were a lot of them, and one thing Halfdan had learned by now was that numbers made a difference. A nagging thought occurred to him as he looked at his men fighting, and he turned, brow wrinkled. Bjorn was not there, and for the big albino to miss a fight was almost unheard of. He felt a chill as his gaze finally fell on his ugly friend. Bjorn was crouched over Gunnhild's bags, rummaging. With a sinking feeling, Halfdan nudged Gunnhild and pointed. 'He wants your powder, for the berserk to take him.'

'Get out of there,' snapped Gunnhild, turning and striding toward Bjorn, but she was too late. As she closed, he rose and turned. He had two dark lines, glistening, smeared down his forehead and a messy blob that had probably been intended as a *valknut* on his cheek. His teeth were bared – gleaming tombstones in the night, with the odd glaring gap – and his eyes were bulging and wild.

'Shit.' Halfdan ran over and grabbed Gunnhild's wrist, pulling her back.

Bjorn stared at the two of them, his eyes dancing with madness, bubbles of snotty powder forming at his nostrils and drool hanging from the corner of his mouth.

'Back, everyone,' Halfdan shouted to the others, waving a finger in the direction of Bjorn, who was circling slowly, looking up into the night sky and issuing a low growl.

'What the fuck?' a voice demanded, but something about the display instantly unnerved them all, even in the middle of a fight. All along the edge of the woodland, the Varangians gave a parting blow and backed away.

The bandits did not press their attack. A couple followed the retreating Northmen, trading blows, but most of them were now looking past their former opposition to the huge, pale, white-haired thing standing in the centre of the clearing and growling at the sky. Just then, Bjorn let out a wolf howl at ear-piercing volume, eerily realistic. The Varangians who had been backing slowly away from the bandits suddenly broke and ran, more away from Bjorn than from the attackers.

'Bear shirt!' someone cried.

Bjorn's hands slowly lowered as his howl trailed off, and he stilled. Halfdan shivered at the sight. Bjorn was utterly lost to the effects of the powder now. As his gaze fell on the pair of them, Halfdan was painfully aware that Bjorn probably didn't even recognise his friends in this moment, and he most certainly wouldn't care. The great albino took a belligerent step toward Halfdan and Gunnhild, roaring.

The young jarl was under no illusion. Had the bandits not done something stupid just then, Bjorn may well have torn his friends to pieces. Thankfully, the bandits had no idea what they were witnessing and one of those at the fore threw a rock, which bounced off Bjorn's shoulder with a crunch. The enormous warrior turned his scarred face on the bandits and even in the gathering darkness, Halfdan saw the man go white as a sheet as he realised he had attracted the attention of what could only be a devil.

Bjorn focused on the man and broke into a jog. The bandit, to his credit, stood his ground for a few moments, until he saw the great, crazed Northman sweep a hand down as he loped right into the burning fire, lifting a blazing orange log.

The bandit ran.

But Bjorn was on him. Even as the hapless brigand fled, the big *berserkr* threw the flaming log. It smashed into the man, sending him, howling, to the forest floor. Two men ran at Bjorn now, both with a short blade in each hand. They dived for this great maniac, four gleaming weapons stabbing repeatedly. Halfdan watched them hit Bjorn, saw their hands rising and falling, and feared for his friend's survival. But then there was a howl of pure violence, and suddenly one of those men was flying backward into the trees, head at an unnatural angle, arms flopping, and the other was trying to run, while a great pale hand gripped his neck, holding tight.

Bandits and Varangians alike watched in awe and horror as Bjorn, bleeding in half a dozen places, lifted the screaming, panicked man, turned, and smashed him headfirst into the nearest tree trunk. The skull burst like an over-ripe fruit, showering both Bjorn and the tree with unspeakable matter.

Someone back in the forest bellowed an urgent call, and the bandits were running, then fleeing, back down the forested slope, cutting their losses. It was not over for them, though. Bjorn, howling again, dropped to all fours and ambled off in pursuit like some great pale bear in the undergrowth. Halfdan watched him go with a resigned expression.

'Should we not try and stop him?' Farlof breathed, stepping close and rubbing a cut on his forearm.

'You can try, but I wouldn't advise it,' Halfdan replied.

The two men fell silent. Indeed, the entire camp fell silent. A gentle breeze shushed the leaves high in the trees, and the campfire spat and crackled, but every ear was on what was happening out of sight down the slope. Periodic screams and shouts of warning were interspersed with occasional clangs of metal and muted thuds, but above it all came the roars and howls of Bjorn as he tore the bandits limb from limb.

'I thought they were a myth,' Farlof said quietly.

'More or less. I think Bjorn was born into the wrong age. Civilisation and him don't get along.' Halfdan grinned at his own comment. Two years ago, he hadn't even known what civilisation was. He turned to Gunnhild. 'I think you might need some healing salves in an hour or so. And something to ease burned hands.'

Gunnhild's face was a picture of irritation. 'Only that giant fool would ignore my curse brooch and go through my things. I shall be having words with Bjorn Bear-torn about his behaviour.'

Halfdan chuckled. 'You might want to keep that pouch on your person from now on.'

As Gunnhild crossed to her packs and began to tidy away the mess Bjorn had left, the rest gathered on the side of the fire where the few bandit bodies lay. Ulfr and his companion joined them.

'Nothing on the far slope, Jarl Halfdan. What happened here?'

'Bjorn happened here,' he replied with a grimace.

As if to illustrate his point, somewhere in the woods, perhaps a quarter of a mile away, a blood-curdling scream rose, only to be drowned out by an eerie howl.

'I've never seen anything like it,' one of the new crewmen whispered, his eyes still wide.

'And you never will again, if I have anything to do with it,' Gunnhild complained, tying the pouch of the precious compound and tucking it away at her belt.

The enemy dead were gathered, just three bandits to show for the fight, and then cast down the slope to feed the scavengers of the wild far enough from the camp to stay out of the firelight.

Gunnhild tended a number of cuts and abrasions, none of which would be debilitating. The worst was the arrow wound that had announced the attack, but even though the Varangian cried like a babe when she snapped off the head and pulled the shaft back through the wound, she announced that it was just muscle and flesh and he would heal. She bound him with a honeyed poultice and told him not to be so stupid next time, which even Halfdan found a little unfair.

It was not long before dawn when Bjorn returned, stumping up the slope like an exhausted bear. He was freezing cold and soaking wet. When quizzed on this, he was unable to explain it, especially given that every river or stream they had come across that day was a seasonal one, run dry until winter. On the bright side, the cold water, wherever he'd found it, had soothed his scorched hand. Gunnhild took the big man aside to tend to his wounds and reported later to Halfdan as Bjorn stumped off, chagrined at the tongue-lashing he'd received. Three stab wounds, none deep enough to leave permanent damage, and a lot of minor cuts. The worst injuries the big berserkr had seemed to suffer were from crashing blindly into trees in his wild pursuit, and he would be a colourful collection of purple and yellow bruises for days. Fortunately, his hand had been covered in dirt when he'd grabbed the burning log, and he'd only held it for moments before throwing it, so the skin was sore and red, but would not cause him long-term trouble.

'So he'll be good by nightfall?' Halfdan asked. 'We should be at Ginosa by then, and we might need him.'

'He'll be sore. And stupid. He's almost terminally stupid. But the worst he'll suffer is from the poison I had on the curse brooch. It'll have worked on him by now and he'll be shitting fire for days.'

Halfdan laughed at that.

Given the numbers that had been against them, they had come out of it well, and Halfdan was forced to admit that it might have been a much harder and longer fight without Bjorn's reckless decision.

Slowly, over the following morning, the new men who travelled with them warily began to come closer, even nodding to Bjorn and nervously congratulating him on a good fight.

As they walked, Gunnhild stripped the small twigs from her stick and peeled it of bark.

'A new staff?'

'Or a spear. I am uncertain.'

A völva's staff or a spear-maiden's weapon. He bit into his cheek. She was on the edge of something. Could he perhaps nudge her?

'It's a bit short for a staff,' Halfdan noted as they climbed the last hill, 'but even shorter for a good spear.'

'Then we will have to see what it becomes, won't we?'

Halfdan nodded. She was still quiet, somehow lost. But he could sense she was struggling with something, some deep decision. 'It is my belief that the goddess will find you and will tell you what it should be.'

Her response was little more than a grunt, yet as they walked, he occasionally caught her looking at him, narrow-eyed, appraising.

As they crested the hill, their objective came into view and he stopped and took a deep breath. Farlof, Ulfr and Bjorn joined the pair, the others falling in behind them and looking ahead.

A cluster of tightly packed grey and brown stone buildings around the tower of a church formed a small town on a rocky spur, surrounded on three sides by the loop of a deep ravine. Even from here, Halfdan could see that the streets on the hilltop had been blocked with rubble, carts and timber, forming defences for want of a city wall. Below Ginosa, myriad caves opened like mouths in the rock, a veritable city of houses cut into the steep slope leading from the town down into the ravine. And there, in the bottom of that defile that looped around the spur on three sides, small encampments gleaming with armour and bearing the banners and colours of Byzantine soldiers.

Ginosa.

Now they could begin.

Chapter 3

'It's sealed tighter than Ulfr's purse,' Bjorn rumbled, as they peered across at the town of Ginosa from the ridge.

'There is a way,' Halfdan replied quietly, eyes still picking out every detail. 'Gunnhild told us to keep looking until we see it.'

'My eyes ache. And my arse aches from sitting on rocks. And my head aches from trying to think of a way through that lot. And Gunnhild is just telling you that because she can't think of it herself.'

Halfdan smiled at the fact that his big friend's voice lowered to a hushed murmur at this last, in case he was overheard. Bjorn was afeared of no man born of woman, but Gunnhild put the shits up him regularly.

Still, he was right that they were no closer to figuring out what to do. They had been at Ginosa for two days now. They had been careful to stay back, out of sight, moving warily around the periphery. Had the Byzantine besiegers been particularly careful and had patrols out, they would undoubtedly have come across Halfdan and the others by now, but they weren't, and they hadn't. Like all Byzantines, their thinking was rigid. To their mind they had their enemy trapped in the town. The Norman wasn't going anywhere, but they needed to watch the town constantly. They didn't see the need to watch the countryside since the lands down to the sea were all in Byzantine hands, and so they remained blissfully unaware of the dangers lurking in the hills and ridges around the town.

Not that it mattered. The Byzantines so outnumbered Halfdan's hirð that any attempt to break into the town would result in carnage, and would be extremely unlikely to succeed. And so, they continued to watch, to learn what they could.

Halfdan could feel in his blood that there must be a way into the town, else he would have walked away by now; there had to be other minor Norman lords he could ingratiate himself with, after all. But this *felt right*. There had to be something he could do, if he could just figure out what it was. And Gunnhild, too, for all the goddess still did not speak to her, was convinced that there was an answer if they were patient enough to wait for it.

'We should just go,' Bjorn said.

Halfdan grunted. 'No.'

'This is a fool's quest.'

'No. If we want to go north, and we *do* want to go north, we have three choices, Bjorn. We go up the east coast, but that's in Byzantine hands, and they're busy launching a civil war. Moreover, a former enemy has taken command there. That's just a mess, and dangerous. Or, we could go up the west coast, but that's all city-states with local lords. There will be no opportunities for us there. It will be costly and slow, and as Northmen we will either be taken for Varangians or for these Normans, and I doubt either will suit us well. That leaves up the middle, inland. And inland is a war zone, dominated by Norman lords. A war zone is a good place to get rich.'

'Or dead,' noted Bjorn.

'I plan on rich. And this Fulk de Courvaudon is our way in. We need to help him so he owes us. And that means getting rid of his Byzantine enemies.'

Bjorn sighed and scratched his privates reflectively as he peered across the ravine. 'So we're back to the start: how to do it.'

Halfdan nodded. 'Fulk is secure. The slopes up three sides of that spur are steep and covered with those cave houses. They have good positioning for dropping rocks and arrows on attackers. The only real approach is along the spur from the west, the gentle climb.'

They both thought hard on that. The western approach had been the first thing they checked. The Norman defenders had fortified that end well, with a ditch, rampart and wooden towers, and behind that there was a wide, open killing zone before the blocked streets of the town. The Byzantines had clearly tried the approach and failed at least once, judging by the mess visible there, and had camped out of missile reach across the rise. Indeed, the Byzantines were organised into garrisons around the city, across that spur approach and along the encircling ravine's base in small camps. Halfdan had pondered the possibility of overrunning one of the camps to reach the city, but there were two problems with that. First, they would just end up trapped like Fulk, and second, the Byzantines were organised and efficient with their signals. Each group was close enough to support their neighbours in case of attack, which meant that any attempt to overrun a fort would mean fighting three of the garrisons rather than one.

Farlof had underestimated the numbers, clearly. There were, by Halfdan's best guess, between 250 and 300 men besieging the town. Far too many for their handful to take on.

'How long can Fulk last?' Bjorn asked.

'That depends on how well supplied he is. If his warehouses and granaries are full, he should easily see this year out and manage until next spring. I'm not sure what the water situation is, but there must be cisterns in the town.'

Bjorn nodded. They had learned the value of water cisterns in the Byzantine capital, where great columned rooms underground stored enough water to keep the city going indefinitely.

'They certainly don't get it from rivers,' he noted, pointing at the dry, dusty bed of the ravine, which had perhaps been a river so long ago no one could remember it. Indeed, the only water they'd been able to find, despite Bjorn having apparently fallen into plenty of the stuff on the night of his rampage, was a small, seasonal stream two miles to the east, which mostly ran underground in the hills, but surfaced a couple of times. It was a matter of great irritation for the men, who drew lots three times a day and had to traipse four miles to fill the water skins.

And that was another thing that was annoying Halfdan. He could assume Fulk had cisterns up in the town, and though it was difficult, Halfdan and his men were managing to resupply from that stream. But it took a lot of water to keep a force the size of the Byzantine besiegers going, and Halfdan simply could not see where they were getting it from. There was certainly no water in the ravine, they weren't using the same stream as Halfdan, and the nearest alternative water source was – according to Farlof, anyway – a small river at least seven or eight miles to the west. They had watched, though, and no party had been sent that way for supplies.

'It's to do with the water,' he murmured.

'What?'

Halfdan turned to Bjorn. 'The answer. The plan I've been waiting to make itself clear. It has something to do with the water.'

'My water wants out,' the big man replied, and stumped away, unfastening his trousers.

Halfdan turned back and watched some more. The sun was now setting on their second day in Ginosa. He had to do something soon. So far the new arrivals were with him, but a jarl only kept the loyalty of his men when he seemed to be winning.

Gradually the sun slid behind the western horizon, leaving the sky a deep, bloody red, which then slowly turned purple, then inky blue. Back beyond the ridge in a dell, the others would now be lighting a fire, far enough away to be hidden from Byzantine eyes. Food would be cooked and wine drunk. Most of the talk would be irritable comments about their situation. Halfdan decided he could wait to eat. He wanted to stay a while longer.

Nothing happened. The Byzantines remained in their camps, loud and bright, with fires and laughter and food and wine, taunting the defenders with their leisure.

After a while, as the veil of night truly fell, the camps' fires were allowed to die down, the music and festivities ended, and the army settled in for the night. Halfdan had almost nodded off with the inanity of his task when he heard footsteps and turned, hand going to his belt. Gunnhild was wandering across to him. In one hand she held her new stick. It was already starting to look impressive – smooth wood, straight and keen; she had begun to carve patterns into it, and had hollowed out a socket of some sort at one end. It would be short for a spear if she attached a blade there, little longer than a sword, but it would be even shorter as a staff. What was she up to? In her other hand, she held a steaming bowl.

'You need to eat,' she said, handing it to him and then sitting on the rock beside him.

He didn't reply, simply tucked into the stew, which was nourishing, warm and flavoured with some of the local flora that Gunnhild had expertly collected, guided by that seemingly endless sea of knowledge she possessed.

Instead, he looked over the top of the bowl, eyes on the now largely subdued Byzantine camp.

'Any moment now,' he said, estimating the time.

Gunnhild frowned a question at him, and he lifted the wooden spoon and used it to gesture across the ravine. 'See? They're changing their sentries.'

While the Byzantines had not bothered to post sentries facing the outside world, they were still keeping a careful eye on the trapped Normans. Scattered along that steep inner slope up to the city, they had picket posts of three men. Halfdan and the others had watched them. They did four-hour shifts, and rotated with other men from the camp, each small position watching some potential route in or out of the town up that unforgiving incline. They changed watches with such rigid timing it was easy to anticipate.

Bored, he watched the three men climb the hill and then the relieved soldiers descend, their place taken, all the time ladling the stew into his mouth until he was scraping around to gather up the last of it. His eyes followed every contour of the landscape, trying to pick out the climbs that each picket was guarding. The upper town was sealed, and what had once been a cave town in the rocks beneath was dark and desolate, probably abandoned when the siege began. The blackened maws of those shelters were scattered all across the ravine side, linked by carved-out walkways and winding stairs. He tried to track the line the descending men followed. They always seemed to go the same way.

He frowned.

'Now that's interesting.'

Gunnhild edged closer. 'What?'

'They seem to have chosen to come down a more difficult route than I would have taken.'

She frowned into the darkness. 'They use reasonable stairs.'

'But there is a straight and gentle slope they could have followed that they do not. Why not use that? Why use the steps?'

He felt his skin prickle. Excitement began to build.

'Why not?' he muttered, straining his eyes. 'Why not?' His gaze found that sloping line again and followed it upward. It passed across a stairway at one point and then disappeared from sight shortly afterwards, though he suspected it continued to climb around round the corner. Twitching with what felt like an important discovery, he now tracked the line back down. It passed the position of the pickets and then stopped rather suddenly, without reaching a door or becoming a staircase. Why?

He noted movement. One of the pickets was wandering down toward the bottom end of the slope he'd been examining. The pickets did move about occasionally, stretching their legs, as was only to be expected, but this sentry walked down to the dead end and then back up with purpose. Halfdan's face broke slowly into a wide smile.

'What is it?' Gunnhild asked.

'He's carrying something from that dead end. I would wager Bjorn's right arm that it's a water skin. That's why they don't walk down the slope. It's not a path. It's a water channel. Like those *aqua ducks* they have in Miklagarðr.'

Gunnhild gave him a warm smile. 'You've found how they're getting their water.'

He nodded. 'That's why it stops suddenly. It empties into a tank there. A cistern. Of course, the cave houses would need water. They have their own supply.'

'But it hasn't rained here in months.'

Halfdan grinned. 'So yes, the channel will be dry, but the cisterns will be filled from the winter. That's why we've not seen them going for water. They have it to hand at those caves. The pickets bring it back down with them. And if there's one cistern, there will be others. Could they be supplying all the water their force needs by just the pickets?'

Gunnhild shrugged. 'There are two camps at the spur and five around the ravine bottom, yes? And there have to be between a dozen and a score of picket positions along the slope near your cisterns. That's maybe three per camp. So each camp is getting water carried by nine men every four hours. That's quite an amount of water on a regular basis. It would seem you have discovered their secret.'

Halfdan turned to her with a wicked smile. 'Now I need poison.'

She nodded. 'Poisons abound in places like this.'

'The goddess will help you find them?' A nudge. A hope.

'My *wits* will help me find them. My wits are all I need for this.'

In a matter of heartbeats, the two of them were moving back from the ravine, carrying the used bowl, hurrying for the camp. As they reached the gathering of makeshift tents, Bjorn turned in surprise. Halfdan gestured to him. 'Go get the other watchers. I think I have a plan.'

–

They began at dawn, the entire group split into two. Seven men were sent to watch the town again, but this time they had a specific remit. They were to trace any water channels they could see and try to identify where any cisterns could be found. While those seven men went to work, another seven scoured the countryside with a piece of stone on which Gunnhild had scratched a drawing of a plant.

They worked throughout the morning, only Halfdan and Gunnhild remaining at the camp. While Gunnhild prepared everything she needed, Halfdan cleared a wide stretch of ground and used a stick to draw a rudimentary map of Ginosa. By the afternoon, he had been to check his details and had a good image of the town, marking everything of interest, including the locations of the garrisons in the ravine. By the afternoon, Gunnhild had a flat slab laid out with mortar and pestle, bowls, a bucket of water, knives and more.

Then, throughout the afternoon, the scouts and gatherers returned. The seven scouts had each managed to locate what appeared to be dead ends for the sloping water channels. They worked with Halfdan to mark their positions on the map. In the meantime, the others began to drift back into the camp with armfuls or baskets full of plants. Each time, Gunnhild took their haul, cast out three-quarters of it for being the wrong plant and threw away others that were mostly frond, for it was the root she apparently needed. She then sent them out once again, with a snapped command to pay more attention and a piece of the correct plant, so they could better know what to look for.

The sun was descending once more by the time Halfdan was content that he had his map just right, and the scouts had been sent to join the gatherers. The light was starting to fade a little when Gunnhild announced grumpily that she finally had enough. She then had the entire party, Halfdan included, working on the plant, cutting off all foliage, chopping, grating and grinding, mixing the powdered root with a number of other compounds from Gunnhild's bags.

By the time the sun dipped below the hills, all was ready.

'What is this stuff again?' Ulfr muttered, lifting one of the small bags of powder.

'Mostly *Mandragora*,' Gunnhild replied, packing her things away and washing the mortar and pestle.

'Never heard of it,' Bjorn put in from where he worked.

'Of course you haven't, you big oaf, because it's not found at the bottom of a beer barrel or in a whore's skirt. It doesn't grow in the North. I learned of it in Miklagarðr. It grows in all these southern lands. The plant is unsavoury enough, but the root is vicious.'

'What does it do?'

'In this dose I believe it will be far from deadly,' she admitted. 'One of these bags would certainly kill a few men, but they must by necessity be dissolved in the cisterns, and that will water it down a great deal.'

Halfdan looked across at her. 'Will it be enough?'

'I anticipate a very uncomfortable night for anyone who drinks the water. Beyond that I can confirm nothing. It is your best chance of putting the entire garrison out at once, though.'

'How do we do this, then?' Bjorn muttered, gripping the bag and peering at Halfdan's map in the gathering dusk.

'We don't.'

'What?'

'Not *we*. *I* do it.'

Ulfr shook his head. 'That's not bright, Halfdan. You can't do it on your own. You'll have to overcome any pickets near the cisterns. That'll be three to one.'

Bjorn nodded. 'For me that's easier than taking a shit, but for you?'

Halfdan reached out and plucked the bag from the big man's hand. 'This has to be done discreetly. If I have to fight anyone, the secret is out, and we've failed. I have to be quick, quiet and unseen. That's easier for one man than a group, and certainly easier if that one man isn't the size of a house and the colour of the moon, with a tendency to ear-splitting farts.'

Bjorn snorted. 'That is no way to describe Gunnhild.'

He flashed a grin at the woman, who paused in her tidying away to throw an icy glare his way. She tore her gaze to Halfdan. 'Come here.'

He did so, obedient as always, and at her gesture held out his arm. She lifted the other, looked at the entwined serpents and measured to the same place on the clear arm. There she lifted the sharpened, charred stick she had been using for drawing, and began to etch in his flesh. He hissed at the pain, for she was digging into the skin deep enough to wound, leaving a black line. Slowly, excruciatingly, she drew the three interlocked triangles of the valknut. When she was done and stepped back, muttering a prayer, he let the arm drop, the sleeve covering the design.

'Loki cunning fills your veins,' she explained, 'but you must have the binding of the Allfather also.'

For the first time since they had landed on the beach, he noticed something in her eye. She had invoked a god. Not Freyja, true, but perhaps it was something. A spark? A rekindling?

Nodding, trying to ignore the burning sensation along his arm, Halfdan collected up the six bags of powder and stepped over to the map. Looking at it for some time, he committed to memory the position of each of the cisterns. The others stood around, looking at him, in awe of what he planned to do. Halfdan steadied himself. It was true that, for all the danger he was about to face, it would be lesser for him alone. But there was another reason he wanted to complete this task without aid. These men had followed him because they saw the Loki cunning in him, but they would only stay with him so long as he proved himself a leader and a warrior. Now was the time to put any doubts about that from their minds. Just as Gunnhild had bound him to Odin, he would bind the others to himself.

Crossing to his kit, he found the darkest of his tunics. Pulling it on, he then moved to the remains of last night's fire and placed his bags down on the ground before dropping and rolling to and fro in the ash, making sure to scrub it into his blond hair and smear his face with it. Rising once more, coughing wildly as the ash clogged his nostrils and throat, he noted the admiring looks of the others. From what little he could see of himself, he imagined he must be truly dark and grimy. Shaking the excess off, he spat and blew black snot from first one nostril and then the other, then readied himself. He drew his sword and, with some regret, wetted the blade from a water skin, then rolled it too in the ash, dulling and darkening the glorious, eagle-hilted weapon so that it no longer gleamed. With that, he swept up the six bags.

He was ready. He carried only a bared blade and the bags, wore only blackened clothes and no armour. As he crossed the camp, he noted with satisfaction that he moved with near silence even here, where he was not attempting to sneak. With his blackened appearance, he would be hard to hear or spot in the dark. He moved across the rocky ground until the town of Ginosa swam into view. Lights were already flickering over there among the houses, and campfires were bursting into golden life in the Byzantine fortifications around the ravine.

On the rock where he had spent most of yesterday sitting, he carefully picked out the cistern he had spotted and allowed his eyes, straining in the gloom, to climb and descend the slope time and again, picking out the best route to it. Then, when he was content that he'd done so, and committed it to memory, he looked right and tried to find the next cistern they'd discovered. Once he located it, with a little difficulty, he worked the quickest and quietest route to it. Then, since he had plenty of time to kill, he did it all over again, several times. Gradually, as he did so, the sky darkened more and more until finally the black of deep night settled across the land. The Byzantines began their evening meal and carousing, and Halfdan rose. This was the moment for which he had been waiting: the time when they were at their most distracted.

Carefully, he began to pick his way down the slope to the ravine. This outer edge was not as steep as the spur upon which the town was built and, though his feet occasionally skidded on loose gravel, for the most part he dropped lightly down between tufted grass and dry mud. In fact, he moved with sufficient speed and grace that he was rather surprised at how quickly the ground levelled out; he reached the bottom of the ravine much sooner than expected.

To each side, he could see the glow of the campfires and the tents of the Byzantines. He could hear them singing and shouting and see black shapes, indistinct, moving back and forth across the orange glow of the fires. Crouching low, he emerged from the undergrowth at the outer edge of the ravine. The open ground between the camps was clear, and spotting someone crossing it would not be difficult. That he was stained black as night would be of some help, but his big advantage was that both camps were busy with their food and wine. They would assume the pickets on the inner slope would be watching for danger, and would not expect anything to be coming from this direction.

He could feel the Loki serpents on his arm itching, and the valknut of Odin was sore where Gunnhild had etched it upon him. He cast a prayer to each of them, and a third to Freyja for good measure, as he crept through the night, feet crunching quietly on the sandy ground. His relief as he reached a small stand of shrubs at the far side and ducked into their cover, without a cry of alarm going up from the camp, was palpable. His heart was racing, and he was starting to wish he'd delegated the task to someone else after all. If only Ketil were here. The man was black as a raven in hair and apparel, and his great long legs would have seen him across the open in half the time.

Pushing aside thoughts of a lost brother, he took another deep breath and began to pick his way up the slope. He had not gone far before he found the straight stairway he had marked as the start of his route. Padding quickly up the steps to the next flat space, he ducked sharply to the left and pressed himself against a wall. The doorways of these deserted houses stood open, like the eye sockets of an old skull. Checking inside for any sign of life, he noted the mess that confirmed it had been occupied until recently, and had then been suddenly abandoned. The people of this cave village had fled with the arrival of the Byzantines. Some of the buildings were whole caves, while others were only partial and had been built out a little with stone walls and a roof in imitation of a normal building.

Moving on, he climbed and jogged left and right, here and there, occasionally dipping into a doorway to catch his breath. He knew he was close to his first goal, and that was confirmed when muted Greek drifted through the night air. Reaching the next corner, he stopped and edged an eye around it. There was a small square here formed by the shape of three houses looking inwards, and the three pickets of the Byzantine patrol were sitting around a flat stone, playing dice. For a moment, he considered darting across the gap, but it was quite wide. Even in the circumstances, distracted as they were and darkened as he was, there was a good chance he would catch their attention. He looked about and smiled. Stepping back away from the corner, he found a narrow alley between two walls and nipped into it. With some difficulty, keeping as quiet as he could, he climbed the slope and stepped out onto the roof of one building, just five feet of flat stone, the rest buried in the cliffside. Edging close to the drop, he could see the three Byzantines below. Holding his breath, he sidled quietly around a corner and onto the narrow edge of another house, and then on again, picking his way around the square above the pickets, who continued their dice game, oblivious.

His foot came down into shadow, and there was a sudden howl and hiss. Pissing himself a little with the shock, instinct took over. He dropped to the narrow roof and flattened himself out, trying to meld with the stonework as the cat he'd trodden on emerged, angrily swiped painful claws across his prone calf, and then moved to the edge of the building and jumped down. His sword was held out at his side, and his muscles ached with the effort of having fallen without it clanging on anything. Halfdan never saw the three men, but he heard them. He heard them react with a shout to the sudden commotion and rise, a clink marking a fallen bottle. He even heard the rattling of two dropped dice bouncing away across the stone.

He held his breath again. One of the men made a rather unkind generalisation about cats and what they could 'fucking do with themselves' and the three men returned to their former spot, arguing about the spilled bottle and the lost dice.

Halfdan began to breathe again. He'd moved quickly enough to be out of sight before they turned, and they had blamed the cat alone. Thank Odin, Loki and Freyja all for that. Still, he lay there for some time before moving, and when he did so, he did it slowly and carefully, on all fours. He had rarely felt as much release of tension as he did when he slid around a corner, out of sight of the picket position, and slowly rose once more. He checked himself carefully. He still had the sword and all six bags of poison were at his belt. He'd succeeded so far.

Biting his lip, he slid on, dropping quietly to the walkway a little further along.

When he finally found the cistern, he was both disappointed and thrilled. It turned out to be a basin maybe three feet cubed, fed by a long, dry channel in the rock. He'd expected something more impressive. And yet that also worked to his favour. The tank was only a third full, and he could see the water line from before the Byzantines had begun to use it. They were running out of water! That meant that the poison he introduced would be much less dilute than they'd thought. He lifted the bag and undid the string, then tipped it out over the small water supply. He was about to throw it all in when a new thought struck him, and he stopped when only half the powder had fallen into the water, slowly dissolving. If all the cisterns were like this, they probably served only two or three houses. But the amount taken from this one would never have kept those Byzantines alive for weeks. And since there was no other river or spring nearby, then the answer was simple: there were a lot more of these cisterns than the seven they had counted. They were small, but there were many. He cursed silently. He would have to be sparing with his poison, and now he would have to search as he went, forgetting his planned route, and simply seeking out each cistern as he moved.

He took a deep breath and one last look into the water tank. Despite the brown colour of the powder, it had become more or less invisible in the slightly murky water. It would certainly not draw attention. How was he going to find all the tanks in the few hours of darkness he could count upon? He rubbed his eyes, then regretted it, for the soot made him blink for a while. As his eyes readjusted, they fell upon the narrow water channel that filled this tank during the rainy months.

A thought struck him, and he smiled.

Instead of following his planned route, he followed the water channel, with some difficulty, stepping carefully. A way back across the hillside, just within earshot of the Byzantine sentries, he found it. A second channel veered off this one, presumably to fill another cistern.

Of course. If you were going to create a water system for a place like this, you would use as few channels to fill as many cisterns as possible. It was highly likely every water channel and tank was connected to another somewhere. All he had to do was follow them and be sparing with his poison.

Odin was with him tonight.

Chapter 4

'Do we go?'

Halfdan turned to Bjorn and smiled. 'I think it's time. The best we're going to get, anyway.'

The pair looked back once more at the ravine below. Their plan appeared to have worked.

Halfdan had located and poisoned fifteen cisterns under cover of darkness the previous night, ranging from small ones two feet across, to another that was so deep he could not see the bottom. There had been a few touch-and-go moments, but once he'd got used to the layout of the cave town, it had been relatively simple to skip around the picket positions without attracting attention. A single figure, blackened in the darkness, he had moved like a ghost through the place, unseen and unheard. There were at least two cisterns he knew he'd missed, which irritated him, but they had been within clear sight of enemy pickets and so he'd stayed away from them. Still, he had poisoned the vast majority of the Byzantine water supply, and then slipped back across the ravine, between the enemy camps, and scampered up to the ridge and the rest of the waiting Northmen, the enemy oblivious to the entire expedition.

Then they had sat and waited as the Byzantine pickets periodically ferried their tainted water supplies down to the main camps with each change of manpower. The sun had risen to show little change in the camps, which worried Halfdan. Had his poison been so dilute as to have no effect? He'd voiced his concerns to Gunnhild, but she had been confident.

'Have patience. The dosage was ample, but it will take time for them to supply sufficient to the camp to bring about the desired effect.'

And so they had continued to watch throughout the day, taking shifts in order to catch up on sleep. Despite Gunnhild's reassurance, the potential faults in his plan rankled, and Halfdan had found himself wondering whether the others were already assuming he had failed. Indeed, the sun was already descending once again when something finally happened.

It began slowly. First, they noticed one of the replacement picket units failed to leave the camp, and they had watched as the three men on guard up the slope paced about until finally they stomped down to the nearest camp to find out what had happened to their relief. Then there had been a surge of activity in the camp. The latrine, which had been dug fresh yesterday morning, was suddenly the focus of much of the camp's personnel. An officer had made his way to the centre of the camp and stood there in the open, bellowing angry orders until he had suddenly folded up and collapsed to the ground. By then it was happening everywhere. The camp was in chaos, men hurrying this way and that, the latrine too busy and men simply crouching and taking a shit outside their tents. The sounds of shouting, wailing, groaning, farting, vomiting and general panic echoed out across the ravine. Most interestingly, odd figures seemed to have abandoned the camp entirely to wander out blindly into the afternoon sunlight alone. And it was not just the nearest camp. The volume of the chaos was such that they could tell similar things were happening in the other camps.

Small pockets of unaffected men were trying to form up and keep their own people at bay with spears, worried about catching whatever was doing this, and here and there an officer desperately tried to regain control.

'There's still a lot of them,' Farlof murmured, 'and a man with the shits can still swing an axe.'

Gunnhild gave him a hard look. 'Have confidence in my preparations,' she advised.

'All right,' Halfdan said, rising from the rock on which he'd been sitting, 'you all know the plan. We hit the camp below and give no quarter. If there's little resistance and no activity in the town, we then split into two groups, one led by me, the other by Bjorn, and we move to each adjacent camp. We keep going until they're done or until this Lord Fuck comes down from his hill. For Odin.'

'Odin!' bellowed the rest, heedless now of being heard in the ravine.

In moments they were running, Halfdan in the lead as usual, Bjorn close at his heel, salivating with the anticipation of violence, Ulfr behind, barking oaths to the gods. They hit the scree at the top of the slope and slowed of necessity, feet slipping here and there, keeping their footing with difficulty as they skittered down the incline and into the hard, tufty grass below. No alarm call went up, despite the obvious visibility of sixteen armoured killers – bellowing the name of ancient gods as they hurtled down the side of the ravine – bearing down on the camp with blades drawn.

Forty, Halfdan reckoned, in this camp. Many more around the ravine, but forty here. A sensible jarl would never pit his sixteen against more than two-to-one odds, but then this was no straight battle.

The sun was still warm and the ground was baking as Halfdan reached the point where the slope levelled out a little and picked his man. There were no shield-wall tactics here, this was a good old-fashioned melee, every man for himself. Each of the attackers, upon reaching the ravine bottom, selected a target and ran at him.

Halfdan's first choice was an officer. It was always good to take on the most important or powerful enemies first. The Byzantine was young for his rank, though in fairness he was probably the same age as Halfdan. Northmen ruled when they had the strength, without having to endure the years of advancing through ranks that the empire required. The man was armoured in a cuirass of gold-coloured scales, red silks and linens visible between the gleaming protection. His face was clean-shaven and unmarked beneath a decorated steel helmet, lined with more red silk, a chain veil hanging from the rear to protect his neck. He had a fine sword buckled at his side, but in his hand he held only a short knife, already gleaming wet and red. Even as he ran to meet the approaching officer, Halfdan registered with some surprise the deep wound on the man's left wrist. He seemed to have made a spirited attempt to cut off his own hand.

'Mother?' frowned the officer, stumbling to a halt in front of Halfdan, face folding into a frown of confusion, blood running from his half-severed hand. The man's face broke into a wide smile. '*Mother!*'

He was still smiling as Halfdan's blade lanced out sharply at neck height, slamming into that unbearded throat and tearing the life from the young man. The jarl ripped the blade free and made to deliver a second blow just to be sure, but the man simply collapsed to his knees, looking up happily at his killer, his mouth forming the word 'mother', though his voice no longer worked.

Off to the right, Bjorn had found a pair of big bruisers who seemed little affected by the poison, and was trading blows with them, bellowing derogatory comments about the size of a Byzantine's manhood. To the left, Gunnhild worked like some battle demon, knife in one hand, short staff in the other, spinning and swiping, battering the life out of a man. All around, the Northmen were scything through the Byzantine unit with ease.

A soldier who had been turning in slow circles, looking at his hand in fascination, suddenly seemed to spot Halfdan. He became focused instantly, roaring a curse in the name of the *Theotokos Pammakaristos* and tearing his sword from its sheath. He ran at Halfdan, who angled to meet him. Then, just before they clashed, the man suddenly stopped dead in his tracks, his dilated eyes widening. There was a strange, loud creaking noise, and suddenly the man soiled himself. Halfdan pulled himself up short from his charge, staring in fascinated horror. The Byzantine lowered his sword, and a look of immense relief flooded his features as watery shit splashed down his legs, soaking his tunic and breeches and running like a river down over his feet. He made a strange, happy, keening noise and chuckled.

The smell suddenly hit Halfdan and he gagged, turning away and leaving this mess of a man for someone else. A small group of Byzantines was gathering, armed and prepared, clearly untouched by the poison, and Halfdan turned and made for them, aware that others were doing the same. As he jogged that way, a man danced out in front of him, no sword in evidence, but his shield held across his front. The man smelled not dissimilar to the unfortunate Halfdan had just avoided, and as he leapt in front of the jarl with a triumphant 'Ha!', his right hand emerged from behind the shield, brandishing a long, wooden ladle.

'Now, you'll pay, Uncle Leo,' the man howled and lunged at Halfdan. The jarl ignored the ladle, rather making sure that the flailing shield with the iron boss and the hide edging came nowhere near him. His sword bit into the man's side, neatly finding a weak spot in the padded gambeson he wore and sinking deep into flesh. As Halfdan turned the blade inside, dealing the most damage possible, the Byzantine laughed gaily and smacked him on the forehead with the wooden spoon.

The young jarl frowned in surprise. He made to pull the sword out, but the soldier had let go of his shield and his left arm came round, gripping the hilt of Halfdan's sword and holding it deep in his side, stopping it being withdrawn. As he kept the tool of his own demise in place, Halfdan struggling to pull it free, the Byzantine continued to laugh like an idiot, repeatedly smacking the wooden spoon on his killer's forehead. Slowly, the smacking lessened as the light in the man's eyes went out, and his grip on Halfdan's blade loosened. Finally, he tore the sword clear of the dying fool and stepped back.

Despite all the danger around them, the stink of death and shit, the heat of the day, and the strain of his muscles, it was the unpleasant throbbing in Halfdan's head that most irritated him. With an angry rumble, he kicked the expiring heap and ran on toward that small stand of healthy Byzantines. Bjorn jogged past him, laughing, a great axe in one hand and half an arm in the other, then veered off with a bellow to Odin when he saw someone big enough to present a challenge. Ulfr was nearby, hamstringing a howling Byzantine, and the rest were all over the camp now, butchering the unfortunates.

Again, before Halfdan could reach that small knot of men, a lone fool ran at him. Drool hung in tendrils from both sides of the man's mouth, dangling from his beard, his mouth wide and leering. He had a sword in his hand, but no shield, and shouted, 'Come to Isaac, young Varangian,' as he leapt.

For just a moment, Halfdan thought this man might be a problem, more *compos mentis* than his fellows, but as he closed, the man threw his arms wide and dived into a hug, embracing the startled jarl. The man held tight, giggling, and it took some work for Halfdan to angle his sword sufficiently to deliver a blow. His grip loosened as the man frowned, a gurgling noise rising in his throat, and as he let go and stepped away, Halfdan delivered a killing blow.

Heedless of the man's last moments, he pushed the hugger away and ran on.

Farlof and two others had already reached the group of eight men who had formed into a small, arced shield wall, their backs to a fence of sharpened stakes. The three were busy exchanging blows with the Byzantines, and from the activity it was clear that these men were not in the least deranged and sick. Perhaps they had not yet sampled the camp water supplies. The eight defenders were focused on the three Northmen attacking them, with that rigidity of combat bred into Byzantine armies, and Halfdan smiled to himself. They felt safe facing smaller numbers with their backs to the defences. More fool them.

Angling away at the last moment, Halfdan ran to engage another of the sick warriors. He attracted only passing attention from the man at the end of the curved shield wall, who then, realising Halfdan wasn't coming for him, ignored him further and turned back to the three men on them.

The wobbly soldier Halfdan had now set his sights upon came barrelling over to him, howling something unintelligible and, miraculously, given the state of him, wielding both sword and shield and even holding the weapon the right way round. Halfdan lifted his own shield ready to block the blow, but the man's swing was hopelessly wild, his vision seemingly blurred from the way he was blinking and failing to focus on Halfdan's face. The jarl waited only a moment for an opportunity to present itself and then stabbed, his ancient blade slicing deep into the man's side below the raised sword arm. The man seemed confused by the blow, looked down with a frown at the sword being pulled out of his flesh, then back up at Halfdan. Then, without warning, he vomited copiously and at range. Halfdan stood no chance. The wave of bile and half-digested food splashed him full in the face and all down his front. Cursing, Halfdan spat and shook his head to remove the worst of it and as he looked back up, his opponent was smiling widely.

'That's better,' the man said, and then folded up and died from the savage wound.

Halfdan turned. The defensive shield wall had dropped to six men, but one of the Varangians attacking them was now sitting on the ground, clutching his side and moaning. Ducking a confused and flailing Byzantine and leaving him for someone else, Halfdan quickly skirted the clash, still spitting and blinking away the mess that coated him, until he passed inside the defended enclosure. The six intact Byzantines now had their backs to him, a defence formed of sharpened stakes like a line of wooden caltrops between him and them. Taking a deep breath, Halfdan walked back eight paces, readied himself, and ran.

Reaching the stake fence, he leapt, praying to Odin that he had the height. He almost fell. As he sailed out over the line of points, his left foot brushed the jagged timber, and had he not reacted in an instant and jerked his leg up, he would likely have ended up a bleeding mess, impaled on the sharpened points. Instead, as planned, he hurtled across the line, sword held out to one side and shield in front of him, braced against his shoulder. He hit the line of defending Byzantines in the back like a catapult shot. Two of them were thrown forward onto their faces, one was pushed onto Farlof's waiting blade, and another was slammed into the Varangian who was trying to stand once more, the pair of them going down in a heap together.

Ignoring the downed men, Halfdan, almost falling himself, skidded to a halt, then turned and swung. It was not a good blow, for he'd not really yet recovered his balance, but it did get the remaining man to turn to face him – a fatal mistake. Behind him, Farlof staggered back, pulling his sword from the dead Byzantine and then neatly reached round and cut this one's throat. The soldier stared in horror and gurgled, staggering left and right. Halfdan ignored him and stepped over to the fallen pair, dispatching them swiftly and efficiently.

Within heartbeats, the one gathering of unaffected soldiers had been dealt with, and Farlof nodded his appreciation to Halfdan for his part in finishing it. Halfdan turned slowly, taking in the situation. There were hardly any of the enemy still standing, and that was only if you counted the pair that Bjorn held upright, one in each hand, smashing their heads together.

His gaze slid past that and into the now deserted camp. *Almost* deserted.

At the centre stood a single tent, larger than the others, presumably the quarters of the commander. In front of the tent, a small, wiry, almost naked man crouched with a wicked-looking spear. He was swarthy and clad only in a dusty, stained loincloth and an iron collar, from which a long chain led to a piton driven deep into the ground. As the figure spotted Halfdan walking toward him, he hissed and turned, the spear dancing as though it were little more than a knife.

Halfdan stalked toward him, his sword and shield ready. The creature spun and whirled the spear with clear expertise. This was going to be a proper challenge, even anchored as he was. Halfdan smiled to himself. Single combats like this were the sort of thing that made men appreciate a jarl. He readied himself. The spear swung out at ankle height as he reached its limit and Halfdan jumped lithely over the weapon. But before he could close to deliver a hit of his own, the spear was somehow whipped around and came again, this time at belly height. Caught by surprise, Halfdan lumbered rather inelegantly out of the way, the creature's strike close enough that he heard tearing as the point of the spear ripped through the cuff of his sleeve. Even as he recovered and turned for another go, that wicked weapon had spun once more and was coming again.

The blow never landed, and Halfdan stared in shock as a pulverized, bloody corpse, missing half an arm, hit the spear-wielding thing full in the face, throwing it back. Halfdan turned, blinking, to see Bjorn striding toward him.

'That thing was mine,' he complained.

'I don't see your name on him.'

'You know all the big ones are mine. It goes without saying.'

'This one is little.'

'You know what I mean,' snapped Bjorn, irritably.

The strange man was recovering fast, pushing off the bloody body and feeling around in the dust for the spear that had been knocked from his grasp. Aware of how dangerous the man was, Halfdan leapt over and kicked at the weapon, skittering it across the gritty surface and out of the reach of the chained man. As he crossed to the weapon and looked at it, Bjorn walked over to the strange figure and reached out. The thing flailed, hissed and rattled off in some other language, trying to claw at Bjorn's face, but the big warrior ignored the scratching and gripped him in both hands, then yanked his head through a half turn, snapping his spine and then dropping him like an eaten chicken leg. The man lay on the ground and shuddered briefly before falling still.

'What was it saying?' Bjorn mused.

Halfdan rolled his eyes. 'We might have found out if you hadn't killed him. He was unarmed and chained.'

'He was annoying. He looks much better with his face on backward.'

Halfdan sighed. 'I don't know, but the language sounded a lot like those Pechenegs and the damned Alani. I reckon he's some mountain tribesman *thrall* of the Byzantine commander.'

'So what was he guarding? Treasure?'

Halfdan snorted. 'Here? I doubt it.'

Walking past his big friend and the broken thing, he reached for the tent flap with his shield and pushed it aside, pausing in the doorway, sword held out ready. His eyes slowly adjusted to the dim interior and finally he made out a figure lying on a cot on the far side of the room. It was barely moving; its chest rising and falling almost imperceptibly. The room smelled dreadful, a mix of diarrhoea, vomit and rotten meat. Halfdan gagged and turned, trying and failing to take a breath of the cleaner air outside.

'Urrrrrrrgh,' managed the tent's occupant.

Halfdan braced himself against the miasma and crossed the tent carefully, his breathing shallow to minimise his exposure to the stench. The man was, as he'd expected, the Byzantine commander. He was unarmoured and unarmed, but lay in his uniform tunic. He was stained and filthy, though. He'd soiled himself repeatedly and was awash with his own vomit.

'The...' the man gagged and coughed. 'The meat?' he managed. 'Breakfast?'

Halfdan shook his head. 'The water.'

'Ahhhhhh,' the man replied, the word tailing off into a sad sigh.

'It was not a noble way to make war,' Halfdan admitted.

The man let out another horrible sigh, accompanied by a fart and a sound like a small stream trickling over rocks, and managed to turn his head. 'Kill me.'

Halfdan shrugged, took four more steps, and delivered the most painless, swift and thorough killing blow he could manage. There was another sigh, but the man had no piss or shit left to expel and simply sagged into his bed. Turning his back, Halfdan stepped out into the light and took a grateful breath.

'Halfdan!'

He turned to see one of the new Varangians waving at him. 'What?'

'The next camp! They're coming.'

Halfdan craned to look past the chaos and could see a small unit of a dozen or so men marching their way, presumably all they could field who were not suffering the effects of the *Mandragora*. He turned, half expecting the same from the camp in the other direction, but there he could see that some shrewd officer had kicked out all the sick, who were staggering about, while he formed up his unaffected men and waited for reinforcements from the next camp along. He turned to Bjorn.

'Take half the men and stop that advance.'

As the albino did just that, calling for men by name to join him, Halfdan gathered the rest at the centre of the camp and prepared to march on the small defensive force. Gunnhild had gone with Bjorn, probably to apply her wisdom and make sure the he didn't do something stupid, but Ulfr and Farlof were with their jarl. On a whim, Halfdan wiped his sword on the least filthy part of his clothing then tucked it into his belt. He would return it to the sheath when it was properly clean. Then, ducking down, he picked up that wicked spear and tested it. The blade was an elongated narrow point, but the edges had also been sharpened to a razor keenness, and the rear of the blade ended in two barbs. It really was a nice piece of work, and had some stylised figure expertly etched into the head. Testing the weight, he nodded to himself. It was a fine prize for a fight, even if Bjorn had ruined it all.

Halfdan and his men strode out of the camp. But as they closed on the enemy – an officer bellowing commands as they readied themselves – a new sound echoed around the ravine.

A horn blast.

Halfdan looked around and finally spotted a distant group of figures emerging from the blocked streets of the town above, dropping to the gravelled slope below and sliding and pounding along stairs, descending the ravine side. There was more than a score of them and they gleamed like men made of silver, their shields the only part of them that was not blinding in the sun – long, kite-shaped things of bright yellow and blue.

Fulk de Courvaudon was joining the fray.

Halfdan laughed aloud and turned to Ulfr. 'Let's kick the shit out of this lot before we have to share them with the Normans.'

Ulfr looked him up and down and sniffed, his face wrinkling in distaste.

'What the fuck happened to you?'

–

In a little more than an hour, it was over. The nearer camps had rushed to lend support to those fighting off this unexpected attack, but so few of the Byzantines remained unaffected by the poison that they came in small, sporadic waves, too few to present much of an obstacle to Halfdan and his men. The Normans had descended somewhere a little further along the ravine and dealt with other camps, taking the pressure off Halfdan's hirð. In the end, half the healthy Byzantines, lacking a disciplined officer to command otherwise, simply fled into the wilderness to escape this nightmare and seek their countrymen closer to the coast.

Halfdan had fought until the danger was past and then set his men to searching the ravine from end to end, putting the sick and ruined out of their misery. Finally, with a chance to pause and take stock, the smell of his vomit-covered body became apparent. If he stood still for any length of time, the stench overcame the general stink of the ravine. He found Gunnhild, who was busily cleaning brains and blood off her stick.

'The water supply… it's not harmful if we don't drink it?'

She shook her head. 'In your case, I think I'd prescribe it,' she said with a half-smile and pulled her scarf up over her nose.

Satisfied that he was not going to end up like the Byzantine commander unless he swallowed the water, he located one of the stockpiles in the camp. The Byzantines had brought it down from the cliff cisterns and stored it in large jars in the centre of their camp for ready access. It took four of them upended over his head to remove the worst of the vomit-stink from him. Even then, when he returned to Gunnhild, she produced something from her bag and scattered drops of it over him.

Halfdan sniffed and wrinkled his nose. 'I smell like a Byzantine whore.'

'And that alone is a vast improvement,' she replied. Every time one of the men came near him for the next half hour, they sniffed and smirked, casting sidelong looks at him. Halfdan was growing weary of the joke by the time another blast on a horn announced the arrival of the Normans on the scene.

Halfdan straightened, wishing he didn't smell quite so fragrant, and the others gathered behind him like a true jarl's hirð. Three of the men hadn't returned from the mopping-up yet, but that was to be expected. They would not only be killing the injured Byzantines, but also taking the opportunity to go through enemy tents, looking for anything worth stealing. He could hardly blame them for that. And he had the important people with him: Bjorn, tall, white and imposing, nursing two new minor wounds; Ulfr, short, barrel-chested and with a beard you could lose a wolf in; Gunnhild, slender and striking, radiating power and wisdom; and now Farlof, unremarkable in every way but for the glint of intelligence in his eye and the scars of a veteran warrior on his skin. They comprised a united front as the Normans approached.

They were on foot, but the man at the front, the only one not wearing a helmet, had that slightly bandy-legged gait of a man rarely out of the saddle. The small force of men was impressive, Halfdan had to give them that. They wore coats of chain that reached down to their knees and trousers of chain beneath, and each had a strong, conical steel helmet with a straight nose guard, though the leader had his tucked beneath his arm. Each had one of those shields, rounded at the top and coming to a point at the bottom, painted with quarters in blue and yellow, and a good straight longsword at their side. Beside the leader, another of the Normans held a pole with a flag hanging from it. As a gust caught the flag, Halfdan saw that it was blue with a yellow lion rampant upon it.

The leader stopped ten paces from Halfdan, looking him up and down. He was tall and broad-shouldered, perhaps eight to ten years older than the jarl. He had a beard, but it had been clipped short, and his hair was little more than a black bowl upon the top of his head, barely reaching down to his ears. Despite this strange look, he cut an impressive and imposing figure.

'I am Fulk de Courvaudon,' he said, 'master of this place. This is my bannerman, Marc. You have done me a service.'

His voice was deep and the accent very thick and hard to follow. Halfdan had to concentrate to pick up what was said, but still, he was relieved. These Normans spoke a tongue all their own, but the jarl and his friends had spent a month learning the basics from one of the Italian campaigners on the *Tyche's Arrow*, and enough of the language bore a resemblance to their own that it made it easy enough to fill in the gaps in their understanding.

Halfdan nodded. 'I heard you were having a little trouble,' he said, hopefully intelligibly.

'Your accent is appalling,' Courvaudon said with a short, barked laugh. 'Yet so few of your kind even try. I am pleased. I am grateful, too. But I also know the men of the North, and I know that you will not have done this out of simple kindness. What is it you want in return?'

Halfdan laughed. 'They say the same of yours. I am Halfdan, jarl of these men. We are travelling north, and that means through the lands of your countrymen. It seemed sensible to make a friend. And if we happen across heaps of gold in our journey we will not be disappointed.'

Now it was Fulk's turn to laugh, and his aide, Marc, chuckled too, beneath that steel brow.

'Forthright and sensible. Good. I like you, Halfdan. So much better to deal with straight men than the oily and untrustworthy Byzantines, or the equally troublesome Italians. And it is good that you are to travel north. I have had my fill of this barren land. I have a mind to return to Iron Arm and demand a more worthy fief. Preferably one not surrounded by Byzantines. We will travel north with you, at least as far as Melfi, where I can pay my debt to you by introducing you to the most powerful man in the peninsula.'

Halfdan simply nodded.

'But,' Courvaudon added with a roll of the shoulders, 'it will take time to prepare for the journey. We have much to gather. It will take a day. Perhaps two. We should be safe. It will take three or more before the Byzantines return in force.'

Halfdan nodded. 'This is good. We also have our gear to gather, and could do with a wash and a night in a bed.'

As the Normans turned and began to make their way back toward the city, Ulfr took a deep breath beside him. 'And so it begins,' he smiled.

Part Two

ᚱᚠᛚᚠᛗᛚ ᛉᚠ ᚩᛚᛁᛏ

The Revolt of Maniakes

Chapter 5

Ketil of Stöð, former owner of the *Sea Wolf*, stood at the ship's rail and looked out at their destination. Dyrrachium stood like an immovable sentinel on a promontory, surrounded by the sea and a large lagoon. The city was fortified with heavy, thick stone walls and numerous towers, the strongest defences Ketil had ever seen outside Miklagarðr. It was a good thing the ships carried an army, for it was immediately clear to the Icelander that one would be required to even think of taking the city.

And take the city they must.

The army of Maniakes had embarked on the coast around Bari, on the south-east of the Italian peninsula – a force larger than any army Ketil had seen. All were determined that the giant general would be the next emperor of Byzantium, replacing the ineffectual and corrupt Constantine Monomachos and his cronies. They had sailed east across the narrow sea in just a day, an immense collection of vessels of all shapes, sizes and origins, carrying men, horses, carts, oxen, supplies and siege engines. The majority of the ships were transport vessels, though, and not warships. Thus Maniakes had made the sensible decision not to sail straight for Miklagarðr and a siege there. Should the emperor gather the full force of the Byzantine navy and meet him somewhere at sea, Maniakes's force would be destroyed before it could ever bring the bastard Monomachos to battle.

So, they had to land on the nearest coast for a direct march on the capital. Dyrrachium was the strongest fortification on the Italian-facing coast, and some of the Byzantine generals had argued against the wisdom of heading straight for it. Why not, they said, bypass it completely and land somewhere rural? Ketil, though, agreed with the general. Better to open hostilities by taking the most powerful fortress between them and their goal. Not only would it send a message, but it would give them a base of operations, secure their supply lines and, most crucially, not leave an enemy stronghold at their back.

All that might be logical, but when a man stood at a ship's rail and looked up at those impressive walls, it seemed like a fool's errand once more. The ship wallowed a little and lurched as the steersman angled them for the beach on the far side of the lagoon. To the north of the city, the coastline was not practical for landing many ships, and the port itself sat beneath those impressive walls, with their archers and artillery. Neither option was sensible, and so they would make a landing somewhere safe and easy off to the south, where the army could marshal itself and prepare to either besiege or storm the city.

'You look sour,' Leif offered from nearby.

Ketil grunted a non-committal reply.

'You still think we did the right thing?'

Ketil spared the Rus a momentary glance. 'I am just sick of these Byzantine ships. They are fat and slow and not at all like a good northern dragon boat. Oh, to feel the cold spray in the prow of a fast longboat, eh?'

Leif nodded, turning back to Anna, satisfied that Ketil was simply unhappy with the transport and that things would improve when they landed. Ketil could not tell him the truth. The canker that gnawed at him inside and had woken him in sweats more than once since they had parted ways with the other Wolves: it felt wrong to be apart from them, however much they irritated him. They were a hirð, even if they were Halfdan's hirð. They had fought giants and dragons and draugar at the edge of the world, had stolen gold from the greatest city in that world and had brought down a foul ruler there, all together. Ketil had always been a loner, and yet now, without the others, he felt oddly naked. Unprotected. Exposed.

He had gone over the argument time and again since they parted. Was there anything he could have said to persuade Halfdan that this was the clear way forward? But he had said everything that could have been said. He had spoken the plain sense of it, and Leif had seen that, being the cleverest of all of them. But Halfdan had been stubborn. He had to go off into the unknown, chasing illusions of riches. And because Halfdan would not come, nor would the others. Bjorn was a big oaf, bound to Halfdan in some way Ketil couldn't quite see. If Halfdan jumped down a well, Bjorn would go with him. And he had Ulfr convinced that he would lead them back to his beloved *Sea Wolf*. And Gunnhild? Well, there was something amiss about the völva these days. Something had changed in the great city, and now she seemed to be allowing Halfdan to lead her, where she had so often led him previously. The whole bunch was determined to follow the jarl, even though he was clearly leading them into the shit.

It frustrated the Icelander. He had given up so much. He'd had a ship and a crew, had been ready to sail for the land of the Finns and raid, taking their wealth and a few thralls for good measure. Like so many things, it had all come down from the gods. A völva back in his homeland had told him straight that he would travel east and fight for riches, and with it would come lasting fame. So, he had left that cold northern isle and used everything he had and could take to secure a willing crew and buy a ship. He'd not had much, barely managing to afford a small vessel and just enough men to sail her, but it had seemed the first step on his woven path.

Then, before he could even put the ship in the water, along had come Halfdan Loki-born. The tricky young bastard had managed to cheat him out of both ship and crew, and Ketil had almost challenged him then. But it had occurred to him that, perhaps, this was part of the weaving, and that Halfdan was merely the second step on his path. He had followed the young adventurer, with a guarded loyalty. He'd never bound himself. He would not make himself Halfdan's servant. He was an associate. An equal.

He should have challenged Halfdan on that Italian beach. Challenged him for the right to lead. A *holmgang*, in the old manner. The Northmen of this weird, warm world might be largely lost to the nailed god, but there was still enough of the North in them that they would have allowed and respected the ancient challenge. And though Halfdan was mickle clever and as lucky as a man could be, Ketil knew his own sword arm and strength; his chances of success would have been good.

But instead, because they were companions, he had chosen words as his weapon, and they had bounced off Halfdan the way arrows would bounce off the fortress that awaited them. He sighed. Once he was a lord of the Byzantines, dripping in gold, he would send men to find Halfdan and offer him the hand of friendship once more. But, for now, there were other matters to concentrate on. If he wanted to succeed, he needed to be at the forefront of this campaign. That, of course, was why he was at the prow, having elbowed his way through the men to the rail.

'Stick with me,' he muttered to Leif as the ships closed on that wide, low beach. 'Maniakes himself is three ships to the right, the great galley with all the flags. If we want an emperor's gratitude, he must know from the outset how much he owes us.'

Leif nodded, though he looked unsure. Anna patted him on the arm and smiled reassuringly. Good. If Anna agreed, then Leif would be as warm wax; easy to mould.

He prepared himself as their ship slowed, and the moment there was a gravelly crunching noise, threatening to slam him into the side had he not braced, he vaulted over the rail, not bothering to wait for the landing ramp. He turned to make sure the others were following, and was irritated to see Leif and Anna waiting for the ramp for disembarkation. They needed to be swift.

'Jump,' he called.

Anna stared in shock, and Leif looked to her, then shook his head. Ketil hissed angrily. This was not going to plan. 'Jump, Anna. I will catch you. Tell her, Leif.'

There was a very brief exchange, which ended with the small Rus placing his hands on her hips, giving her a kiss, then lifting her with some difficulty up to the rail. She braced, crossed herself, then leapt. Ketil took two steps forward and reached out, catching her as she dropped. He was tall and strong, yet he almost missed as she plummeted into his arms.

'What?' he grunted as she glared at him.

'Put me down, now.'

'I thought you didn't want to jump into the water.'

'It was the drop I didn't like. Not the water. Put me down.'

With a snort, he did so, and she smoothed down her skirt as best she could and waded with some difficulty ashore. Leaving Leif to follow, he sloshed through the water after her and finally staggered up onto the sand.

He would have liked to have had his shield with him already, be ready for battle in an instant, but the Byzantines planned everything to the smallest detail, and his kit was stored in one of the carts on a cargo vessel, along with everyone else's. He didn't worry for its safety, even with so much gold buried inside, for the Byzantines would not pry into a man's gear. But still, it meant he wasn't prepared.

A few moments later, Leif was at his side, coughing out salt water, soaked to the hairline. The little man barely came up to Ketil's armpit, and had seemingly submerged before he could struggle up onto the beach. His *sax* and throwing axe would need some cleaning later, as well as any leatherwork, before it got pitted and salt-damaged. For now, though, there were other things to think about.

The ships were starting to unload, but the three Wolves of Odin were among the first figures to stand on the sand, and all the others were either officers or their standard bearers or bodyguards. Taking a breath, Ketil gestured to the other two, pulled his axe from his belt, and trudged swiftly across the soft sand beneath the afternoon sun, in the direction of the giant Georgios Maniakes. More and more men were gathering in that area of the beach, all those close to Maniakes in the archaic, colourful uniforms of Byzantine officers.

Ketil braced himself. He had to be noticed. Had to be owed. It was the only way this was going to work. It helped, of course, that he stood a head above almost everyone else on the beach, with the exception of Maniakes. As he closed on the group, Leif and Anna at his back, the two men stood proud of the sea of heads, and it was no surprise that, as he turned, Maniakes spotted the approaching man. Still, despite the passing glance, the general went back to whatever he was doing, and Ketil was forced, none-too-politely, to elbow his way through the gathering of officers in the direction of the commander.

Accompanied by curses and complaints in Greek, he finally pushed his way into a small clear circle at the heart of the gathering, where Maniakes was in consultation with two senior officers, both of whom looked like parchment-skinned vultures in armour. The general had drawn a rough map of the situation in the sand with a stick and was jabbing it, murmuring with the two ancient officers. All three frowned and stopped mid-conversation as one of the officers Ketil had just elbowed aside called him something unflattering, quite loudly, and swatted him on the shoulder. The kerfuffle having drawn Maniakes's attention, Ketil took two more steps toward him in the clearing.

A collection of heavily armed bodyguards were suddenly in evidence, coalescing from the gathering and bearing down on Ketil. He stood his ground, a short but safe distance from the trio, throwing a silent challenge. Maniakes chewed his lip as he regarded the three lessers who had burst into his meeting, his brow furrowing. Perhaps realising he was in no danger, or perhaps content that he was one of the most physically imposing men on the entire beach and could flatten most attackers with a punch, the general waved to his guards to stand down. They did so, though they did not retreat, and their weapons remained bared.

'I know you,' Maniakes said, a touch of suspicion in his voice. 'Where from, though?'

Ketil fixed him with a level look, the only man on the beach able to meet him eye to eye without craning. 'The rising against Kalaphates. A crew of Wolves.'

Maniakes nodded slowly. 'Alongside that mangy dog Harðràði.'

'The mangy dog who breached the palace and saved the empress,' Ketil reminded him.

The general nodded. 'I remember you all. Brave. A little foolhardy, but certainly brave. I am surprised to find you in my army. I presumed you had all gone with the Norseman, back to his snowy lair.'

Ketil snorted. 'Why seek hills of snow when there are mountains of gold to be had?'

This finally made Maniakes laugh out loud. 'Well said. But what brings you and your friends to interrupt my business? I have no mountain of gold here,' he added, patting his belt pouches theatrically.

Ketil had not planned anything. Indeed, he'd had no idea what he was going to say or do beyond getting close enough to Maniakes to stand out. Which is why he cringed inside when his ears caught up with his mouth.

'Give me fifty men and I will give you Dyrrachium.'

What the fuck had made him say that?

Ketil clenched his teeth. That had been a ridiculous thing to say. Utterly moonstruck of him. Damn it all, but he wished he had Halfdan here. *He* would have known exactly what to say. The Loki cunning of the jarl would be so useful. Better than blundering into mad promises like that. Still, he knew enough to know that he could hardly go back on it now. It was said. It had to be done. He could feel Leif staring at him in astonishment, and could hear a little strangled whimper that had clearly come from Anna. Fighting his own nerves, Ketil held himself straight and tall, continuing to meet the general's gaze.

Around them, officers snorted and laughed. One slapped his thighs with amusement. Even the two old vultures smiled. Maniakes, oddly, was not smiling.

'Go on,' the giant said, gesturing to him.

A plan. He needed a plan. He had no plan. Of *course* he had no plan. There could *be* no plan. The very idea of this boast was preposterous. And yet, Maniakes seemed to be taking Ketil's claim at face value. Ketil fought down the nerves that fluttered at the edge of his reserve. He cleared his throat.

'There is nothing more to say. I have an idea.' *No, no I don't.* 'I will not tempt fate by sharing it. But I give you my oath, the word of an Icelander, that your fifty men and I will bring you the city.'

Maniakes continued to peer at him in silence, one eyebrow arched, thoughtful. Slowly, the laughter and gaiety among the officers faded until an odd silence held the crowd, the only sound the breeze whipping across the sand and the distant unloading of an army.

One of the vultures cleared his throat, a scratchy, papery sound. 'Surely, General, you are not considering this?'

A murmur rolled across the officers, like a wave breaking on the shore.

'As it happens, I am,' Maniakes replied. He turned to Ketil. 'You will need nothing else?'

The Icelander was about to shake his head when next to him Leif cut in. 'Ropes and grapples. Fifty-two of them.'

Another snort of derision arose among the officers, but Maniakes waved them to silence. 'I believe I can provide those, once the supply ships have begun to beach.'

'Good, because I will also need my shield and byrnie from the supplies.'

'Sir,' the other vulture said, lurching forward, 'you cannot throw away resources on such foolishness. This is only the start of the campaign.'

'But it is the most important step, with the exception of the last. We must have Dyrrachium before we can proceed, and the faster we take it, the more momentum we can create with our advance.'

'But it is *insane*.'

'You, Alexi, are not a gambling man,' the general noted. 'I, on the other hand, have been known to make a wager here and there when I think the stakes warrant it. Heavens, man, but I owe some of the glory of my military career to gambles that paid off. I can spare fifty men and fifty ropes if it saves me weeks of siege and the potential loss of thousands.'

He turned back to Ketil. 'I will give you your men and your ropes. Give me the city, and I will make sure you are rewarded appropriately.'

Ketil bowed his head, gestured to Leif, turned and marched away, the gathering of officers parting to make way for them. It was not until they were on the open sand that he let out an almost explosive breath.

'What the fuck was that?' Leif demanded as they stopped.

'I was spinning yarn straight from the sheep.'

'You were spinning yarn from a *bear*, Ketil. There is no way to do this without getting killed. You *know* that.'

'No, I do not know that. I have a destiny, Leif, and it is not to end my days dead beneath the walls of a city. I shall live long past this, the greatest völva in Iceland told me so.' He sagged. 'What was your thought with the ropes and grapples?'

Leif snorted. 'Not so much a thought as a process of elimination. We will not be able to break the gate down, so we will have to go over the walls somehow. Hence the ropes.'

Ketil nodded. 'Well-reasoned, my friend.'

They stood for some time at the edge of the beach, on a slope where tufty dry grass had formed, the sun beating down

73

and making them sweat. As they waited, Ketil peered off at the great citadel hunched atop the rise above the lagoon, a narrow causeway with a bridge crossing the water between them and it. A gate stood some two hundred paces from the far end of the bridge, flanked by strong towers and resolutely shut. The towers were only a little taller than the walls from which they rose. With long enough ropes, they could probably reach the towers as easily as the walls. Of course, the city would have a garrison of thousands, and the lion's share would be concentrated near this gate, facing the threat. What fifty-two men and a talkative woman were going to achieve by climbing the walls remained to be seen.

His attention was finally claimed by the approach of armed men and four pack horses. He was pleased to note that there were fifty armoured figures, which confirmed they were the men Maniakes had promised, but he was even more pleased to realise that they were Varangians, Northmen like himself – either Svears or Geats or Rus, most likely. They would be more likely to work well with him than Byzantines would have been. And he could see his shield hanging from one of the pack horses, too.

'I am Boldin,' the foremost of the warriors said. 'In Constantinople I was the Pentecontarch of these men. I have been ordered to serve under you,' he added, with a mix of suspicion and distaste. 'I want you to know now that I am not pleased by the duty assigned us.'

Ketil gave the man a feral smile. 'I don't give a shit what pleases you, Boldin the penter-whatever-it-was. All I want is your obedience and your sword arm. We're going to take Dyrrachium.'

'How?'

That, of course, was the problem. 'With ropes and grapples.' *Time to make it up as he went. To spin yarn straight from the bear, as Leif had noted.* He saw the look of disbelief on the Varangian's face. 'We are going to move as though we have no fear. We will

74

take a few Byzantine standards. Leif here will dress as though he is a herald or some such. As we approach the gate, it is my belief that they will not attempt to destroy us, for they will presume us to be some deputation from Maniakes. Once we are close enough that they cannot bring their artillery to bear, a stone's throw from the gate, we will run to the walls. Once we are next to them, it will be difficult for archers to aim so far down, so close, even across the gate. We will divide, half to each side of the gate, and use the grapples to reach the two flanking towers.'

Even to him, it sounded dubious at best. Boldin was giving him a withering glare. 'What then?' the Varangian demanded. 'What will the six survivors do when they reach the wall top and enter a fully garrisoned city?'

Spin, spin, spin…

'Each half will then divide again. Some will enter the tower and take control. Others will defend against enemies coming along the walls. The rest will descend. There must be stairs. They will break out to the inside of the city and seize the gate. Once the gate is opened, we only have to hold it long enough for the lead elements of Maniakes's army to reach us.'

'Only?' demanded Boldin with a snort.

'Do you have a better idea?'

'Yes,' the Varangian answered. 'Dozens of them, in fact. And they all involve long sieges where the Greek soldiers do all the dying while we sit in tents and wait.'

'I thought not. We follow my plan, then.'

'That is not a plan. It is a dream, perhaps fuelled by eating the wrong sort of mushrooms. You're going to get us all killed.'

'No. That's one thing I truly know. I am not.' Of course, that was a little lie. The völva back home had told him that he was going to be famous, but that didn't mean everyone else would live.

'Do we go?' one of the other Varangians asked, directing his question to Boldin. The leader hawked and spat into the sand. 'What choice do we have? We pledged to Maniakes, and he assigned us here. May the Theotokos preserve us, we will do our duty.'

Ketil sent Anna back to the general, warning him to be ready to move into the city the moment the gate opened. She was to stay with the commander. She argued, of course, but when Leif begged her to stay out of danger, she acquiesced, with a look that suggested they would pay for this. For half an hour, then, they armed up from the pack animals, retrieving their shields. A priest came by and delivered a blessing for them in the Greek tongue, for which Boldin and his men knelt, as did Leif. Ketil surreptitiously kissed his Mjǫllnir pendant and sent up a swift prayer to Thor and to Odin and, because this was foolish and unplanned and he needed all the help he could get, to Loki, Freyja and even Tyr, too. Then, finally, they were ready.

Bearing half a dozen impressive-looking flags, and with Leif now clad in rich Byzantine robes, they set off for the bridge. Each man had a rope and grapple over his shoulder, and the fact that no one had yet realised that it would look really strange for a parley deputation to be thus equipped was something for which Ketil could only thank the gods.

They were going to need the most extraordinary luck for this to work.

The tension among them gradually increased as they crossed that long bridge and set foot upon the low slope of the headland upon which Dyrrachium sat. Even Ketil was straining almost unbearably with it all by the time they climbed the slope and bore down upon the gate.

'Strange,' Leif murmured beside him.

'What?' the Icelander asked, eyes raking the walls ahead, and settling on the very closed gate.

'The artillery is silent.'

'They think we're a deputation.'

'But even if they were not going to shoot, wouldn't they at least move? Wouldn't the soldiers manning them turn the things and keep them trained on us?'

Ketil frowned, his gaze rising to the parapet once more. The Rus was absolutely right. Nothing was happening up there. The artillery was all still pointing out toward the beach. Moreover, there was not a sound from up there. His skin prickled as he realised he couldn't see flags, or the smoke from braziers. Gods, but he couldn't even see the shapes of any men looking down at them.

'I think,' he began, but fell silent as there was a heavy thud, like a tomb door closing, and then a long, ligneous groan. As he stared in wonder and surprise, the city's gate slowly opened inwards. He braced, as did the rest, waiting for a sally of slavering, angry Byzantines, but nothing emerged.

'How did you know about this?' Boldin breathed nearby. 'This *was* your plan, yes?'

Ketil nodded. He didn't quite trust himself to speak. What was going on?

Finally, figures appeared in the shadowy archway and emerged from the gate, stepping out toward them. They were not soldiers. Indeed, none of them were armed. The leader was impeccably dressed in rich silks and draped with jewellery. A politician in the town? A merchant?

Leif stepped forth ahead of the others, and Ketil moved to his shoulder like a bodyguard.

'Where is the garrison commander?' Leif demanded in an imperious tone.

The local threw him a disgustingly obsequious smile. 'Blessed lord, I am the nearest thing to a garrison commander, until you choose to install one, of course.'

'Explain,' snapped Leif.

Ketil smiled. The little Rus was playing the role perfectly.

The local gave a nervous cough. 'The forces of the treacherous, false emperor Monomachos fled the city the moment your sails appeared across the water, great lord. We have heard, of course, of the coming of the noble katepan Maniakes, liberator of Byzantium. I, for one, am delighted that the garrison fled, and I welcome our saviours.'

'A sentiment that would undoubtedly have been reversed had the garrison chosen to stay,' Leif noted.

'Ahahahaha,' the noble laughed, weakly. 'The city is yours, gracious lord. May you find its delights a welcome distraction until you continue on your way to liberate Constantinople from the false emperor.'

Ketil turned to look down at the beach. The vanguard was already on the move, the banners of Maniakes among them. He heaved a sigh of relief and kept a smile to himself. He'd delivered on his promise. Perhaps not in as martial and heroic a manner as the general would have expected, but he could hardly deny that Ketil had secured the city for him.

He had taken the first step toward his goal. And now, Miklagarðr awaited.

Chapter 6

'I don't understand why he keeps us so close,' Ketil murmured, glancing across at the general, who was poring over a map of the region spread across a large table in the centre of the headquarters. 'I was actually embarrassed to hand him a city that had panicked, emptied of soldiers and fallen over itself to surrender. He could have sent a raddled donkey up to the gate and they'd have begged it for mercy.'

Leif chuckled as Anna smiled and poured them wine. 'He sees you as some kind of lucky charm, Ketil. They were expecting some great battle or siege at Dyrrachium, and he was prepared to lose weeks and a lot of men, but you turn up with your offer and the next thing he knows, the most powerful Byzantine stronghold in the west just surrenders.'

'He is easily influenced, then.'

'It's not just that, Ketil. Like all Byzantines, Maniakes is extremely superstitious. You have no idea the store they set by signs and omens. You gave him Dyrrachium, but I have been watching, and there's more. You remember that *ikon* we found in the church the next day?'

'The picture of the god–woman? What of it?'

'The Theotokos, yes. The mother of God. It is a priceless and sacred icon. It is a coup for a Byzantine army to bear such a thing. You found it and handed it to them.'

'I didn't want it. It was just a picture of a woman. I kept the gold.'

'But to Maniakes that icon was worth a ship full of gold.'

'Then I gave it away too cheap.'

'No. You bought yourself value. Even the priests, who know you for a pagan, are murmuring about how God watches over you and works through you. After all, the Divine plan is ineffable to man.'

'You are ineffable to man,' Ketil grumbled, accepting the cup from Anna and peering into it suspiciously.

'It's good wine,' she said. 'From the *theme* of Boleron. Drink it.'

'Wine is a woman's drink,' he replied, a little too loud, for he earned a glare from half a dozen officers nearby with cups in their hands. 'At home, we wouldn't use this stuff for watering the seed beds.'

'I can get you beer if you give me time. There are local brewers.'

'The beer here is even worse. It tastes like it's been drunk once already,' he complained. Nothing seemed right today.

'Hello, what's this?' Leif muttered, looking up at the doorway. Ketil followed his glance to see, in the door arch, a pair of the general's bodyguards standing at the shoulders of a dusty, travel-worn man in the uniform of a Byzantine imperial messenger, his leather satchel over his shoulder. The murmur of conversation among the officers assembled in the room drifted to nothing and all eyes turned to the figure.

Ketil tried to make a rough calculation in his head, based on the number of days they had now been moving across Bulgarland in the direction of the capital and the distance that was said to remain. He concluded in a breath or two that, if a man rode as though the ice giants were at his heels, he could just about have heard of the revolt and reached this place from Miklagarðr. He was not surprised, therefore, when the bodyguard announced that the messenger had just arrived from the emperor himself.

'No pomp or splendour?' Leif mused. 'I've seen imperial messengers before, sent from the palace. Even in the midst of a war they arrive with fanfares and a glorious escort. The emperors like their messages to look and sound imperious.'

Anna shivered. 'Monomachos is frightened,' she muttered. 'So panicked that he sends a rider as fast as he can go.'

Maniakes had now straightened and paced to the centre of the room. 'You have a message for me.'

The dusty rider bowed low and reached for his satchel.

'Ah, ah,' admonished one of the guards. 'I'll do that.'

The messenger frowned, but held his hands high and let the guard rummage in his bag. It was, after all, feasible that the man could be an assassin, close enough for a thrown dagger to strike home. The bodyguard fished out a scroll case, bound with the imperial seal. With a warning look at the messenger, he crossed to the general, head bowed, and proffered the message. Maniakes was about to reach for the scroll when one of his officers intercepted it. Tearing the seal and upending the tube, he lifted the rolled-up message within and shook it, perhaps testing for scorpions or poisonous snakes enclosed. Satisfied that no wildlife had been sent to kill the general, he first sniffed the scroll, shrugged, and then ran his fingers across the surface, including the seal and the ink. The officer straightened slowly.

'What is he doing now?' Ketil frowned.

'Testing for poison on the page,' Leif replied. 'You spent a year in the city. You know how the Byzantine court works.'

Ketil nodded. Brave man, then, that officer. Offering his own life to test for poison and protect his master. The man, satisfied that the message was just that, turned and held it out for Maniakes. The general took it and unfurled it, reading down the lines. His face remained expressionless until he finished, when he let it roll up once more and pulled himself up to his full height.

'His Majesty the Basileos Constantine the Ninth makes us an offer,' he announced to the room full of officers. They looked at him, tense, expectant. Maniakes sucked on his teeth. 'Every soldier who has taken up arms against the throne is to be granted amnesty and to keep his rank and position. Every officer above the rank of *decarch* will receive the same treatment, but with a donative to celebrate their renewed loyalty. Every senior officer on my staff will be required to lay down his military position, but will receive a court or civil administrative position of equal or higher status, along with new estates in the themes in Asia. And finally, I am to be pardoned, offered high position, and granted lands and titles galore.'

He looked around the officers. 'What is to be my reply to this?'

A surge of refusals rose across the room. One of the older officers looked toward the messenger. 'You should send the false emperor a reply. An offer of your own. Maybe give him the choice between being roasted in the bronze ox or being thrown from a column in the hippodrome.'

Ketil looked at the reedy messenger and thought back over the dangerous lands they had traversed since Dyrrachium. He leaned closer and whispered to Leif. 'How unlikely is it that the emperor would send a messenger on his own?'

'Very unlikely. And I still find it hard to believe this is true, with the lack of pomp. It smacks of a trick. I'd have expected an assassin – poison probably – just like these men did, yet nothing has happened.'

Ketil nodded. 'Then what is this? It makes no sense.'

Leif scratched his neck, frowning. 'It does if this is a distraction. That's all it is, I think. Puppetry. Pantomime. The message is too good to be true. No man offers so much to his enemies without a reason. And you remember Monomachos? He is not likely to abase himself so quickly, especially with men like Romanos Skleros advising him. This is a trick. It is meant to delay us.'

The room fell silent and Ketil looked up to see Maniakes waving his hands for quiet. 'Take this message to your master,' he began, wagging a finger at the messenger, but he was interrupted before he could continue.

Again, Ketil silently cursed himself for not thinking things through before committing. It was something Bjorn ribbed him about regularly, labelling him dangerously unpredictable. Ketil was starting to see the big man's point as he strode out to stand between the messenger and the general.

'What?' Maniakes snapped, eyes narrowed dangerously at this unseemly interruption.

'This is a trick,' Ketil said. 'A delaying tactic. It is a cloak, covering something else.'

Maniakes folded his arms. 'What are you talking about, Varangian?'

Ketil held up a finger, suggesting the general wait a moment, and paced over to the messenger in the doorway. He gestured for the guards to step out of the way. They did so only when the general nodded his consent, leaving Ketil and the messenger facing one another in the arch.

'Do you use your left hand or your right?' he asked.

The messenger frowned. 'Right,' he said quietly.

Ketil nodded, reached out and gripped the man's right hand. The messenger struggled for a moment, trying to pull away, but the Icelander was strong and had a solid hold of the man's wrist. He reached down and snapped the middle finger so that it pointed up at a right angle, the bony crack echoing across the room. The man screamed. A number of officers stepped forward, but Maniakes, still frowning, waved them still.

As the messenger's scream died to a pained whimper, Ketil took a breath. 'That was so you know I mean business. Right. What else has the emperor done other than send this message?'

The man shook his head. 'I don't know, master. I am just a rider.'

'Wrong answer.' With a jerk, Ketil snapped another finger. The man howled in agony. The Icelander waited until he fell into panting silence. 'Now, we shall try again. What other orders has the emperor given?'

'Please?' pleaded the man, desperately.

'Wrong,' Ketil said.

Jerk. Snap. Screech.

Again, he waited for pained silence. He gripped the fourth finger tight. 'Shall we try again?'

'I will be killed,' the man begged.

'You well might. Here, if not in the city.'

Another snap. When the howling was over, Ketil grasped his thumb.

'No. Please, no.'

'The emperor?' Ketil urged.

The man sagged, tears streaming down dusty cheeks. 'The army of Byzantium has been gathered.'

A murmur of surprise rolled around the room. Now Maniakes was stepping forward. 'Go on,' the big general said.

'When do they march?' Ketil asked.

'I don't—' the messenger began, but screamed as his thumb snapped, leaving his hand permanently maimed. Ketil let go and grabbed the left instead.

'When?'

The man whimpered. 'They have marched already.'

Gasps echoed around the room. 'When?'

'I don't...'

Snap.

The man just keened quietly now, the pain already so intense that this break only made a small difference. 'The advance units were already mustering as I left the city,' he said. 'Two days behind me. Three, perhaps.'

Behind Ketil, Maniakes hummed. 'This was supposed to distract us. If the army already musters, Monomachos never had any intention of honouring such promises. We would spend precious time considering the matter and corresponding, all while he gathers more and more men to stand in our way. But he has failed, thanks to my friend here.' He grinned and clapped a hand on Ketil's shoulder, then turned. 'We send the message. We send the messenger's head.'

The man in Ketil's grip pulled away, fresh panic filling him, but the tall northerner had a firm grasp of him still. He turned to the bodyguards. 'The rider was alone?'

The guards nodded. 'He rode into the town on his own.'

'Unlikely. Country roads are lawless and a single rider could easily fall foul of bandits.' Ketil turned back to the messenger with a very unpleasant smile. 'Where are your friends?'

'I don't know what—' the man began.

'Your escort,' clarified Ketil as he broke another finger.

Once the screaming faded, the man, shaking, rattled out words. 'Two miles—'

'Yes?'

'Two… miles, from the town gate…' He heaved a shuddering breath. 'In a tavern… in the nearest village.'

'How many?'

'Twelve. All… *excubitores*.'

Ketil nodded. 'Thank you.'

His other hand moved suddenly. No one in the room, even the man in his grip, had seen that hand drop to his belt and pull out the sax. The sharp, straight blade jabbed upward, sinking into the man's throat beneath his chin, angled straight up through mouth, nose and brain. The messenger stared in horror as the steel passed through his head until it touched the inside of his cranium.

Blood washed down the blade and across Ketil's hand to spatter over his clothes and onto the floor. As he pulled the knife free and let the dying messenger collapse to the floor and shake his last moments out, fresh waves of blood washed over their feet. Even the two bodyguards nearby stared in surprise.

Ketil turned at an angry bark from Maniakes.

'What do you think you are doing?'

He shrugged. 'What needed to be done.'

Leif darted forward as the general puffed up ready to explode, waving his hands, trying to calm the situation.

'Ketil is right. Send the emperor nothing. No offer, no threat, no head. No message. If you do, he knows where you are and what you have decided. Send no messenger and he can have no knowledge of whether his letter even reached you. He will be unsure where you are and whether you still march. You now know roughly where his army will be. With no reply, he will be blind to your movements.'

Maniakes nodded slowly. 'Well-reasoned, Varangian.' He stepped back over to the map. Ketil paused, nodding his thanks to Leif as two servants arrived with a bucket of water and cloths. One dragged away the body while the other began to clean the archway. Ketil took a wet cloth from the man and wiped his hands, then his blade, and slid the sax home. He turned, looking like some dreadful blood-drenched battle spirit, and joined the general and his officers at the table. It was, perhaps, a measure of how his standing was changing that no one challenged his right to be there.

'The army mustered here,' the general said, tapping the map somewhere in the east, not far from the capital. 'They will have been marching for five days at least, eight at the most. Their natural speed will be slower than ours, but they will be at forced-march pace to catch us before we do too much damage to the lands between. We will have to fight the odd garrison, no doubt, but if we meet little resistance, by my reckoning, we will encounter the main enemy force somewhere near Thessalonika. If we can defeat them there soundly enough, Constantinople will be open to us. The emperor will not have time to raise another force to hold us out. There will only be the city garrison, and Monomachos has enough enemies in the city that I anticipate the gates being thrown open to us within a day.

'One great battle, gentlemen, and we all know how strong this army is. There are more veterans in this force than across the rest of the empire together. Even if Monomachos fields every soldier in Byzantium against us, we will still be stronger. God is with us, my friends. Constantinople will have a new emperor soon, one who cares for the empire as more than just a source of gold.'

'I need permission to take my fifty and leave the city,' Ketil said suddenly, looking up.

'You do?' Maniakes replied, arching an eyebrow.

Ketil nodded. 'You heard the messenger. He had twelve imperial soldiers with him. I would wager that if he does not return by sunset, they will ride for Constantinople, or at least for the Byzantine army and tell them that the messenger failed and you refused his offer. We can buy days of preparation and advance without the enemy's knowledge if no reply reaches the city. The excubitores in that tavern have to die.'

The giant general smiled slowly. 'See, gentlemen, why I allow this heathen among my staff?' He turned to Ketil. 'Go. Take your men and my blessing and stop the message being sent. I will have the pickets and gate guards informed.'

Ketil turned and gestured to Leif. The Rus shook his head. 'You don't need me for this. But I can help here with logistics.' As the general frowned at him, Leif grinned. 'I was an ambassador to the court from Kiev under half a dozen different emperors. Few men have as good a grasp of geography and troop movement as me.'

Ketil nodded and left the room, stepping over the mess still being cleaned up in the doorway. This Byzantine city – Ketil had been told the name several times, but it never seemed to lodge in his memory – had been largely evacuated of civilians and all the buildings given over to the general's military for the past two days. They had been waiting for supplies to catch up before moving on, though now it seemed likely they would move in the morning regardless.

He crossed the square where soldiers were arguing over a cart full of supplies while the teamster stood by impatiently, and two whores were touting for trade with every armoured man who passed. A drunken soldier wallowed in a gutter, but he would not enjoy himself for long, for an officer was marching his way across the pavement with a face like thunder. Turning down a side alley, Ketil located the warehouse given over as accommodation for his men.

He was surprised to find the place empty, but for two men left behind as guards, both of whom stared in surprise at their blood-soaked leader in the doorway.

'Where are the others? Where is Boldin?'

The man frowned in surprise, but then pointed vaguely west. 'Church,' he said.

Ketil harrumphed. What was it with these Christians and their finicky need to fawn over their nailed god at specific times every day? Surely Christ had better things to do than spend six hours a day listening to his followers telling him how wonderful he was and how unworthy they were. A true Northman respected Odin and the other gods, but he'd even tell the Allfather to go fuck himself if Odin demanded a ritual before breakfast.

'Gather your things. We have a job to do.'

Leaving the two men, he retrieved his shield and axe and then emerged into the open air once more. The sun had become paler and more watery over the past three days, and hazy grey cloud was slowly coalescing in the sky. He could feel on his skin the faint mist that foretold rain by nightfall. He would want to be back inside by then. For just a moment, he had to acknowledge how he'd changed over the past few years in the south. Back home, he'd always enjoyed the rain. It was refreshing and natural and he liked it running down his face. But something about spending time in the almost endless warmth had made him less enamoured with the experience these days.

Faintly irritated with this revelation, he jogged down the street. He ignored the first chapel, despite the singing he could hear from inside. That place was too small to hold forty-eight men. His Varangians would be two streets over, where the church of Saint Olaf was sizeable enough to fit them, and the saint was a Northman himself.

Sure enough, as he pushed open the doors and the droning atonal misery of the nailed god's songs washed over him, he could see men he recognised, including Boldin near the front.

It took a few moments for the song to peter out to silence, even when the priest himself stopped singing, looking with a mix of disgust and surprise at Ketil.

Once the church was quiet, the priest held out a hand. 'Pagan heretics are not welcome here. May you burn in the fires of eternal damnation for your endless sins.'

'Fuck off,' Ketil replied casually, and then ignored the priest entirely. Half the Varangian congregation crossed themselves at this, but Boldin stood. 'What is it?'

'We have a job to do. Now.'

The priest shook his head. 'The Lord demands obedience and love. It is not acceptable to leave halfway through devotions, no doubt to stain your hands with the blood of the innocent.'

Ketil snorted. 'I am not new to Byzantium. You could kill a hundred men at random and not find an innocent among them. But the men we must kill are bound to the false emperor Monomachos.'

The priest seemed conflicted for a moment. Uniformly, every church in the city, as with the other cities they had passed, had pledged their support to Maniakes and cursed the emperor as an apostate and a puppet of the devil. Killing his men would, it appeared, actually be the work of the nailed god. Boldin looked expectantly at the priest, who sighed and lifted an elaborate gold cross, studded with precious stones, raising it to head height.

'O Lord Jesus Christ our God, the true and living way, be thou, O Master, my companion, guide and guardian during my journey; deliver and protect me from all danger, misfortune and temptation; that being so defended by Thy divine power, I may have a peaceful and successful journey and arrive safely at my destination. For in thee I put my trust and hope, and to thee, together with thy Eternal Father, and the All-holy Spirit, I ascribe all praise, honour and glory, now and ever, and unto ages of ages. Amen.'

Boldin and the others bowed their heads in respect. The blessing, and its reception, seemed to go on far too long for

Ketil, who stood there, drumming his fingers on the rim of his shield until the priest glared at him, at which he drummed even more loudly.

As the Varangians began to file out, each in turn crossing himself before the priest, Ketil stood outside. Boldin emerged first. 'What must we do?'

–

Half an hour later they were leaving the city. The guard at the gate had been warned and they were permitted to leave the walls without issue. With only two miles to travel, they had no need of horses and as many of them could not ride, that worked in their favour. As they moved out onto the road at a mile-eating pace, Ketil turned to them.

'There are twelve. They must all die. None are to get away. We do not know who else in the tavern is associated with them; they may have slaves or servants, drivers or guides. Everyone in the inn and its stable will have to go. They will be nervous, this close to the general's army, so they will be watching. If we march along the road, they will see us coming, mount up and ride off. Divide yourselves into four groups. The fastest among you will come with me. We will leave the road and move through the fields at speed. Then we will circle around and come back at the tavern from the far side. The slowest will bring up the rear, marching along the road toward the inn. The rest will divide and move out along both sides in the fields, moving a little ahead. We should be able to encircle them and stop them getting away. If just one escapes, the enemy will be told of our approach. You understand?'

There were nods and a rumble of assent, and with a little discussion the fifty men divided themselves into quarters. Trusting the others to do what was required, Ketil took the tallest and leanest, the fastest runners, and led them off the road, crossing two fields and then running along a hedgerow, keeping an eye on the road. With satisfaction, he saw two groups veering off, behind his own runners, but ahead of those who remained on the road. They should be able to keep just about within sight of each other and coordinate the attack. Leaving them to it, Ketil and his dozen men raced on ahead, along the field boundaries, keeping out of sight but close enough to see the road and the sparse traffic on it. Few civilians had any interest in being out and about with the prospect of military action around them.

They had only been running for a few minutes when Ketil spotted the small village ahead. It was little more than a cluster of houses hugging the main road, with fields stretching out all around. It was not hard to identify the inn. The houses were all ramshackle, single-storey timber affairs, poor quality and old, while the inn was considerably larger with a ground floor formed of stone and an upper of wood. A small stone church in the centre of the village was the only other building of note.

His keen eyes picked out a man sitting on a rock close to the road at the eastern edge of the village. Undoubtedly a look-out for the excubitores. The man looked bored. Ketil smiled to himself as they skirted unseen around the man and passed the village. At the far side, he could see no such watcher, and so they gradually moved back toward the road. From there, they advanced slowly, carefully. Ketil reached back and touched the war axe at his belt, but changed his mind and pulled the throwing axe from its looped thong at his side.

'Close in. No one gets away.'

They were not far from the village when a warning shout went up. Gritting his teeth, Ketil waved his axe to urge his men on and they picked up the pace, closing on the nearest houses. They had just reached the dwellings when activity broke out. The rearguard had been spotted on the road and the excubitores had run for their mounts in the inn's stables, saddling up. Now, the dozen riders emerged out into the street and looked about. They spotted the Varangians approaching from the west, then

Ketil and his men closing in from the east. An officer barked unheard orders and the unit burst like a dropped fruit. Riders disappeared between the houses to either side, clearly hoping to escape that way. Ketil prayed to Odin that his men had managed to move into position to catch them. They should have done. Four men rode toward Ketil and his men, kicking their horses into speed. They intended either to ride down the Varangians or jump them. They would be disappointed.

Off to the left, one of Ketil's men threw a spear, a beautiful cast that plucked a rider from his horse's back and sent him down to the dirt. Another horse, to the right, charged at them, but the men formed a wall with their shields and brandished long axes on great poles, and at the last moment the horse refused, terrified, rearing, its rider fighting for control before falling. The central horse ran straight at Ketil and he could see that this beast would not turn aside. Teeth bared, Ketil pulled back his arm, levelling his axe by his ear, and at the last moment flicked it forward. The weapon cartwheeled through the air and struck the horse right between the eyes. There was a strange moment when the beast continued running, and then its nerves told it that it was dead, the blow having smashed the skull and killed the beast. The horse collapsed in a screaming tangle of legs. Its rider, a deft and apparently very lucky man, leapt free at the last moment. As he staggered to rise, he took a look at the dozen men in the road, then turned and ran back into the village. As half Ketil's men finished off the fallen, he gave chase to the runner with the rest.

The imperial guardsman kept looking over his shoulder, then suddenly turned left and disappeared into the church. His pursuers scattered to a halt outside the building. Ketil looked about. The rearguard had left a few men at the edge of the village and had disappeared into the inn to butcher the occupants, just to be sure. Past the church, Ketil could see more of his men out in the field, fighting other riders.

'He's claimed sanctuary,' one of the Varangians said, pointing at the church. 'What will we do?'

'Leave this to me,' Ketil grunted and stormed forward, pulling the door open.

The solider was at the far end of the church, sword in hand, limping, while an elderly priest turned to face Ketil. 'You have no business here. This is a house of God. Take away your weapons, son of Satan.'

Ketil walked purposely forward. 'I have no argument with you, old man, and no wish to hurt you. Get out of my way.'

The priest stepped closer, holding up a hand to halt him. Ketil reached out, grabbed the priest and moved him aside as gently as he could. The man might be another of the endless nailed-god followers, but he was venerable and had done nothing wrong. As the priest blustered and argued, Ketil marched past and bore down on the soldier. He could see by the way the man moved that he'd not only damaged his leg, but apparently broken a rib or two as well.

'Stay back.'

Ketil shook his head. 'You have to die.'

He closed on the soldier, pulling his war axe from his belt. He lifted it high, ready for an overhead blow. As the soldier reached the end of the small chapel, unable to back away any further, he raised his sword to block, wincing and hissing at the pain in his side. At the last moment, Ketil changed his grip and the great, heavy axe swung back and down then forward and up. The soldier tried to adjust, to bring his sword down to parry, but he had no time. The great axe blade bit into his nethers, splitting his pelvis with a crack that echoed around the church. As he howled and collapsed, sword falling from his hand, Ketil dropped the axe and pulled his sax free. In a heartbeat, he cut the man's throat, picked up the axe, turned and strode from the church.

'May you be damned for all eternity, murderer,' hissed the priest as he passed. Ketil spared him not a single glance. By the time he had cleaned his blades and stood, breathing hard, in the middle of the road, his men were emerging from doors and side streets. He had lost two, their bodies being carried by friends, but they confirmed all twelve guards were dead, along with every living soul in the inn. No message would go to the authorities. Maniakes could march on, and the emperor would be blind to his progress.

Boldin gave him a weary smile as they looked out west along the road.

'Constantinople, here we come.'

Chapter 7

'That is the imperial army?' Ketil eyed the enemy with disdain.

'No,' Leif corrected him. 'That is *an* imperial army. In fact, those are the forces of the katepans of Hellas and Thessalonika, the local imperial governors.'

Ketil nodded. That made more sense. What made less sense was these katepans sending such a limited force to stop the rebels, rather than combining their own troops with those they now knew the emperor to have dispatched somewhere further east.

'Why do they not join the emperor?' he asked.

'Self-preservation. If they marched their men east to meet the main army, they would leave their themes wide open for us to ravage, and they cannot afford to do that. If they waited for us, they could have ended up besieged by our troops. They more or less had to march against us, despite the lack of numbers.'

Another nod. But, Ketil thought to himself, the main Byzantine army would not be far behind them. Maniakes's huge force had been marching east for days now, virtually unopposed. They had had to deal with a few small, defiant garrisons, but in most cases, the imperial troops had either taken flight at the army's approach or had thrown their lot in with Maniakes and joined the rebels. In fact, their ranks had swelled considerably since landing at Dyrrachium, despite the conflicts they had endured. Now, they had finally descended from the highlands, passing the city of Edessa, a place of fortresses, ruins and impressive waterfalls, and emerged onto the plains. Leif had explained that they stretched all the way to the sea, and most of the way to Miklagarðr.

And here, on those plains, two imperial governors had gathered their forces to try and stop the usurper and save their cities, buying extra time for the emperor in the process.

But it would not buy *much* time.

'Thousands of men,' Ketil murmured to himself.

'What?'

He turned to Leif. 'Just thinking. It's a lot of men.'

In the days before Halfdan had led the Wolves into Georgia and the midst of a civil war, Ketil had never seen a warband of more than a hundred warriors. The very notion of a thousand men standing together for a battle would have stunned him, as it had, in fact, when they had met the army of King Bagrat. It was a sign of how they had all changed that he now considered the several-thousand-strong imperial force awaiting them to be little more than pitiful.

Indeed, Maniakes had decided not to bother fielding the majority of his army. Upon seeing the gathered forces waiting on the plain, he had announced that he could sweep them aside with just one *tourma*, a little over two thousand men. His officers had persuaded him to an attacking force of treble that number, just to be sure, but even then that was only a small fraction of the general's impressive force. In the end, Maniakes had committed to the battle with seven thousand men, drawn from the various lesser units who had yet to see action, allowing precious rest for those who had led the advance thus far.

The general himself would join the fight, of course. Ketil approved. It was just one more reason Maniakes deserved the throne and the support Ketil had offered. He was no yellow-spined officer who stood at the back with a flag and ordered his men to die for him. Maniakes was always in the thick of it with his troops. Indeed, he was a fearsome spectacle in a fight, probably the only man in the army who could boast a similar height to Ketil, but also powerful across the shoulders, with a build like Bjorn's. Consequently, he eschewed the small, fast ponies favoured by the Byzantine cavalry and instead rode an enormous stallion. He towered over friend and foe alike, a god among men in battle.

In theory, Ketil should be back with the staff and the waiting reserves. The Varangians in their entirety had been stood down to rest, only Byzantine regulars and a few local levies taking the field. But Ketil had strode out with the others despite that, and no one had argued, given the value the general now placed upon him. Anna had argued against Leif joining them, but the Rus had been adamant: if Ketil fought, Leif would be by his side.

'For God and the Empire!' Maniakes's voice rang out across the gathered men like a peal of thunder, raising a roar in response. With that, the general urged his horse forward. In what was apparently an ancient tactic, he had placed infantry at the middle of the line, with a cavalry force on each flank, though he and a small mounted guard held the very centre. Despite the potential speed of the cavalry, at the general's signal the entire force moved out at a steady marching pace. The valley that led down from Edessa onto the plain opened out between slopes roughly a mile apart, and Maniakes's force, even though it was but a part of his army, still almost reached each incline.

Ketil and Leif marched along with the infantry, close to the general. They had been offered horses, but Ketil felt much more at home in a fight on his feet, and so he had declined.

Leif was puffing and panting a little.

'You should have… taken the horses,' Leif managed between breaths.

'I can move faster than a horse. You must have done something to piss the gods off to be born so short.'

'Just the right height… for hamstringing lanky bastards,' he managed again as they marched.

Ketil just answered with a grin.

The imperial forces braced as their archers loosed a flight of missiles. A Byzantine officer somewhere close to the general bellowed an order that Ketil didn't quite hear, but the nature of the command was clear and, like everyone else, the Icelander lifted his shield and covered as much of himself with it as possible as he advanced. The cloud of arrows fell into the attacking force and, while the lion's share of the shafts thudded into wooden boards, here and there men disappeared with a shriek, falling away as their mates leapt over the downed bodies to continue their advance. Ketil gritted his teeth as he felt an arrow thud into his shield, the very tip of the head emerging on the inside, not far from his hand. A strangely slithery noise announced the release of a second volley even as Ketil lowered his shield to see how close they were, and he raised it in time to catch a second arrow meant for his chest.

A quick glance told him that Leif was still with him, and then the shields came down once more. They were almost on the imperial forces and, at this close distance, the archers could not target them for fear of hitting their own. Ketil eyed the waiting enemy, but twenty paces away now.

Like most of the Byzantine military they were lightly armed and generally expendable infantry. Armoured only with padded coats and a long shield, some wore small, round helmets, but most just a cloth cap or turban. Each had a sword at his side, but had prepared for the fight with a spear perhaps twice the height of a man. The front line was readied in a crouch, their spears braced in the dirt and lancing out at groin height in a lethal hedge. Behind them, the second and third lines held their spears braced below their armpit and jutting forth at chest height, adding to the line of points. The rest of the lines held them high in readiness. Such a defence would be excellent against a cavalry charge, and probably also against a standard infantry unit. They were not so well prepared for the giant Maniakes and his guards, nor for the two battle-hungry Northmen.

The rebel force gave a roar and broke into a run. The enemy braced. They looked neither happy nor confident. At that moment, Ketil lost all sense of what was happening to the rest of the attack, for his own attention was focused on the men in front of him. As he charged, he angled carefully. The three spears at each point along the line left little room for an attacker to actually reach the enemy, but Ketil had already settled upon his plan the moment he had seen them lined up.

As he reached the sharpened steel line, he thrust his shield out with his left hand, angling it so that the edge faced the waiting infantry. The shield smacked against the two spears angled out at chest height, knocking them aside even as his axe came down and sheared the head from the one at groin height. In a heartbeat he was inside the line of the enemy spears, unharmed and howling curses. He could hear Leif complaining, for in knocking the spears aside, he had simply moved them in front of the Rus, but the little man had compensated swiftly, like the clever bastard he was. Shorter than anyone else in the line, he had ducked his head and come in underneath most of the waiting spears, smashing the bottom one aside with his small, round shield.

The Byzantines panicked. They were largely conscript levies, rather than professional soldiers, and far from the born-and-bred warriors of the North. Ketil hit the front line like a charging bull. The beard of his axe fell onto the long shield of the front man and he yanked, pulling the defensive board out and to the side. The soldier gave a terrified cry, which was cut off in moments as Ketil's head connected with his. The headbutt was not a common battle manoeuvre, but the Icelander wore a good steel helmet with a wide nose guard. Ketil heard a series of crunches as the heavy steel brow caved in the soldier's face, and with little effort he brought round his shield and used it to push the mangled man out of the way. The soldier fell, gurgling, and brought down two of the men closest to him. Someone swiped at Ketil from his left, but he heard Leif curse and then a blood-curdling scream, and he could sense the space opening up beside him as the Rus went to work. A momentary glance to his left told Ketil all he needed to know about his friend. Safely inside

99

the hedge of sharp points, Leif had dropped his shield and was now laying about himself with wild abandon, hand axe in one grip, razor-sharp sax in the other. Even in that brief glimpse, Ketil saw a soldier fall with an agonised cry, the tendons at the back of his knee slashed through by the Rus blade.

Turning back to his own opponents, Ketil roared and stepped over a knot of fallen men, being careful to actually tread on the one who was rapidly recovering and making to get back up. His boot hit the man's ribs with audible cracks, guaranteeing the soldier would stay down, and then Ketil was into the next line. Behind the fallen man, a spear wavered and wobbled, and men in the enemy reserve, lines four, five and six, were trying to bring their own spears down, but there was no longer room as Maniakes's killers waded into the mass of beleaguered soldiers.

Ketil swung overhead, his axe slamming down into a man's shoulder even as his shield smashed out, pushing the injured infantryman back. The spear fell from his ruined arm and the man spun with the twin blows, staggering into the soldier beside him. The two men were dead before they hit the ground as a pair of rebel soldiers, who had now caught up with the Icelander, slashed and hacked, bellowing some battle chant of the nailed god.

Ketil was lost now to the rhythm of war. His shield lashed out, shoving enemy soldiers back and aside, while his axe slammed over and over into chain, wood, wool and flesh, bringing back with it a warm mizzle of Byzantine blood each time. The press smelled of butchered meat; of shit and of death. The world had become a dizzying whirl of panicked faces, falling bodies, blood and flashing steel. Ketil fought on. He felt blows land on him twice, but neither penetrated his chain shirt, and he would have only bruises to show for it later. To his left, Leif cut and sliced, always moving low, dealing out horrifying wounds at ankle, knee and groin height, felling man after man. Ketil could remember only a few short years ago, when the Rus had been a scholar and a politician, with little experience of or desire for battle. Whether it was constant exposure to men like Bjorn that had turned Leif into a killer, or perhaps his northern blood shining through at last, somehow, over the months of sailing and fighting with the Wolves, Leif had become a far greater warrior than most men could ever hope to be.

Ketil was so caught up in the ebb and flow that when the enemy broke, he almost went with them, dragged along with the momentum of killing. He pulled his blood-soaked axe from a staggering, glassy-eyed spearman and stepped back, heaving in breaths, as the forces of the emperor fled the field.

Clearly the katepans of Hellas and Thessalonika had decided the battle was over not long after it had begun. They had only been fighting for a short time, less than half an hour, but already their small, colourful band and expensive horses, surrounded by bannermen and musicians, were so far from the field that they were almost lost to sight. The enemy officers were dashing around, bellowing commands, trying to turn a rout into an orderly withdrawal, but they were being universally ignored by the defeated Byzantines. The surviving troops flooded across the plains, heading in a score of different directions, casting away weapons and shields, unburdening themselves in order to run faster. Ketil snorted as he watched those desperate officers. What army could be made to stand when their commanders had run at the first sign of trouble?

The rebel army cheered, the congratulatory surge swiftly giving way to jibes and insults hurled across the plain at the backs of the fleeing imperial army. The jeering only died down as the imposing Maniakes, still on his great charger and soaked in blood, lifted his sword in victory.

'The day is ours,' he bellowed. 'And the door to the capital has been opened.'

Another round of cheering. As the officers and guards around the general began to issue orders for the creation of a camp nearby and the clearing of the field, burning of the dead and gathering of any salvageable supplies, the giant general turned, his gaze falling on Ketil and Leif.

'Where was my good luck charm in the press of battle?' he said, eyebrow arched.

'You seem to have won anyway,' Ketil replied, gaze straying across the carnage. One body in seven was a rebel by his brief estimation. It was not just a victory, but a slaughter.

Maniakes gave a snort and nodded, then turned and spoke to his officers. Cavalry units were dispatched to harry the retreating infantry, to carve them up even as they ran and to be certain they did not have the chance to rally for a second attempt.

'The emperor's army will be a different matter,' Leif said to Ketil, cleaning his sax on a piece of cloth torn from a corpse. 'It will be a lot larger, and led by men specially chosen by the emperor. They will not run so easily.'

Ketil shifted his axe to the same hand as his shield, rolled his shoulders, and massaged one where he could feel a bruise already forming. 'How long 'til we meet them, I wonder?'

Leif peered out east, as though he might see past the field of corpses and spot the emperor himself. 'Soon. Very soon. I was working it out this morning with one of the general's logistics officers. At the pace we've set and with a good estimate of the date of their army's departure and the rate at which it will move, we should be almost upon them already. Thessalonika is but forty miles away. Since we're camping here now, I think we'll reach it the morning after next. I would not be at all surprised to find the emperor's forces waiting for us there. If not, they will be very close by.'

'Is the place that important then?'

Leif nodded. 'Thessalonika is the empire's second city after Constantinople. Emperors have stayed there, campaigns been launched from there. Should Thessalonika fall to Maniakes, the emperor will have some explaining to do back in the capital. It would not only be dangerous for Monomachos, but also extremely embarrassing. So I can assure you, my friend, that if there is any way the emperor can stop us reaching that city, he will do it. We may be fighting the greatest battle of this campaign tomorrow, or perhaps the day after.'

'Then let us pray that the Allfather is watching over us these coming days.'

Leif gave him an odd smile. 'And while you offer prayers to old gods, I'll personally advocate for you with the Theotokos and Christ himself. I know you're a pagan, but even *your* sorry hide is worth saving to some of us of the True Faith.'

'I'm starting to see why Bjorn was always arguing with you.'

The two men staggered from the field, ignoring the activity around them. Officers were bellowing orders all over the place, but none of them commanded the two Northmen. Somewhere back in the rest of the army, Boldin and his men waited, having been kept back with the rest of the Varangians. As Ketil and Leif wearily approached the lines, Anna came hurtling out into the open space. She ran toward Leif and he responded, breaking into a jog to meet her. As they closed, he threw out his arms, but she skittered to a halt and wagged her finger at him.

'Oh no, Leif of Kiev. I am no Rus woman to cling to a filthy, blood-soaked warrior. I am a daughter of the empire and a civilised woman. You can hug me when you've bathed and changed.'

As Leif gave her a weak smile, her brow rose. 'I am assuming all that gore belongs to other people?'

'I think I got a cut on my shin. Nothing bad, though.'

'Good. Now get yourself cleaned up so that I can be certain of that.'

Leif threw an apologetic smile at Ketil and then tottered off in Anna's wake. Anna might be a civilian and relatively poor-born, but there was something strong about her. Back in Byzantium, as Gunnhild's maid, she had been outspoken and headstrong, but since leaving the city with the völva, that had seemed to blossom into something more powerful. In an odd way, she reminded Ketil of Gunnhild, and that might not be a good thing. Did the world really need two of them? As she marched off toward the baggage train with Leif in tow, great grizzled warriors melted out of her way as she cut through the army like a dragon ship in placid waters. Gunnhild's influence had changed her, even as proximity to Bjorn had changed Leif. *Ketil* had not changed, at least.

He continued to tell himself that all the way back to the others. By the time he got there, he almost believed it.

Boldin was pleased to see him. The fifty had begun to gain something of a reputation, a certain notoriety, even. Their leader's apparent favouring by Maniakes stood them in higher stead than most units and they were given a great deal of latitude to do as they pleased, so long as they were ready when needed. Ketil had bound them to himself swiftly. Had he done that with the crew of the *Sea Wolf* before Halfdan got his hooks into them, he might still have been making a very successful career as a raider of Finn lands.

'That was short,' Boldin said, bluntly.

'Cowards. Their leaders ran first. Didn't take the warriors long to follow. Leif seems to think we are about to meet the main force. He reckons we'll face them before we get to Thess-something-or-other, so when we make camp tonight, and in the coming days, I want us on the edge of the camp, and I want every man sleeping with his equipment by his side. We'll double the usual watch but halve the times, so every man should still get enough sleep. Should they come across us in the night, I want to be able to be up and fighting by the time you can snort and spit, and I want us where we have room to rally or run, not trapped in the middle of a huge camp.'

Boldin nodded his agreement. 'We'll be ready. You'd best get yourself checked for wounds. I can hardly see any skin under all that blood, but you've got torn links on your shoulder, so someone must have hit you hard.'

Ketil nodded, shook hands with his second, and then wandered off. After a little discussion with a group of scouts sitting on the edge of the army, he was directed to a stream at the southern edge of the valley side. Filthy, blood-covered men were already there, stripping down to their underwear and sitting in the chilly flow, scooping up water and using it to wash off all the gore. Indeed, as Ketil looked downstream, he noted that as the water passed every man, it became a deeper shade of pink. With interest, he reasoned that by the time the stream reached its end, presumably somewhere across the plains to the east, the waters might well look entirely like blood. What rumours might reach the waiting ears of the empire's second city at the sight of rivers of blood flowing from the west?

It took some walking to pass all the others and find cleaner water upstream, and he could see other men following him, doing the same. If he wanted clean water without their blood in it, he was going to have to be quick. Reaching the bank, he dropped everything, peeled off his chain shirt, hissing at the fresh ache in his shoulder, stripped out of his clothes and then dropped into the two-foot-deep stream. It took only a few moments to scrub off the worst, and then he knelt at the edge and, before anyone could pollute the flow, quickly rinsed out his tunic and trousers.

As he stepped back on the grass, he nodded in satisfaction. He and his gear were far from spotless, but they were a lot less bloody now. He would try and have a proper bath later. On the way back to the new camp, where the tents were already being raised for the commanders at its centre, he made the decision to err on the side of caution and visit the medics. His shoulder was only bruised, and he was sure enough of that, but he couldn't raise his left arm above shoulder level without a great deal of pain, so it was worth a second opinion. The Byzantine army medics confirmed that there was no real damage done. They looked him over and found a number of minor injuries, but proclaimed him fit to fight and sent him on his way after just a little poking and prodding.

From there he found a group of soldiers busy sorting out foodstuffs from a cart, in preparation for the evening's meals across the camp. A few coins managed to persuade them that he had the right to pick and choose before the rest got their hands on it. He managed to grab a little salted meat, some bread, a few pieces of fruit and a small jar of wine. Laden with his prizes he wandered over to one of the few open spaces he could find and sat down, eating his feast.

By the time he finished, he had made a decision. Clearly Maniakes still remembered and valued his lucky Icelander, but if the coming battle was going to be the big one, as seemed very likely, he needed to be with the general throughout, along with Leif, Boldin and the rest of the men. This might be their big moment to make their worth truly known. To make an impression that he could later exploit when Maniakes was on the throne. To do so, he was going to have to hold a position close to the general in the fight, which would mean at the centre, in the very heart of the battle. That was the prime position, and other officers would be expecting to be placed there. He took a swig of the sharp, cheap wine, winced, and strode off toward the command tents.

Two big Varangians, with those great, long-handled axes, stood at the sides of the door to the general's tent. Even as Ketil approached, taking another slug of the wine, a clerk emerged from the tent, sour-faced and clutching a pile of documents.

'I'm here to see Maniakes,' Ketil announced.

'He's not seeing people,' one of the guards replied.

'He's seeing fucking scribes. I'm more important. Let me past.'

'Come back later.'

Ketil allowed his face to crease into what he knew was a belligerent scowl, and stepped close enough to the guard that he almost trod on his foot. The two Varangians had been chosen for their size, but neither of them could match Ketil in height, and the guard found himself looking straight at the Icelander's chin. Slowly, his gaze slid up to meet Ketil's eyes. He did not look cowed, but some of the haughtiness had gone from his stance.

'You try and stop me, and I'll send you to meet your fucking nailed god in person.'

The other guard changed his grip on his axe and took a step forward, but as they squared up, a voice called from within. 'Who is that?'

'Me, Ketil,' he called.

'Let him in,' sighed Maniakes, and the two Varangians stepped back into place, throwing black looks his way. He met them with a tight smile containing no humour, and then marched in through the tent flaps.

The general's tent had only recently been put up and most of the furnishings had yet to be unloaded from the wagon, but a brazier, table and chair had been swiftly provided. Maniakes was seated, looking over a set of records on the table. He glanced up and nodded at Ketil. 'Go on.'

The Icelander looked at the general. Something about the big man seemed different. Usually, when Maniakes took meetings in his tent, he was more at ease. Today, he had yet to unstrap his armour or even wash off the gore; only his hands were clean so far, a bloody towel on the floor nearby. Maniakes owned a great copper bathtub that would be brought into his tent and filled with heated water before nightfall. But he could have taken his armour off, at least.

Ketil shrugged off his observations and straightened. 'I want pride of place in the coming battle.'

Maniakes frowned. 'I have already concocted a rudimentary battle plan. I have you on the left flank, supported by the Macedonian cavalry, and next to another unit of veteran Varangians. Though any sensible man would choose a good tactician to face me, I doubt that will be the case with Monomachos. In fact, I will be very surprised if I am not facing Stephanos, and the man is as strategically minded as an ape's behind. Stephanos has lost more battles than he's won, and to my knowledge has never employed a new tactic. He will place the *hikanatoi* or the excubitores, or both, on that flank. They are among his best troops, and so I want the most vicious bastards in my army facing them. When they break, the heart will go out of the enemy. That is my plan. That is where you will stand. Not with me at the centre. The flank will be more important.'

Ketil chewed his cheek, thinking this over. He would not be visible to Maniakes, but perhaps, if that flank was going to be as critical as the general believed, he could gain more glory by leading the fight there. He straightened. 'All right. But don't forget me, just because you cannot see me.'

Maniakes gave a short, barked laugh. 'Unlikely, my lucky Icelander. You shall bring good fortune to the whole army by winning the battle for me.'

Ketil took a breath, but Maniakes was moving. Slowly, he rose from the chair, then gave a salute and gestured toward the tent door. 'And now, I think I shall rest,' the giant announced.

Ketil turned and strode from the tent, but as he did, a suspicion was forming. Something about the way the general had moved suggested that something was wrong. He had leaned slightly to the side, and Ketil could have sworn he winced, if only for a fraction of a moment.

It was probably something amiss with his armour.

Chapter 8

'Mean you to fight in the dark, Basileos?'

Maniakes turned in his saddle to look at the officer who had spoken, the late evening sun hovering just above the horizon, lending him a golden glow across his bronze scaled armour. 'Do you underestimate our strength so much, Demetrios? No, I intend to crush them and to be master of this field before the last of that gold disc is gone below the hills. This should not take long.'

'He's certainly confident,' Leif murmured to Ketil as they watched the imperial army manoeuvring. 'They must outnumber us by two men to our one.'

Ketil shrugged. 'Maniakes knows his battles. He's not stupid. The enemy is mostly conscripts or untested guards, shiny nobodies from the city. The army we travel with has been tested in war across Italy and boasts many Northmen. They outnumber us two to one, but each of our men is worth four of theirs.'

Leif looked unconvinced, but Maniakes had apparently heard the comment and turned to them. 'The critical thing is those banners at the rear. See them? They are the standards of the *Sebastophoros* Stephanos, the very fool I thought they would send. He is unimaginative, predictable and altogether not very bright. See how the far flank gleams bronze and purple? They are the palace regiments, just as I had anticipated. Even now he lines up his men exactly as I knew he would, and he will pin his hopes on that formation, as expected. You, and my fearsome

Varangians, will break them, and the horse will follow up in support.'

He leaned back in his saddle. 'The only surprise is the *scholae*. I did not expect them to be fielded. I was sure Monomachos would keep them in the city to guard his walls against my arrival. He has committed them, though. See the cavalry in the centre. They are the other crucial enemy unit to beat and I shall lead personally against them. My northerners will break the excubitores on the flank, I shall rout the scholae, and the enemy army will collapse in its entirety. Now, let us take them before they are ready. Sound the advance.'

The rebel army was already in position. The wily general had spent the last day moving forward in a wide formation, making use of the great, flat plains so that his army had been in place for battle the moment the advance scouts had warned of the enemy army ahead. Conversely, the arrival of Maniakes and his troops had clearly taken Stephanos by surprise, for he was still deploying his units in a hurry, much of his force still arriving on the field from the travelling column.

As the calls went out and Maniakes gathered his own heavy cavalry, Ketil and Leif turned and ran across the front of the lines. Some eight hundred paces away, Boldin and their fifty waited, along with a huge force of Varangians, ready to move. Indeed, even as the two men fell in at the front-centre of the unit, they were already advancing in response to the calls.

Maniakes was not a man to balk at danger. Ketil turned at shouts and blasts to see that the giant general and his heavily armoured cavalry had already pulled ahead of the battle line, charging headlong at the gleaming ranks of the emperor's elite guards. By the time the Varangians had crossed but half the distance toward the ranks of the imperial force, the general had hit the enemy. It was truly impressive, Ketil had to admit. If ever a man was born to lead an army in battle, that man was Maniakes. He and his riders hit the enemy centre like a winter wave crashing over the sea wall. So hard, in fact, that they broke the lines instantly, and in heartbeats were among the press of the enemy, chopping and hacking with fury, slaying any man who came within sword reach.

The imperial unit was equipped with solid, bowl-like helmets with plated neck guards, shirts of gleaming scales over long, padded tunics, large shields shaped like teardrops and long, straight swords. They were formed with perfect precision, each shield in a line with the rest, swords up and ready to strike, every bearded face sporting a grimace. They might have frightened any other enemy, but these attackers were Northmen.

Moments later, those Northmen joined the fight, Ketil and his warriors, along with each other *bandon* of Varangians in the army. There was no strategy here, no need for manoeuvres or signals. Every man on the flank, whether he prayed to the Allfather or kissed the cross, carried the song of the North in his veins, and battle came as naturally as breathing.

Ketil hit the wall of shields hard and with an immediate three-pronged attack. His shield came up at the last moment to block the falling sword of the imperial soldier opposite, his axe slammed out, biting into the top of the man's shield, dragging it to the side, and his left foot stamped down hard on his boot. The soldier's sword skittered off the round northern shield even as the bones in his foot broke and his shield was forced aside, exposing his belly.

Ketil did not have time to take advantage of the man's predicament, for Leif took the opportunity, leaning slightly – even as he blocked a blow with his own shield – and sliding his sax into the man's belly, just under the bottom edge of the scale shirt. He ripped it to the side as he pulled it out, opening a bloody smile in the man's midriff. Blood and organs spilled out and Ketil simply pushed the man aside and stepped in to take the next, promising himself that he would punch Leif later for taking the kill.

Boldin was suddenly beside him, roaring imprecations as his axe bit into a Byzantine shoulder, the blow so hard that the scale armour did little to protect its wearer, the blade sinking deep into flesh and bone. Boldin's victim screamed and fell to one side, and Boldin cursed as the axe was pulled from his grip, tightly wedged in the body. Growling, the Varangian also let his shield go and drew a sword and a sax from his waist, launching himself at another man in the press.

Ketil was suddenly being pounded with a sword from the side, but managed to move his shield in time to block all but the first blow, which had hit him hard, bruising him badly and possibly even damaging a rib. Gritting his teeth against the discomfort, he took the repeated blows on the shield, his arm aching more with every thud. He managed to get his own axe down in the press and, with some difficulty, swung it upward into the unseen attacker. He could not get much momentum behind the blow, but the nethers of these men were poorly protected and the blade slammed up into a groin covered with only tunic and breeches. The pounding on his shield ceased in an instant as the mortally wounded man disappeared, howling.

Given a little space once more, Ketil shouldered his shield and cursed the fresh pain in his side, which pulsed every time he tried to lift the boards. An excubitore leapt from the mass, bellowing some insult in Greek and swinging a blade. He managed to catch the blow with his axe, trapping the blade between the curve of the head and the haft, and jerked the axe aside, ripping the man's sword away. As the Byzantine blinked, Ketil hit him hard with his shield, the iron boss slamming into the man's chest. Scale armour could turn a blade and stop an arrow, but was little use against blunt force, and the crack of the man's sternum breaking within the armour was audible even over the din of battle.

The Icelander had no chance to take stock of the situation, even as the man fell away, for another warrior hit him from the side. He turned even as he was pushed back to see that Boldin was kneeling on the ground, moaning and clutching his ribs, and his comrade's attacker had now moved on to him. The soldier was big, strong and determined, and Ketil was driven back step by step, the man too close for him to bring his axe to bear.

Hurt by the damage to his ribs, Ketil managed to get the shield between him and the soldier and tried to anchor his foot. The man was still too close to swing an axe, but Ketil managed to lift his weapon above the struggle and brought the end of the haft down on him, where shoulder met neck. The pressure pushing him back relented as the soldier snarled and staggered away for a moment. Ketil turned and hefted his weapon, ready to try for a strike.

He never saw the blow coming. Whether it came from axe, sword or some other edge, a tremendous strike slammed into him. He felt his helmet crumple under the weight of the blow, and the sudden white-hot agony of a wound to the face.

He reeled, his world suddenly an explosion of pain and disorientation. In a heartbeat, he had dropped both axe and shield and had reached up, gripping his damaged helmet. He couldn't see. All was black and red and fiery. As he tried to pull the helmet from his head, there came a fresh wave of hurt in his left temple and the side of his face. The crumpled iron had creased under the blow and driven into his head. He struggled, blind and panicked. A blow landed on his back, but he ignored it. Somehow, screaming violent curses, he managed to pull the helmet free of his head, but he was sure part of his scalp and face had come away with it.

Ketil dropped the helmet too now, dizzy and weak. He vomited copiously, and every tiny movement sent waves of searing pain across the left side of his head. He couldn't have said how long he stood there, stunned, unseeing and inactive, simply enduring the agony, trying to get a grip on his shaking body.

With some surprise, he realised that he was squeezing his eyes shut. Was that why he couldn't see? What was he doing? He opened his eyes, and immediately wished he hadn't. Only one worked. His right eye sprang open, blinking away the blood that seemed to coat him. His left eye either hadn't opened or, if it had, no longer worked. He was blind to his left. Reaching up gingerly, he touched the left side of his face.

The extraordinary pain that even that tiny touch sent arcing through his head made him throw up again.

Heedless of the danger, even standing in the midst of battle, he stood still, allowing his body to settle, trying to master the excruciating sensations coursing through his body. Slowly, the swimming, blurred vision in his one good eye came into focus. He was no longer in the thick of it. The Varangians had pushed back the excubitores and were on the cusp of totally breaking the flank, just as Maniakes had planned. His darting eye briefly caught sight of the body of Boldin, face down in the blood and mud.

Another figure suddenly appeared in front of him. It was Leif, and he was shouting at him.

He couldn't hear what the Rus was saying, but the man seemed urgent, desperate. Ketil tried to say something, he wasn't sure what, but it made no difference, because the moment he opened his mouth, he just threw up again. He felt something in his fingers and swivelled his eye to try and see, lifting that hand. He dared not move his head just yet. Leif had pushed his axe into his palm and was closing his fingers around the haft.

'Can you walk?'

Ketil was so surprised to suddenly hear the words that he involuntarily turned his head to look down at the Rus, and the pain washed over him afresh. He nodded instinctively in answer and immediately realised what a stupid thing that was to do.

'Yeagh...' he croaked. 'Think so.'

'Your face is a mess. Can you see?'

'Little.'

He turned, very slowly, taking in the battle. The rebel army was clearly winning and impressively so. The enemy lines were in utter disarray, this flank all but crumbled, the centre hard-pressed by Maniakes and his armoured cavalry. Desperate calls were going out all across the imperial force.

Strangely, despite the deafening noise of the battlefield and the pulse of his own blood, which thumped like a hundred drums, Ketil heard the bird. Even knowing the pain moving his head caused, he found himself looking up. Two black shapes flitted about above the battlefield, cawing repeatedly. He stared with his remaining eye. Birds did not fly across a battle. They were always in evidence afterwards, feasting on the remains, but during the fighting itself they never flew across the field. He felt his skin prickle with the presence of *Seiðr* on the plain. The gods were at work here. Odin's birds were watching.

Leif was shouting at him again, but he ignored the man, waving him down with his free hand even as he concentrated on the two birds, waves of hurt striking the cliffs of his resolve again and again. He could hear the cries.

Death, they were calling. He knew that it was the birds' own language, but he could hear the word in their cries as clear as anything. *Death*.

He closed his eyes, willing this to be a dream or an illusion, and opened them again, hoping to find no birds. But the two black omens continued to chant *death* above the field, and he could see shapes forming in the late evening sky. They were indistinct, just a blur in the deepening gloom, but he knew what they were: Odin's handmaidens were coming for the fallen.

Well, Ketil of Stöð was not fallen. He was in agony, half-blind, and troubled by even basic movement, but he breathed, he stood and he reasoned, so he was still very much alive. No *Valkyrja* was going to take him to Odin's hall just yet. But the meaning was clear. Odin's ravens called *death* and the Valkyrjur were gathering. The rebels had all but won, but somehow that was not meant to be. He lowered his gaze once more, fighting the waves of nausea, and settled his one good eye on Leif the Teeth.

'Find... others. Find men. Pu— pull back.'

'What?' Leif stared at him. 'Why? We've won!'

'No. Lost.'

With that he turned, his wounded gaze sweeping across what should have been a glorious victory. He was just in time to see it; he might have been the only man on the battlefield who did. Maniakes fell.

Ketil, a head above every man between himself and the general, had an unusually unrestricted view of what happened. The great warrior, claimant to the throne, the only man who could have ended the terrible sequence of emperors that plagued Byzantium, a man they had all followed from Italy in this bid for power, died in that moment.

The distant giant had swayed in his saddle, sword falling from his fingers. His hand went to his side and he looked down. The details were hazy across the clamour of battle, but in the darkness of his own head, Ketil saw once again that evening in the general's tent. Maniakes rising from his chair, wincing and leaning to one side. The general had taken a wound in that last fight, but had refused to stop, knowing that victory was so close. Ketil knew how that worked. A wound that had not yet healed could not cope with violent movement, and it was certain in his mind that Maniakes had been slowly leaking out his life's blood even as he fought to victory on this field.

As the general toppled from his horse, he disappeared from view and a roar of dismay arose from the heart of the battle.

'What is it?' Leif demanded, still close by.

'Maniakes fall,' Ketil replied, pulling back his gaze, swallowing, trying to speak through the pain. 'Fallen. Battle lost. War lost.'

Sure enough, as that great wail of disaster rippled through the rebel army, shaking them, cracking their resolve and their morale, cheers of victory arose from the serried ranks of the imperial army. In a heartbeat, the flank, which the Varangians had broken and won, was being recovered. The rebels were being driven back now, step by step, forced to retreat across the field as fresh energy and hope spread throughout the excubitores. Maniakes had been the heart and soul, the driving force of the rebel army. His fall changed it all.

Another moan drew Ketil's attention and he could now see, in the distance, a small shape atop a pole, waving around at the centre of the field. It was too small to make out clearly, but he knew what it was: the head of the would-be emperor, Georgios Maniakes, had been hacked free and mounted on the tip of a spear.

Already, the centre had turned into a rout. The enemy was roaring and fighting with renewed fury, taking heads and crushing the rebels. The general's heavy cavalry, which had been utterly destroying the scholae beside their master only moments earlier, was now on the run, racing for safety. Confused calls went up as some rebel officers tried to rally their men while others took up the order to retreat. Chaos exploded across the field.

Only the Varangians alongside Ketil continued to put up any kind of resistance, but the fight had gone out of them, too, and they would not hold for long while the rest of the army fled.

Ketil and Leif turned to the pressed ranks of the Varangians, unable to find their own men among so many similarly clad warriors in the confusion. After a short pause, Leif cupped his free hand to his mouth and bellowed at the top of his lungs.

'Odiiiiiiin!'

Ketil turned, surprised to hear the god's name from the mouth of Leif, whose adherence to the nailed god was unshakable. But quickly he realised what Leif was doing. Only their own men on this field would respond to the call. Moments later, Ketil was yelling alongside him.

'Odiiiiiiin!'

The two men continued to shout for what seemed like hours. Somehow Ketil seemed to have gone numb; the pain was just as bad, but now oddly muted. He still felt sick, though.

Gradually, figures emerged from the press, pulling their way free of the fight. Most were at least scratched, and some seriously wounded; many had lost their shields and some their axes, too. Even as they emerged, though, they were dying. Two fell as they tried to clear to open ground. The imperial force was totally ascendant now, breaking even the Varangian ranks. The centre was gone, and presumably the far flank too, and while the rebel army fled across the field, the imperial forces were already in pursuit, flooding over the bodies of the fallen and chasing the panicked rebels.

'Heavens,' Leif said suddenly, eyes wide as he turned.

'Wha?' Ketil replied, turning with him to look back across the field.

The fleeing rebels were running in any direction they could, seeking somewhere to hide from their pursuers, but a force of mounted scholae was bearing down already on the undefended baggage train at the rear of the rebel position. More than a hundred wagons carried all the provisions, supplies, ammunition and tents for the army. And with them were the teamsters, the servants, the army's wives and children...

And Anna.

Before Ketil could say anything, Leif was running. He was only small, but desperation lent him unprecedented speed and he raced off across the churned mud and blood of the field at a pace Ketil had never seen. The Icelander turned to the dozen or so men who had managed to pull clear of the fighting and were looking to him with bleak expressions, willing him to do something to save them.

'Follow,' he said, and turned.

He ran, for a grand total of ten steps. Then agony overwhelmed him, the nausea returned with a vengeance, and he collapsed, drool and vomit flowing. As he recovered slowly, he realised the others had stopped too and were watching, concerned. There was no way he was going to maintain a run in this state. His shaky gaze fell upon an abandoned cavalry horse wandering nearby, its coat bloody with evidence of its owner's fate. Swallowing pain and queasiness, he rose, staggered to the horse and, with the help of one of his men, pulled himself up onto the beast.

'Follow,' he said again, and turned the horse, racing away from the field, the motion bringing a whole new level of sickness. His men pounded along in his wake and he knew he was leaving them behind. Still they followed on as they could, even as Ketil rapidly caught up with Leif running ahead of him. Ketil's fingers gripped the axe Leif had pushed into his hands.

He rode.

Guilt flowed through him now. He had been wrong. He had argued with Halfdan because the lure of Byzantine gold and the impressive figure of Maniakes had turned his head. He had asked the others to come. Had they done so, now all the Wolves of Odin might have been staggering, wounded and bloody, across this field of failure. He had gambled on Maniakes, and he had lost.

And he could have swallowed the bitter draught of that failure, had it been only him. But he had begun to think himself a jarl. He had started to think he had replaced Halfdan and was doing a better job. In the silence of his soul, he had pitied those friends left behind with the young jarl – walking into the unknown while Ketil played out his guaranteed plan for riches and fame. He had been wrong.

Worst of all, he had taken Leif and Anna with him. They could have been safe back with the others in Apulia, but instead they were here, on this field of death, beneath the gathering Valkyrjur. He had led them to this.

He gritted his teeth. He was wrong, but he was man enough to admit it. Odin had given an eye for wisdom, and so it seemed had Ketil. Only now, running for his life and for those of his companions, did he see clearly how Halfdan had always been meant to be the jarl, and that Ketil had made a dreadful mistake forging his own path. An eye for wisdom.

Now he had to make things right. He had to find Anna. He had to save her and Leif. And the others, all those men pounding across the field behind him who had gradually become his men rather than the empire's. No one in this rebel army would ever see Miklagarðr again, but he could save his own; *had* to save his own.

In moments he was past Leif, his horse thundering across the grass. It took some time for him to see Anna, for she was to his left, and he now had to turn his head to look in that direction. She was sprinting *toward* them, the crazy woman. She should have fled, found somewhere to hide, but instead she was running toward disaster, shouting her lover's name. The Rus, not far behind him, was calling out to her, too.

Most of the enemy were racing for the wagons. They cared little about the camp followers and civilians, though as night fell, as sure as *Ragnarok*, there would be rape and murder across the land. For now, however, the victorious imperial troops had their eye on plunder. Those wagons would carry great prizes and an ambitious soldier would want to secure his share before the senior officers arrived and put an end to the looting.

But one man had seen Anna and had veered in her direction. His horse was tired from the battle, and flagging, but he forced it on anyway, bearing down on the fleeing woman. His sword came out to his side, blade still gleaming with blood from the battle.

Ketil could hear Leif, further and further behind with every stride, praying for her.

The Icelander pushed his exhausted horse on, trying to ignore the discomfort every strike of its hooves sent through his body. He rode like he had never ridden before. He had always been his own man, even when he'd taken an oath to Halfdan. He'd always been out for himself, prepared to do what he must to survive and to win. Only now, with the closing of an eye and the arrival of wisdom, did he realise that he was, and would always be, one of the Wolves. For the first time in his life, he was fighting for something more important than himself.

He ignored the pain. He rode. He was close now. Almost on the rider. But the enemy was closing on Anna. Ketil realised he couldn't get there in time. The man would kill Anna before he could do anything.

He lifted the axe Leif had forced into his hand. It was a heavy thing, a war axe, not a weighted throwing weapon. It would take the muscles of Bjorn to cast such a weapon with any hope of accuracy.

That was all Ketil had now: hope.

He threw the axe with all his might, begging the gods that they guide it and carry it through the air.

It struck the enemy horse low, on the rear right leg. The throw was clumsy, but Odin was with them, and perhaps the momentum of his own steed had added to the pitch. Whether the blow broke the horse's leg, or just surprised it, causing the exhausted beast to trip, it fell, a tumble of mount and rider, legs flailing.

Ketil, thanking the Allfather as he rode, closed on the soldier. Anna ran past him without a glance, hurtling into the arms of her Rus. Ketil, though, needed to finish the cavalryman. The horse was alive, if hurt, for it rolled a few times and finally came up again, unsteadily, and staggered away a little. The rider lay shaking on the ground. As Ketil closed, he realised the horse had rolled across the man's lower half. He was broken, done for. Ketil reined in and slid somewhat gracelessly from the saddle, pulling his sax free from his belt. He dropped, the sudden movement even more dizzying than the run, and cut the man's throat.

When he turned and rose, Leif and Anna were together, and eleven of the fifty Ketil had led since Dyrrachium were following close on. Behind them – *worryingly close* behind them – came the forces of the victorious emperor, Constantine Monomachos, seeking blood and riches. They had only moments.

The others skittered to a halt, panting.

'What now, sir?' one of the Varangians asked, worry evident in his voice.

Ketil straightened. He was no jarl, knew now that he never would be, but he had to play that role as best he could for a little longer, to save these people. He squared his shoulders. 'We leave.'

'The bags,' Leif said meaningfully, pointing at the wagons that were even now being stripped by whooping imperial soldiers.

Ketil closed his eyes for a moment. Their kit was on those wagons along with everyone else's. But unlike the others, *their* kit held the gold they had won at such cost in Miklagarðr. Its loss was just another reminder of Ketil's failure.

'Bags are gone. Gold is gone. All we have is our lives. We have to get away from here before the enemy comes for our heads.'

'Where do we go?' another Varangian muttered, hope absent from his voice.

'West. The east is closed to us now. But to the west we have friends. I abandoned them once, but I think they will take us back.'

Leif nodded, reaching for Anna, whose sad gaze was locked on the eastern horizon. There would be no homecoming for her after all. She turned with him, reluctantly. West it had to be. Halfdan would surely not hold a grudge. The Wolves of Odin had to gather once more.

Ketil hauled himself back into the saddle with some difficulty, then turned his mount and the fourteen of them made for the last, blood-red rays of the setting sun.

Part Three

�ᛒ ᛟᚠ ᚱᚢᚾᛁᛏ

City of the Fugitive

Chapter 9

'Hold. Something is amiss,' the Norman said, quietly.

Halfdan held up his hand, his small hirð coming to a halt in an instant. Bjorn took another step forward to stand by the jarl's side as Fulk and Marc consulted, peering ahead.

'Why have we stopped?' the big man rumbled, frowning. 'There's nothing wrong.'

But Halfdan had already come to trust the Norman's instincts in the four days they had travelled together. Fulk de Courvaudon knew the area well, having spent years fighting here, allied to one side or another, as most of the Normans had. Moreover, he knew the tactics and habits of the locals and of the Byzantines. He had also made every effort to visit the villages and inns they passed, wearing simple travelling clothes and asking for any local news of forces nearby. Three times already they had avoided walking into large Byzantine columns on the move, or Apulian lords travelling with their households, because of Fulk's caution. It did mean they had moved with infuriating slowness, but it was better to progress slowly and safely than to become embroiled in one of the many small wars that still raged in the region, even with Maniakes and the bulk of the imperial forces gone. On this occasion, though, Halfdan could feel it, too. Something was amiss.

'Listen.'

Bjorn grunted. 'I am. I can't hear anything.'

'Exactly.'

There is a certain kind of silence that results from a group of people being carefully quiet, and this was most definitely that kind. The hair rose on the back of Halfdan's neck.

The stillness was shattered by a flock of birds suddenly startled into flight from a tree somewhere off to their left.

'Bandits?' Halfdan queried in little more than a whisper.

Fulk shook his head. 'No one I have spoken to mentioned local bandits, and a group of such outlaws would surely have taken us while we were still moving. Bandits are opportunists and there are too many of us to take on in a straight fight. No, not bandits. And not Byzantines. The Greeks are incapable of such quiet. An officer would be shouting commands by now.'

'Let me handle this,' Gunnhild murmured, stepping past them, her carved stick gripped tightly. Halfdan watched her walk out ahead and despite his misgivings, he felt a certain pride. Even if the goddess never spoke to her again, she was a magnificent sight: her piercing green eyes sharp; ash-blonde hair braided from her temples and tied at the back of her head; long, green dress seemingly melting into the woodland surroundings.

'Wait,' Fulk warned her, but she waved his concern aside with a hand and disappeared into the undergrowth by the side of the road without looking back. Halfdan smiled at the look of surprise on the Norman's face as he watched her, for as the young woman disappeared among the trees, there was hardly a sound. The undergrowth seemed not to move with her passage, as though she drifted *through* the plants, rather than across or around them.

'She unnerves me,' Marc murmured at their shoulders.

'That's natural,' Halfdan smiled. 'She does that to everyone. But if that's how her friends feel, imagine being her enemy.'

The bannerman simply nodded, watching the edge of the woods. The rest fell in behind them, waiting, quiet, a dozen Varangians and a score of Normans all armoured and ready for trouble. At the rear, a small string of pack horses carried all their gear, and Courvaudon's horse walked among them, the Norman travelling by foot alongside his men and the Varangians.

They stood for some time in silence, and when Gunnhild reappeared it was so sudden that even Halfdan jumped a little. Striding across to them, she came to a halt, shouldering her stick.

'Fourteen men,' she said in a quiet voice. 'They are in a clearing almost a hundred paces from the road. They are hiding, waiting quietly. They do not look ready to launch an attack. I believe they are waiting for you to pass by, aware of your superior numbers.'

Halfdan looked across at Fulk and shrugged a question. The Norman lord drummed his fingers on his belt. 'What did they look like? Did they bear colours?'

'Red and yellow,' she replied. 'Stripes like the rays of the setting sun.'

Fulk continued to look thoughtful, perhaps even uncertain, which was new in the normally confident Norman.

'Who are they?' Halfdan prodded.

Fulk sighed. 'Soldiers of Salerno. Their master, Guaimar, is one of the most powerful of the Italian lords. Much of the land north and west of here belongs to him. The nearest city is Potenza, just a few miles away, and it has been contested between Guaimar and the Byzantines for years now. I could not say offhand who currently controls it. I have been rather cut off in the south.'

'This Guaimar. You speak of him as an enemy, yes?'

Fulk gave an odd laugh. 'In this land, Halfdan, everyone is at least a little bit enemy. Even your friends. *Especially* your friends,' he added with another chuckle, and Halfdan spotted something in his eyes then that gave him uncomfortable pause.

'Answer plain,' Halfdan grumbled. 'Is he friend or enemy?'

'Both,' sighed Fulk again. 'He has supported some of our lords, including Iron Arm himself. It was Guaimar who gave

Melfi to Iron Arm. But it has been less than a year since we were at war with Salerno and the alliance is shaky at best. Some of our lords still fight with Guaimar despite the change. Alliances here are written on water and change with every tide.'

Halfdan frowned. 'Your men fight an ally? Do not obey their jarl?'

'God in Heaven, Halfdan, but you are a relic of a lost age, aren't you? Every Norman here with a fief of his own is his own lord with his own goals and his own plans. Iron Arm rules us all because he is the strongest, but still he is only the lord because we voted him to it. He *rules* us. He does not *control* us.'

'Then where does that leave us with the men in the woods?'

'It is a problem. If Salerno has driven the Byzantines from Potenza then the city is in their hands. That means they have control over the area, and we would be wise to avoid trouble with them. If they are in small numbers, though, and the Byzantines still hold Potenza, then...' He scrubbed his head with his hand. 'Gah, but things were easier when we were just at war with the Byzantines. Now everything is so... political.'

Halfdan turned to Bjorn. 'You're ready?'

'*Always* ready,' the albino replied with a gappy grin.

The jarl turned back to his Norman ally. 'They are fourteen. We are more than twice that number. We deal with them.'

Fulk shook his head. 'But if they are hiding, we might be better avoiding trouble.'

'We cannot avoid trouble, Lord of Courvaudon. Trouble travels with us. He stands over there, pale as snow and picking his nose, and he's ready for a fight. One thing is certain in all of life: unless you can truly trust a man, never allow him to get behind you with a knife. If we cannot trust these Salerno men, we deal with them before we move on.'

'But the political ramifications...'

'Are unimportant.' Halfdan was starting to feel frustrated. Why was Courvaudon being so cagey? 'If they all die, then no one can lay the blame with us, so we must attack in such a manner to catch them all. Your men are the loudest,' Halfdan smiled. 'You sound like an army with all your armour and gear. Keep marching, then turn off the road at the next rise and fan out through the woods, coming back toward them. Make sure no one gets away. We'll jump them from this side. Together, we will trap them.'

Fulk still looked uncertain, but finally he nodded, and the Normans set off once more, traipsing along the road, rattling and clanking. Halfdan gave directions to his men with just hand signals, and the sixteen of them melted into the undergrowth beside the road at speed, leaving the pack horses walking on, making plenty of noise.

The jarl waved to Farlof and Ulfr, flashing a splayed open hand at each and pointing left and right. In response, the two men took five of the others and spread out, creating three groups moving through the woods carefully and in a line, like thralls driving prey through the forest toward the huntsmen. As they moved further and further from the road, they slowed, taking care with their movements, avoiding breaking twigs where they could, holding shields up, away from the undergrowth, gripping scabbards to stop them slapping against hips. They were so quiet that they were almost upon the waiting Italians before the enemy soldiers knew they were there.

A collection of shapes in red-and-yellow striped coats, wearing conical steel helmets and gripping tall spears, was just visible through the foliage. Halfdan waved a hand and in an instant the entire group came to a halt, breathing lightly, looking ahead. The Italians were not watching them. Indeed, their attention was clearly focused on the far side of the clearing. In the silence, they could hear the telltale, if sporadic, noise of armoured men moving through undergrowth. Halfdan had known Fulk long enough already to know that such a level of noise could only be their Norman friends deliberately making a din. Not only would they attract the attention of the hiding soldiers, but the distraction also allowed Halfdan and the others to plot their rough position. The northerners waited, eyes drifting back and forth between the oblivious Italians and Halfdan leading them.

Halfdan held his breath, counting silently, working out how far away the Normans would be. When he reckoned they were only a little further from the clearing than the Wolves, he lifted his hand and motioned for everyone to be ready. When the last of his men nodded his agreement, the jarl raised the short, eagle-hilted blade he had taken in Georgia and swept it forward, toward the soldiers.

With a roar, the sixteen northerners ran the last ten paces, ignoring the foliage and thin branches that whipped around them. They burst into the clearing like a wave of iron-coated death.

The Italians were stunned, caught by surprise. Indeed, half of them seemed to be unaware of this fresh danger, still at the far side of the clearing and peering off into the woods, watching for the approaching Normans. The rest had turned at the shouting and were diving for shields left leaning against rocks or running to meet the threat.

Halfdan leapt a fallen log to meet the nearest of the Italians. The man held his spear out in front, gripped in both hands with his shield on his forearm. The tip of the blade was thrust at Halfdan, but it took little effort to bring his own wolf-painted shield up and turn aside the point. With a cry to Odin, he slammed into the man, knocking him back into the clearing. The winded soldier almost fell, struggling to keep his feet under the attack. Even as he barrelled the soldier across the clearing, Halfdan identified the weakest points of the man's unarmoured torso and lifted his blade. The point punched through the striped coat, angled so that it slid with relative ease between two ribs to drive deep into the body, cutting through the vitals within.

The soldier let out a wheezing gurgle and the resistance went out of him in a moment. Careful to retain a strong grip on the hilt, Halfdan pulled his sword back and the dying soldier fell away, the yellow stripes of his coat rapidly swelling to the same colour as the red. The body hit the ground and lay there as the man gasped his last, but Halfdan was already moving on. His men were engaged with the rest, and Gunnhild was making a most non-magical use of her stick. Indeed, she shouted something surprisingly base as she yanked the point back out of an Italian's eye, the last part of her imprecation lost beneath the screaming of her victim.

The attack had been overwhelming already. Only six of the fourteen soldiers in the clearing had come to meet them, and all six had been put down in the opening moments of the fight. At the same time, the remaining eight looked about, struggling to decide what to do. Three of them settled for facing the noise of armoured men approaching in the woods, bellowing at the remaining five in their incomprehensible local language, though from the fact that one of them jabbed a finger toward Halfdan it was clear the five were being told to engage and to take on the northerners. The dithering men looked first at the soldier who'd given the order, then at Halfdan and his warriors climbing over the red-and-yellow corpses, and bolted.

They did not get far. As Halfdan led his men across the clearing, sending half of them after the runners and taking the others against the defiant three, it became clear that Fulk had been smarter than even Halfdan had expected. The approaching din turned out to be only eight of the Normans, led by Marc, making an inordinate amount of noise. As those eight broke clear of the undergrowth, trapping the three soldiers against the Wolves, Fulk and the rest appeared in a cordon, emerging from the trees all around and driving back the five men who'd tried to flee but had merely run headlong into more attackers.

It became clear that Halfdan was going to face no one else, as the remaining Italians fought for their life against Fulk and his Normans, an armoured machine of mayhem that hacked and battered them into submission. A thought struck him, and he ran across the clearing to where one of the Normans towered above a wounded and disarmed soldier. The Italian was on his knees, eyes closed and palms together in prayer as the Norman's heavy sword rose for the downward swing that would end his life.

'Wait.'

The Norman didn't hear him for a moment, and the sword began to descend before the warrior became aware of Halfdan running toward him, shouting. The sword stopped as Halfdan reached the scene, and the Italian soldier opened terrified eyes and looked up at the killing blow that had not come. He smelled of urine. 'Tie him up,' Halfdan told the Norman, who looked across at Fulk for confirmation. The lord nodded, and by the time the last of the men in the clearing was down, the prisoner had been hauled over to the trunk of a tree and tied to it, arms encircling the bole behind him uncomfortably, wrists bound there.

Finally, as the fighting stopped, the gathering closed on the scene. A brief headcount suggested no losses and only three men were gripping or probing injuries. Fulk crossed to Halfdan with his bannerman close by, and Gunnhild and Farlof joined them too, as the others moved around the clearing, thrusting blades into bodies to make sure they stayed down.

'You speak their tongue?' Halfdan asked the Norman. He had to, of course. He'd been making enquiries as they travelled.

Fulk nodded.

'Ask him about that city you mentioned.'

The Norman rattled off a number of questions in that strange tongue. The soldier was defiant for only a few moments before something Fulk said made him blanch in horror. A heart-beat later, panicked explanations were spilling out of the man. Courvaudon translated as they came.

'Potenza is in the hands of the Byzantines still, but it will not hold out much longer. Guaimar's forces encircle the place and have been pounding it with artillery. He gave a lot more detail than this, but that is the meat of it.'

Halfdan frowned. There had been a lot of speech for such little information. 'Why is Potenza important to Guaimar?'

Another exchange, and Fulk translated again. 'Guaimar has claimed Potenza for some time, but it seems that the forces of Benevento are also moving in. It appears that both princes are looking for someone known to be in the area.'

Halfdan narrowed his eyes. Fulk was holding something back. 'Slow down. You're talking in riddles. Where is Benevento and who is this man they are looking for who is important enough to draw the attention of two kingdoms?'

Fulk looked unusually flustered. Halfdan folded his arms. The man was still being cagey, withholding information. 'Whatever you are not telling me, now would be the time. You have friends here, Courvaudon. Don't make enemies of them.'

The Norman sagged. 'You've not been long in Apulia. You've not heard of Atenulf?'

Halfdan shook his head.

'So you don't know about the katepan Doukeianos?'

Halfdan was starting to feel rather frustrated by the whole conversation. 'Just explain.'

Fulk sighed. 'Even trapped in a small city in the south, information reached me through rumour and spies. Doukeianos was a Byzantine katepan here before your Maniakes came. He was captured by the forces of the Duke of Benevento a couple of years ago. No one knew what to do with him. The Byzantine emperor would lose face with his nobles if he left Doukeianos languishing in Benevento, so when Maniakes came as the new katepan, he agreed to pay an enormous ransom for his predecessor.'

A frisson of destiny rippled across Halfdan's skin at the word 'ransom'. He felt a slow smile crossing his face even as Fulk continued.

'Pandulf, the Duke of Benevento sent his brother, Atenulf, to arrange receipt of the ransom.'

'And Atenulf and the gold have disappeared, yes?' Halfdan could sense something important here.

Fulk nodded. 'At first, Benevento blamed Guaimar of Salerno, but it turns out that Guaimar didn't even know the ransom had been arranged. Somewhere in Apulia, Atenulf is at large with a small force of soldiers and a king's ransom in gold. Katepan Argyrus is furious and blames Maniakes, and the Byzantines are looking for Atenulf. They want their gold back. But as far as the Duke of Benevento is concerned, the gold is his, and he wants it, else there is no point in him holding on to Doukeianos anymore. And, of course, Guaimar wants it because he could really do with a healthy treasury right now, given his costly disputes with Benevento and the bribes he continues to pay my countrymen for their support. And above all this, Iron Arm has offered lands and titles to any man who brings *him* Atenulf and the gold.'

Halfdan gave him a sour look. 'You were well informed for a prisoner in your own city. So that is why you were so happy to abandon Ginosa when we broke the siege. You want the gold, too.'

Fulk shrugged. 'More accurately, I want the land and title Iron Arm will grant me in return for it. But yes.'

Halfdan turned, sword still in hand, and swiftly dispatched the tied man. The entire Italian unit was gone now. 'No witnesses,' he said. Fulk nodded.

'All right, everything is now out in the open,' the jarl said. 'A local lord has gone to ground with a fortune in gold. Every man and his dog on the peninsula want to find him, including you.'

Something clearly occurred to Courvaudon and he stepped back, his sword grip changing slightly. Halfdan laughed. 'Settle, lord of Ginosa. Yes, I want the gold, but sixteen of us can only carry so much. Thirty-eight could carry more. You need our strength, I think, but we need your knowledge. Together we stand a greater chance of finding this runaway thief.'

Fulk nodded slowly, but it took a longer moment for him to lower his sword.

'If we are to travel together from here, then, Halfdan of Gotland, I would ask you to swear on the Holy Scriptures that you will not betray us, that we are allies in this. Like you, my people are ever hungry and not unknown to have their heads turned by profit, and I would have your word.'

Halfdan gave a short bark of a laugh. 'Your Christ book offers little security for us.' Ignoring the disapproving look the Norman threw him, he sank his sword into the soft grass and reached up, lifting the Thor hammer pendant around his neck. 'But a Northman would sooner break his own neck than an oath he gives in good faith, and I give you my oath in the sight of the Allfather that neither me nor mine will betray you, unless you give us good cause.'

Fulk nodded slowly. 'I, however, set great store by an oath on the Holy Book.' Beside him, Marc produced from somewhere unseen a thick, well-worn bible. The Norman lord removed his glove and placed his hand palm-down on the tome. 'I swear loyalty and good faith to Halfdan of Gotland and his men.'

'All right,' Halfdan said as the rest gathered around in a circle. 'What next?'

Fulk scratched his chin. 'Everywhere west of here is Salerno's lands and they're creeping eastward all the time, now that so much of the Byzantine army has gone. Beyond Salerno, the lands are those of Benevento. Neither man can be trusted, and it is highly unlikely that Atenulf is to be found there. The last place he would want to be found is in the lands of the coastal lords he has betrayed.'

'So we steer north and east a little, staying clear of this city of yours.'

'Potenza, yes. But we cannot afford to press too far to the east. Everywhere east of Lavello was still in Byzantine hands last I heard. Neither you nor I will be welcomed by the Byzantines and the chances of finding Atenulf in the lands of the men from whom he stole the gold are tiny. So that's roughly thirty miles from each coast that are out of the question.'

Halfdan thought back to the only map he had seen of the Italian peninsula, in Fulk's hall at Ginosa before they left. A thought struck him. 'How wide is this peninsula?'

'Between here and Melfi it narrows from around a hundred miles to just under eighty.'

'Eighty miles across, and we cannot go within thirty miles of either coast?'

'That's about it, yes.'

'That doesn't give us a lot of room to manoeuvre.'

'But it also limits the places where Atenulf and his gold can be hiding,' Fulk noted.

'True.'

There was a long pause, finally broken by Bjorn, scratching an armpit reflectively. 'So we're looking for gold, then?' he said.

'Yes, Bjorn. We're looking for gold.'

'Good. Do I get to pull the arms off this Atenulf when we find him?'

'I see no reason why not.'

The albino grinned. 'Let's get moving, then.'

'Don't be too hasty,' Fulk said. 'The twenty- or thirty-mile corridor we will use to move north is still plenty wide. We could quite easily slip past Atenulf without knowing he was there.'

'And that,' Halfdan added, with a sidelong look of under-standing at the Norman, 'is why we've been moving at such a slow pace so far, isn't it, Courvaudon? You were not being alert to danger, but seeking news of this thief and his treasure. You've been careful not to miss Atenulf even when we didn't know you were looking for him. Very sly. And lucky that none of us speak the local tongue.'

Fulk shrugged, without a hint of guilt or remorse. 'That was certainly part of it. But this is the situation: we know he has to be somewhere north of us and he cannot realistically be within thirty miles of either coast, and so we advance carefully once more, checking every rumour and looking at every possible hiding place. Melfi is only thirty miles north of us, so we have a limited area to search. Wherever he is, it will have to be defendable, large enough to house a military escort and a number of wagons and carts, and somewhere not controlled by anyone who is looking for him. That cuts down where we must search to a surprisingly narrow field.'

Halfdan pursed his lips. 'All this is assuming that you are correct on each count. Perhaps the Byzantines are playing some strange game and have taken this Atenulf in, for they're a tricky people. Perhaps they even only pretended to pay the ransom in order to save face. Maybe the gold does not exist and everyone is looking for a Byzantine fantasy. Or maybe Atenulf has already done a deal with this Guaimar and the gold has gone to the coast. Or maybe Atenulf has simply moved faster than you anticipated and he is already gone to the south coast and on a ship.'

'I do not believe that. I am certain he remains in Apulia, and somewhere north of here.'

'I like to be sure there is prey when I hunt,' Halfdan muttered, then turned to Gunnhild, a request in his expression. She looked back at him, challenging. Ever since that day in Miklagarðr, her talents had remained untested, and both she and Halfdan knew that the goddess may never speak to her again.

'What?' she said, her tone flat.

'I was hoping you would cast for knowledge, Gunnhild.'

'No.'

He winced and rubbed his hands together, walking past her and standing there, between Gunnhild and the woodland she observed. She had wavered. He'd seen it. She had still not put a blade on her stick, and that suggested to him that she had not yet fully turned her back on her old life. Perhaps now was the time to drive her into a decision?

'This is important,' he pressed.

There was a long silence, and slowly Gunnhild's gaze swept down from the trees and fell on Halfdan's face. 'No.'

Crossing to her, he took her elbow, which clearly annoyed her, but she did not fight him as he steered her away from the others until they were practically alone.

'Tell me,' he murmured, not unkindly, but with a hint of impatience. Gunnhild had been quiet and waspish ever since they fled the great city. Bjorn had tried to cheer her up, but had quickly learned that she was not in the mood and abandoned his efforts. It was something to do with Harðráði, he was sure, and it wasn't just infatuation. It was deeper than that. Whatever had happened had shaken Gunnhild to her very soul and seemed to have drawn a veil between her and the goddess. But now that they were in new lands and with plans to make, he needed her. With Leif gone, he needed her more than ever.

Still, she was silent.

'Is it Harðráði?'

She closed her eyes, an angry flash washing across her face. He could tell she was struggling to keep herself calm, and when she opened her eyes, she just shook her head.

'Tell me,' he muttered again. 'Gunnhild, we are friends. And after our arguments in Miklagarðr, I swore we would never fall out again. We are a hirð. We are together and we rely on each other. Tell me what happened. I can help.'

Again, there was a long pause. Then, finally, she seemed to sag a little. 'No, you cannot.'

'Then tell me, so I understand.'

Gunnhild reached up and scrubbed her face with her hands. 'The goddess has left my side, Halfdan. I had a path, laid out by the Norns. I knew it, saw it clearly. But I did not follow it. I followed *you*.'

He blinked. 'Me?'

'Yes, you. And since that day, I cannot hear the goddess. I cannot feel her.'

He shivered, but straightened and cleared his throat. 'This is not new to you. You were never fully a völva after all, even before,' he noted, pressing for a reaction, one he felt sure would come.

'I walked with the *goddess*,' she snarled angrily, predictably. 'I *should* have been völva. I would have been had I not left Hedeby with you.'

An uncomfortable silence fell again. Halfdan started to move the information around in his head, like pieces of a puzzle. He felt there had to be an answer here, and it was just out of reach. Gunnhild had abandoned a path laid out for her. But it was the Norns that would make her pay, surely, and not Freyja? She had been hovering between his world and the world of the völva since the day they met, and twice now he had been responsible for her changing her course.

'How do you become a völva, then?' he asked, finally.

'What?' she snapped.

'You know so much. I have heard you sing your songs. The goddess spoke to you. Why were you not already völva?'

'I was not ready,' she said, flatly. 'When the mother in Hedeby decided I was ready, I would have been given a true völva's staff of power. Then I would offer my whole life to the goddess.'

'So do it,' Halfdan said in a matter-of-fact tone.

'What?'

'You know what a völva's staff is, and you have one in the making. We've all seen it. It's too short to be a spear and you know it. You are ready,' he added, pointing to her carved stick. 'If you weren't, you'd have put a spearhead on that already. Devote yourself.'

'Halfdan, Freyja doesn't talk to me anymore.'

'And if *I* didn't talk to you, what would you do?'

She frowned. 'I would shout at you until you did.'

'That's what I thought.'

The frown deepened. 'I turned my back on—'

'The Norns,' he interrupted. 'You turned your back on the Norns, not the goddess. Maybe the weavers will relent and weave you a new path, or maybe they will weave you a descent to *Hel*, but whatever that fate, it is not the work of Freyja.'

She took a deep breath. 'You are not supposed to be wise, Halfdan. That's why you need *me*.'

'I need Gunnhild,' he said quietly, encouragingly. 'I need the Gunnhild who guided a fleet to the edge of the world and brought down a kin-slayer. I need the Gunnhild who tried to save us from the corruption of Miklagarðr. You are that Gunnhild still. I know it. Cast your runes.'

Her brow creased in frustration and worry. 'What if I try and I cannot? Halfdan, it is better sometimes not to know.'

'Only if you have reason to believe it will fail. I believe you will succeed. You are the most powerful woman I have ever met. The most powerful person I have ever met.'

The confidence in her eyes was still wavering, but he watched her resistance crumble and finally, as though accepting terms from an enemy on the battlefield, she nodded. 'Very well. But I can guarantee you nothing, Halfdan. You know that.'

The Northmen nearby fell into a respectful silence. Gunnhild stepped to the edge of the clearing and turned a slow circle, drawing a line in the ground with her staff. She looked about, then crossed to a tree on the edge of the woodland, stepping over a fallen body. There she rummaged in the foliage, her back to them, doing something unseen. When she returned to her circle, the tree had been marked with an intricate design, drawn with a small blade in the bark. She now had runes marked across her forehead in brown smudges, which Halfdan presumed had come from the bag of powder she'd taken from Bjorn.

Then she sang. Halfdan had seen and heard it many times now, and yet every time she did this, he was entranced. It was part prayer, part song, part display, part oration. It was power in its rawest form, and he felt the Seiðr flowing out across the clearing. Gunnhild rose until she was on her toes and twirled, her carved shaft dancing in her fingers as though it weighed nothing, or had a life of its own. When the tip thudded down into the earth, a small collection of bones, hacksilver, coins and shiny stones fell with it, scattering into a pattern.

Gunnhild fell silent and dropped to a crouch, looking down. Halfdan had seen this before, and it made him extremely nervous to note something new. A frown of trouble. Of difficulty. A squint as though even with her eyes closed she was trying to see through thick fog. Was the goddess there, or was the völva's sight truly blinded?

On impulse, Halfdan glanced around him. The Normans were drawing crosses over their chests repeatedly, bearing worried looks. Fulk also looked a little disturbed, but there was an element of fascination to his gaze as he watched this display. He and his kind might be solidly Christian, but somewhere deep inside they still carried the blood of the North.

Finally, Gunnhild gathered up her fallen trinkets, tipping them back into a purse. Rising, she pulled her staff from the soil and used the tip to scrub the circle out, ravaging the ground. She then crossed to the tree and defaced the sigil there, too. All done, she paced over to Halfdan once more.

He could see the weariness, the struggle and the fear, in her eyes.

'Do you...?' he began. 'Did you...?'

She paused for a long moment and finally nodded. 'The goddess hears me, Halfdan. Freyja walks this land, though she does not wish to. She resists, and the path the Norns wove for me is no longer there as my guide and my lodestone. This is not their world, nor Freyja's, and for bringing her here I owe the goddess much.'

'I will pay it,' Halfdan said hurriedly. 'What did you see?'

'*I* will be the one to pay,' she said. 'We have a difficult time in the coming days, my jarl. The gold you seek does lie ahead, but with it comes much peril. I see a wolf in a gilded cage. I see death and disaster, wolf pelts on the skinning bench and fire and roasted flesh. But I also see gold and glory. It is... it is still confused.'

Halfdan clenched his teeth. That was even more convoluted and unilluminating than usual. 'But in the end?'

'I cannot *see* the end. There is something else there. Something uncertain is yet to come. I cannot say whether it will help us or cause further harm. It reminds me of the shadow that obscured Yngvar's end.'

Behind Fulk, the Normans were crossing themselves again. The troubled lord looked from Halfdan to Gunnhild and back. 'This witchcraft unsettles me.'

'You would do well always to heed what Gunnhild tells you,' the jarl replied. 'She speaks with gods far older than yours.'

Fulk shivered. 'You are content, then, that I was right? That Atenulf and his gold still lie ahead of us?'

'I am. But we should proceed with a great deal of care. Something is not right about all this.'

'Agreed. Then let us leave this butcher's yard and return to the road. At the next village I will ask a few questions. Perhaps we can pick up the trail, and together we can track the gold.'

Halfdan nodded. Perhaps. But even as they returned to the road and set off north once more, he could not rid his mind's eye of the image of a wolf in a golden cage.

Chapter 10

'What did you say this place was called?' Bjorn rumbled, as he looked across the golden fields to the city that rose on a strong ridge from the surrounding landscape, a grey-and-white walled warren of roofs and streets.

'Acerenza,' Fulk replied with a relieved smile.

'And why are we pleased?' Halfdan asked.

The Norman gave a small chuckle. 'Four days through unfriendly terrain, squeezed between Greek lands and the coastal duchies, and the moment we find allies, you begin to get nervous? Halfdan, my friend, Acerenza has been in the hands of my people for over a year now. It is a bulwark against the troubles to the south. It was conquered by Guiscard himself, and given as a prize to his right-hand man, Armand.' His mouth twisted into a smile. 'Armand happens to be a cousin of mine.'

'*My* cousins are all nasty fucks,' Bjorn said. 'Wouldn't trust any of them further than I could shit a dragon boat.'

Courvaudon threw a strange look at Bjorn. 'Colourful fellow, your bear over there.' He straightened. 'But this is the place our fortunes will change.'

'That, I do not doubt,' Gunnhild murmured from behind them.

Fulk ignored her and gestured toward the fortress-city with its powerful walls. 'Acerenza is important. So much so that the Byzantines fought for control of it for years. It is a hub for trade, as well as a great fortress and a centre of Godliness. There we will find our rumours of the missing gold. I am certain of it.'

'The walls look new,' Farlof noted, squinting into the morning sun.

'Very perceptive. Yes, Guiscard gave Armand sufficient funds to fortify the place. It is a statement. The Greeks will never retake Acerenza. She has the strongest walls in the region. And with all the traders, market holders and farmers from thirty miles about converging here, we will be sure to hear rumours here, but we must be subtle how we go about our enquiries. If it was common knowledge, my countrymen would already have found the gold, so we must be careful. Indeed, I would have liked to have entered the city quietly and unnoticed, but a column of this many men draws attention and we will have to present ourselves to Armand as soon as possible. With luck he will find us suitable accommodation.'

'Turn back,' Gunnhild said, eyes narrowed.

'What?'

'No good will come of this place. Find somewhere else.'

Fulk gave a disbelieving snort. 'You are mistaken, good woman Gunnhild. This is my cousin's city and we shall be safe here.'

'I am not a good woman. And you are mistaken. Your cousin, he has a royal banner?'

The Norman frowned, glancing across for a moment at Marc. 'He does. Of course he does.'

'It bears a red cock.'

Now, Fulk frowned. 'Your eyesight is a marvel, Gunnhild. I can just make out there are banners atop the walls, but no detail upon them. Yes, Armand's colours bear a red cockerel.'

'This is bad. So very bad. Halfdan, tell him how bad this is.'

Before the jarl could oblige, Bjorn let out a chuckle. 'A red cock is always a bad sign. This one time, I met a whore from Daneland…'

Halfdan silenced him with a glare that just had his friend's face slide into a leery smile. He turned to Courvaudon. 'The cock is a bad omen. Gullinkambi is a cock that crows in *Valhöll* to signal the end of this world. The war of gods and giants.'

'You pagans speak in so many riddles.'

'Ragnarok, man. Has your northern blood become so diluted you do not remember the most important of things?'

'Halfdan, I am a child of Christ. A lamb of God. I do not give credence to these ancient tales of giants and of battles among gods. They are fictions that should have been overwhelmed by now in the glory of the Lord.'

'Bollocks. The Allfather watches us. I have seen his birds, Huginn and Muninn, as we travel.'

Fulk sighed. 'Armand owes me, and he is a loyal man of the Hautvilles, Robert Guiscard and Iron Arm among them. We shall be safer now than at any time since we left the south. And here we will learn about the gold. Believe me.'

Halfdan turned to Gunnhild, a question in his expression. She was extremely troubled, and he could see it. She shivered. 'I believe he is correct. I think you will find more about the gold here. But the danger is too great. I see disaster in every window of that city.'

'But we will find out about the gold?' urged Farlof, hunger in his voice.

'Do not let your love of treasure blind you to peril,' she replied.

'Can you consult Freyja?' Halfdan asked, quietly.

'No,' Fulk put in. 'Please, no. It was a fascinating display of ancient witchery, but it makes me extremely uncomfortable. Witnessing such rituals imperils our mortal souls, Halfdan. My men will not stay for it.'

Gunnhild shrugged. 'I do not need the goddess to tell me this place is trouble.'

'Trouble or no, we need Acerenza,' Fulk said. 'Not only is it the only place we are likely to track down the information we seek, but we need provisions. If we are to press on toward Melfi, we will have several more days to travel and we are down to meagre enough supplies even for one meal, let alone days on the road. And if we are seen passing through Norman lands and do

145

not present ourselves to Armand, we will appear suspicious. He will want to know why we are avoiding him. No, my friends, we must enter Acerenza.'

'Then be on your guard,' Gunnhild said, still eyeing the city on the hill.

And Halfdan was. If there was one thing he had learned about the woman who had walked beside him in mountainous Georgia and glittering Miklagarðr, it was that when she said something, you paid attention. She had guided the Wolves through the perils of that strange eastern land with her wit and her uncanny connection to the gods, and had he listened to her more carefully in the great city, they might have left with a ship and a crew. Of this he was certain: he would never shun her advice again.

Consequently, his gaze played sharply across all their surroundings as they climbed the road toward the city of Acerenza. The gravel thoroughfare wound this way and that across the slope, a ribbon of grey as it ascended toward the powerful new Norman walls. At the top, a strong gateway beside a heavy, square tower stood waiting, its dark arch beckoning them like the maw of some great stone giant. Halfdan shivered at the image. Giants and Ragnarok. Just what he needed.

Indeed, he could sense something of what Gunnhild perhaps felt as they approached those defences. There was nothing obviously untoward. The gate stood open, the sound of everyday city life arose from within the walls, a shepherd nearby watched them warily from his grassy slope full of animals, and figures in the red and white of the local Norman lord were just visible here and there atop the walls. It was all so ordinary.

But something was slightly off. Of course, he reasoned, he could easily be fooling himself into believing that, influenced by Gunnhild's words, and yet somehow he still felt it was real: a very palpable sense of danger despite there being no overt sign. As they moved on, he turned to the others. Gunnhild and Bjorn strode behind him, then Farlof and Ulfr behind them, the rest stringing out in pairs along the road. There was room for four men abreast, the road broad enough for carts to pass one another on the way to and from the market, and so Fulk de Courvaudon's men walked in pairs beside the carts, the lord himself and his bannerman at their head.

Marc was whistling some jaunty tune. Halfdan frowned at him, then spoke to the Wolves.

'Something is amiss. Something is odd, dangerous. I know you felt it, Gunnhild, but I feel it now, too. Be on your guard and ready to move at a heartbeat's notice. As we pass inside, note the position of every guard, every door and arch. Be aware of every exit and every point of danger. If we pass through that gate and find trouble awaiting us, I want to be able to be back out and away from peril in the blink of an eye. Hands on weapons, wits about you. Tell the others.'

Gunnhild did so, and Halfdan turned back to the ever-steepening slope ahead. That gate was looking more and more like a mouth with every step. The gates were open, pulled inwards into the dark tunnel. As they neared the top of the hill, approaching the entrance, Halfdan could make out a little more. The arched tunnel through the walls was about the same width as the road, and some thirty feet long. There were two sets of gates, one outer, one inner, both wide, each manned by a pair of guards in that red-and-white livery, leaning on shields, looking bored. Beyond the dark passageway he couldn't make out any detail other than the bright light of the Apulian morning inside the city.

Still, nothing was out of place. He had been to enough cities these days to know how such gates were manned. There were no artillery pieces on the parapet, tracking their movements. No archers drew bows along the top. Just two pairs of bored-looking guards.

He was twitching now. His fingers reached down to the pommel of his eagle-hilted sword, playing across its beautiful carving, ready to pull it and deal with anyone who came at him. He could hear Bjorn's heavy breathing behind him as the big man readied himself for anything, could feel the alertness emanating from Gunnhild.

He dropped back briefly as they stepped into the gateway. Just a single pace, letting Courvaudon take the lead. This was his world, and perhaps he was right. The jarl moved into the darkness, blinking, momentarily blinded by the change after the bright morning sun. As his eyes adjusted, he noted the two guards as they passed. They hadn't moved, made no attempt to stop or even challenge these armed visitors. Was that normal? More than thirty armed and armoured men entering the city without being at least questioned? But then it was a Norman city, and they walked alongside a Norman lord with his banner on display. Perhaps this was normal in their world.

He felt a palpable sense of relief as he neared the bright light of the city within. He narrowed his eyes, squinting, so that the sunlight would not completely blind him as he emerged. Inside the gate he could see an open space, perhaps forty feet across, beyond which lay houses, streets marching off into the city. No army awaited them. No unit of archers stood with their bows levelled, arrows pointing at the arch. No horsemen. No Greek fire. No blockade. The city was open and clear. Indeed, he could see a beggar by the roadside now, and a man wheeling a small handcart. Two more guards stood beside the inner gate. One nodded at Fulk, a gesture of familiarity and greeting.

Halfdan emerged into the light and slowly let his eyes widen once more, taking it all in.

There was no warning when it came.

A single rock bounced off the ground just in front of Halfdan, but it was only the first of many. Of their entire group, perhaps a dozen had made it through the inner gate when a barrage of stones came from the wall above. Halfdan's shield went up over his head in an instant, as did those of the Wolves behind him, each of them tense, ready for danger. The thuds and clonks of masonry bouncing off the boards became a rumble of thunder and Halfdan's arm vibrated and ached with the pounding. His gaze snapped back and forth to see that Fulk had been struck on the shoulder, but was still standing. Marc had leapt forth, dropping the banner he carried and raising his shield to cover his master and himself. As Halfdan turned, taking stock of their situation in an instant, he could see the two men at the gate pushing the outer doors closed, even as the visitors in the passageway struggled to force them back open. But stones were raining down inside the passage, too, and the fight was impossible. The guards were hurriedly closing the inner gate and just for a moment, Halfdan caught sight of the light back at the outer end of the passage narrowing as the external gates were also closed, trapping the men inside.

Indecision struck him for just a moment. Two-thirds of their number were caught between those closing gates, trapped in the dark passage and being pounded with falling stones through the murder holes above. Realisation came swiftly. Those men were lost. There was nothing he could do for them and if they did not get away from this place, the falling stones would surely be the least of their worries. Why they were being set upon in such a manner he could not yet determine, but the reasoning was for another time. Now, survival was all that mattered.

'Run,' he bellowed, and began to do so. Rocks continued to bounce off his shield, but the frequency of the blows decreased as he moved away from the walls. As he got halfway across the small square he risked turning back and looking up. A line of men with baskets of rocks were slinging them down, and already the paved ground beneath resembled a scree slope more than a city square. The soldiers who had closed and barred the gate had now pressed their backs against it, shields up and swords out, though anyone wishing to attack them would first have to brave more of those falling rocks. With a heavy heart, he knew he had lost the men in the passageway. The pack animals would not yet be in the trap, they and perhaps one or two survivors remaining outside the city. All their gear, and a not inconsiderable sum of gold, was out there, at the mercy of whoever was behind this.

His gaze turned back to the city ahead. There were two narrow streets leading into the urban mass, one ahead, and one angled off to the right, as well as another marching off along the inside of the walls. That last was not an option, for it would put them once more beneath the parapet and its vicious projectiles. The one to the right curved around another set of heavy walls, which looked to be a smaller fortress within the walled city. Though he had no idea about the layout of this place, any fortress would surely hold more armed men, and so passing close by such a place would be perilous. That left the street straight ahead, for which he now ran, the others at his back. His instincts had played him right, clearly, for as the falling rocks stopped with their increased distance from the gate, he could see more men in red and white emerging from some door in the city walls further along, and another group spilling out of a gate in that fortress.

For a moment, he feared that the trap was complete, as a couple of red-and-white figures emerged from the side of the remaining street ahead of them, but it took only a moment to understand this was simple coincidence. The two men had strolled out of a tavern, and one was busy settling his helmet in place even as the other turned, wide-eyed, and spotted the Northmen racing toward them.

There was shouting now behind them at the gate, and beneath the cries they could hear the screams, muffled and echoing, of men being battered to death in the dark. His lip curling into an angry twist, Halfdan vowed that someone was going to pay for this.

He and Fulk hit the two soldiers at full pelt, swords out. The Norman had no shield at the moment, his bright teardrop-shaped defence back on the pack animals, but he wore his chain shirt and he snarled as he leapt forward. Halfdan was having a little trouble keeping his shield high in front of him, his arm numb and painful from the repeated pounding of rocks. His sword was out now, and as he hit the man, who, taken by surprise, was still struggling to draw his own weapon, he felt renewed shock in his arm from the shield barge. The soldier staggered back with a squawk, struggling to stay on his feet, but Halfdan gave him no time to recover. He leaned back to allow sufficient room, then with a grunt of effort lifted his shield and slammed it into the man's face. The Norman's helmet had a nose guard, which certainly saved him having his whole face caved in by the iron boss, but still the damage was immense. The soldier bellowed in pain, and as his fingers let go of his half-drawn sword to claw at his face, Halfdan saw his opening.

Unlike his own chain shirt, which reached down to cover just the groin, the Normans wore a longer garment to protect their legs while on horseback. But to allow for sitting astride the beast, the shirt was divided by a split from hem to waist. When on foot, however, this arrangement provided a fortuitous opening for an observant and skilled attacker. Halfdan's sword was shorter than most, and designed as much for stabbing as swinging; it lanced out like a striking viper between the two sides of the mail skirt, slamming into the man's privates. Between the trousers beneath, the underwear and the flapping chain shirt, Halfdan could not be sure how vital his blow had been, but as he ripped the sword back, it came out glistening with red.

The man gave an unearthly howl, his shield now falling away, his battered and bruised face forgotten as both hands came down to cradle his ruined manhood. Halfdan stepped back a single pace and delivered another blow, this time to the neck, which silenced the soldier. The mortally wounded man fell, and the jarl pushed him aside without a further thought.

He turned to see that Fulk had dispatched the other man, his own sword unsullied by blood. His blows had been hard and swung against chain, breaking bones rather than puncturing flesh, and his victim was lying on the floor, leg at an unnatural angle, clutching a similarly broken arm. The Norman threw him a quick glance and nodded, and they ran on. As they raced along the road, ever further from the gate and the men they had lost, Halfdan could hear Bjorn behind him, grumbling about being left out of every fight, and Gunnhild calling the big man some very unfriendly things.

'Do you know this place?' Halfdan panted as they ran.

'No,' Courvaudon replied. 'I was here once, more than a year ago when it was captured, but only for a few hours.'

'Then follow me.'

With that, Halfdan turned right into a side alley, the others pounding along behind him.

'Where are we going?' Fulk breathed.

'To find somewhere to hide while we think. That street was leading toward a market. Too many people, and soldiers, too, probably.'

Reaching a crossroads of narrow alleys, Halfdan slowed and the others followed suit. He came to a halt and peered cautiously around the corner. Back in the direction of the gate, he caught a brief glimpse of red and white. That likely led back toward the small fortress inside the walls. That would be where the men were coming from. The other two directions were clear.

His thoughts whirled. The guards here had been prepared enough to spring a trap, but not enough to ensure its success. If they had truly been waiting for Fulk, Halfdan and the others, they would have had a full garrison out and ready to contain them. Instead, they had closed the gates, cutting the column of men in half, giving them easy targets in the passageway, but risking those who had already entered running to safety. And these Normans used archers, just as the Byzantines did. Had they been well prepared they would have had archers on the walls. Likely the baskets of rocks were already up there as part of the standard defence of the city walls.

The men of Acerenza had had little warning. They had probably seen the travellers approaching over the last quarter-mile or so, and that had only given them time to react, rather than plan. They couldn't possibly have identified Halfdan and his friends as Northmen, nor as followers of the old gods, not in that time and from that distance. The only thing they could have seen that might make them react was Courvaudon's banner.

'Your cousin has turned on you,' he told Fulk as he tried to decide on a path. Left would take them on toward the market, and right back toward the fortress. Straight on it was. He ran again.

'What could have caused such a thing?' the Norman grunted as they ran.

'I don't know, but it can only have been the sight of your banner that started this.'

They reached a corner and turned with it, and then, with Halfdan peering carefully each time, turned again and again. Always he kept his eye on the shadows cast by the high buildings, which told him which direction he was moving as he disappeared ever further into a tangle of narrow alleys. Finally, he came to a stop outside a building. The door, like most here, stood resolutely shut, and the window beside it was shuttered. But a small flight of steps next to the house's entrance led up to another door and, as he looked up, he could see that it was slightly ajar.

'Here,' he said, pointing.

'Why?'

'This place is disused.'

'How can you tell?'

'Look at the muck on the steps.' Thick dust and detritus coated each stone on the staircase, mute evidence that it had been some time since any foot had fallen upon it. Sword still out, Halfdan crept slowly up the steps. Reaching the top, he squinted in through the narrow opening. The place was dark and empty, and Halfdan looked this way and that along the alley before putting his shoulder to the door. It creaked inwards with a surprising amount of noise, old wood scraping loudly on the stone flags. A cloud of dust billowed up at the disturbance, but Halfdan ignored it and dipped inside, beckoning to the others. As he waited beside the door, he counted as they entered. Thank Odin and Freyja, his friends were still with him, Gunnhild, Bjorn and Ulfr, as well as the solid Farlof and three of the Varangians he had brought from the beach. Fulk was accompanied by Marc and four of the Normans. Fourteen of them, of the thirty-seven they had had as they approached this cursed place.

Once the last man was inside, Halfdan stuck his head back out through the door, checking the way they came. No one seemed to have observed their arrival. Indeed, they had been immensely lucky to have moved through that warren of alleys without bumping into anyone. Seemingly the market was the focus of most of the town's activity, drawing the life from the smaller streets. Carefully, as slowly and quietly as he could, he pushed that door closed once more. Reaching up to the one window in the place, he pulled aside its tatty and threadbare cover to allow light in.

The place was not particularly large, this room sporting only one door that led to another of similar dimensions. It would house the fourteen of them, but the accommodation was hardly salubrious. A broken bench was the only seating, one leg at an angle such that when Farlof attempted to perch on it, it sagged with a warning creak and the leg bent a little more. Piles of old sacking and broken timber formed the rest of the decor, along with a thick layer of dust.

As the rest stood massaging aching arms, shields propped against the walls, Halfdan rolled his shoulders and took a breath.

'When Gunnhild tells you something,' he said in a meaningful voice, looking Fulk in the eye, 'you listen to her. I take it you now understand that?'

Courvaudon looked distinctly uneasy. 'She is a pagan, man. A witch. Demons whisper in her ear.'

Halfdan could feel irritation rising in him. 'Yet she knew this was coming and you led us blindly on. I don't care what you think of her, she is völva. She walks with Freyja and the goddess guides her. And until your nailed Christ starts to talk to you personally and give you advice, you will listen to a woman who *does* speak with a goddess.'

The Norman said nothing in reply. His eyes were lowered, either unwilling or unable to look at Gunnhild. Halfdan sagged.

'All right. Why would your cousin take against you so much that he launches an attack on you on sight?'

The Norman lord looked to his bannerman. Marc shrugged. 'Maybe the balance of power has changed up here, my lord? Maybe Iron Arm is no longer lord of Melfi? We've been trapped in the south. Maybe while we were there, the coastal lords have done new deals?'

Fulk shook his head. 'It's nothing political. Even surrounded by Byzantines we managed to hear tidings of the north. Anything as important as a change in alliances would have reached us. The Byzantines would have used it to try and pry us from the town. No. This is something else. Something personal. But Armand and I have been on cordial terms since the day we both travelled south. Our allegiances are to the same lord, we are both sons of the Church, there is no conflict in our fiefdoms, and we owe one another nothing but familial fealty.'

'Would you slow down when you talk?' Halfdan complained. 'I'm still getting used to your tongue and when you talk fast and use words I don't know, it takes me a while to piece it together.'

Fulk nodded his understanding. 'Apologies. Simply: I can see no reason why Armand should turn on me. I just do not understand.'

Halfdan jumped at a noise, his hand reaching out toward his sword, which was propped against the wall, before he discerned the source of the noise and stood down.

Gunnhild was never crowded. Wherever she was, she always had space around her, for those who knew the truth of what she was had too much respect to press her, and those like Fulk's men, who were at least half afraid of her, kept away for their own reasons. The völva now crouched in that circle of clear floor, looking down at the scattered beads, bones and trinkets. Her finger extended and began to draw lines between them in the dust, linking the debris into intricate patterns that Halfdan would never understand had he three lifetimes to study them.

The room fell utterly silent, the only sound that single finger dragging through the dust, drawing futures. Finally, she lifted her hand and then her face, looking up at Halfdan and Fulk.

'The gold is here.'

Fulk's face folded into a frown. 'How could you know that?'

Halfdan coughed. 'Given all you have witnessed, are you *still* going to question this?'

'But I don't see...' the Norman began, before falling silent.

'Your Atenulf,' Halfdan said quietly. 'He's here. That's why we've not found him so far. He is in Acerenza. And if he is here, with a small force of men and cartloads of gold, that means the man who runs this city – your *cousin* – knows about him. Either Atenulf is now in league with your cousin and the two of them couldn't risk you finding out about the gold, or your cousin has already done away with the thief and taken the gold for himself but, again, cannot risk you uncovering his secret. Gunnhild was right about this place. Now I am a wolf in a golden cage. And you are all here with me.'

'We are still free,' Marc noted.

Halfdan cast him a black look. 'Are we? Trapped in a city that is now looking for us? Most of our men gone, dead or captured, all our goods and gold lost. We have only what we carry, and there is no one in this city likely to help us.'

'We don't need them.'

Halfdan glanced around at the statement to see Ulfr looking directly at him, arms folded in confidence. 'What?'

'We have fourteen strong sword arms. We have Gunnhild's wisdom, your Loki cunning and luck, my skills and Bjorn's size. We were trapped in Miklagarðr with less, and we escaped. We are in the same place as enough gold to make us kings. All we have to do is find it and get out of here.'

'That's all?' Fulk snorted.

'You can have no faith in your nailed god,' the shipwright snapped, 'but we have faith in ours, and in our jarl. We will beat this.'

And Halfdan's mind was already turning this over. They were trapped. But the gold was here.

There had to be a way.

Chapter 11

The first patrol came round a little after noon. Halfdan and Fulk had kept their people in that upper room as bells tolled around the city, marking a general alarm. It had seemed prudent to remain hidden at least for the time being, until they could formulate some sort of plan of action. They had been skulking for an hour when they heard the rattle, shush and clonk of arms and armour, as a small unit of soldiers in red and white came along the street, banging on every door and demanding of the residents they found any news of armed strangers. Where there was no answer, the soldiers tried the doors and either pushed them open and searched or argued about the viability of breaking in before eventually moving on.

As the patrol neared their position, Halfdan carefully pulled the tattered blanket back into place and examined the door. It had a lock, but the key was long gone, and no bolt or latch prevented it from opening. He murmured a vow to the Allfather, hoping the patrol simply passed by, as Fulk quietly gathered everyone into the back room, into the darkest corners, out of sight of the door.

Outside, the patrol hammered on the door below, by the bottom of the stairs. When they received no answer, Halfdan could hear them murmuring, trying the door, murmuring some more. They seemed to split up, then, for some of them were pounding on a door across the narrow street, while others were still outside this place, still debating among themselves. Halfdan, the only one still in the front room, leaned toward the window and peered as best he could through the most threadbare part of the covering. Three men stood across the street talking to a bent and frail old woman, while three more were looking at the steps. One then turned his face up, peering at the upper storey, and Halfdan leaned back away from the window, his heart thundering like the coming of Thor.

The steps. He had known the room would be safe from the thick layer of detritus, but now they would be covered in recent footprints. If the guards were bright, that would trigger some kind of alarm. He held his breath. Then he heard the first booted foot on the stone step. Risking another glance, he leaned forward and looked through the window. One of the men was climbing the stairs. Cursing silently, Halfdan backed across the room at a quiet shuffle, moving through the doorway and into the back room where the others lurked in the darkness. In a heartbeat he was beside Gunnhild, pressed into the shadow, breathing as shallowly as possible and hoping for the best.

He heard the door grate open on the stone. There was no call or challenge from the visitor, but Halfdan could hear his presence, the slight shuffle of feet, the swing of a chain shirt, controlled breathing, as the man stood in the doorway, peering into the building. The step that would bring him into the room never came. As they waited – every hand on a weapon hilt, but none daring to draw it, for the slightest sound might reveal their presence – the man in the doorway looked around. He peered toward the dark room at the back, and finally turned and clomped away down the steps, apparently satisfied that the place was empty, without having delved into every corner. Halfdan heaved a sigh of relief. Quite apart from the steps outside, a truly observant searcher would have spotted the various prints in the dusty floor of the outer room.

They listened carefully for some time until the sounds of knocking and searching faded down the street. Finally, Halfdan signalled to the rest and then moved out into the other room and ducked his head through the open door. The patrol was some distance away now, close to a corner, so he gestured for the others to join him and everyone returned to the main room.

Ulfr moved toward the door, reaching out to close it.

'No, don't,' Halfdan murmured quietly.

'What? But we might be heard.'

'And if that patrol comes back, they might be surprised that an abandoned door closed by itself. They have to think this place is empty.'

Ulfr nodded his understanding.

'We could have just broken his neck,' Bjorn said in a huffy tone.

'And the five outside?'

'Them too.'

Gunnhild turned to the albino. 'Are you planning on being an idiot for your whole life? We cannot kill a patrol. If we do, it will just draw more attention to the place they were searching. Kill those six and we'll have sixty in the street within the hour.'

Halfdan nodded. 'For now, we need to stay hidden. What do we know about this place, about Atenulf and about your cousin?' he asked, turning to Fulk.

'If Armand has managed to find Atenulf and overcome his forces to take the gold, it will be safe within the vaults of his fortress and the chances of getting to it are almost nil. In such a case, he would have had to dispose of all evidence of Atenulf and his men's passage. He will receive occasional visitations by Iron Arm's men, and he cannot afford to be found out, else the most powerful lords in the peninsula will turn on him. In truth, I cannot believe Armand has done such a thing. I have always considered him something of a coward.'

He huffed. '*Cautious* is perhaps a better word. He is not the sort to take such action without a good reason. To kill Atenulf and steal the gold is committing to a course of action that could land him in a disastrous position. No, I think, if you're right and the gold *is* here, that Armand has come to an arrangement with Atenulf. The thief is passing through with his gold, and he has bribed my cousin to let him do so without incident.'

Halfdan nodded. 'And we arrived unexpectedly at the most uncomfortable moment, when they were both in the city. You had your flag flying, so they knew it was you. He had a moment of panic when he could not decide what to do. He could attempt to keep Atenulf and the gold hidden, greet you and hope you would go away quickly. Or he could turn on Atenulf, kill the thief and then welcome you – but then you would know about it, and he would have to hand the gold over to this Iron Arm of yours. Or he could kill or capture us all, which sounds like something of a panicked decision.'

'And that sounds most like Armand,' Fulk sighed. 'So we work on the assumption, then, that Atenulf and his men are in the city and that at some point shortly they will attempt to take the gold south, leaving a percentage with Armand for his aid. Armand gets a little richer and Atenulf gains safe passage to the south.'

'You say your cousin is a cautious man?'

'Most certainly. In fact, it will have been his caution that led the Hautvilles to install him in such a critical position. Better to have a man who overthinks things and will do everything he can to keep the status quo than someone too inclined to fight and expand, who might put the place in danger.'

'Your cousin will presumably live in that fortress near the gate.'

'I imagine so.'

'But he will not want Atenulf's soldiers in that fortress, if he is cautious. He will place them somewhere where he is not at risk from a sudden attack. And if the soldiers are elsewhere, that means the gold and Atenulf himself must be, too. I wish we knew this city better.'

'My lord,' murmured one of the surviving Normans, crossing toward Courvaudon.

'Yes?'

'There is another option,' the man said, and Halfdan narrowed his eyes at the way he licked his lips nervously. The jarl's hand went to his sword hilt.

'What?'

'These men are Varangians. Greeks. The Greeks are the enemy of us all, Atenulf included. We might buy our own freedom with their heads.'

Bjorn took a fierce step forward, hand going to the axe at his belt. 'Six of you and eight of us?' he grinned. 'Let's dance the dance of blades, little man.'

Fulk stepped forward, one hand held up, palm forward to forestall Bjorn, the other pressed against the chest of the man who had spoken, separating the two. 'That is no option, Aimery. I gave my oath on the Bible, and I am a good Christian and a man of my word. What's more, these men saved our lives down in Ginosa, and you should have more loyalty than this. No. Whatever awaits us, we meet it together.'

'Well said,' Halfdan agreed, hand sliding from his sword.

The Norman soldier looked faintly disgruntled, but nodded and stepped back into place.

That one could be trouble, Halfdan thought to himself as he turned back to Fulk. 'Sitting here does us no good. If your cousin cannot afford to let us leave, then he will keep his men searching, day and night. Others will come, including men who will look closer than the last. We will be found. And the longer we delay, the more likely it is that Atenulf, if he lives, leaves the city with his gold and heads south. We need to locate the visitors somehow. That means moving through the city and paying attention.'

Fulk nodded. 'But very carefully. How do we move unnoticed?'

'We split into small groups. They will be looking for fourteen armed men. We strip down our kit and leave armour and anything that identifies us in the back room. This is a nailed god city, so they will ring their temple bells when it's time to sing your awful songs, yes?'

Fulk gave him a look of arch disapproval, but he nodded.

'Then they ring the bells at dusk.'

'Vespers,' noted Courvaudon.

162

'We meet back here when those bells toll and decide on our next step.'

'Your giant cannot go,' the Norman lord said, pointing at Bjorn.

The big man grumbled and frowned. 'Why?'

Halfdan turned to him, nodding. 'There is no disguising you, Bjorn. You stand out too much. We cannot risk you going out into the city. The rest of us can just about pass for locals or Normans if we mess up our hair and dress right, but we can do nothing about you unless we paint you brown and cut down your legs. You will have to stay here.'

Bjorn began to bluster and argue, but Halfdan held a hand up to him, as he turned to Fulk. 'You, too.'

'What?'

'You are known, to your cousin at least. Walking you through the streets is too much of a risk.'

The Norman looked as though he might argue for a moment, but sagged and folded his arms. He looked across at Bjorn. 'You and I must occupy our time carefully, arranging everything in here to form a small hidden area where we can lurk and not be seen, even if a searcher comes in through the inner door.'

Bjorn continued to grumble, but Halfdan ignored him. 'That leaves twelve. We split into threes, each group formed of both your people and mine. Marc, you come with me. Ulfr, Farlof and Gunnhild each take a group.'

As the gathering murmured and started to plan, Halfdan moved close to Gunnhild and leaned in to whisper. 'Take the man who wanted to sell us to the enemy and keep a very close eye on him. If he tries anything, you know what to do.'

Gunnhild nodded, her hand straying to the knife in its small leather sheath at her belt.

Moments later, as everyone grouped up, Halfdan moved to the door and looked through it, up and down the street. Once more it was deserted. Listening, attempting to block out the chattering in the room, he paid attention to the rhythm of the city. There were sporadic shouts and bells, signalling that the search was, indeed, ongoing, but the majority of the city's noise remained the hum and bustle of the market.

He turned to Fulk. 'Your cousin's colours are the red cock on a white shield. What about Atenulf?'

The Norman pursed his lips in thought. 'Red and yellow are the colours of Benevento, with a boar, though I cannot say for certain that Atenulf uses his brother's arms, and likely his men are kitted as mercenaries anyway. They have been fleeing south and are unlikely to have been advertising their presence with flags.'

'Then we must note anything suspicious,' Halfdan nodded. 'See you here as the sun sets.' And with that, he, Marc and a Varangian named Sveinn shrugged from their chain shirts and deposited their helmets and shields in the back room, smoothing out their plain tunics, adjusting sword belts and then stepping out into the afternoon sunlight.

Without further ado, they pattered down the stone steps and turned in the direction they had yet to try. As they strolled down the street, the three men did their best to settle into a natural stride, as though they had not a care in the world.

'Where first?' Marc asked, quietly.

'To the market, I think. You should do all the talking. You sound like a Norman. I keep struggling to find some of the words for your tongue, and I speak not a word of the Italians' language. Sveinn, like all those that joined me in the south, has too much of a Greek accent. He and I shall remain quiet.'

The three men strolled along the narrow street and turned the corner, hoping not to catch up with that patrol; they breathed sighs of relief at the sight of a street devoid of red-and-white tunics. Two old men sat on a simple bench outside a door, leaning on sticks. They looked up in vague interest at the men striding past. One nodded a silent greeting. Marc returned the gesture and said something brightly in the local tongue that

Halfdan had no hope of translating. Once they strolled on, he murmured, 'I wish I'd had time to learn a little more of the language.'

'Wouldn't do you much good until you're used to the place,' Marc smiled. 'Every city has its own dialect and most of them are different enough from each other to almost sound like different tongues.'

They strolled on, occasionally nodding at people they met, more and more as they closed on the heart of the place, though each was just a commoner, no arms or armour or lordly colours about them. A number of times, they caught sight of buildings that looked very familiar, suggesting they had become turned around more than once in their wanderings. The problem now was that, with the sun almost directly overhead, using the shadows for direction-finding was almost impossible. The last corner they rounded led them to the market place; the noise hit them like a wall.

The square was packed tight with stalls attended by the folk of Acerenza. Halfdan was slightly overwhelmed to begin with, uncertain where to start. He leaned closer to Marc. 'Keep your eye out for any trader who sells either weapons or arrows, or any sort of kit a man travelling for days might need. Those stalls may have seen our friend Atenulf's men. I think we should split up and look around, then meet up in about half an hour over by that big doorway. We could do with buying a few things since we now have no food.'

'You can't speak the tongue,' Marc reminded him.

'How do I say "those" and the numbers one to five?'

The Norman walked Halfdan and Sveinn through the words several times until they were content that they'd memorised them, and then the three parted ways. Halfdan meandered here and there between the stalls. Once or twice, he spotted a white-and-red uniform in the crowd and turned away, casually, being sure not to look panicked and suspicious. He found himself at a fruit stall and looked about. There were many fruits he recognised and a number that were completely unknown. As the stallholder came to him, he pointed at the apples and asked for four. The man nodded and said something. Assuming it was a price, Halfdan reached into the purse at his belt and fished out a collection of small coins, holding them in the flat of his palm while he struggled to hold the four apples in his other hand. Noting which coins the man took, he flipped another at him and picked up a strange yellow fruit. The man shrugged, put away the coins and then went on to serve someone else without a further glance.

Trying not to drop the five pieces of fruit, he wandered on. As he reached the end of a line of stalls, close to the edge of the square, something caught his eye, and he focused on a gateway. Three bales of hay sat to one side, and the entry was coated with dried horse manure. A pitchfork stood against the wall near the hay. A sign above undoubtedly labelled the place a stable, though Halfdan could not read it. Turning, he spotted Marc after some searching and took a moment to catch his attention, then waved him over. The Norman converged on him, his arm full of two large loaves of bread, and Sveinn was not far behind, assuming the summons was for him also. Once they were together, Halfdan thumbed over his shoulder.

'A stable, I think. It strikes me that Atenulf will have plenty of horses, and carts too, for the transport of his gold. He will have to stable his horses somewhere, and even if that is with Fulk's cousin, he will need plenty of supplies if he is planning to move south. Can you make some subtle enquiries?'

Marc frowned, nodded, and stepped into the gateway, Halfdan and Sveinn following on. They ignored the young lad sweeping the flagged yard, their Norman companion making straight for a man in a well-cut tunic and cote. Catching the man's attention, he rattled something off in the local tongue. There was a brief exchange and Marc nodded a number of times. Halfdan's eyes, however, were on the other man. Even without being able to understand either side of the conversation, Halfdan could see enough in the stable owner's expression to formulate a solid, and worrying, opinion.

After a few moments more, the man nodded to Marc, turned and wandered away into one of the doorways leading off the yard. The Norman turned to Halfdan with a smile. 'He has catered for a visiting lord's baggage animals. Not the nobles' beasts or the soldiers', but the pack and cart horses. He has a ledger that contains all his information on them. He's gone to get it.'

Halfdan shook his head. 'I don't know what he was telling you, but whatever it was, that was only half of it. I saw his eyes. They moved constantly, shifting. He has secrets he keeps, and he was not happy to be talking to you. We need to go.'

'But if he has what we need—'

Halfdan dropped the apples he was carrying and grabbed Marc by the upper arm. 'He's not getting a ledger. He's getting the guards. Come on.'

With that, he turned and marched out of the stable yard, eyeing the boy with the broom warily as they went. With Marc and Sveinn at his heel, he emerged out into the market square once more. Immediately his hackles rose up. Despite the din of the crowd, he could hear soldiers. His eyes swivelled to the right to see a small unit of men in the city guard's tunics, jogging around the edge of the stalls.

'Shit.'

With the others in his wake, Halfdan dived between two stalls, pushing customers out of the way and leaping baskets of goods. Assuming the others were with him, but not sparing the time to check, he ducked this way and that, dodging, jumping, running at a crouch, and was rather relieved when he burst clear of the far end of the market square and looked left and right to see no soldiers coming to cut them off. He turned to see the other two right behind him. Sveinn, at the rear, had been tipping over stalls and baskets as he ran, to provide obstacles in their wake. Consequently, the men in red and white were still only two-thirds of the way through the market, trying desperately to catch up.

Satisfied they had a sufficient lead now, Halfdan charged on down the narrow street directly ahead. He reached the second turning and took it. As they ran on down that alley, a grizzled-looking man with a long face emerged from a rickety gate ahead, pushing a wooden barrow. As they neared the gate, the man turned off into the next, more major, road and disappeared. Knowing they had only moments before the soldiers caught up, Halfdan took a chance, pulled open that gate and slipped inside, holding it open until Marc and Sveinn were through, then pulling it shut.

It was only as the gate closed once more that the smell hit Halfdan and he realised what this small enclosure was. Three buildings had windows overlooking the small dead end, separated from the street by the gate, and all three clearly emptied their shit pots through those windows. The three men were standing almost ankle-deep in human waste. Though he was now gagging and had thrown up into his mouth a little, Halfdan could only find gratitude that the man with the barrow had clearly been removing some of the contents, for otherwise it might have been up to their knees.

They struggled to hold their breath and stay silent, and moments later they heard the guards pound past the gate. Halfdan waited as long as he could bear and then pushed the gate open slowly and looked outside. The alley was empty, and he turned and led them back the way they'd come to avoid the greatest risk of meeting their pursuers.

In moments they were back out on the first street, breathing deeply to clear their lungs of the terrible stench. He ran on until they found a building that looked familiar. Moving more carefully now, guiding their route by the few landmarks they could pick out, the three men traversed alleys and streets until they saw the end of the one in which their hiding place lay. They approached the alley, and Halfdan almost jumped as a voice hissed from somewhere nearby. Jerking to a halt, he looked all around. They were back away from the centre now, and this street was deserted. It took him some time, and a second hiss, to identify the source.

Brow furrowed, he crossed the street and tried to peer through the minuscule gap in the shutters of a house from which the noise seemed to have come. Unable to make anything out, he moved across to the door and reached for the handle. The door slammed open, smacking painfully into his hand, and as he swore and pulled back his arm, a pale, meaty fist emerged from within, grabbed him by the tunic front and pulled him into the darkness.

As the other two followed, Halfdan stared up at the serious face of Bjorn.

'What's happening?'

Fulk de Courvaudon replied, stepping out of the gloom. 'They found us at the place with the steps. We had to kill three men to get away. Fortunately your big friend here seems to think that fighting fewer than three men at once is unmanly, so we didn't encounter much difficulty. But we had to run, because others were coming. The whole place is out of our reach now, including all our gear. We had to find somewhere to hide where we could hopefully see anyone running past.'

'Thank you,' Halfdan breathed. 'We too ran into trouble. We found a stable man who had dealt with Atenulf's horses, but he was suspicious and called the guard. We had to run. This is not turning out to be a good day.'

Bjorn snorted. 'Maybe not for *you*. I had fun.' His nose wrinkled. 'It was bad enough to make you shit yourself?'

'Long story.'

Halfdan became aware that they were not alone, as other figures emerged from the gloomy shadows at the edge of the room. He was relieved at the sight of Ulfr, along with the two men he'd taken. 'We had less trouble, but learned nothing,' the shipwright grumbled. 'We stumbled across a patrol and had to run, but they either didn't see us or weren't interested enough to follow. Saw nothing to the west, though, anywhere back toward the gate we came in. Don't think the thief can be in that quarter.'

'You heard what I told Fulk?'

Ulfr nodded. 'You realise, of course, that the noose is going to continue to tighten all the time we stay here.'

Halfdan nodded. Sooner or later they were going to get caught, but even if they managed to escape the city, they would lose their chance of catching the gold. Halfdan was perhaps unusual among his crew and friends for being less concerned about the acquisition of gold and silver than of survival and honour, but even he balked at the idea of having arrived here with saddlebags full of gold from Miklagarðr, but leaving without a bean to their name. That was not merely a lack of success, but an abject failure. He found that a niggling part of his mind laid the blame at the absence of Ketil, Leif and Anna. While none of them individually might have made a difference to all of this, together they were a wolf pack. Alone they were at risk.

The afternoon wore on. Some time as the sunlight turned that late golden colour, Gunnhild and her party appeared. In that uncanny way of hers, she made straight for their door before anyone had to hiss to grab her attention. The three of them ducked inside, making the count of survivors now eleven. She delivered a report succinctly. They had found a rich-looking house with a stable attached. The stable had been full of noblemen's riding horses. It seemed highly likely to be where Atenulf was staying.

They waited on, and Halfdan was starting to fret, when someone called out. Farlof was staggering down the street, exhausted and nursing a wound on his forearm. They caught his attention and dragged him inside. He confirmed that his group had found the same place and traced the tracks of carts across town to a warehouse, but there they had met soldiers and only Farlof had managed to get away.

The sun went down on their first day of being trapped in Acerenza, and the situation looked nothing but bleak. Halfdan was assailed again and again by the image of a wolf in a gilded cage. Despite the protestations of some of the Normans, Gunnhild sang her song and cast her bones, but whatever it was she saw, she refused to speak of it, and her face remained grave.

Not long after dark, they ate what little they'd managed to procure from the city. It turned out that the only thing Halfdan had managed to retain in his run was something called a lemon, and he spent almost an hour regretting biting into it. A fight broke out in the tense darkness after a while, as two of the Normans launched a stream of bile and accusations at the Northmen, stating flatly that they'd have been better staying under siege in Ginosa than here, trapped in just a house. Bjorn had broken a nose before the arguing parties had been dragged apart by Fulk and Marc, Halfdan and Ulfr.

The tension returned an hour or so later, when shushing chain shirts and clonking scabbards and shields sounded in the street outside, as a patrol made its way past, down the street.

Halfdan should have seen it coming. All the signs had been there. He cursed himself for not having predicted it, as Aimery, that Norman who had earlier suggested selling the Northmen out, and who had instigated the later argument, suddenly burst to his feet and ran to the door, shouting to the city guard.

The room exploded into action. Aimery never had a chance to regret giving away their hiding place, for even as he reached the door, Bjorn was on him. Both big, pale hands grabbed the man's head over the ears and he wrenched his entire skull round, breaking every bone in the neck and almost pulling the head free in the process. He let the body drop, and by that time both Halfdan and Fulk were bellowing orders.

They had to hold the door now. All they could do was defend and hope.

Chapter 12

The street outside burst into life and activity. The trapped fugitives could hear men shouting orders in a weird mix of the largely intelligible Norman tongue and the baffling local one. With Bjorn already at the door, standing over the quivering body of Fulk's traitor, Halfdan immediately focused on that, while Fulk hurried over to the shuttered window.

Between them, Fulk and Marc held the shutters closed as men outside began to pull on them, attempting to wrench them open. The other Normans huddled beside them, and managed to pull daggers from sheaths and jam them between the latches on the shutters, holding them closed for now. The twin wooden boards were not perfectly fitted and as the guards rattled harder and harder, trying to dislodge the knife and open the aperture, the Normans began to jab their blades through whatever cracks they could find, discouraging the attempts outside. A few yelps suggested that their tactic was working, at least temporarily.

There was no way to lock the door, and though it was latched, the only thing holding it shut was Bjorn, who, the moment the Norman had fallen, had slammed his considerable bulk against the timbers, heaving it against the jamb. Outside, just as at the window, men were hammering and slamming against the door, trying to open it. Bjorn's weight was preventing entry for now, but the door shook and bucked with every battering, and it was only a matter of time before the guards managed to push hard enough to force a gap. The latch clattered up and down as men tried to gain entry while

Bjorn repeatedly slammed it back into place even as he leaned on the door.

Ulfr and the two Varangians hurried over and threw themselves against the timbers, adding their own weight to Bjorn's and, for the time being, this seemed to overcome the increased attempts to open it from outside. Still, it was only a matter of time, and there was no doubt in that dark room that the guards out in the street had sent men running for reinforcements. In no time, the patrol out there would multiply into a small army.

Halfdan looked around, his eyes falling on a woodworm-riddled old table and bench upon which several of them had passed the last few hours. With a gesture to Farlof, the two men lifted the heavy table and carried it over to the door. With nods of timing, they prepared. Bjorn slipped aside amid the flurry of blows on the door, making sure the latch was still down, and in a heartbeat the two men had slammed the table end-on against the door in his place. Bjorn now added his weight to the table, while others hurriedly located a piece of twine lying on the ground and used it to tie the latch in place, preventing it from being lifted without some superhuman effort.

The bench was brought over and added to the weight against the door. Halfdan watched as the defence deepened every moment, his gaze slipping to the window, where Fulk and his men had added another dagger wedged into the shutter latches, helping keep them shut.

The Norman turned, scanning the dark room, looking for Halfdan until his eyes fell upon the jarl.

'That's all we can do here. If you have a clever plan up your sleeve, now would be the time.'

Halfdan chewed his lip. 'Nothing leaps to mind. We're trapped like rats in a dragon boat.' He pointed at the window and door. 'They won't hold for long, and when they get inside we're fucked. There are eleven of us. I know we're better than them, but I'd bet there are enough guards in Acerenza to swamp us.'

Fulk nodded. 'A straight fight is unlikely to go our way. On the other hand, if we're going to die, I'd rather fall to a blade like a man than starve to death in here. Maybe we should take our chances with them.'

Halfdan raised an eyebrow. 'If I didn't know better, I'd wonder if you were related to Bjorn.'

The big man snorted. 'Even *I* don't want to fight a whole city.'

'Quite.'

'If you have all finished,' Gunnhild said, standing with her arms folded in the gloom, carved half-staff leaning against the wall.

The two men, and indeed most others in the room, turned to look at her. 'Yes?' Halfdan asked.

'As you have said, a straight fight is not the way. We will be overrun, killed or captured, and many will die in the process. Remember what the goddess has shown me. A wolf in a gilded cage.'

Halfdan shrugged. 'What are we in now, if not a cage?'

The völva shook her head. 'I did not see a wolf run through with a sword. I saw a wolf in a cage. There is more yet to come, but we must go on. We must survive. Open the door and lay down your arms.'

'What?' Fulk held his arms wide. 'Surrender?'

'Unless you intend us all to die here, that is your only choice. You either die tonight or you buy us a tomorrow. When there is a tomorrow there is always a chance.'

Fulk snarled. 'My slimy bastard of a cousin turns on me for shiny gold, the city plays host to the biggest thief on the peninsula, and you suggest we bow our necks beneath the swords of such men?'

Halfdan was looking back and forth between them. 'You know I trust you, Gunnhild, but there must be some other way.'

'No, Halfdan. There is no other way. You are a caged wolf, or a dead wolf. Which would you prefer?'

'No,' Fulk barked. 'I have no intention of bowing to the bastards. If I must die, then I must die, but I am Fulk de Courvaudon, Lord of Ginosa, liege man of William de Hautville, and I do not surrender to criminal traitors.'

Farlof stepped out from the edge of the room, looking a little sheepish. 'I am inclined to agree with him, Halfdan. If we surrender, they might just butcher us on the spot. If they are willing to turn on us just to hide their secret alliance, we are of little use alive. I have no faith in their nailed god, and if I die like a thrall, I will not sit beside my kin in the Allfather's hall. Better to die with sword in hand, standing my ground.'

Halfdan found himself wavering. It was a persuasive argument. He turned back to Gunnhild, a pleading look in his eye.

'A wolf in a cage, not a wolf on a spit,' was all she said, brows creased, eyes piercing in the darkness.

He turned to Fulk. 'She is rarely wrong. You should listen to her.'

'No,' the Norman said. 'We will escape this.'

With that, he dashed over to the other side of the room. 'See this alcove? The stone wall here is old, the mortar crumbled. We can pull this wall down. Your white giant could do it easily. There is always a way out, Halfdan.'

The jarl looked across at Gunnhild, but her expression betrayed a great deal of scepticism. He looked back to Fulk, then to Bjorn. 'Help the man.'

He flinched as he glanced back at the völva. The look he saw on her face was neither disapproval, nor anger. It conveyed impressively the suggestion that whatever he was doing was utterly pointless. That she knew the end result, no matter what he tried. It was an extremely disturbing expression, and even as he turned away to help, he couldn't shake the after-image of it from his mind.

It took perhaps a quarter of an hour. The mortar might be crumbling and old, but the wall was thick and the stones large. Bjorn worked like a beast, with three others helping, while the rest continued to hold the shutters and door closed against the men battering them. To make matters worse, over that time, they heard repeated increases in the force outside, more voices adding to the cacophony, more fists pounding on the door. He was already estimating well above a hundred men in the street now. Every heartbeat that passed tipped the balance more in favour of the lord of Acerenza.

The sense of dispirited failure washed over them all, as a pivotal stone was removed from the crumbling wall and Bjorn finally revealed their precious escape route. It led into a small courtyard, not more than eight feet wide in each direction, formed of blank-faced walls, just an unused recess where buildings met. There was no magical, gods-granted way out of there.

Gunnhild huffed. 'Buy our lives. We still have time.'

Halfdan chewed on his lip again, deep in thought. 'Can anyone remember what this place looked like from outside?'

'What do you mean?' Fulk asked.

'Up top. If we climbed, could we get away across roofs?'

A smile spread slowly across the Norman's face. 'Maybe. The city is carved up into small blocks of maybe ten houses or so, separated by these alleys. There won't be a way down into any of the houses. The roofs are tiled and pitched, not flat. But if we could get across them, we might be able to jump across one of the alleys and get away.'

Farlof winced. 'I think I'd rather fight here or give up.'

'What?'

'I am not good up high. Even the thought of sloping tiled roofs and jumping over streets makes me want to shit myself.'

'Live to fight again,' Gunnhild said flatly.

'I'll go up and have a look,' one of the Normans said, crossing the room. 'I spent my youth climbing every tree and wall in Fresney.'

The man pushed his way past Bjorn and heaved into the small space between buildings. Halfdan had no fear of heights himself, but as he looked up into that narrow space, even he shivered. The houses were all two-storey and it seemed a very long way up from this angle. The Norman scanned the wall opposite, looking up, and selected a place that looked to Halfdan just like any other. Without further ado, he gripped two of the more jutting sections of stone and hauled himself up, his feet finding a toehold with ridiculous ease. The man scurried up the wall like one of the lizards Halfdan had seen all over this dry, warm land, climbing with short, sharp and decisive movements. In a time Halfdan could hardly credit, the man was at the top of the wall, some twenty feet up, and reaching up over the eaves of the building. He seemed to grip something out of sight, and a moment later hauled his legs up and over.

Halfdan strained to listen, hoping to hear something positive from the Norman, though all he could hear was optimistic murmuring from his friends at ground level, playing over the constant banging and shouting outside the door and window. Before the man up top could report back, Halfdan's attention was drawn back across the room as a horrible wooden crack boomed out across the dark room. The amount of dim light creeping in around the left-hand of the two window shutters had increased worryingly. The wooden boards were beginning to give, and it would not be long before the window was open.

Halfdan looked up again, a sense of urgency stealing over him. He almost leapt with relief as the man appeared at the edge of the roof once more.

'Well?'

'It's as milord de Courvaudon said,' the man replied. 'Maybe eight or ten houses in a block. This one is at the middle of them. There's a whole street full of guards out front now, and I don't know what they're up to, but more are on their way and they're bringing a horse and cart.'

'What about escape?' Halfdan urged.

'It won't be easy. I reckon the narrowest alley is maybe ten feet across. I've found no way down into any of the adjacent houses, and the other blocks look very similar, so there's a good chance we will have to jump more than one alley before we find any way down. Here and there are towers sticking up another storey above the roofs, and they mostly have flat tops. If we could get to one, we might be able to climb it and then get down inside.'

'And then what?' Gunnhild demanded, arms still folded defiantly.

'What?'

'We are still trapped in the city, and the guards will just follow your progress across the roofs and trap you inside another building.'

'You have seen this?'

'Halfdan,' she sighed with strained patience, 'it does not take communion with the goddess to see such things. Simple common sense is all I need. Men will die scrambling across the roofs and jumping alleys, and at best you will end up the same as we are now. There come moments in life, young jarl, where the *'tafl* board is inescapable and the jarl is trapped. Now is one of those moments.'

'I found a way past Ketil's men on the board,' he insisted, rather petulantly if he was forced to admit it.

'Your cunning cannot find you a way out here, and nor will your sword arm. But in the coming days your Loki cunning and my sense might find us another way out, assuming we live that long.'

'I think we can—' began the Norman on the roof, calling down to them with his hands cupped around his mouth, but then he stopped, mid-sentence, and straightened suddenly. Without a further sound, he slowly toppled forward and pitched into the open air, falling into the courtyard. Bjorn leapt back, knocking Halfdan to the side as the unfortunate Norman hit the packed earth floor and exploded in a messy tangle of broken limbs, blood and brains. Halfdan stared at the corpse and at the arrow standing proud from his back, between the shoulder blades, having pierced the padded tunic that was all his protection. He had landed on his face, and so the arrow jutted up, unbroken.

'Shit.'

'I think that answers that,' Farlof said, a touch of relief creeping into his tone at the thought that he would not now be required to climb to the roof.

'They have archers somewhere,' Fulk snarled. 'Must be on one of those towers he mentioned.'

'Then the roof is not an option, after all,' Halfdan sighed, sadly.

Before anyone could say more, the window shutters suddenly gave way in an explosion of splinters and shards of rusted iron. The two men who had still been holding them closed fell away, crying out, one thrown clear by the blow, the other screaming in agony at the spikes of torn wood peppering his face. As the shutters crashed in, torn from their hinges, so too came death. Spears were suddenly lancing in through the opening, and the tips of wavering swords. An unfortunate Varangian who had reacted instantly and leapt forward to try and stop the shutters falling away was taken through the cheek with a spear, smashing through his teeth and pinning the back of his throat. The man gave a strange-sounding scream, hampered by the metal filling his mouth, and fell away.

In response, all those available now leapt forward, close enough to act, but not close enough to follow the last man to Valhöll. Their swords slashed and stabbed, axes swinging, preventing anyone from attempting to climb in through the window, but equally they were doing no damage to the soldiers outside.

Halfdan felt hope die. It was only a matter of time now. The door was taking a fresh assault; from the sound of it, it was now being pounded with a tree trunk, perhaps what they had brought forward in that cart. It would not last much longer and once the door was open, the tide of soldiers in red and white would not be held back for long.

He turned to Gunnhild, the only one in the room so far not to have tried to do something at window or door. She had a resigned and fatalistic look on her face, but as she swung to meet his gaze there was no recrimination or smugness there. Just a simple question. He hated nodding his agreement, but he could see no alternative, now. There was no escape, and to fight on was to die. Every man of the cold North wanted to die with a sword in his hand, spitting curses in the eye of his enemy, but not if there was still a chance of living. Only an idiot sought death as a favourable alternative.

He turned to shout to the others, and his eyes widened. He ducked just in time as two arrows whipped in through the window, shots of opportunity taken between the struggling shapes. One arrow clattered off the wall, the other took a piece out of Ulfr's shoulder, causing him to cast a stream of eye-wateringly biological curses at the attackers as he reached up to nurse the bloody wound.

They were done.

And if he had ever to that last moment thought otherwise, what he saw through the gaps in the window sealed it. Behind the red-and-white figures at the window, and past that second group with the bows, he caught sight of a third wave of attack, and this one made him shudder to the core. Men in dun-coloured cotes carrying bundles of brushwood and armfuls of thin logs, and behind them, a line of men with torches ablaze, creating a golden glow in the darkness of the street, enough to reveal what the future held for the luckless defenders.

In that split second, his mind's eye cast him back over the months, drawing him over the space of a single heartbeat right across the leagues of open sea and back to the hippodrome of great and fabled Miklagarðr. There, he had watched impassively as that bastard Ari Karsten had burned. It had been a fitting death, and well-deserved, and Halfdan had not shied from watching it, but he had not, until this moment, realised what it had done. That scene, the crisping flesh, the shrieks and wails, the popping of fat in fire, had somehow buried deep in Halfdan's heart a new and brutal fear.

He was, in that moment, unmanned, and he'd never expected such a thing. The jarl of the Wolves of Odin feared no one. He would face man, giant, dragon or god with a blade in his hand, and he had always thought that to be the pinnacle of bravery and as far as a man could go. But to suffer Ari Karsten's fate…

'Stand down,' he shouted. Only he noticed just how much his voice wavered.

'What?' came a number of shocked replies. Bjorn, Fulk and Farlof all took a step toward him.

'Gunnhild was right,' he said, trying to keep the strength in his voice, praying to any god who might be listening that he didn't piss himself, for while he spoke commands his mind's eye was still replaying scenes of Ari's death in the darkness of his soul.

'Better to fight than—' began Bjorn.

'No,' Halfdan said. 'No it isn't. Because we're not going to die fighting. We're not going to take the bastards with us. They're about to burn us.' He thrust a finger toward the window and, as if to illustrate his point, the archers had parted in the street and men were coming forward now with their kindling in the torchlight.

Many eyes turned to this new sight, and the sense of fatalistic bravado in the room trickled away, leaving an aura of fear and hopelessness. Halfdan gestured to Fulk. 'You speak their tongue well. Tell them we surrender.'

Fulk wavered for a moment, but Halfdan nodded toward the approaching men, and even at that moment a collection of sticks and straw came over the heads of the nearest attackers and through the window, loosely tied with twine so that it burst open on contact, scattering combustible material all around. Many more of those and it wouldn't take much for the fire to gain a hold.

'Tell him.'

As Fulk crossed to the window, waving his arms and offering surrender in the tongues of both Norman and native, Halfdan turned to the others.

'Get rid of your Mjǫllnir or valknut. Anything that ties you to the gods. Throw them away. Hide what you cannot get rid of,' he added, pulling his sleeve down to cover the Loki serpents on his arm.

'What?' Ulfr said. 'Why?'

'Because this is all about greed. Atenulf turned on his own people to steal a jarl's ransom in gold. Fulk's cousin turned on him for just a share of that gold. But greedy men can be bought. There is always a chance we can argue a way out of this, but these men are all nailed-god men. Do not give them a reason to refuse us. Fulk can do any talking and I will find us all a way out of this, I give you my oath. But if we want Christian lords to consider anything we say, we want to look as though we are Fulk's men, sons of the nailed god one and all.'

Gunnhild, her face displaying sourly just how she felt about that, had no choice but to nod her agreement. 'The Allfather will understand. It is no dishonour to him, only a trick to outwit your enemies.' As the Wolves in the room reluctantly untied thongs and lifted them over heads, muttering charms of protection as they threw the symbols of gods into the corner of the room, Halfdan tried not to feel perturbed that Gunnhild did not seem to be following the same advice. She did not wear a hammer of Thor about her neck, of course, and her symbols of the goddess were all etched into her very being rather than worn as apparel, yet she seemed to do nothing to cover them.

As Fulk continued negotiations at the window and the others prepared themselves, Halfdan watched Gunnhild with a frown. She stepped back into a corner, into the shadowy recesses, where he was surprised to see her bend at the waist and peel off her dress. A couple of the others turned and started to watch with interest until Halfdan gave them a glare, yet even as he stopped others watching her strip, he turned back and guiltily did just that.

'Hold my belt,' she hissed, and he reached out and grabbed it as she made a swift flourish of her hands – suddenly her green dress was inside out. The lining was a drab brown colour, and with ease she shrugged herself back into it. Once it was in place again, she pulled on a hood she seemed to have acquired from nowhere and jerked it up over her head, hiding her features in the darkness within. She took her belt, slid the pouches to one side and then fastened it inside out, so that the pouches were largely lost in the folds of dull brown dress and beneath her arm. Satisfied, she reached out and swept her short staff from the wall. Gripping it tight, she dropped the tip to the floor; suddenly it was a harmless walking stick as she affected a lean. Finally, she crossed to one of the Normans nearby.

'Apologies. You can have this back later.' And with that she pulled the crucifix on its thong up and over his head, replacing it around her own neck and settling it against her chest.

Halfdan stared. Mere moments ago, Gunnhild the völva, daughter of Freyja, who emanated power and confidence had stood before him. Now, unless he looked hard, she was a lame old priestess of the nailed god.

'Fuck me with Odin's staff,' Bjorn breathed, crossing to them, eyes wide.

'I'll fuck you with *mine* if you don't lower your voice,' snapped Gunnhild. 'The last thing we need now is for anyone to draw attention to me or to call on anyone but the nailed god. For now, Christ on his cross is your only lord. Odin will understand. And, Bjorn Bear-torn, pass the word. Everyone is to address me as "sister".'

Still wide-eyed, Bjorn stepped away and whispered as much to Ulfr. Halfdan leaned a little closer. 'Can you do this? You said you would pay a price for what you did. Dare you risk such a thing?'

'My debt will be paid in the North, Halfdan, and it will be for me alone. Worry not about me. And you would be surprised how blind even the most perceptive of men can be when faced with their own faith, so just follow this. Just remember: *sister.*'

The negotiations seemed to have concluded, and Fulk turned back to the room. 'Throw down your weapons everyone. We have been promised that no one will be killed until the lord of Acerenza has heard our case.'

'Very reassuring,' Farlof grumbled as he threw down his axe and sword.

'He is my cousin. He might be a treacherous bastard, but I will talk our way out of this,' Fulk said, dropping his own sword.

The others followed suit, no one very happy with the command, but all very plainly aware of what was at stake, given the kindling all across the floor and the torches burning outside the window. As the Norman lord pulled the door open, Ulfr leaned close and murmured something to him. Fulk threw a confused look toward Gunnhild and stared when he saw her. She turned to Halfdan.

'Give me your sword.'

'What?'

'I cannot hide everyone's weapon, but yours is short.'

Quickly, Halfdan slid his scabbard from his belt and refastened it. By the time he looked up, the buckle closed once more, there was no sign of his blade. He blinked. How she had hidden it so thoroughly and so quickly he had no idea, but he suspected he might not want to ask the question of her. The bustle of men moving drew his attention, and he looked back to see that Fulk de Courvaudon had stepped out through the door into the open. Someone outside was demanding that he raise his hands, but he did nothing of the sort. Marc followed his master out, and Halfdan hurried across to be the third, gesturing at Ulfr as he did so.

'Escort the priestess out,' he hissed.

The jarl of the Wolves emerged into the city air trying to look downcast and defeated, but not enough to draw specific attention. Some sort of officer was standing with a group of armed men, archers nearby with arrows nocked and ready to raise. The officer was glaring at Fulk.

'Raise your arms,' the man repeated, angrily.

'Mind who you speak to in such a manner,' Fulk replied, brow knitted and eyes bright. 'I am Fulk de Courvaudon, cousin of your master, lord of Ginosa and liege man of William Iron Arm. I have laid down my weapon and will speak with my kinsman, but if you treat me or mine with anything less than the respect due our rank, when this is over I shall have you peeled raw, tied to the back of a mule and dragged across a salt flat.'

Whether the titles impressed the officer or the threat perhaps suddenly seemed worryingly likely, the officer made no further demands. The entire group, now down to nine bodies, shuffled out of the building and past the lines of armed men. Halfdan turned, close to Fulk, and saw Ulfr escorting what looked to be a brown-robed Christ priestess out of the building.

As she emerged, Halfdan was once again struck by the sheer brilliance of the woman. She even moved like an old woman – her foot turned slightly in, walking on the outer edge, giving her a weird limp that accounted for the stick she thumped along with. Somehow even the intricate carvings in the wood seemed to fade to the eye, hardly noticeable. As she moved out with the group, the soldiers in red and white used their free hand to draw a cross on their face and chest in the usual manner of Christians. He marvelled at how no one seemed to see the real Gunnhild, but then reminded himself that even *he* had to concentrate on her, and force himself to remember it was her, to see the stick in her grip for what it was and to notice the seams visible on her inside-out dress. He hoped that when the light came and there was less obfuscation, she would still find it as easy to hide what she was.

Moments later they were being turned and marched away along the street.

Halfdan looked about him. There really was no way out now. He was a wolf in a gilded cage, just as Gunnhild had predicted.

Now he had to trust that innate Loki cunning that had seen him from a poor orphan to the jarl of a ship of men.

It was not over yet.

Part Four

ᚹᛟᛚᚠᛖᛋ ᛟᚠ ᛟᛞᛁᚾ

Flight to Freedom

Chapter 13

'We need to stop,' Leif gasped between heaving breaths.

'No,' Ketil grunted. 'Not until we reach the next river. The river will stop *some* of them following, at least.'

'Ketil, *you* might be able to run a hundred miles in a day, because your legs are as long as a horse's, but the rest of us are exhausted. We need to stop.'

The Icelander turned in the saddle. It was clear the others were struggling, Leif most of all, but even the taller Varangians with them were puffing and panting, red in the face. Ketil had been keeping his horse at a slower pace than he'd have liked to allow the others to keep up, and so it seemed unfathomable that they might be struggling, yet they were. He fought the irritation. They had passed a river somewhere back here on the way to the battlefield and he really wanted to reach it. He remembered it being roughly chest deep; the fourteen fugitives might be able to struggle across in armour, but any pursuing units would think twice about trying it just for the sake of mopping up a few survivors. But it was increasingly clear that they were not going to reach the water together – and if he rode off ahead, he would leave them all behind.

That was not acceptable, and he was surprised at his own reasoning. Some time ago, he'd have thought principally of himself and his own chances of survival. He'd have seriously given thought to leaving them for the Byzantines and running ahead to safety, perhaps even abandoning Leif and Anna, let alone the Varangians he did not know that well. *That* Ketil seemed to have died on the battlefield. Now, not only was he reasoning that their best chances of survival involved staying together, but he also discovered that he was unwilling to leave a man behind. Or a woman. Was this what it was like to be Halfdan? He wasn't sure he liked such a noble attitude. It made life more complicated, and that was another reason why he would only play the role of jarl until he found Loki-born once more.

He slowed, and the others did the same with visible relief.

Unfortunately, once he was not suffering the nauseating bouncing in the saddle, the pain in his face flooded in and filled the space. He thought he blinked, but he couldn't really tell, for his eye was clearly gone. Not just blinded, but gone. He'd thrown up a little as they ran, when he'd reached up tentatively to prod it, and found he could put his finger in the socket. Still, he was like the Allfather now: half blind, but so much wiser. He would endure the pain, for it would fade with each passing day, while the wisdom was now his forever.

'All right,' he said, taking a deep breath and coming to a halt. 'We stop.'

As the others stumbled to stillness around him, bending double with their hands on their knees, panting and coughing, Ketil peered off east and listened.

There was nothing in sight, but that was no consolation, for the light was now almost gone and he could still hear activity. Fleeing the battlefield, they had raced west for a solid hour now as the sun disappeared and the inky darkness grew, but they were still some way from safety, he was sure of that. The Byzantine general, realising he was victorious and that the rebel army had broken, had released his men to chase down and capture or kill anyone they could find. The 'great' emperor Constantine Monomachos had hated Maniakes, and would not be forgiving of rebellion. Anyone who had taken up arms against him would find themselves made an example of, and Ketil had no intention of being tortured to death in the hippodrome of Miklagarðr for the entertainment of the masses.

And he could still hear it. Even an hour from the battlefield, he could make out the sounds of victorious Byzantines hunting down escaped soldiers. Most of the rebels who had fled the field had done so on foot, Maniakes's cavalry having been largely cut down the moment the battle turned against them. The Byzantine horse, however, had made it through the fight largely intact, and so now riders hunted fleeing infantry.

Even now, as Ketil wondered what they would do, he could hear screaming not more than a quarter of a mile away, back beyond a stand of trees that was visible only as a blacker mass in the gloom. The fourteen of them were lucky in that they had been among the first to get away, and potential pursuit had been distracted by the presence of wagons to plunder; they had got further than most. Still, they needed to be far enough away from the field that the Byzantines believed there could be no more routed soldiers running.

Damn it, he wished the others could keep up with him, that they *all* had horses.

The light was gone now, the night becoming truly dark. Regardless of the gloom, Ketil was finding it hard to see with his one remaining eye, for the constant throb of the wounded socket interfered with his perceptions.

His painful gaze fell upon shapes he suspected of being buildings. A village? At least, perhaps, they might be able to find food, if not somewhere to hide and rest for an hour or two. He beckoned Leif, whom he knew to have good eyesight – and two eyes to see with.

'Can you see over there? What's that, a village?'

The Rus squinted into the night and sucked on his teeth. 'Whatever it is, it's ruined and uninhabited.'

'How can you tell that?'

'It's dark and there're no lights there. If it were occupied, they'd have lamps or fires lit by now.'

Ketil took a deep breath. 'It's as good as anywhere, then.'

'For?'

'For the night. If we're going to lie low for a few hours, we might as well make it the whole night. If we do nothing to draw attention, anyone else should take it for unoccupied, as you did. We'll stay there and set watches. By dawn, I reckon they'll have stopped looking for survivors, so if we make it 'til then, we can set off and feel fairly safe.'

Leif nodded, a relieved look on his face. 'Tell the others,' Ketil said, and as the little man did just that, he turned away, ostensibly scanning the horizon. In reality, the pain in his face was cresting once more, close to unbearable; he was crying tears from his remaining eye, and unspeakable matter from the empty socket. He was their jarl for as long as he had to be. He could not let them see him in anguish. He clenched his teeth and fought the agony. Pain thumped him in the face with every beat of his heart. If only Gunnhild were here, she would undoubtedly have some poultice that would lessen the pain. Why had he been so stupid and prideful to lead them east into this mess?

Taking a breath, he fought it down. He had to remain in control. He turned, hoping his face was sombre and straight, and that the darkness hid the worst of his tears. Leif was looking at him. Ketil was sure there was sympathy in that gaze, which only served to irritate him.

Now they had rested for a few moments, he gestured onwards with his arm, and the whole group began to move again, much slower now, tired muscles stiff even after such a short rest. Ketil forced himself to stay with them, and the bouncing gait of the animal once more drove the pain in his face into the background, making it easier to manage. They moved down a slope and past a small copse, eyes mostly on the ground in front of them, for a single rabbit hole could break a leg in the dark.

It took almost a quarter of an hour to reach the buildings. As they approached it became clear that it was much smaller than a village: just an old, abandoned farmstead. The main house, just a single storey of six or seven rooms, sat within a low boundary wall that had enclosed what appeared to have once been well-tended gardens, now overgrown and gone to seed. From the state of the roof, Ketil surmised that it had been empty for a number of years. Two barns stood nearby – both missing their doors and at least some part of their roofs, one having completely fallen in – and several smaller sheds or shells thereof were visible dotted around, as well as a smashed chicken coop.

'Into the main house,' he said.

Leif cleared his throat. 'Might the barn not be safer?'

Ketil frowned, then promised himself never to do so again, for he almost fainted with the pain it caused. As he recovered slowly, shaking, he focused as much as he could on Leif. 'Why?'

'Well if anyone else *does* come looking, just as you did, they'll focus on the house. If we're in the barn we're less likely to be discovered straight away.'

Ketil straightened. He'd almost nodded, but that would probably have been a terrible idea, too. 'Good thinking. One of the barns is more intact than the other. Come on.'

Leading the way, with Leif and Anna close behind and the others following on, Ketil hurried across to the better-preserved of the two barns. Reaching it, he dismounted and ducked inside. It was truly gloomy within, and even had he still both eyes, he doubted he'd be able to make much out. One thing that he noticed, though, was the ruined doors, which lay on the ground just inside. A patch of murky light at the far end betrayed the existence of a second, smaller door. As the others gathered around behind him, Ketil turned to Leif. 'Go check the other door. See if you can block it up somehow.'

Leif nodded and gestured for the nearest of the Varangians to come with him, creeping through the darkness, wary of tripping over unseen hazards. While they did that, Ketil brought his horse inside and tethered it, waved over the others. 'Let's get these doors propped back in position. Just leave enough of a gap for a man to fit through.'

The Varangians did as much, and Ketil breathed quietly, grateful he did not have to bend and help, for he was fairly convinced he would pass out. Instead, he tried to ignore the pain in his face as he took in what he could of the barn's interior. It was filled with rubble and detritus, which would make it uncomfortable, but could also perhaps help hide them if required. As the rear door was gradually blotted out by Leif and his friend, and the Varangians heaved the broken doors up, ready to prop them in place, Anna crossed to Ketil.

'I am just going through the gardens.'

'Don't be daft, woman. It's pitch black out there and there are angry Byzantines about who would gut you, and probably rape you first. Stay inside.'

She narrowed her eyes dangerously. 'Don't think to command me, Ketil the lanky Icelander. I'm not one of your soldiers.' She sighed and relaxed a little. 'I'm not going far, just out into the gardens here. There are things I need.'

Before he could argue, she was out, wandering among the ruined gardens, peering down at the plants all around her. He watched her, worried, as she occasionally stooped and then rose, finally disappearing around the corner of the farmhouse. He was trying to work out what to say to Leif if the Rus returned while she was gone, when she reappeared around the far side of the building and continued to bend and rise, an armful of foliage growing as she moved.

'What is she doing?' Leif murmured, reappearing with startling silence.

'I have no idea.'

The two men stepped back as the doors were raised between them and the outside world, leaving a gap just two feet wide in the middle for ingress and, more importantly, egress. They started at the sound of metallic scraping and turned to see sparks as one of the Varangians struck flint on steel.

'Stop that!' they both hissed at once, and the soldier turned, frowning in the last, brief flash.

'No lights. No fire. Do you want to draw the emperor's cavalry down on us?' Leif snarled. In the darkness they could almost feel the chagrin emanating from the man. Slowly, the whole group gathered near the entrance.

'All right,' Ketil said, 'there are fourteen of us, but I will not task Anna with a watch. Who is the most wounded or exhausted?'

There was an odd silence, finally broken as one of the men coughed. 'Er, you.'

'*Apart* from me,' Ketil grumbled.

'Ubbi,' someone said. 'He's been running for an hour on a wounded leg. He's about ready to pass out.'

'No I'm not, you cheeky fuck,' snapped a voice in the darkness.

'Oh yeah? Then come over *here* and tell me that.'

There was a resigned grunt. Ketil straightened a little. 'Fine. Anna and Ubbi with the not-wounded leg are out of the watch cycle. The rest of us take turns in pairs. Six hours, one hour per watch, one man at this door, and one at the back. No noise, no fire, no light. Make sure you stay awake and alert. Leif and I will take first watch, 'cause, frankly, I'm bollocksed and I need a rest, so I'll get my stint out of the way now. The rest of you, organise yourselves into watches and the two up next make yourselves known so that we can wake you in an hour, and then get what rest you can.'

As they broke up into small groups, Anna reappeared in the doorway.

'Sit down,' she said.

'What?'

'I need to look at your face.'

'Leave me be.'

She glared at him. 'Don't be a baby. You don't spend a year buying, mixing and administering healing balms for Gunnhild without learning a thing or two. I've found a few plants I can use.' She turned to Leif. 'You still have your flask of wine?'

He frowned. 'This is hardly the time.'

'I need it, not just for drinking, Leif.'

Reluctantly, he pulled a small flask from his belt and handed it over. 'That's all I have until we find some money.'

'Then at least you'll be sober for a while,' she tutted and jabbed a finger at Ketil. 'Sit.'

He did so, still confused. The pain was back in force now, though, and if she had anything in mind that might lessen it, he was willing to give her the benefit of the doubt. She *had* been apprenticed to Gunnhild, after all. He watched as she produced from the bag at her side a mortar and pestle and began to grind up plants into a powder. Content with what she had, she placed it on the ground, produced a small copper bottle and tipped some of the wine into it. Into the metal container she poured a fine powder that smelled very garlicky, and then found another small pot in her bag and added some of its contents as well. She then put on the lid and shook it well. Satisfied, she opened it, poured it into a bowl, and then added honey, stirring the mixture until it became a light paste.

'Hold on to something,' she said.

Ketil had almost formed the word 'why,' when his world exploded in horrifying agony. He may have cried out, or at least whimpered, as she liberally daubed her mixture into his ruined eye socket and all across the wounds on the side of his head. The pain was unbearable, far worse than the wound, as far as he could remember. As he tried to pull away, she kept hold of him in a surprisingly powerful grip and continued to work.

It was only when he came around, groggily, that he realised he had passed out and she had continued to work on her unconscious patient. His face still stung and ached horribly, certainly. It felt no better than before; perhaps even worse.

'What did you do?' he gasped.

'Garlic and wine in copper becomes a substance that helps prevent wound rot setting in. I've seen Gunnhild apply it a hundred times, though never to an eye socket. *That* was an experience I'm in no hurry to repeat.'

'You and me both. That was agony.'

'That was probably because I added salt.'

'*Salt?*' he hissed.

'Also good for preventing such infections. And the honey will finish the job.'

'I thought you were going to numb the pain.'

'No. I was just going to make sure you didn't go rotten and die on us.'

'Odin, but you're a cold one, woman.'

'Relax. In the morning, when there is light, I will see what I can find that might help with the pain. For now, I just want to prevent any wounds festering. I have needle and thread, so I can try to stitch up injuries, too, though I'm not very good. Gunnhild always did that.'

'Then I'm bloody glad I don't need stitches.'

She gave a humourless laugh, then went off inside, asking for anyone with injuries in a quiet voice. Leif passed on the names and rough locations of the next stint, then went off to the back door and settled for his hour on watch.

Ketil did the same, listening to the low murmurs of the others inside, along with the occasional hiss and curse as Anna administered her treatments with the bedside manner of an outraged bear. He hated to admit it, but gradually his face was numbing a little. Perhaps that was the result of her ministrations, or possibly she had driven him beyond some hitherto unknown barrier of pain. Whatever the case, he was able to breathe and sit in calm repose for the first time since the tide of battle had turned.

His mind whirled as he thought back on everything that had happened. He knew now that he had made a poor decision, and that choice had almost cost them everything. He knew that it was important that the Wolves remained a pack, and that Halfdan was their leader. He wondered if his obstinate refusal to follow had cost the others back in Italy as much? As he sat scanning the night with his one remaining eye, he also lifted the Mjǫllnir pendant from his neck and made a number of vehement promises to Thor and Odin both, if the gods would help them get back to the others.

He could not have said how long it was before he heard the trouble, but the moment he did, he was alert. For three or four heartbeats, silence fell once more, and he wondered if he'd imagined it. Then it came again. Shouts. Whoops. The thunder of hooves? Quite distant still, but too close for comfort.

He chewed his lip. There was a good chance they would not even see the farm, of course. But then figures burst from the treeline only half a mile away, on foot and running. They were heading straight across the field, in the same direction Ketil and his men had been taking originally, but then someone clearly spotted the buildings, for they turned and began making for the farm.

Ketil rose, took two steps inside and called quietly. 'Trouble. To arms, all of you.'

As the men rose and retrieved weapons, Leif came hurrying over. 'What is it?'

Ketil pointed and Leif squinted into the darkness. 'Byzantines. On foot, running. They might be friendly, useful even? Safety in numbers and all that?'

'I hear horses. They are being pursued.'

Leif nodded. 'Oh. What's the plan?'

'It's their problem, not ours. We hide in the barn and let them sort it out.'

If Leif disapproved, he didn't show it. Instead, he moved back inside and passed the word to the others. Similarly, Ketil stepped back into the shadow within the barn, peering out through the gap they had left between the doors. There was no doubt now. Maybe twenty or so men were making for the farm, a few with weapons, most unarmed and running in terror. They were definitely Byzantine, and given their speed and the air of panic, they had to be fleeing rebels. Even as Ketil watched, a dozen horsemen burst out into the open behind them.

'Don't lead them to us!' Ketil cursed in a whisper.

But that was exactly what was happening. The runners outnumbered their pursuers, but they were routed, panicked, largely unarmed and clearly exhausted. As they came closer and closer, Ketil stepped back a little more, making sure he was entirely shrouded in darkness. One of the rebels pointed at the barn and shouted but, much to the Icelander's relief, the rest ignored him and they all ran on to the main house.

It was clear to Ketil that any fight would not last long. They seemed to know as much, too, for they piled into the ruined building and, within moments, those with weapons were at the windows and door, the rest hiding in the darkness. Ketil turned and looked in the direction from which they'd come. The riders were close now, coming at a gallop. They were only light cavalry, a few in chain shirts, most in plain tunics, armed with spears and round shields. An idea arose and, before he could reason it through, he had already made a decision. He turned to the darkness behind him. 'Get ready. When they attack the rebels, we hit them from the rear.'

'Why?' someone hissed. 'Let them fight it out themselves.'

Ketil grinned in the dark. 'With the Byzantines we have them outnumbered three to one, and they're not well armoured. You could all do with a horse and some fresh equipment. Whatever they're carrying is ours if we take them down.'

The notion settled with some satisfaction among the others in the dark and, in moments, the entire armed gathering had moved up to join Ketil – only Anna and Ubbi, the patient with an injured leg, remaining back in the room.

Ketil watched as the riders, sensing an easy victory, approached, only slowing once their mounts had leapt the low boundary wall, crossing the garden with jeers and threats at the trapped infantry. Within moments they had reached the farmhouse, still mounted. Some men threw their spears through the windows and were rewarded with the odd cry of pain as they drew their swords. Others, as they closed, used their spears to stab from the saddle into the open windows and door, forcing the poor defenders to back away.

Ketil stepped out into the starlight, threw his arm forward, and he and the others ran.

The riders, who were now milling about at the house walls, were concentrating on trying to get to the men hiding inside. Not one of them was paying attention to their surroundings.

The Icelander was the fastest, of course. He leapt the low wall with the same ease as the enemy horses, axe in one hand, sax in the other. The first that the imperial riders knew of their presence was when Ketil hit them from behind. He could feel the impetus of Thor pulsing through his veins as he struck, pushing away pain and weariness and replacing it with the fiery euphoria of battle. His axe slammed into the back of one unarmoured man and he let it go, leaving the blade buried horizontally in the man's spine as he reached up and jammed the fighting knife into the thigh of another rider. The first of Ketil's victims howled in agony, lolling in his saddle as he rocked about, the weapon still jammed in him. His current victim screamed and turned, looking down at the blade in his leg and the hand still gripping the hilt. His cries only increased as the tall Icelander used it as a handhold to pull himself up, free hand slipping round the rider's neck as he settled onto the horse's back behind the man. As the rider choked and gagged, Ketil pulled the sax free of his leg and then casually drew it across his windpipe, pushing the man to one side, off the horse.

Ketil had a mount, now, though wielded only a knife. As the rider to his right turned with cries of alarm to face the Varangians now running at him and bellowing, Ketil leaned across and punched the man in the face with the fist still wrapped around the sax hilt, then plucked the spear from the rider's surprised hand.

He turned, spear poised to cut down another man, but was confronted only by the dying man with the axe buried in his back. The rest were now fighting the other Varangians, and fresh help was coming, too. Even as the riders, their victory turned to defeat in an instant, fought for their lives against this unexpected surprise attack from behind, the armed infantry who had fled into the farm now reappeared, snarling and lashing out with swords and spears. Trapped between infantry and Varangians and hopelessly outnumbered, the riders tried to make a break for it, but failed dismally. One by one, the pursuing imperial soldiers died. The Varangians were careful to try and avoid damaging the horses.

When it was over, mere moments later, it was clear what a massacre it had been. Twelve riders lay dead, and only one horse had fallen in the attack, while just one of Ketil's Varangians and two of the Byzantine infantry lay on the ground, shaking their last.

'Who are you?' one of the fugitives from the farmhouse asked in easy Greek.

'Like you,' Ketil replied. 'Survivors.'

The man nodded. 'Thank the Holy Mother you were here. I thought we were done for.'

'Don't be too thankful. I did this for the horses and the equipment, not for you.'

The Byzantine shrugged. 'The result is the same. We owe you.'

'Save your breath. You'll need it in the coming days. Now, piss off.'

The man blinked. 'What?'

'We don't need your lot slowing us down.'

'Are you moonstruck? Together there are near thirty of us. That's enough to be sure of safety from random patrols. Safety in numbers. Where are you bound?'

Ketil pointed vaguely. 'West.'

'Then we go west.'

'Listen, I don't *want* you. We are men of the North, of the grey stone lands of snow, forged in Odin's grasp. We don't need broken Greeks.'

He became aware of someone tugging at his arm. He turned to see Leif giving him a very meaningful look.

'What?'

'Stop moralising your pagan ways at people, Ketil of Stöð. You don't speak for me. I was forged in Kiev in the sight of the Holy Mother. These men are soldiers and comrades. They come with us.'

Ketil sighed. He might have argued, but he knew that look in Leif's eye. Any debate would be long and difficult, and the loquacious little bastard would win in the end. He straightened. 'All right,' he growled in annoyance. 'You take the house, we'll take the barn. Strip the horses, share out the weapons and equipment as best you can, then tether the beasts inside. Get rid of the bodies, set watches and we'll move at first light. We find the nearest village, barter whatever we can raise for food and then move on. We head west, the way we came. Hopefully Dyrrachium is still in rebel hands, and we can get a ship there. I have friends in Italy. We find them, and all will be well.'

As the men went about their business, Ketil looked first east, where an enemy sat on the Byzantine throne, unopposed now, and no doubt sending out messages to hunt down any rebels and bring them to justice. Then he looked west, where days of difficult travel awaited them, even if they could travel unmolested. And once they reached the sea, they would have to secure passage. Then, if they got to Italy, they would have to try and find Halfdan and the others.

A long journey lay ahead.

Best get some sleep.

Somewhere nearby, a man screamed as Anna tended to his injuries.

Ketil smiled grimly.

Chapter 14

'What do you think?' Ketil murmured.

Beside him, Leif peered off into the early morning, hand held over his eyes for shade as the post-dawn sunlight from alleyways cut golden lines across the road.

'There's definitely a garrison. Maybe a large one, too.'

Ketil nodded and looked up the street. The gate at the top of the long incline was topped with battlements and above it he could see the gleaming figures of armoured men, the banners of Byzantium snapping in the breeze. Imperial control had come back to Dyrrachium. Ketil stamped weary feet. It would have been nice to have ridden the horses this far, but they had been forced to sell them the previous day to buy food for the ongoing journey.

'Why don't we just try somewhere else?' Anna asked.

Leif turned to her. 'Anywhere with a port large enough to have merchant vessels that cross the open sea will have a garrison. And the smaller the port, the less likely we are to secure passage, especially now that there are so many of us. No, I think unless we all split up and go in pairs or trios, it has to be Dyrrachium. But that means getting past the officials here.'

'They're letting other people in,' Anna muttered, watching carts and travellers climb the street between the houses and shops that had grown up outside the city walls, on the road down to the lagoon bridge.

'*Other people*,' Ketil noted, 'are not coming in numbers and bearing weapons. City guards tend to frown on things like that.'

'And there are other problems,' Leif added. 'The imperial courier system is second to none, and you can be sure the authorities here already know about the battle and the death of Maniakes. There will undoubtedly be a standing order to check for any rebel survivors. But the main issue is the bureaucracy. To put to sea here, our names will have to be in a number of ledgers and documents, and will be checked up on. It's a thorny problem.'

'Maybe,' Anna murmured, 'maybe not.'

'What have you seen?'

Her hand came up, pointing off to the left. Ketil's gaze followed the gesture a short way up the road to a large inn, two storeys high and arranged in three wings. There would be a courtyard around the back, between the wings, and there had to be stables, for outside the front sat a carriage and a number of horses, tended by servants in Byzantine-looking dress.

'You have a wicked mind,' Leif admonished her.

'She's right, though,' Ketil added, looking at the coach with his remaining eye. The wounded one had settled into a gentle but constant ache now, the pain receding gradually over the days of travel, aided by poultices and concoctions brewed up by Anna with surprising skill.

The carriage meant someone rich and powerful was at the inn. During their time in the Byzantine capital, Ketil had quickly come to understand that rich men were also politicians. There seemed to be no dividing line. Gold equalled power. That meant that the owner of the carriage, whether he was here for business or pleasure, would be able to sweep past guards and clerks alike. Moreover, a man in his position might well be travelling with a military escort, especially given what everyone would now know had happened in the region.

Ketil turned to look at the men behind him, a smile gracing his lips. Each and every one was either a Byzantine soldier still wearing his uniform, or a Varangian who had served in Miklagarðr. To the average eye, they would look as imperial as anyone.

'How do we do this, then?' Leif muttered.

'We can't leave any witnesses, especially from his entourage. Fortunately, he's leaving the inn.'

'How do you know that?' Anna asked.

'Because it's early morning. When a man like that travels, he spends his nights in a comfortable bed and then moves on. He can't have just arrived. The carriage out front means he's been there overnight and now he's leaving.'

Leif nodded. 'He probably arrived after dark yesterday. The city gates will be locked up when the sun goes down, so he had to rest here and wait for morning.'

'We need to get everyone he is travelling with off the street and out to the back somewhere.' Ketil turned to the others. 'There are alleys either side of the inn. Move into the nearest one and wait for us. The moment you see us leave the inn and go to the coach, come up and join us like a proper escort. Leif and I will handle this.'

Anna was a little miffed as they told her to wait with the soldiers, but she did so with a glare as Ketil and Leif moved into the doorway of the inn. For better or worse, there was no going back now.

'So, what's the plan?' Leif hissed as they entered.

'No idea. Follow my lead.'

He ignored the worried look from the Rus. In Ketil's experience, planning things like this was highly overrated. Plans could go wrong, and usually did. When you had no plan, the plan couldn't go wrong, so nothing surprised you. He'd had no plan last time they were in Dyrrachium and they'd breezed into the city like kings.

The main room of the inn was one large chamber filled with benches and tables. A fireplace stood at the end, though nothing burned at this time of day. The smell of freshly baked bread wafted in from somewhere, and there were sounds of activity coming from most of the doorways leading off the room. A man dressed impeccably in a long blue robe, with a red and gold patterned tunic and a red cloak pinned at the shoulder, stood in the middle of the room, playing irritably with a curl of oiled black hair that kept escaping his red felt hat. There was no mistaking the owner of the coach.

Near him, a well-dressed servant and two guards in chain shirts stood talking to a man who was clearly the innkeeper. Half a dozen other patrons were sitting around the room, safely back from the nobleman for fear of upsetting his guards. As the two new arrivals paused in the doorway, the stylish lord lifted a cup from the table beside him and drank from it.

The pair slipped inside, trying to achieve an air of innocence as they looked about, seemingly waiting for the opportunity to speak to the owner. Ketil looked down at Leif, and the Rus motioned to him with a gesture that seemed to say, *Patience*. He knew Leif. He knew the man's mind was churning through ideas and plans as they stood. Ketil would never be a man for plans, and so he simply took in their surroundings like a general observing the ground before a battle.

As they waited, Ketil's gaze was drawn by the way the nobleman was tapping his foot rhythmically. He might just be bored. Or he might be starting to feel the need... Maybe he was a man for plans, after all?

'Follow my lead,' Ketil whispered. 'When you hear a call out back, follow those three,' he added, pointing discreetly at the guards and the servant.

Leif did not look impressed, but he nodded as Ketil led him across the room. As they came close to the gathering, near the bar, the taller man stretched, opening their little charade for the benefit of the occupants. 'Get us a drink,' he said loudly to Leif. 'But I have to go and drain the dragon first.' Then, insolently cutting into the conversation at the bar, he waved to the owner. 'You have a latrine?'

The man nodded, irritated at the interruption. 'Out back, on the right, doorway in the corner. Follow the smell.'

Ketil smiled at him and walked toward a doorway, through which he could see the light of the courtyard. He walked deliberately slowly, making low murmurs about how desperate he was for a piss. Sure enough, as he emerged into the light, he heard the lord address his men. 'I had best unburden myself before we leave.'

The courtyard's only occupant was a young serving boy with a broom, dusting leaves into a pile in the corner. Several doors led into the other two wings of the inn and an archway at the far end, large enough to admit a coach, led to the stable and rear exit. As the owner had noted, it was not difficult to locate the latrine from the aroma that clung to its corner of the yard. Ketil crossed to the doorway and dipped inside, wrinkling his nose at the strong smell of ammonia. The inn was large, and probably crowded of an evening, and so the latrines were capacious. There was a communal four-seater at the far end and two individual ones in their own little cubicles, all served by the same channels beneath, but allowing some division between the genders for modesty. A bowl of clear water, fed by a pipe from the wall, allowed for the washing of hands and faces. The whole place was perhaps ten paces across. There was no door, which was a shame. He would have to be quiet. As he rounded the corner and the courtyard disappeared from sight, Ketil drew his sax.

The nobleman entered calmly, blissfully unaware of the danger awaiting him. Ketil leapt the moment the man was out of sight of the courtyard. One hand gripped his wrist, pulling it painfully up behind his back, while the other brought the point of the sax up to rest on his neck, just below the jawline. The man let out a surprised squeak, but before he could shout in alarm, Ketil was breathing in his ear from behind. 'Scream and it will be the last thing you do.'

The man in his arms tried to nod, but couldn't do much with the sharp point so close.

'Good. Now, shout for your guards. Tell them you need a fresh tunic.'

'That's ridiculous,' the man said quietly.

'Do it.'

Swallowing nervously, the nobleman called out for his men as Ketil had demanded. The moment he fell silent, the Icelander pushed on his knife, driving the blade up through the neck, beneath the chin and into the man's mouth and brain. His victim was so surprised he never even gasped as he died. Ketil was careful to keep hold of his arm and shoulder so that he lowered him to the ground on his front, face over the drain from the sink, so that the flow of water carried away the blood from the wound. What mess there had been was largely lost amid the red of the man's garments. *Some* details, Ketil *did* plan.

As he rose once more, he could hear fast footsteps crossing the yard, more than one pair, but not running. They were not suspicious yet.

Again, Ketil took up position against the wall, just inside the doorway. This time, he pulled the axe from the back of his belt, too.

The first guard to enter the latrines started to speak as he moved inside.

'I've sent Lexi to fetch your spare—'

He got no further, for at that moment the Icelander's axe was buried in his neck, almost beheading him. Ketil yanked on the axe haft even as it lodged – not to pull it free, but the action jerked the man forward and into the latrines, where he fell face first. Ketil cared not a jot for his condition. The second guard, following on from the first, had too little warning to do anything. As his friend suddenly died and then disappeared in front of him, a bloody sax whipped out from round the corner and buried itself in his face. Ketil grasped the man's shoulder and pulled him inside, out of view.

As the pile of bodies in the latrine grew, Ketil stepped into the doorway and risked looking out. The boy sweeping the courtyard was staring in shock toward the latrines, eyes wide. That was the downside of insufficient planning, of course.

He was saved a moment later by Leif, who had been following the guards. He took a swift step to his left, clamped a hand around the boy's mouth, lifted him and carried him, broom and all, to the latrines.

'You leave a mess everywhere you go,' he noted as he entered, eyeing the pile of guards and the richly dressed corpse in the drain.

'You want to get to the port or not?'

'The other servant is on the way with the tunic.'

'Kill the boy and let's dump these bodies in a cubicle,' Ketil said, ignoring the stifled cries of panic that emerged from the lad.

'No,' Leif replied. 'The others died for a reason. This lad's done nothing.' Letting go of the boy, but with his hand still over the mouth, Leif drew his own sax and smacked the pommel down on the boy's head, driving the wits from him in one blow. He collapsed in a heap.

'He could wake up and alert everyone to what's happened,' Ketil noted.

'I think the game will be up the moment a woman wants to go for a crap and finds three bodies in the way,' Leif retorted. 'Now change and let's get moving. I'll deal with the servant when he arrives.'

'Hardly,' Ketil replied. '*I'll* deal with the servant. *You* change.'

'I'm a head shorter than the man. His clothes won't fit.'

'And I'm a head *taller* than him,' observed the Icelander. 'It's easier to tuck bits in and roll bits up than to stretch them to cover long legs and arms.'

Grumbling, but unable to fault the logic, Leif quickly climbed out of his outer clothes. Complaining about sticky patches, he carefully peeled the outer garments from the first body in the pile. As he was beginning to pull them on, the servant arrived with a fresh tunic. He turned the corner into the latrine and died by sax in that instant, his body adding to the mass on the floor. As Leif finished dressing in the lord's fine clothes, Ketil retrieved his axe and hefted all four corpses into one of the individual cubicles. They only just fit, and Ketil carefully removed any pouches from belts first. Satisfied, he pulled the cubicle door closed and threaded the bags onto his own belt, refastening it. Leif was dressed now and looked remarkably good – if a little short. Finally, they lifted the unconscious boy into the other cubicle, sitting him on the toilet as though he was enjoying a little personal time.

'Do you not think the owner will notice how his guest shrunk in the latrine?' Leif murmured, looking himself up and down.

'Maybe it was a *really* big shit,' Ketil said with a snort. 'We'll not go back through the inn. We leave through the back gate.' Before they departed, he carefully washed his axe and sax blades in the gutter from the washbowl, then tucked them back away, drying the knife on his trousers first.

Trying to walk nonchalantly, they stepped out into the inn's courtyard, where a breeze was busily whipping all the carefully swept leaves back across the stones. A man appeared from the main inn doorway, one of the other patrons, strolling toward the latrine.

'Pray to your nailed god he doesn't want to use one of the private cubicles,' Ketil breathed as they moved through the archway, passed the stables and slipped through the large gates out into the dusty ground behind the inn. The rear exit let them out into the other alley at the far end of the inn from their initial approach. As they moved around the side of the building and made their way back out to the main road, exploring the pouches they had taken as they walked, they stepped over a gutter that ran with a faint pink tint, carrying away the inn's waste.

'What's in them?' Leif asked, pointing to the bulging containers at Ketil's belt.

'Coins, by the sound and the weight. Lots of them, too. Hopefully enough to buy passage to Italy.'

'I can probably help there,' Leif added, holding up a palm full of bejewelled gold rings he'd taken from the nobleman. 'They're too big for me anyway. There were gold coins in his pouches,' he added, 'and, best of all, this.'

Ketil looked down and took the proffered tube. He undid the end and slid out the contents. 'You know I can't read the Greek tongue.'

'I know you can't read *any* tongue. They're imperial authorisation documents. They are what allow a man like me free travel using the imperial courier system, and free accommodation at any official mansion. They should also get us in or out of anywhere.'

'Good,' Ketil said, jamming them into his belt. Edging out toward the street, Ketil could see three men at the carriage. One was a driver, the other two clearly lowly servants.

'What now?' Leif muttered.

'Now, threats should carry us the rest of the way. Wait out of sight until we control the coach.'

With that, leaving Leif in the side alley, he strode out toward the carriage. Once he was in the street, to his relief, the Varangians and Byzantine deserters emerged from the other side road and moved up the street in front of the inn toward him, Anna striding along at the rear. Ketil waited until they reached him, then fell in with the men, the woman stepping aside into the alley with Leif. 'Take the two servants into the carriage at knifepoint and stay in there with them. I'll handle the driver. The rest of you form up as though you're a proper military escort.'

Two dozen men strode up to the carriage and fell in alongside it in neat rows, Varangians to fore and aft, regular infantry at the sides. The three men at the carriage looked around in surprise, not sure what was happening. This was not expected, but the new arrivals were clearly Byzantine. Perhaps they were from the city? The driver looked down in interest as Ketil reached the running board and used it to vault up beside him.

As he did so, two of his men suddenly grabbed the two servants below and bundled them into the carriage, quickly enough that the act went unnoticed by passersby among the gathering soldiers. The driver turned in surprise, his mouth opening. Then he looked down at the sax, its point resting on his rather wide midriff, just below his ribs.

'Hold your tongue. We're going into the city and straight to the port. You drive us there without any trouble and you'll be able to tell your wife what an interesting day you had. One wrong move or unexpected sound, though, and your widow will wonder what happened to rob her of her love. Do we have an understanding?'

The man nodded. 'I want no trouble.'

'Good. Me either.'

Turning, he nodded to the alleyway and Leif, dressed as well as he ever had been, crossed to the carriage. The soldiers opened the door and he climbed inside to sit with the two servants, who were being held at knifepoint behind the curtains.

At a gesture from the Icelander, the driver shook the reins and clicked his tongue, geeing the horses up and setting the carriage off, rolling gently up the slope toward the city walls. As they approached the gate, the general populace moving in and out of the city veered to the sides of the road, out of the way. No one got in the way of a nobleman's carriage in the empire, especially not one accompanied by a sizeable armed guard.

As they moved into the archway that led through to Dyrrachium itself, one of the gate guards, along with one of the ubiquitous bureaucrats in an official-looking uniform, stepped out and waved them to a halt.

'Where are you bound?'

'The port,' Ketil called back in lightly accented Greek.

'And your master's name?'

Ketil cleared his throat. 'The katepan of Strymon,' he announced, hoping his luck would hold. A katepan was a high-enough ranked official that few bureaucrats would mess with one, and Strymon was the name of the next region they'd have reached had they won the battle near Thessalonika. He didn't know whether Strymon even had a katepan, but was banking on the fact that neither would an average provincial nobody.

212

He tried not to roll his eyes in irritation, for he could hear from within the coach Leif's muffled curses at Ketil's pronouncement.

There was a long pause as the official ran his eyes down a list in a ledger. 'Your master is not expected.'

'Perhaps not by you,' Ketil snapped. 'He is expected in…' he ran his memory over that brief time he'd spent in Italy. He'd heard the names of a dozen cities, but they all seemed to have escaped his memory right now. Eventually, one leapt to mind. 'Berry.'

'Bari?' hazarded the bureaucrat.

Ketil glared at him. 'If you are responsible for the katepan missing the morning tide there will be serious repercussions.'

The official was less than fazed by this. 'You have documentation?'

Ketil was starting to lose his temper now, but before he could say anything, the carriage curtain was twitched aside and Leif leaned out, red hat perched precariously atop his head. 'Is there a problem?' he demanded in a refined voice, but a very sharp tone.

The bureaucrat frowned. 'Apologies, my lord, but—'

'Give him the authorisation, Varangian, and if he is not out of the way by the time I count to twenty, let your men deal with him.'

With that, Leif ducked back inside and the curtain flapped closed. Around the carriage, two dozen hands closed on weapon hilts. Ketil gave the man a nasty smile as he proffered the scroll case. 'Don't push my men. They've travelled for days with little sleep. There are still rebels in the hills, you know?'

For the first time, the man exhibited some sign of nerves as his eyes darted around the irritable-looking armed men. He took the tube, slipping out the document within. For a moment, he looked rather suspicious. But whatever he suspected, he clearly decided to ignore, for he nodded, replaced the papers and passed the case back up to Ketil.

'You know the way to the port?'

Before Ketil could answer, the carter snorted. 'Drive downhill until the horses get wet?'

The official threw a glare up at them, then stepped back and waved them on.

As they passed through the walls and out into the street, Ketil turned to the driver. 'Thank you.'

'Fucking bureaucrats. The same everywhere you go. Hate 'em.'

Ketil smiled. He'd actually been planning to kill the man the moment they left the carriage, but now he found himself more kindly disposed toward him. Perhaps he wouldn't, after all.

'When we get to the port, we'll leave you.'

The driver nodded and they moved through the streets, angling off to the south, heading down to where they could already see the multitude of masts sticking up and the blue sea beyond. The port was extremely busy. Ketil looked about, his gaze falling upon another inn, close to the water though separated from it by the wide dock. A stable beside it drew his attention.

'Go in there,' he announced.

The driver did as he was told and the escort formed up outside the stable as the carriage rattled through its gate. The stablehand, clearly a servant of the attached inn, strode over to them. 'Can I help you?'

Ketil nodded. 'We need to put this in stables for the night. We'll be staying in the inn, but need to visit the ship first and confirm our journey tomorrow.'

The man nodded uncertainly, but became a great deal more helpful as Ketil pressed a silver coin into his palm. 'Look after the horses well. The carriage will be fine in storage.'

The driver stepped down, Ketil close by, the sax still in his hand, a warning look on his face. The stablehand and his lad unhooked the horses and the boy led them away. Leif and the two guards descended from the carriage, the stablehand bowing low in respect to the noble. As Ketil closed the door, he noted the two unconscious servants on the carriage floor. They would be out for a while. The stablehand and the two guards pushed the carriage back into one of the wide stalls, before the former strolled off to find a chitty for them, Ketil turned to the driver and smiled. 'Say hello to your wife for me.' With a single, powerful movement, he smacked the man in the side of the head with the hilt of his sax. The driver folded up and the two guards had only just shoved him inside the coach with the others when the stablehand returned.

As Ketil thanked the man, paid him and took the chitty, the guards closed the door to the stall and the entire entourage strode out of the stable and onto the dock.

'I hate it when you improvise,' Leif growled quietly.

'It got us here.'

'We had best hope we can find a ship quickly. I don't know which alarm will reach the guards first – the servants in that coach waking up or the bodies being found back in the inn. Either way, I think we'll want to be a few miles out to sea by the time it happens.'

'Where do we want to go?' Ketil muttered, looking along the dock.

'Pretty much anywhere on the Apulian coast. We don't know where Halfdan will be yet, anyway.'

'Shouldn't be too hard to find,' Ketil replied. 'He won't go into lands controlled by the Greeks, nor probably the coastal lords I've heard about. He'll be going north, somewhere in the middle. And he'll be looking to get rich. Rumour should drag us to him.'

'Bari for preference, then. That's north enough that we can get a bit of a head start.'

'See, I told the man at the gate it was Berry we wanted.'

'For the love of God let me do the talking, Ketil. It's nearly as bad as having to work with Bjorn.'

Ketil once more took a secondary place then, walking alongside Anna with the soldiers and Varangians at his back. With a few minor enquiries, Leif located the port authority building and there spoke to half a dozen Byzantine clerks, who checked their lists and ledgers and finally directed them to a ship called *Sea Dove*, bound for Bari with a mixed cargo and due to sail within the hour.

They found the ship at its jetty and located one of the sailors, who introduced Leif to the owner. A few questions were asked. The merchant was not comfortable with the number of men asking for passage, each of whom would displace some of his precious cargo. When a large number of coins changed hands, however, the trouble eased. With each handful of tinkling gold and silver, the merchant's concerns over his cargo lessened, and in no time, sailors were once more unloading some of the gear they had loaded only that morning. Each of Ketil's men now carried only his own kit and, without the horses, they could manage with only a small berth. The merchant was pleasantly surprised that the nobleman joining them seemed quite happy to stay with his men and did not expect to be given the captain's cabin.

The journey, they were told, was some hundred and fifty miles and would take three days.

Relieved, the refugees from Maniakes's army boarded the ship and were shown to their place for the journey. Ketil sat with them, eye constantly on the hatch that led up to the deck, ears alert for trouble, half expecting the angry shouts of guards at any moment. He only relaxed at the sound of sailors pulling in the plank and loosing ropes. Within an hour of having secured their passage, the *Sea Dove* slid out from its berth and began to move calmly through the water toward the open arms of the harbour walls.

The sounds changed as they put out to open sea and left the port behind: the ship rocked gently with the waves, the sails filled with an audible crack and men hurried hither and thither at their tasks. Somewhere in the distance, Ketil could hear bells. Warning bells. Perhaps the bodies had been found.

He leaned back with a relieved sigh, hands behind his head, and relaxed. Whatever lay ahead, at least they had escaped the emperor's clutches.

Chapter 15

'I see sails,' Leif said, a touch of tension in his tone. Ketil could understand that. It had been a nerve-wracking journey.

They had maintained the fiction that Leif was an important Byzantine official, though they had kept his name and rank quite nebulous when the subject came up. Better to be vague than caught out, was Leif's opinion. All this subterfuge rather went against Ketil's straightforward approach to such matters, but he knew when to bow to Leif's wisdom, especially with this newfound wisdom of his own.

And so the atmosphere on board was tense, the crew unsure of precisely who they were transporting. Furthermore, it seemed that there was a superstition in the south that women on a ship were bad luck, and so Anna's presence did little to improve matters. Ketil, at least, was safe from too much questioning. His ravaged face and empty eye socket gave him such a fearsome appearance that most of the sailors turned away at the sight of him, never mind showing any undue interest.

Then there had been the traffic on this sea. The ship they sailed upon was a fat, slow merchant. It was infuriating to a man of the cold North, used to a fast dragon ship that cut the waves like a knife, to watch the waters ponderously ambling by, the ship's wake little more than a roll of white on the deep blue. Almost any ship they spotted moved faster than them.

Given that they had caused so much trouble in Dyrrachium, and their existence had now almost certainly become known to the garrison and its commander, Ketil and Leif had half expected Byzantine *dromons*, powered by myriad oars, to come

218

racing after them, intent on hunting down the murderers of a Byzantine lord. Thus, any large, oar-powered ship they spotted from a distance set their hearts pounding.

Just after noon on that first day of sailing, Ketil had lurked low behind the rails and watched as one of those very same imperial dromons surged after them from the coast. His relief when it passed by and then powered off west without incident was truly palpable. As the ship passed them he'd looked across at it. The vessel had been armed with artillery in both the bow and stern, with a squad of soldiers aboard, as well as a small unit of archers. He'd not seen a sign of the dreadful Greek fire throwers, but it was a reasonable bet that the dromon carried just such a ship-killing weapon. The long and the short of it was that, no matter how fierce and brave the fugitives proved to be, if an imperial dromon decided to take them on, the result was a foregone conclusion. So later that day, when another came past them – this one cutting across at a tangent, north-east to south-west – all the fugitives had hidden from sight in case any curious sailors on the other ship noticed them.

That night had been tense. The ship's owner sailed directly across the open sea rather than hugging the coast. It would save the trader at least a day on his journey, which, of course, maximised profit, but it presented its own risks and difficulties: it meant spending two nights at sea in open water.

As sunset neared that first night, they had watched what appeared to be a wall of grey off to the north, which slowly grew as it approached. Beneath those foreboding clouds, the sea turned black.

'Can we weather a bad storm?' Ketil had asked one of the senior crewmen.

The man had shrugged, gaze averted oddly so as not to fixate on the Icelander's empty socket. 'With some hard work and a shitload of luck.'

'What can we do?'

The man had snorted. 'We're forty miles from land! Fucking pray.'

So, as the evening light faded, they prepared as best they could for the danger to come. All was made safe, the sails furled, the rudder tied off securely and anyone not required for essential control of the ship went below and found somewhere among the cargo to try and sleep.

Ketil was as at home on the water as any man born to an island full of raiders and merchants, yet even he had trouble sleeping that evening. The storm hit them almost two hours after the night truly consumed the sky. He remained below with the others, so he did not witness that grey billowing mass engulf the ship, but he had seen enough storms at sea to know what it looked like, how it went. Ran's daughters battered the hull, a constant crashing, groaning and creaking that echoed through the lower decks.

Ketil clutched at the Mjǫllnir pendant around his neck until it bit into the flesh of his hand, asking Thor repeatedly to pull his storms away from them, to leave this ship untouched, for he could feel the claws of Ran herself pulling at the keel, trying to drag the *Sea Dove* down to the depths. The moment he heard a timber break, he was ready to race to the deck and seek something to cling to, for he had no intention of spending his afterlife in the goddess's cold, dark abode beneath the waves, when Odin's feast hall awaited him.

He must have drifted off at some point despite the rocking and the noise, for when he woke all was silence once more, apart from the gentle creak of the timbers. He struggled up to the deck to find a quiet, dark night all about them. The storm, it seemed, had largely missed them, heading south. The *Sea Dove* only caught the edge of it, making it through without any real damage. The merchant and his crew gave thanks that night and early in the morning, shouting out their droning dirge-songs to the nailed god and his all-important mother. Leif joined them, while Ketil quietly and privately thanked Thor for having blown his storm off course and saving the ship. For when faced with such things, who could believe that a strange Serkish spirit had anything to do with their survival when the lord of thunder himself had so clearly intervened? To be charitable, Ketil thanked Thor on behalf of Leif and the misguided crew.

The next morning was uneventful and Ketil began to relax, thinking that the journey's perils had clearly passed. Then came the cry from the lookout, late in the morning. Sails had been seen. Triangular black sails, atop two fast galleys that raced across the open sea, white spray marking the speed of their passage.

An old sailor with a face like a cracked leather satchel shivered. 'Pirates,' he said.

Ketil felt his heart lurch. Piracy was a new concept to him. Back in the North, when he had first commissioned the *Sea Wolf*, he had planned to use her to raid the Finns, for that was what a strong warrior with a ship did. Oh, he would trade too, but when opportunity presented itself, he would most certainly take ships, sack coastal settlements and steal booty and thralls when he could. Piracy did not exist back home, because it was an inherent and expected part of life on the whale road.

Here, they terrified even burly, experienced sailors.

In the south, the seas were regimented and controlled. Ships were either traders, or fishers, or warships, not all three at once, and so raiders were classed separately, too, and given the name of 'pirate'. What that meant, though – and this was what unnerved Ketil – was that these 'pirates' were purely hunters and thieves, nothing more.

A ship built for war, filled with men whose single simple objective was to kill whoever they found and take what was not theirs.

'Who are they?' he demanded of another passing sailor.

The man turned, flinched at the sight of Ketil's wounded visage, and then looked off across the water. 'They're Illyrians, from an island north of Dyrrachium. They don't usually get this far south, with Byzantine warships patrolling.'

'But now the empire's fleet is too busy to stop them,' Ketil finished for him, nodding. 'Can we outrun them? Evade them?'

The sailor threw him a look that suggested he was an idiot. Of course they couldn't. The speed the pirates were making was impressive.

'Our only hope is to find an imperial dromon.'

'What?'

'Either one of those that passed us yesterday or one coming the other way. If one of those we met has had to slow for any reason, there is a chance we'll catch up with them. The pirates will think twice if they see a Byzantine warship. Or, through luck, we might meet one coming the other way.'

The captain was bellowing now. 'Trim the sails. Make me a course due west. Raise the imperial flag. They might not risk it if they think we're imperial and not private. Ready for action. To your places, lads.'

Before he ran off, the sailor took a deep breath and focused on Ketil's surviving eye. 'We can't outrun them, but we might be able to stay ahead of them long enough to find a dromon.'

That was no relief to Ketil. The idea that they might be saved a harsh fate at the hands of pirates, only to be executed by imperial forces for crimes committed back in Dyrrachium, was not a pleasant one.

He waved over to Leif. 'Have a quiet word with everyone. I want everyone armed and ready, but we've more to worry about than war. If the pirates catch up with us, I want imperial uniforms on display and weapons ready. The captain seems to think they might not attack the empire's ships.'

Leif nodded. 'But if we catch up with a dromon that all changes. I heard what your friend said. We'd best be ready to jettison anything that ties us to Byzantium too.'

Caught between Fenrir and Jörmungandr. To be eaten or crushed. What a choice.

They spent two hours racing westward, changing tack whenever the winds shifted, using whatever breeze they could to pull them ahead. But the black sails drew ever closer and their chances of bumping into a dromon were diminishing, for the winds forced them to head further north than originally intended, away from the direct shipping lane to Bari.

The Northmen gripped their weapons, fingers testing edges. The tension was cutting through the whole ship. Every sailor watched those black shapes with a nervous eye. The captain was muttering under his breath the whole time, prayers to his nailed god.

A fight with savage pirates, inevitably followed by a drowning, or capture by angry Byzantines. Ketil once again cursed his decision ever to have left Halfdan's company.

Time dragged on. Every time he stared out toward that pirate vessel they seemed to have moved alarmingly closer.

'Ship ahoy,' bellowed the lookout. Ketil hadn't realised he could feel any more tense until his chest tightened at the announcement. A dromon, then. But what to do? Pirates on one side, Byzantines on the other, neither likely to give quarter to the fugitives. He ground his teeth and waved to the sailor he'd been talking to earlier.

'A dromon, or another pirate?'

'Neither,' the sailor told him. 'It's Venetian.'

A surge of hope. Neither? 'What's a Venetian?'

'They're men from a city to the north. Traders mainly, but aggressive bastards, and not above a little piracy themselves when they feel like it. They don't usually come this far south, but what with the Byzantines having pulled away from Italy…'

Ketil found himself once again cursing that whole matter. And not just his part in it, either. He had followed a fool's crusade and was still paying the price for it, for it was Maniakes's decision to try for the throne that had stripped the region of much of the military that had kept pirates and brigands at bay.

'What will they do?'

'Your guess is as good as mine. That Venetian's a rough match for the two pirates. The captain might decide to leave the black sails to their prize. After all, it's really none of their business. Or he might decide to frighten them off and take our cargo for himself. Who knows?'

Ketil became aware of Leif beside him.

'Can you signal the Venetian?' the Rus asked.

'We can try.'

'Venice trades with the empire. I've seen their ships in the Neorion Harbour in Constantinople. If they know you're carrying a Byzantine official, they might feel honour-bound to help.'

The sailor frowned. 'Venetians *have* no honour,' he grunted, but then nodded. 'Apologies, *kyrios*. I mean no disrespect. Perhaps they will weigh your good faith against our cargo.'

With that, the sailor bowed and hurried off to the captain. Ketil looked up at the flag still snapping in the wind, noting the double-headed eagle banner of the Byzantines. There could be no disguising the allegiance of the ship. Anyone within sight would know them for Byzantine. Ketil wondered for a while what a private trader might be doing with an official Byzantine flag, but whatever the man's reasons, he was grateful.

The great Venetian galley, red and gold flags streaming, was still making for them, closing faster than the pirates, for it was coming south-east, cutting across their path. They remained that way for a while, all three ships closing on them.

At the last moment, with the pirates and Venetians both close enough to see their crews running about the decks, a decision was made aboard the galley, and the great ship with the bright flags turned sharply, the wave it caused racing toward the *Sea Dove* and making her rock. The Venetians, who were clearly excellent sailors, raced now toward the two pirate ships. That the *Sea Dove*'s crew raised no cheer at this development reflected how uncertain they all still were of the Venetians' intentions.

The black ships came on, the Venetian bearing down on them, cutting off their path to the traders. Ketil had to hand it to these hunters, for it took guts to race into battle with a vessel of that power. Archers were brought up to the front rails on the black ships. If they could deal enough damage, thin out the Venetian crew sufficiently, they might just have enough edge to take the fight.

There was a loud crack, and an arrow the size of a man's arm arced out from the bow of the Venetian vessel, plopping into the water only two ship lengths ahead of the lead pirate. Still they came on, not too far from bow range now. Ketil tensed, fingernails biting into the rail as he urged the Venetians on.

A second shot from the great ship's artillery found a target, and the rail at the nearest pirate's bow exploded into shards of timber that peppered the archers, killing them in droves even as the captain raised a shout of alarm and the black-sailed ship suddenly slewed hard to the left.

That was it. The Venetians had taken the edge and the black ships broke. The prize upon which they had set their sights had now become too costly to be worth the danger. They peeled off, one to each side, turning with impressive sharpness, and in moments they were racing away in slightly different directions, presenting the Venetians with a choice should they feel inclined to pursue. The galley chased them perhaps half a mile and then turned and hurried after the *Sea Dove*. The Venetians pulled alongside and matched speed, and their captain came to the rail.

'Hail Byzantine vessel! You fly a mighty powerful flag for a fat trader?'

There was an air of suspicion in his voice, and well there might be.

The trader turned, casting a hopeful look at Leif. The Rus, still dressed in his rich Byzantine robes, crossed to the rail. Anna followed, assuming her former role as a maid, while Ketil and half a dozen Byzantine soldiers provided a solid guard for him. The Venetian captain's eyebrow rose at the sight of the troops and what appeared to be Varangians in the background. Varangians meant either military activity or a mission for the emperor's court. Ketil tried not to smile. The captain would be congratulating himself now for saving them.

'I am the katepan of Strymon,' Leif announced, resuming the role Ketil had thrust upon him in the city gateway. 'In the wake of the failed revolt of Maniakes, the imperial throne is safe and strong once more, and I bear instructions for the forces in Apulia. I am bound for Bari and I thank you for your timely intervention.'

Ketil could see the Venetian weighing it all up. It was suspicious, such a nobleman aboard a low trader and not an imperial dromon, and yet his story seemed plausible. He was clearly a Byzantine noble and with imperial military support, and given what had happened near Thessalonika, there could be any number of explanations.

'Please convey my best wishes and warmest felicitations to your counterpart in Bari from the Duke of Venezia and Dalmatia, and from the esteemed Cornaro family.'

Ketil smiled to himself. Throwing in a powerful name to give himself extra legitimacy, as well as his own name so that they could tell the Byzantines how useful the Cornaros had been. These Venetians were political animals, clearly.

Leif exchanged a few further pleasantries with the man, and finally the Venetians bade them good sailing, turned and made north-east, perhaps in hope of happening across those pirates for a little fun.

–

The rest of the second day passed without incident and Ketil began to relax. That night the temperature rose a little and the air was warm enough that they slept in comfort, the sea little more than a gentle rise and fall.

The next morning, Ketil had risen from his blankets and made his way up into the breezy sunlight, yawning and shivering, to find the trader and his helmsman in deep discussions.

'There's a problem?' he prompted, walking over to them.

'Not so much a problem as a delay,' the merchant grumbled. 'All that tacking with the wind yesterday bought us the time we needed to get away from the pirates, but it's driven us off course. We are now considerably north of where we should be.'

'And?'

'The winds are not right for turning and making directly for Bari. We'll move slower than a priest leaving a banquet table. Ideally, we don't want to spend another night at sea. Quite apart from the fact that my factors in Bari are waiting for us – for customers await our cargo – we had supplies aboard only for our three-day journey, and half of that was jettisoned for weight and speed when we met the pirates. This will be a hungry night if we do not put into port.'

'What do you intend?'

'We must make for the coast wherever the wind carries us, which is north of Bari. I am not entirely sure where we will land. The cloud obscured the heavens last night, and so my navigation is not precise. We should make landfall somewhere between Bari and Siponto. We'll make for the nearest visible port and take on an extra day's supplies, then hug the coast down to Bari.'

'None of this presents a problem?'

The merchant shrugged. 'When I was last here two months ago it didn't. But the emperor had an army here then and the empire controlled the coast north, way beyond Siponto. Now, I can say nothing for sure. Bari will still be imperial, for it is the heart of the katepan's domain, but war has been raging across the region. We must hope and pray.'

And so, on their third day – theoretically the final day of their crossing – they made for land and hoped for the best. The helmsman and the trader peered into the haze as the white ribbon of land gradually coalesced into something identifiable, discussing what they could see, and finally the owner seemed satisfied.

'That,' he said with confidence, pointing to a dark blotch amid the white, 'is Barletta. Barletta is maybe thirty miles north of Bari. We will overnight there and then arrive a day late at our destination.'

Ketil took this news below to Leif, who, along with the help of a sailor checking on the cargo, drew a rough map in the dust on a beam. He marked Bari, the centre of Byzantine power; Taranto in the south, where the Byzantine navy operated; Salerno and Benevento, two of the most powerful lordships in Italy; Melfi, which was known to be the centre of Norman power; and finally that smudge on the shore, Barletta. Their destination, if the map's dimensions were correct, was at the northern edge of the land they would expect to search for Halfdan. That he might have gone north of Melfi without having become known to the Norman lords there seemed unlikely. If they could find no trace of their friends' passage on the coast, they would try Melfi. If there was no news there, they could gradually backtrack south toward where the crew had separated, and undoubtedly they would find tidings of them somewhere. Even if Halfdan and Gunnhild were cunning enough to move without discovery, the notion that Bjorn, ice giant that he was, might march north through Italy unnoticed was laughable.

'Then we begin at Barletta?' Ketil said.

Leif nodded. 'It's as good a bet as Bari.'

They informed the trader that they would put ashore at Barletta, and the news was greeted with satisfaction. The ship would need to take on considerably fewer expensive rations without the Byzantine noble and his soldiers. The trader's profit margin, which had been shrinking with the delay, began to look a little healthier once more.

Now, as the *Sea Dove* made for that dark patch of shore that marked the port, Ketil felt a tingle.

'I see sails,' Leif said again.

They all squinted out across the water. A ship was coming their way. It was no grand Byzantine dromon, powering through the waves with the rise and fall of many oars, but neither was it a smaller pirates' vessel, dart-like, with black sails racing across the surf. It was no Venetian galley either. It was a sailing ship of a not dissimilar size to the *Sea Dove*, but faster and less heavy in the water. Not a trader, then. It had a flag that was hard to make out.

A curse arose from the helmsman.

'What is it?'

'It's a patrol ship out from Barletta, but it's not imperial. The port has changed hands.'

Ketil frowned. It no longer hurt too much to do so, thanks to the regular ministrations of Anna, as well as the salty sea air. 'Who, then?'

'I don't know the flag, but if it's not the empire, and it's neither Benevento nor Salerno, which it isn't, then it's Norman. They've been expanding their territory out of Melfi and Byzantine lands are easy pickings. Some Norman lord now owns Barletta.'

The trader looked up sharply.

'Get the imperial colours down, for the love of the blessed Maria.'

The sailors hurried, doing just that. If Byzantine Barletta had been taken by Normans in the past month or two, arriving under the imperial flag would hardly be a good start. It was just possible the patrol ship had not seen the flag before it was removed, amid the rigging and sails. They had to hope.

'Shit,' Ketil said suddenly. 'Get everyone down below.'

Leif looked down, realisation dawning. A Byzantine nobleman might make a rather lucrative prize for a Norman captain. Ketil took a quick look at his own getup. A chain shirt, no shield, no colours at all apart from his ubiquitous black tunic. He could be any type of warrior or mercenary, really. He looked across at Leif. 'I'll stay here. Tell the men below to drop any shields with designs and for fuck's sake tell the Byzantines to take off their tunics, strip down to their basics and keep their mouths shut. And you… just get changed. There's an empty barrel near where I was sleeping. Put all the tunics and Byzantine clothes in there and weigh it down with something, then tip it over the side opposite the ship. Hopefully we can get away with this.'

As Leif disappeared and the last visible signs of Byzantine allegiance disappeared from the *Sea Dove*, Ketil watched that ship coming closer and closer.

'What will you tell them?' he asked the trader.

'The truth: I'm a merchant out of Dyrrachium bound for Bari and blown off course. The Normans aren't pirates. They're not really at home on the sea,' the man said with a huff of breath. 'They won't be particularly interested in a merchant, no matter where he's from. I doubt they'll do more than look at us. They might decide to search us, which could be a problem with your master aboard, but they might just extort money from us and then go away.'

Ketil looked over at the hatch. 'The katepan is busy making himself look most un-Byzantine.'

'Good. Then we might get through this without trouble.'

The patrol ship came closer still, slowing now, and Ketil examined it carefully with his remaining eye. There were maybe a dozen men in chain shirts on board, no more. The rest were all sailors and unarmed. One of the armoured men wore a tunic of blue and white and seemed to be giving the orders. As the Normans came alongside, Ketil worked at readjusting his perceptions. He'd been learning the Norman tongue on the ship from Miklagarðr all those months ago, and fancied that he'd become quite good at it. It was, after all, not a great shift from their own northern language. But he'd not heard or spoken it for some time while he'd been off in Bulgar-land fighting Greeks for other Greeks. He listened carefully and was relieved that he could make out nine words in ten, and easily get the gist of what was being said. The sailors were speaking the local Italian dialect, but the armoured Normans were using their own tongue.

'Be on your guard,' the officer said to his men. 'Watch for trouble, but there shouldn't be any. It's a slow merchant.'

A scraping noise attracted Ketil's attention and he turned, eyes widening, to see two of his men trying to drag a barrel full of Byzantine uniforms up to the deck to cast over the side. He'd totally forgotten he'd given that order. Shit, but he really should think more about plans before he put them into action. His gaze snapped back and forth between the Normans on the ship now alongside, matching the steady speed, and the two men with the barrel. The foreigners had not yet spotted the unusual activity. Ketil's eyes caught those of the merchant, who was staring in horror, and felt panic rising. The moment the Normans spotted what was happening, they would want to search the ship, then they would find a small Byzantine army on board and this would turn into a bloodbath. Ketil was content they could win such a fight, but the consequences of butchering a patrol ship of Normans in sight of their own city might be too much to deal with.

As he looked again at the barrel – now clearly visible and being dragged along with a lot of grunting and scraping – Leif appeared in the hatchway, back in his miscellaneous leathers and chain shirt. Leif's eyes went to Ketil, to the trader, to the Normans only forty feet away, and then, bulging with shocked realisation, back to the barrel.

Leif lashed out with a foot, kicking the man beside him with the barrel. The man yelped and let go. As he reached down to his shin, the barrel bounced and crashed back down into the hold below, pulling down the other man holding onto it.

Ketil turned to find the entire complement of armoured Normans looking across at the ship, their attention drawn by the noise. The fact that they hadn't already drawn their swords told Ketil that the barrel had disappeared before their gaze had fallen on the hatch. They'd missed the pantomime. Ketil tried not to explode with relief, for the Norman commander was staring at him and Leif, who was now stepping out onto the deck, with a furrowed, suspicious brow.

'What was that?' the Norman demanded.

'My crew, such as they are,' the trader said with an air of bitterness. 'The war has stripped the coast of good men, all taken for the empire's navy. In their place I have clumsy fools.'

As the Norman digested this, one of the crew translating for him, the suspicion still in place on his face, the merchant gave a low chuckle. 'On the bright side, I can pay them less. Profits are better, or will be, if I still have any undamaged cargo when I arrive.'

The Norman snorted at the translation of this. 'What do you carry to the Greek citadel of Bari? Not military supplies?'

'Far from it,' the merchant replied. He rummaged in the cupboard near the rudder and produced from a waxed, waterproof sack inside, his manifest. Approaching the rail with it, he held it out. The Norman looked at it in bafflement, but the steersman of his ship hurried over, took the manifest and opened it to the current journey. He read it with some difficulty and the sailor who spoke both tongues translated to the commander.

'*Sea Dove* out of Dyrrachium, bound for Bari. Ninety tons of cargo, including Thessalian wine, cedar wood and linens from the Arab lands, and pottery from the Euxine region. Nothing suspicious or dangerous.'

'And nothing particularly valuable,' the commander added, with a touch of disappointment in his tone. Ketil privately formed his own opinion as to how close to piracy these Normans could come. They may have emigrated halfway around the world and changed their tongue, but this man would have been at home on a dragon boat, burning Finnish homes and stealing their silver. Apparently you could take the man out of the North, but taking the North out of the man was a tougher proposition.

'Lucky for you that you came across us and not some greedy local,' the Norman announced as, with a gesture from him, the sailor snapped the manifest shut and tossed it back. 'There will, of course, be an additional fee. Patrolling this coast and keeping it free of thievery costs money.'

Ketil fought the urge to point out the irony in that, and stood silent as the merchant handed over a small pouch of coins for the 'protection' of the Norman patrols. With a reminder to keep his nose clean, the patrol boat pulled away from the *Sea Dove* and went off in search of richer merchants to 'protect'.

Once they were safely out of the way, the merchant heaved in a relieved breath. 'Don't take this the wrong way, but I'll be quite relieved when we part ways,' he said.

Ketil laughed. 'It would appear, despite storms, pirates and Normans, we have still reached Italy. I don't know whether your nailed god watches over you, but I tell you this: more ancient gods have watched over us this journey.'

His frankness had numerous sailors crossing themselves.

Once they were out of sight of the Normans, the patrol vessel just a small spot on the endless whale road, the others climbed up to the deck, assembling there. They watched the port of Barletta sliding toward them.

The sense of relief was tangible among them all as a ramp was run out to the dock, and each of them stepped down and arrived in Italy, alive and truly free of the Byzantine yoke.

Now they had to find their friends.

Chapter 16

'May God go with you,' the trader called from atop the ramp.

'They will,' confirmed Ketil as he turned away and crossed the short distance from dockside to city. Barletta was obviously an ancient place, its stone buildings venerable as they marched off in narrow streets from the waterfront. The slender white spires of nailed-god churches rose above the roofs, across the skyline.

Off to the east of the port, a strong stone tower was being constructed, cranes and scaffolding all around it. Men in bright tunics and shining chain shirts, glittering in the sun, moved about giving orders to the labourers. Byzantium had lost Barletta to the Normans, and the city's new lords were already stamping their mark upon it. Instinctively, Ketil turned and looked at the others. They no longer looked Byzantine. Indeed, given their piecemeal collection of armour and weapons over miscellaneous tunics and under drab cloaks, they could be anyone. That would last until they opened their mouths, of course. The Varangians had all been serving in Apulia before the revolt, so many among them might be able to carry enough of an Italian twang to get away with it, but the regular Byzantine infantry spoke Greek almost exclusively, which would identify them as imperial.

'What's the plan?' Leif asked.

Plan? How long had the Rus known him now? He chewed on his lip.

'The first thing is to prevent trouble. If anyone asks, we're sell-swords, mercenaries. That can account for the Greeks

234

among us. We most certainly are *not* from the empire. If anyone asks who we work for or whether we're for hire, we need an excuse, a name. Who do you think we can work for?'

Leif shrugged. 'I don't know anything about the Norman lords. Make something up. A made-up name and a made-up town can't be denied. We're bound for... Siletta. There, we're to take up service with lord Arne. I'll pass on those names, so that everyone has the same story. But still, what's the plan?'

Plan. Plan. Ketil's mind raced. Firstly, if they were going to make enquiries, only he, Leif and Anna knew who they were looking for, and taking a sizeable military force into the town was asking for trouble. Yes, it would have to be just the three of them. The others should stay out of sight. And where was the best place to gather information? Where people got drunk and their mouths ran away with them. He smiled.

'We need to find somewhere for the others to wait while the three of us ask around.'

Leif nodded. 'There will be bunkhouses near the port for the sailors overnighting here. They'll be cheap.'

'Good. Then we start to try the mead halls in the city and listen to men who've had too many drinks. We ask questions and find our friends. Once we know where we're going, we join the others at the bunkhouse for the night and then set off at dawn.'

'And what do we ask? We can't exactly ask about Varangians. That's not going to go well here, I'd say.'

'Wherever Halfdan is, he'll be chasing gold. We find out where there's gold, and we'll find the others. There's a likely-looking drinking hall over there. Get the others settled and then come find me.'

Leaving Leif and Anna to find one of these 'bunkhouses', Ketil checked his weapons, adjusted his tunic and cloak and checked the pouch of coins at his belt, diminished somewhat since its acquisition in Dyrrachium. Satisfied, he walked to the Mermaid, for that was the name of the drinking hall. There was something refreshing about not being in imperial-controlled territory anymore. They had disembarked, stepped around a few piles of goods on the dock, edged around a puddle filled with dead, dismembered fish, and then been presented with the city. No officious, self-important bureaucrat with an armful of records had hurried over to write down a thousand details and charge them for the privilege. This was more like the ports at home: busy and chaotic.

The door to the Mermaid stood open and he walked in, letting his eyesight adjust. It was perhaps an hour before sunset now and already the place was filling up. From the noise emanating from a few of the patrons, it seemed highly likely that a number of them had been in here since at least noon. Like port taverns everywhere, it was mostly filled with sailors and dockers. Ketil strode across to the bar, where the innkeeper was busy laughing with a big, tattooed man about something in the local Italian tongue. He paused, turned to Ketil and said something that was clearly a question.

'Öl,' he replied, presuming the man had been asking what he wanted. It was a gamble, speaking the tongue of the North, but he hadn't really thought about it beforehand.

The innkeeper seemed to understand. Probably the Normans used the same word, though that one hadn't come up during their education on the ship. Sure enough, a big mug of foamy ale clacked down on the bar in front of him. Ketil pulled a collection of coins from his purse and held them out. The barman took a few and then went off to help someone else.

Ketil nursed his drink and turned to take in the place once more. He listened carefully. He could hear conversations in the Italian languages, none of which made any sense, two in the Norman tongue, which he could follow pretty well, and even one that he thought might be Serkish, coming from two dark-skinned men in a corner. No Greek. He concentrated on the conversations he could understand, listening in on the two Norman exchanges.

One was about the difficulties of carting trade goods across the peninsula's interior when every city seemed to change hands weekly. One of the speakers was dismissive, putting forward the notion that soon Iron Arm and his kin would extend Norman control over everything in the south, barring Salerno and Benevento. Then things would be easier. The local lords would have to accept the way things had changed. The Byzantines were done in Italy, in his opinion. Their main strength had gone now, and the rest would not last for long. The other speaker patiently explained that this might all be true, but it didn't help him trade in the short term.

The other conversation seemed to be about the construction of the new fortress near the port. Apparently, the supplies of stone kept being waylaid for one reason or another. Work was slow and behind schedule, and the new lord of this place was getting irritated and taking it out on his men.

The latter conversation seemed unlikely to yield any results, and so he focused on the first. Leaning on the bar, he hummed quietly, a ditty Leif whistled habitually, which got into your ear and burrowed there. He listened for perhaps half an hour, but the conversation never seemed to move on. The two men were drunk and seemed determined to labour the same points over and over again.

At one point he shivered and turned to look at the room. He'd had that strange feeling of being watched, but as he glanced around, nothing had changed, nothing stood out. He frowned at the door. It was closed. The door had been open when he arrived and every time he'd looked at it since. When had it been shut?

His contemplation of the matter was quickly put aside as the door opened and Leif and Anna walked in. Ketil turned and beckoned to the innkeeper. As the man came, the Icelander scanned the room once more. The sense of being watched had gone. He shrugged and asked for a second öl, and two *vin*. The ale and wine arrived and he paid.

'Anything?' Leif asked in the northern tongue.

'Nothing of use. Let's have this and move on.'

Anna, being largely a Greek speaker still, and certainly having a strong accent, kept silent and sipped her wine. The two men murmured to one another about mundane matters for another half hour, listening all the while. Since nothing else arose in that time, when they had finished they returned their mugs to the bar and the three of them moved out into the last light of the sun.

'Let's hope we have more luck elsewhere.'

'We might have to direct the conversation,' Ketil suggested.

'You mean interrupt some Normans and ask them where the nearest pile of gold is, or whether they have heard of a group of pagan Varangians rampaging around Apulia? I think we need to be considerably more subtle than that, Ketil.'

'Let's get away from the port. Most of this lot are sailors anyway.'

After a little further discussion, they traipsed at length through the streets of Barletta, making for the road that led south-west: inland. On that road, further from the bustling port, but still close enough to the centre to be busy, they located another tavern. This one had a lean-to outside where horses were tied to a rail. The three of them pushed open the door to be greeted by a warm fug, a miasma of alcohol, sweat and smoke from the fire burning in one corner, making the place far too hot, given that it was already a warm evening.

'Did you feel anything when we were outside?' Leif asked.

'What?'

'Like… like someone was watching us.'

The hair rose instantly on Ketil's neck. He'd not noticed, but given the feeling he'd had in the Mermaid, this was hard to ignore. He quickly explained what he'd noted earlier and the two men decided to stay as alert as they could to their surroundings.

Half a dozen different groups sat in here and the three of them listened carefully as they crossed to the bar and bought drinks. Ketil's spirits sank – every conversation here was in the local language. They were all native Apulians. Likely they had more useful and pertinent information, given that many would either have just come into town or were planning to leave in the morning along that inland road. But that was of little help, since none of the three could understand a word that was being said.

They managed half an hour before giving up and deciding to move on. As they approached the door, it burst open and three men in long blue-and-white tunics, with heavy swords at their sides, swaggered in, laughing. They had a quick exchange in the Norman tongue and laughed again, then walked toward the bar, shoving a seat out of their path, causing the occupant to tip his drink across the table.

As the three men crossed the room, Leif and Anna stepped aside, knowing they didn't want to draw unwanted attention. Ketil, however, was in no mood for such niceties and as the man who'd shoved the chair walked past, almost knocking him aside, Ketil *accidentally* trod very hard on his foot.

The Norman cursed and turned, angry. Some of the ire melted away from his expression as he came face-to-chest with Ketil and had to strain to look up into the Icelander's remaining eye.

'You trod on my foot,' the man snapped, but his voice wavered with uncertainty. Almost two head-heights taller, Ketil presented a fearsome appearance, his hollow, raw eye socket fixed on the man, the lines of healing wounds across his temple.

'He didn't mean to,' Leif said, stepping in.

'Like fuck I didn't,' Ketil snarled in the Norman tongue. 'Go drink your drink, little man, but remember that you are far from the biggest fish in this pond.'

The man nodded hurriedly and ran over to join the other Normans as they approached the bar. The man whose drink had been spilled nodded his appreciation to Ketil, who nodded back, and the three left.

'We might have to rethink our approach,' Leif sighed. 'I was assuming we would be in Bari and the bulk of conversations would be intelligible. This is hard.'

'Perhaps we'll have more luck in the centre of town?' Ketil muttered. Agreeing, they strode back up the street, where here and there beggars called to them or ordinary folk hurried home before arrogant, drunk Normans found them and caused trouble.

As they walked, Ketil once more felt that strange tingle of being the object of someone's attention. He nudged Leif.

'Yes. I sense it too.'

Ketil closed his eyes as he walked. His eyesight was pretty restricted these days anyway, so better to rely more on his other senses. He could feel it. Could almost hear the quiet breathing of someone trying not to be heard. He reached out subtly with his right hand and tugged at Leif's sleeve. 'Keep walking and talking.'

Leif knew enough not to waste time with questions and picked up his murmured conversation, wandering on with Anna.

Ketil took two steps to his left and slid into a dark alleyway, drawing his sax. There he waited, lurking in the shadows. He could sense the approach and, moments later, a cloaked figure flitted across the alley mouth. Ketil leapt. One hand went around the figure's neck, the other gripping the sax with the point coming up to rest against the figure's chest. It was only as he did this, the blade nestling in a fleshy defile, that he realised with some surprise that the figure was a woman.

'Why are you following us?' he hissed in his own language, close enough that a Norman could follow it.

The woman made a stifled sob. 'I don't speak that language,' she said, in little more than a whisper. In Greek.

Ketil blinked. The language was such a surprise that he let go of her neck, his blade slipping away.

'You are from Miklagarðr?' he said in the Greek tongue.

She frowned in confusion. 'I don't know where that is. I'm from Barletta, at least these past years.'

'Why are you following us?' Ketil repeated. Leif and Anna had appeared at the alley entrance now and slipped in. Anna looked distinctly unimpressed.

'I heard you,' the woman said. 'In the Mermaid.'

'You just said you could not speak the northern tongue.'

'You weren't speaking,' she said, then pointed to Leif. 'You were humming.'

'What?'

'The tune you hummed. It is a lullaby from Constantinople, one I have known all my life. No Norman would be singing such a thing.'

'How could you be so careless?' Anna hissed at Leif, saving Ketil the job of chiding him.

'I never thought.'

'And you,' she hissed, turning on the woman, her fingers moving to the hilt of the eating knife sheathed at her side. 'What Byzantine lady would sneak around like this?'

'All of them in my experience,' grunted Ketil, trying to take control of the conversation again.

The woman in front of them shivered and her brow creased. 'You speak the northern tongue and the language of the empire. You are Varangian!'

'*Quiet,*' Leif hissed. 'We *were* Varangian. The empire has changed recently. The *world* has changed recently.'

'I know. I have friends. You… *you* have friends,' she said.

'I have few friends, and I trust even fewer of them,' Ketil replied, cagily.

'The sons and daughters of the empire are not wholly welcome in Barletta. Merchants are tolerated in the port, but few come any further into the city than the Mermaid. Iron Arm's men control the city now. They are like a plague.'

'We will be fine,' Ketil said. 'We're not staying.'

'Three of you alone will be in danger in Apulia. Much of this land is now under the control of one Norman lord or another. The empire's hold shrinks daily. You could use my friends.'

'We are not three, but nearer thirty,' the Icelander said, earning a look of warning from Leif. He shrugged.

'Please,' she said. 'Just come with me.'

Ketil opened his mouth to object, but Leif was shooting him more warning looks.

'Where?' the smaller man said.

'A house. Not far from here.'

As the woman slipped past them and padded along the dark passage, the other three fell in together a little further back. 'I don't trust her,' Anna murmured.

'Nor I,' Ketil replied. 'She reminds me too much of you,' he added, earning a narrow-eyed glare from Anna.

'She is Byzantine,' Leif interrupted, 'in a world where the Byzantines are the enemy now. She is no spy, for she came upon you by accident and wouldn't even have done that had I been bright enough not to hum Byzantine songs in public. I am intrigued. Just be on your guard.'

They followed the woman around several streets and to a run-down house not far from the western coastline. There, the woman approached the door and rapped on it, a complex staccato rhythm. Ketil saw a drape move at a window and fancied he saw a bow move in the dimness, briefly.

'If this is a trap of some kind, I—'

But he had not finished before the door opened. A fat man of advanced years was holding up a short but stout length of ash, ready to defend himself. A look of relief passed across his face and the club was lowered.

'Cassandra. We thought you lost. And where is the food you went for?'

Another Greek speaker.

'I have something better,' the woman called Cassandra replied. 'Let us in.'

As the man disappeared inside, lamps were lit, illuminating the interior, and Cassandra followed him in, beckoning. The three of them followed, Anna closing the door behind them. A collection of a dozen or so people stood around the edges of the room. They were a varied cross-section of city life – old, young, male, female, fat, thin. Only one looked to be of a military background and Ketil's eye at the window had not deceived him, for there was indeed a bow slung over the man's shoulder. Another, Ketil took to be a smith from the size of his arms and barrel chest. The one that truly caught the attention, though, and sent Ketil's spirits sinking into the deep once more, stood at the centre of the crowd. Ketil recognised the priest from the long black robe that so neatly complemented his long white beard and the circular black hat atop his head.

'What are you all doing here?' Leif asked them.

Cassandra swept out a hand, indicating the gathered folk. 'The Normans have been fairly lenient with the people of Barletta,' she said. 'The imperial garrison, or what was left of it, pulled out without a fight, leaving at night. We woke one day to find the Northmen in command of the city. The locals have been allowed to go about their business as normal, and the merchants and traders allowed to continue their travels. But one thing they are adamant about is that we worship God in their manner, for they follow the dictates of Rome. We are the congregation of the Holy Mother Church in Barletta, which has now been given over to the Roman rite.'

'And what do you want of us?' Ketil grunted. He was struggling a little with what Cassandra had said. He couldn't really give a wet shit about the plight of a bunch of Christians who were arguing with another bunch of Christians over which songs to sing or some such. But at the same time, he found that the idea of the Normans imposing their way of worshipping the nailed god on anyone, even this lot, irked him.

'We need to leave the city.'

'So leave.'

'You don't understand. Everybody here protested openly to the new lord about the closure of our church. We were to be arrested, but we got word and fled, went into hiding. We dare not show our faces in the city. I have been going out alone, cloaked, to source supplies.'

'I think you overestimate your worth to these men,' Ketil snorted.

'You do not understand,' Cassandra repeated.

'You want us to get you out of Barletta. What then?'

'Once we are out of reach of the authorities here, some will make for Bari, where we will find others like us. Others might like to travel with you. We have no home here now.'

Ketil fought the urge to point out that Bari would probably be under Norman control too before very long, the way things seemed to be going. 'I do not want passengers,' he said dismissively. 'What can you offer us for our help?'

Leif shot him an angry glance. 'We will help them, Ketil of Stöð, because it is the right thing to do.'

'No,' Ketil replied with a flat expression. '*You* will help them because it is the right thing to do. *I* will help them for appropriate reward.'

'We do not have much money,' Cassandra said in a worried tone. 'We will see what we have between us.'

A thought struck Ketil and he narrowed his eyes. 'What do you know of gold?'

'I'm sorry? I don't understand.'

'We are seeking gold. And no small amount, either. Where might a man find a fortune in this place?'

Cassandra frowned still. 'The Norman lords have their gold. And the dukes of the west coast. I... I don't know how you will find gold, though, other than signing over to service with a rich lord.'

'I think he means the *missing* gold,' one of the watching men said, taking a step forward. Ketil's ears pricked up. He glanced at Leif, whose eyes were suddenly gleaming. The pair could have been Odin's own wolves, Geri and Freki, the ravenous and the greedy, the way their eyes had lit up.

'Tell me about the missing gold,' Ketil said, stepping close to the man.

'The ransom. We know nothing more about it than anyone else.'

'Pretend I know *nothing* about it, and explain.'

'The prince of Benevento,' the man replied, apparently surprised to have found someone who didn't know about it. 'Atenulf, brother of Duke Pandulf.'

'Am I going to have to drag this out of you?'

The man hurried on. 'The duke was given charge of the imperial katepan a few years ago when he was captured in battle. Atenulf arranged a ransom from the imperial coffers to get him back, but then disappeared with the gold.'

A smile spread slowly across Ketil's face. 'But no one knows where this Atenulf and his gold are?'

The man nodded.

Leif stepped in now. 'If he has cheated the lord of Benevento out of the ransom, he will not be on the west coast, where his brother rules. And if the missing gold was imperial, and the katepan was not returned, then the empire has also been cheated, so they will not be in imperial lands. From what we hear of the Norman lords, they are unlikely to let this pass without seeking to get their own hands on such a large sum of gold. And Melfi is the centre of their power, so by my reckoning this Atenulf and his gold have to be somewhere in the region bounded by Byzantine, Beneventan and Norman lands. Somewhere in the middle.'

'And that,' Ketil grinned, 'is where we'll find Halfdan and the others. Be sure of it.' He turned to the man. 'I presume you've heard no rumours of ice giants?'

The man frowned in total incomprehension.

'No one has seen Bjorn, then.'

'We have found our trail,' Leif smiled. 'Somewhere to the south-west of here, our friends are to be found. There is no

245

way rumours of such a prize have not reached them. Where we find the gold, we will find Halfdan.'

Ketil snorted. 'The closer we get the more likely it is that someone has seen Bjorn. It is Bjorn who will bring us to Halfdan. And when we find Halfdan, we will find the gold.' He straightened. 'We will come for you when the sun rises. Be ready. We will leave the city and see you on the road for Bari.'

'You will just leave us,' said the man who'd told them about the gold.

'Michael, be quiet.'

'Look at him. He's a Northman, like the Normans. Now he has what he wants, we'll not see him again. He'll be off after the gold and without another thought for us.'

Ketil narrowed his eyes dangerously, hand going to the haft of his axe. He tried to radiate indignation at this slur on his name, though in truth, it had crossed his mind – and he'd not yet written off the possibility of doing just that.

One glance across at Leif and Anna, though, told him how unlikely such a course was. Both of them shared the same faith as these people, and Leif was already far too sentimental for his own good. Even Anna, who seemed not to trust Cassandra, seemed ready to help.

'Be charitable, Michael,' the old priest said, stepping forth now for the first time. 'The Lord has seen fit in our time of need to bring us salvation. This man is our Moses, come to part the waters to allow us to return to the land of our fathers.'

It may have been utter bollocks as far as Ketil was concerned, but the priest's words seemed to have the desired effect on the man, who settled into a suspicious silence.

'You will have to travel in ordinary clothes,' Ketil said, gesturing to the priest. 'Squeeze that lot into a bag and take it with you.' The old man nodded his understanding. 'All right,' Ketil went on, looking around. 'Be ready at dawn.'

As they left the house, Leif cleared his throat. 'For a moment there, I thought you *were* just going to leave them.'

'How little you know me, Leif the Teeth,' Ketil grunted, though he kept his eye away from the Rus for fear of revealing the truth.

They walked all the way back to the port and the bunkhouse Leif had organised in silence, lost in their own thoughts, with Anna unable to speak out in the open anyway for fear of attracting attention. When they reached their destination, they each sought their bed, ready for what could be a long and troublesome day ahead. Leif took a few moments first to pass on word of what they had found.

That night, Ketil slept badly, repeatedly assaulted by dreams in which priests of one type or another kept whipping him with thin, sharp branches and demanding that he side with them. He awoke feeling groggy and irritable, almost an hour before dawn. Gradually, the bunkhouse came to life and men washed in the water barrel provided, then wearily pulled on their clothes and weapons.

'Where are we bound?' Ketil said finally, addressing the gathered Greeks and Varangians.

'Siletta,' came the sporadic reply.

'And who do we serve?'

'Arne.'

'And who does *he* serve?'

'Lord Iron Arm.'

Ketil nodded in satisfaction. Tired, achy, he stretched and tried to work out the knots in his muscles, and then straightened. 'We collect the civilians, then leave by the east gate, heading along the coast. Once we are four miles from here, and away from the Normans, or when we see the first Byzantine soldier, we let them go on their way and we turn and make inland. Our first target is a place called Melfi. If Halfdan and the others have not been there, we start to make our way south, listening to rumours as we go.'

He felt oddly official as he led more than a score of armed men out of the block and began to hike across the city with them, Leif and Anna at his side. They caught a number of odd and suspicious looks from the occasional Normans they saw in the street, but soon they were in the periphery of the place, away from such eyes, and they had found the house where the fugitives dwelt. At a call, they emerged, nervous, looking about themselves. All had dressed very sensibly for travel in miscellaneous and drab clothing, even the priest.

'Good. As we leave Barletta, I want you all spread out among my men, in the middle, though, not out at the sides where anyone can get a good look at you. If anyone asks you, you are in service to Lord Arne of Siletta.'

'Who?' one of them asked in bafflement.

'Precisely. Lord Arne of Siletta. That is where we are bound.'

Ketil took a deep breath. He would be quite pleased to be rid of this lot.

And then they could find Halfdan.

Part Five

ᚠᛜᚱᚠᛗᛋ ᛜᚠ ᛜᛈᛁᛏ

The City of Thieves

Chapter 17

'Aimery was right,' Turstin, the last of Fulk's Normans said, eyeing Bjorn warily, his eyes sliding to Halfdan and then Gunnhild.

'Aimery was a fool,' Fulk retorted. 'It was his betrayal that put us in this mess.'

'No,' Turstin snapped. 'No, it wasn't. Aimery showed you a way out and you wouldn't take it. You could have bargained for our release with these pagans, but you hold your own honour more precious than the lives of your men.'

The soldier squawked as Marc slapped him hard around the jaw with a leather gauntlet.

'Quiet, turd. You don't speak to your lord so.'

The man fell into resentful silence, massaging his jaw. Halfdan looked across at Gunnhild, who was watching the outspoken Norman with narrowed eyes. Fear did different things to different people, and it was almost to be expected that someone would once again raise the spectre of selling out the Northmen for their own skins. Neither Fulk nor Marc seemed inclined to break the pledge, but Turstin now sat in a corner glaring at them, suggesting that he was of a mind with his friend.

They had languished in this place for six days now, a single large room of stone with a solid timber ceiling, above which was a room filled with guards. There was just one door, locked from the outside, and no window. They were fed two meals a day, both plain and small and supplied by an armed party that took no chances. Every time the food had been delivered, Halfdan and the others had demanded to speak to the lord of Acerenza. Every time, they were denied.

It would be all too easy to feel doomed and fated, to think this was the end, but Fulk's adamant belief that his cousin would still see them freed gave him, gave them all, the hope to go on.

His eyes slid to Gunnhild. Why was she here? Why had she not taken the line thrown to her? As a priestess of the nailed god – a nun, as they were seemingly called – she had been separated from the others and a room had been arranged beside one of the chapels in the city, where she would be watched, but would be safe and have access to a church. She had declined, telling their captors that it was her duty to stay with her 'flock'. She had gone on to cite all sorts of Christian quotes, which had surprised Halfdan immensely. Apparently she had spent time in the great city reading the nailed-god book and arguing its falseness with priests and the empress. Her familiarity with it was paying off now. But she had determined to stay with the others. Whatever fate they faced, they would face it together.

For perhaps an hour the room lapsed into sullen silence once more, Bjorn and Gunnhild both watching the outspoken Norman with disdain, until Farlof, sitting close to the door, rose and stepped back.

'Visitors.'

The others climbed to their feet, too. It was hard to even estimate times in this place, other than by the bells they could hear across the city, muted by their prison. But it had only been a couple of hours since they had been delivered bread and some sort of watery broth, so this was unlikely to be a food delivery.

They could hear footsteps approaching, the hard boots of soldiers, and a number of them. With a couple of clunks and a rattle, the door was unlocked and pulled open, a beam of light falling across the fetid interior of the straw-floored room. At least a dozen soldiers stood out there, fully armed and armoured, their weapons out, anticipating trouble. An officer stepped into the doorway.

'Come,' was all he said as he paced back out.

The prisoners looked at one another, shrugging, and began to shuffle toward the door. The order in which they emerged was deliberate. Fulk, as a Norman lord, went first, with his bannerman, Marc, at his shoulder, then Turstin. Then Gunnhild as a nun, followed by Halfdan, Bjorn, Ulfr, Farlof and Sveinn for by now all attention would be on those who emerged first, minimising the risks.

Down the passageway they were marched, and then through a door into the sunlight. Once they were out in the courtyard of the fortress, they looked about. More soldiers awaited them here, and the gate that led to the city was well manned and well protected. There was precious little chance of escape. At the officer's gesture, Fulk led the way and they strode across the courtyard and in through another doorway.

Fulk marched with his chin high, every inch the lord. Halfdan took in their surroundings, repeatedly confirming the minimal chances of making their way to freedom. They were led into a large chamber and told to wait there. The banners of the lord of Acerenza hung upon the walls, along with tapestries and drapes, and a large wooden chair, resembling a throne, sat atop a dais up three steps. Guards stood at strategic points around the room. Counting their escort, they were now outnumbered at least two to one, the local soldiers both well armed and armoured. The lord of Acerenza was taking no chances.

Behind them, the doors were closed and men stepped in, surrounding them. They did not have long to wait before another door opened at the far end of the large chamber and in walked a procession of figures. Halfdan mentally checked them off as they came. First, some sort of herald, followed by a tall man with a sombre face, dressed in rich colours and with hair cut into that strange Norman design, a scar running from his nose down past the corner of his mouth to his chin. This was clearly the lord of Acerenza. Behind him came a couple of serious-looking men in armour, one young and bearing a familial resemblance to the lord. Then a stockier man in a tunic of red and yellow with a richly embroidered cloak. He wore his golden hair long, and his moustache drooped. His eyes were sharp and gleaming as they took in the array of prisoners. This, Halfdan decided, had to be Atenulf, thief-prince of Benevento. Behind the prince came several more of Acerenza's soldiers, a couple of servants, and a priest in his rich robes.

Halfdan sized up the situation at a glance. Atenulf may be currently sheltered by the lord of Acerenza, but there was no love there and no trust. Not one man in the room was Atenulf's. A number of questions and possible answers ran through his mind now as the party gathered, the lord taking a seat on the throne and arranging his garments carefully, the Beneventan prince noticeably standing more than a sword distance from the seated man and with two guards close enough to stop him should he do something precipitous. Indeed, the priest seemed to be given a lot more deference here than the thief-prince.

Why was Atenulf still here? It seemed unlikely that anything would impede his journey south at this time, so there was no clear reason why the thief would have delayed his departure this long. That suggested that Atenulf of Benevento was being delayed in his departure, presumably at the whim of the lord of Acerenza, and that, in turn, suggested that Atenulf was little more than a prisoner himself. This was an interesting development.

Why, then, was Acerenza not either letting the man go, or stealing his gold and doing away with him? It seemed likely that these men were as complicated and political as the Byzantines, and so it may be that Acerenza was playing some game of his own. Perhaps he was waiting for something? Had he been approached by Iron Arm and warned about the gold? Was the lord currently negotiating with another party? Whatever the case, while Atenulf may currently have control of the gold, clearly Acerenza had control of Atenulf. Whatever happened now would be at the whim of Fulk's cousin.

The lord of Acerenza cradled his chin lazily in a claw-like hand and dragged his gaze across them.

'What to do with you all,' he mused.

Fulk took a single step forward and every military hand in the room went to the hilt of a sword and stayed there.

'Might I suggest, cousin, that you release us, and I will look the other way at the appalling treatment you have levelled upon your own kin and a noble of this land, as well as his entourage, companions and even a woman of God.'

This did not seem to impress the lord of the city, whose mouth twisted in a half smile. 'You were never my favourite cousin, Courvaudon. Indeed, I have dogs of whom I am more fond. And I suspect that even were I to simply do away with you and word reached our mutual liege lord, the fact that you were found in the company of members of the Byzantine imperial guard would negate any goodwill he might feel toward you. You *are* aware that we are at war with these people?'

Fulk snorted. 'As a man who, like me, came to this land an impoverished mercenary, and who has fought for Italian lords and Byzantine masters alike in his time, you of all people should understand that not every warrior cleaves to a flag. These men have served as Varangians, but they are sell-swords now, and ones who broke a siege in the south and freed me and mine from Byzantine control. You seek reasons to justify your unlawful arrests.'

Acerenza's fingers drummed a tattoo on the arm of his chair, though his expression did not change. 'Your presence here is… *inconvenient* at best.'

'Because I now know that a katepan's ransom in stolen gold hides behind the city walls and every power in this peninsula would tear down those ramparts and climb over your corpse to get to it.'

The drumming increased. 'Your disappearance would be the most convenient solution, though there are complications.'

'Are you mad?' Atenulf said suddenly, in the Norman tongue, but thick with an Italian accent. Acerenza turned to the prince, brows raised in surprise. Atenulf grunted. 'Execute the lot of them.'

Halfdan frowned. Perhaps the prince was not *quite* the full prisoner, then?

'It would be convenient,' Acerenza repeated.

'If you execute a woman of God,' the priest standing nearby suddenly announced, face folded into a disapproving frown, 'then you will be damned for an eternity to the lake of fire.'

Acerenza simply nodded and the drumming of fingers slowed. 'And if I let the nun leave, then knowledge of our situation is free to spread, and it matters not if the others survive. A thorny problem. I cannot easily condemn these people, even if the Varangians follow the dictates of Constantinople and not the rule of Rome. But to let them leave the city would be to broadcast to every power in the land the presence of the larcenous prince and his wagons of gold.'

'And you have yet to decide whether to keep them,' Fulk concluded.

'I am inclined to do so,' admitted Acerenza. 'Once you have stepped knee deep into the river, you might as well get wet and swim. I am committed to some extent.'

'But,' Halfdan said, suddenly realising something, 'the matter will never close then, will it? Everyone will continue to look for the gold and you will never be at ease. Whereas, if you take a healthy cut and let Atenulf go, then when he inevitably gets caught or is spotted elsewhere, all the pressure will be lifted from you and you can enjoy the gold you have already taken.'

Acerenza nodded slowly and the drumming ended as he turned a look of dislike on Halfdan. 'I have no idea who your Byzantine rat is, nor how he feels it is his place to interrupt his betters, but he is astute, I'll give him that. I have many decisions to make.'

'Then let me help you, my lord,' said Turstin, stepping out away from Marc and Fulk. Halfdan felt his heart sink. What was it with these Normans, who could not hold their treacherous tongues for anything? He instantly regretted not having told Bjorn to break the man's neck the moment he spoke against them.

Marc made a move to stop the man, even as Fulk turned angrily toward him, but the Norman was already out of reach and Acerenza's guards were closing on him. He was safe from reprisal and his face took on a triumphant look as he turned to the lord of the city.

'My lord, these men are not what they appear.'

'Oh?'

Fulk levelled a finger at his man. 'Be quiet, Turstin.'

'Let the man speak,' Acerenza advised, flicking a gesture at the Norman traitor.

'My lord, my master and I are, as you know, good men of the North, loyal to the powers of this land. But these Varangians are not what they purport to be. Each and every one is a filthy pagan, following demonic gods. They deny the Christ. Do not be fooled by their false piety, and do not allow their lies to save them from the executioner's blade.'

The look of victory that swam across Atenulf's face made Halfdan want to break it. Acerenza's however, remained silent and thoughtful. 'How does a woman of God tolerate their presence?'

'She is no nun,' Turstin spat. 'She is the worst of all of them. A witch, I say. I have seen her witchcraft with my own eyes.'

'Indeed?' Acerenza leaned forward, peering at Gunnhild. 'And I take it there is more proof of this than your mere word?' he asked the Norman as he looked the völva up and down.

'Evidence is plentiful, my lord. Look to the house where we were taken and you will find their false idols and heathen symbols. Look upon their flesh and you will find them, too.'

Acerenza still had not taken his eyes off Gunnhild. 'Do you have anything to say for yourself, sister?'

Halfdan felt the wave of failure break over them. Their subterfuge was gone. It had held well until broken down from the inside by one of their own. Gunnhild's expression changed now, and Halfdan realised that the völva had decided that the time for pretence was gone. She straightened a little.

'I am Gunnhild of Hedeby. I shall say no more.'

The richly dressed priest's face was twisting with uncertainty, not sure what to do, whether Gunnhild was truly what she claimed. Finally, the priest leaned toward Acerenza and whispered something to him. The lord thought for a moment on what was said and finally nodded, then leaned back, hands going to the arm of his chair again.

'The bishop here reminds me that it is my duty as a good Christian to protect the Faith. This means that he is adamant that I both forgive children of God and punish his enemies. As such, before I make any rash decisions, I give you each the opportunity to demonstrate your devotion to the Church.'

As he spoke, the priest stepped forward with two servants at his heel. He was lifting a cross of silver almost a foot high, etched with decoration and inscribed scenes of the nailed god's miserable life. One servant carried a flat loaf of unleavened bread on a silver platter, the other a silver cup and a jug. They stopped first at the nearest prisoner, which happened to be the traitorous Turstin.

'Kiss the cross of our Lord,' the bishop instructed. The Norman wasted no time in doing so, and when he was offered the bread and a mouthful of wine, announced as the flesh and blood of the Christ, he took them almost eagerly. Satisfied, the bishop moved on. Fulk repeated the ritual, and then Marc. As the priest turned and made toward the others, Halfdan caught a look flashed at him by Fulk, almost pleading him to conform.

Halfdan looked at the approaching priest. Would the Allfather forgive any further subterfuge? Odin was a wily one, after all. Such trickery was not above him, so surely he would forgive them playing this game? He glanced at Gunnhild, who gave him the slightest of nods.

The priest held out the cross and, trying not to recoil, Halfdan leaned in and kissed the cold metal. He hoped the bitter flavour in his mouth was his own distaste and the tang of metal, not a warning from the gods. When offered, he took a torn piece of bread and consumed it quickly, washing it down with a small cup of wine. He could see the evil looks of disbelief Turstin was throwing him.

'This is a farce,' the Norman spat, 'a fallacy. That man is a pagan idolater. That he doesn't care about kissing the cross proves nothing.'

But the warning look Acerenza shot him silenced him as the priest and his men moved on to Ulfr. The shipwright hesitated for only a moment and then followed the nailed-god ritual, wiping his mouth afterwards with his wrist and letting a small belch echo through the room. Farlof followed suit without argument.

The bishop came to Gunnhild, only Bjorn and Sveinn now remaining. Gunnhild regarded the cross for some time and then reached out. As she did so, the priest let go of the cross with one hand, his eyes bulging. His free hand grasped Gunnhild's arm and yanked it so that she staggered forward for a moment. The bishop hissed and stared. 'The Devil's marks are upon you, woman!'

Halfdan winced. As her arm had come up, the sleeve falling back, a number of tattoos had been revealed, including the valknut, the ward against elves from their time among the draugar and the *Gibu Auja*. There could be no denying their nature, and the bishop recoiled, pulling away from her, spluttering, leaving the two servants looking panicked.

'Fuck it,' Bjorn boomed, stepping forward. 'I'd sooner kiss a goat's arse than your god's cross,' he snapped. Reaching out, he snatched the jug from the white-faced servant. 'But wine? Now wine, I never refuse.'

He upended the jug, managing to catch roughly half the contents in his mouth, the rest flowing down over him. Once again, there was no point in maintaining the fiction. Gunnhild had been revealed for what she was – the priest would never believe her now, and Bjorn had denied the Christ God to stand by her. It took only a moment for Halfdan and then Ulfr to step to their sides. Farlof was not far behind.

'Very well,' Halfdan said. 'Call us pagans and believe what you will, but I will say this in the sight of all the gods, even your poor nailed one: we are men and women of our word, who have fought openly and for our comrades. This room contains only two proven criminals, and it is those two thieves who think to sit in judgement on us.'

Gunnhild threw him a look and he was surprised at the irritation in it. 'I might yet have talked this down, young fool,' she hissed out of the corner of her mouth. There would be no denying it now, though. Halfdan had hammered in the final nail.

'An unexpected and troubling development,' Acerenza said at last, sucking in his cheeks and resuming the drumming of his fingers. 'I find I am now beset by witches and demon worshippers. Only four of you have any real claim to follow the true Faith, and yet even you, cousin, are guilty of willful association with witches and demons. I suspect that rather supersedes your kissing of the cross.' He glanced across at the bishop, whose lip was wrinkling.

'The city,' the old man said, 'and every soul in it are in danger while these creatures poison our very air with their devilry. Death is just the *beginning* of their punishment, for the Lord shall see them burn in *aeternum* for what they are.'

Acerenza nodded. 'I had a feeling that might be your position.'

'Burn them all,' Atenulf snapped. 'Do you need any further reason?'

The lord shook his head. 'I am inclined to be merciful to the extent such a thing is possible. My cousin and his men should be given the opportunity to atone for their misdeeds. I feel they should be given the option to take Holy Orders and join the ranks of the Church, making reparations to God with the rest of their time in this world.'

Fulk stared in disbelief and even Turstin the traitor gasped. He had sold them out for nothing.

'As for the others, I cannot condone their ways, but I am also aware that they have gone some way to redemption. They have partaken of the eucharist and shown devotion to the cross. I cannot commute their sentence. They will have to die, but I will give the order that it be fast, and the executioner's sword be razor sharp for the occasion. This is my pronouncement.'

Halfdan felt the anger rising. How dare this thief... no, this thief who even thieved from *thieves*... presume to judge *him*?

'There remains the matter of two admitted pagans, one who profanes the eucharist and another who stands accused of witchcraft. I cannot lessen any sentence on such creatures, for what precedent would that set?'

'Burn them,' growled Atenulf.

'The witch will burn,' Acerenza confirmed with a flick of a finger toward Gunnhild. 'The giant, though... I feel we should have some entertainment from him. He looks strong and I fear he prides himself upon it. We shall see how long he can rely upon that strength while horses endeavour to tear him apart.'

Halfdan looked across at Gunnhild.

'Give me my sword,' he hissed quietly.

'No.'

'Better we die here in battle than we let these thieves torture us to death. I will not let you burn, Gunnhild of Hedeby.'

'I do not believe I will burn, Halfdan. In fact, I will not let such a thing happen, even if the Norns have woven it. But remember being trapped in the house? Death offers no second chance, while capitulation can buy time.'

Halfdan gritted his teeth. He'd said he would never ignore Gunnhild again, but surely even she must see the time to act was now? She'd talked about defying the Norns, for fuck's sake. Perhaps if he ignored her advice, it might even be for her own good, if she would challenge fate.

'Give me the sword.'

'No.'

He glared at her in frustration.

'Return them to their incarceration,' Acerenza said, gesturing at the gathering. 'I will consult with the good bishop and set a day for the executions. It must be soon, I think.'

The guards began to gather, weapons out, herding them back toward the hall's entrance. Halfdan stood protectively by Gunnhild's side. Again, as they moved, Halfdan took in everything he saw, hoping for even a hint of a weakness in this place he could exploit to escape, but it was in vain. They were trapped, overpowered and helpless. He was the wolf in the gilded cage – though not for much longer, by the sound of it. Execution by sharp blade would clearly be better than what the lord of Acerenza had in mind for Gunnhild or Bjorn, but the fact was that in the end he would be just as dead, and none of them would join their forefathers in Odin's hall.

Back across the courtyard they were marched, and thrown into their prison once more, shut away in the gloom as the door was slammed behind them and bolts slid into place.

As they spread out in the room, Turstin shuffled uncomfortably away toward Fulk and Marc. Bjorn looked across at Gunnhild, and Halfdan caught the look in the giant's eye. When Gunnhild nodded, the big albino looked then to his jarl. Halfdan gave his own nod and in a heartbeat Bjorn was stomping across toward the traitor who had sold them out for his own skin, only to fail in the end.

Turstin saw Bjorn coming and backed away with a moan, moving to the protection of Fulk and his men. The Norman backed into Marc, but then cried out again in fear as Fulk's bannerman gave the unfortunate traitor a hefty shove, sending him back toward Bjorn.

Turstin panicked. The Varangians were each looking at him with murderous glares, and his own lord had turned him away. Now a great, white-haired, pink-eyed monster with arms like tree trunks was almost upon him.

'Please. I didn't want to die.'

'Oh, you'll regret that you didn't live long enough to meet Acerenza's sword,' Gunnhild said with some cold confidence.

Turstin gave a little whimper. 'I'm sorry. I'm so sorry. What can I do? There must be *something* I can do.'

'You can fucking die,' Bjorn growled, reaching out and grabbing the man. The Norman squawked, flailing helplessly in the big warrior's grasp, babbling promises and pleas. Bjorn looked up, then across to Gunnhild.

'Can Huginn and Muninn see through roofs?'

'Odin's ravens are watching, Bjorn Bear-torn,' she confirmed.

'Good. Then let the Allfather witness.'

As Turstin babbled and shrieked – urine soaking his crotch and leg in fear, tears streaming down his face – Bjorn lifted the Norman with as little effort as he might raise a drinking horn, and slammed him down to the flagged floor, face down. They all heard a number of nasty cracks as the man's nose and teeth smashed against the stone; soon he would not worry about such things.

Halfdan almost looked away, but made himself watch. Some things were important not because they were done, but because they were observed. He had never seen this, nor heard of it done in living memory, even on his home of Gotland, yet he knew what was coming. Horrors from the stories of old *skalds*.

The Norman gave a muffled scream, half drowning in his own blood and snot as the albino knelt on the back of his thighs, holding him down. Bjorn turned to the others and Halfdan reached out a hand. Gunnhild slapped into it that glorious eagle-hilted blade she had kept hidden from their captors, and he took three steps and proffered it to the big man.

Bjorn took the blade with a nod of thanks. Turstin had recovered enough of his wits to struggle once more now, and Bjorn snarled 'Quiet, you,' and used his free hand to grab the Norman's neck and force him to stillness. Using his immense strength to hold the man down, Bjorn tore away Turstin's shirt with the blade, revealing his bare back. Muttering under his breath, the big man began his work.

Every figure in the room watched in dreadful fascination as, amid the screams of agony, Bjorn drew with the tip of the blade, fashioning an eagle on the man's back, wings outspread, reaching up toward the shoulders, fanned tail on his lower back, talons out to his sides, all carved in flesh, the blood welling up to gradually obscure what was, to Halfdan's surprise, a very artistic shape.

Turstin was howling now, wailing with exquisite pain, but Bjorn was far from done. Tongue poking out of the side of his mouth, he passed the blade back to Halfdan, who took it and retreated a step. When Bjorn peeled the eagle away from the traitor's back, they wondered if the screaming could possibly get any louder. The Normans were now drawing crosses on their chests, though they did not move to stop this ritual, nor did they look away.

With eye-watering cracks, Bjorn broke the man's ribs near the spine, and that was how Turstin died. The pain was too much, and he was still and lifeless even before the last rib snapped. His spirit had left his shell before the albino buried his hands in the Norman up to the wrists and with a grunt of effort pulled out the lungs, leaving them wobbling on the man's back where the wings should be. The lungs were not moving. No breath for Turstin the traitor.

The job finished, Bjorn stood. There was a small bucket of water for drinking that they had been careful, at least from day two, not to confuse with the piss bucket. Ulfr was still apologising for that. Bjorn tipped out a little water to wash the worst of the sticky blood from his hands and lower arms. When he turned, he looked up as though he could see the azure sky through the heavy timber ceiling.

'Hear me, oh ravens of Odin. Tell the Allfather that a traitor has died a traitor's death. May Odin curse his memory.'

Fulk had gone white, his eyes wide. He looked at Gunnhild.

'It is called the blood eagle,' she said. 'It is an ancient thing. It was never common, even in the days of the old ones, and never is it done in these times. Sometimes, though, death is just not enough.'

Fulk nodded slowly, uncertainly, swallowing repeatedly, his eyes slipping down to the body every now and then. Beside him, Marc was wiping sick from his chin with the back of his hand.

'We have days at most,' Halfdan said, breaking the grisly spell as he straightened, wiping his blade on his trousers before handing it back to Gunnhild. 'If we are to find a way out, the time is upon us.'

'What way out?' Farlof said, sagging slightly. 'There is no way we can leave here. We are in a locked prison room inside a walled fortress, within a walled town, all controlled by our enemy, who outnumbers us considerably.'

'I think we had already brushed aside the idea of fighting our way out,' Fulk said with bitter irony, slowly recovering from what he had just witnessed.

'It may be that our salvation lies with the very thief who demanded our death,' Halfdan mused.

'What?'

'I think Atenulf is being held in Acerenza yet. It may be that we share a mutual enemy in the lord of this place. If there were some way we could manage to speak to the thief-prince, we might be able to persuade him that we are his best bet to get away with his gold.'

'And then steal it later,' Bjorn added, with an air of satisfaction.

'I tell you this,' Halfdan said, 'if Acerenza lets him go, it will not be for long. Fulk's cousin needs Atenulf to be found with the gold, but he doesn't have to be alive. Say Acerenza keeps a quarter and the thief takes the rest. Then Acerenza's men hunt him down and kill him somewhere public, where he'll be found. The body will be identified, the gold recovered, and Acerenza will be congratulated by the very lords he has cheated.'

Fulk nodded. 'It may be as you say, but I cannot see a way we can get to speak to the thief.'

Halfdan took a deep breath. 'Perhaps, Gunnhild, it is time for you to see if Freyja walks this land once more.'

Chapter 18

Halfdan couldn't help but smile at the sight of Fulk and Marc watching Gunnhild. Their expressions reflected an uneasy mix of horror and fascination. Their eyes were wide, hungry, eager, yet their mouths were pursed and taut, their knuckles white where they clasped hands tight in prayer to their Serkish god, occasionally unlocking them to draw a cross over their chest even as they took in every wondrous detail of the völva's work. Christians, Halfdan was coming to realise, were always happy to denounce something they disapproved of, yet there was nothing they liked more than to secretly watch those very blasphemies.

Gunnhild was singing now, her voice ephemeral, like aural filigree; so delicate and otherworldly that even if Halfdan could understand the ancient words, he would never be able to follow them. Her song drifted higher with each stanza, as though her words climbed Yggdrasil, leaving *Midgard*, the land of men, and climbing the great tree of worlds to reach *Vanaheim*, where Freyja dwelled in her magnificent hall. And then suddenly the goddess was with them all.

Halfdan was no weaver of spells, nor any sort of priest, yet he felt his skin prickle as Gunnhild's song joined two worlds and the völva walked with Freyja. He felt the Seiðr all around them, crawling across the walls and floor and ceiling like a silvered ivy growing at frightening speed. Even his hair crackled with the power filling the room. The reverent looks on his friends' faces suggested that they felt the same, and the Normans' eyes bulged as they crossed themselves repeatedly and fervently.

As the song wavered, coming in ripples like a stone dropped into a pond, echoing out from the völva at its centre, Gunnhild changed with the melody, twisting, turning, spinning, sometimes seeming tall and untouchable, her reaching, twining arms the branches of the world tree, her feet the roots that bound the realms below. And then she was returning, coming down that tree from the worlds of gods, folding in on herself like a flower wilting at speed until she was crouched and still, the last strains of her song echoing around the walls as the fragments of silver, of bone, of beads and feathers spilled out before her. She swept out an arm and grasped her staff, waving it over the scattered items, a blur of wood, and then leaned on it, breathing heavily.

'God in Heaven,' murmured Fulk, still watching her.

'What have you seen?' Halfdan asked, a sense of urgency in him, his skin still prickling.

'Do not rush me, son of Gotland.'

He fell silent, impatient, waiting. Finally, she rose to her feet with languid ease.

'The magpie picks over a corpse, but it is too intent on its work to see the wolf pack closing upon it.'

Fulk frowned. 'What?'

Halfdan waved a hand to quieten him. 'Atenulf is the magpie, yes? He has to be. The thief.'

She nodded. 'The wolves close in.'

'So we will move on Atenulf?'

She threw him an irritable look and he stopped questioning her and waited.

'There is no gilded cage, and so it seems as though we must be the wolves. I can see nothing beyond this.'

Halfdan turned to Fulk, a look of relieved satisfaction on his face. 'See. We are not bound for death. This is not to be our end. The cage opens, and we move on the thief-prince.'

Fulk was chewing on his lip. 'You must have heard a different witch to the one I listened to. What I heard was that the cage is gone and that a thief is about to be torn apart by wolves.

Of course the cage is gone, because the next time you leave this room it will be to lose your head to an executioner's blade. And wolves? What makes you think you are wolves? This is witchcraft, but it is vague, useless.'

Gunnhild glared at him and Fulk faltered for a moment. 'I mean no insult,' he added hurriedly, crossing himself again.

'You do not understand,' Halfdan said to him. 'You have been gone from the North and your people too long. Your blood has thinned, diluted, and you have lost the strength of ice and of grey rock that fills every Northman. You have forgotten the tales of your forefathers that have nursed our people for a thousand years and seen them cross worlds and survive when even empires have died.'

Fulk shook his head, but Halfdan wagged a finger.

'No. You have lost your way. You no longer see the world around you and your place as part of it, a single piece on a great game board. To you, just like the Byzantines, the world is the backdrop and your people are the centre. We are no more than a part of it all, like the animals, like the gods, like the morning mist and the jagged mountains. It is all one, and yet you are now blind to it.'

He threw out an arm, indicating the others in the room. 'We are Wolves of Odin, like Geri and Freki. And like those two great beasts, we are hungry and rapacious. We are a pack, even if some of our number have strayed, and like a wolf pack, we are strong together. The magpie is a lonely bird. We *are* the wolves. Atenulf *is* the magpie. The gilded cage is open, and the thief-prince had better beware, for the pack will close in on him now.'

Fulk snorted. 'How? How will the pack close in on him? Are you going to walk through the walls and escape? Is Gunnhild going to magic the door open? This changes nothing, Halfdan. You have a nice new prophetic story, but we are still in prison, and when they come for us next, you will all die and we will be given the choice of joining you or spending our lives in a new prison of tonsures and cloisters and evensong. Nothing has changed.'

'*Everything* has changed,' Halfdan insisted.

'Then I await your magical victory, but I shall not hold my breath.'

Fulk stood, glowering, and Halfdan felt the frustration and the impotence rising. He could not explain to this man how the Seiðr changed things, how the world was woven into a tapestry by the Norns, how Gunnhild could see those threads leading out somehow, with the help of the goddess. He could not explain how it was possible to *know* that things were changing. And the reason he couldn't explain it to the man was because he couldn't quite understand it himself, for all that he *knew* it to be true. Somehow, they would not meet death and they would turn on Atenulf, and yet he could not see how such a thing could possibly come to pass.

The hours slipped by, Halfdan thinking over and over about any way he could bring about their escape. The Normans had spent their time in their own huddle, praying to their god and trying to come up with any new idea. Ulfr had been picking his nails with the tip of his knife, something he only did when the tension was getting to him. Gunnhild had a worried look that she surely was not aware of, for she'd have changed it if she knew. Sveinn tapped relentlessly and Farlof wouldn't stop pacing. Bjorn... well, Bjorn seemed no different, apart from what might be nervous farts. Or that might just be his usual fare.

They *had* to escape. If the gilded cage was now open and the Wolves were to close in on Atenulf, then clearly they had to get out of here, somehow. They could not break down the walls or door, the ceiling and floor were solid. Thus, the only way they were getting out was when the door was opened, and whenever that happened they were confronted with plenty of guards.

They would have to surprise and overwhelm those guards. That was all there was to it. Soon, the evening meal would be brought. Yet more bread and broth. Their water bucket would be refilled. A couple of servants would do this, while armed men watched on from outside the door. The prisoners would have to pull the servants aside and make it out of the door before it could be closed, and then they would be free to deal with the guards. That would be a hard fight.

After hours of thought, Halfdan could see no alternative. Gunnhild had said she would save them somehow, but she had suggested that she would have to defy fate to even try. She could not be sure. And if they were defying fate, then fate and the gods were against them now, which meant they had to fight for themselves, for no one else would do it. Perhaps in doing so, he could save Gunnhild from her own problem? Finally, he took a breath, straightened, and laid out his plan, such as it was, for the others.

Bjorn, of course, was all for it. 'I cannot understand why we have not tried to break their heads before,' he grunted. 'We could have been out of here days ago.'

'You are unarmed,' Fulk noted.

'You're blind, then,' Bjorn snorted, clenching his fists. 'Once, I pulled a man's spine from his body with one hand.'

'No you didn't, you lying shit,' Ulfr said, laughing hollowly.

Bjorn turned on him, eyes slitted. 'One more comment from you, bearded dwarf, and I'll show everyone what *your* spine looks like.'

'I fear we are being sidetracked,' Fulk said with strained patience.

Halfdan nodded. Ulfr was for it, and Farlof and Sveinn, the remaining Varangians, could see no feasible alternative. As for the Normans, both consented that it was better to at least try, and die in the attempt, than to submit and live or die at the whim of the lord of Acerenza. It was when he came to Gunnhild that Halfdan found himself up against a wall of ice.

'You are supposed to be the one with Loki cunning,' she said. 'You are the jarl, whose plans and whose luck see us from disaster to triumph. Yet where is the wisdom in this? The chances of us overcoming the guards are minimal. And what then, if we somehow succeed? We are in a courtyard held by the enemy, filled with his men. Around that courtyard are high walls. And outside those is a city filled with the enemy, surrounded by more walls. What do you hope to achieve?'

Halfdan turned on her. 'I am not challenging your words, Gunnhild. You tell us we'll live, but not why or how, that you will see to it even if it means defying the Norns. What if this is what the Norns have for us? What if this is our escape? You have seen what will be, but unless you explain *how* that will come to be, it is down to us to make it happen. You say I should use my cunning, but there is no other way, Gunnhild. I have pondered on this for all these hours past, and there is no alternative.'

'Then be patient. Trust in the weaving. Trust in the goddess.'

'We have to try *something*, Gunnhild. This might be what Freyja wants us to do.'

Just then they heard noises outside – clattering and footsteps in the passage. The meal was coming. Halfdan turned to Gunnhild. 'You want no part in this?'

'I will wait.'

'You will not lend your spear to our struggle?'

'No.'

'Then give me my sword.'

'No.'

The footsteps were getting close now, settling outside the door.

'Gunnhild, give me my sword.'

'No. If I give you your sword, when you fail you will also lose your sword.'

'Gah!' he hissed in frustration. She was being obstinate. This was an odd echo of that time in Miklagarðr, when the two of them last came to odds. He'd known there was no way to leave the city, and yet she'd insisted it be done. Now she insisted he wait, passing up their only opportunity. For one brief moment, he even considered trying to wrestle his sword from her, though that would not only mean turning against her, which he was loath to do, but also rummaging in her skirts to find the hidden blade, which he could not imagine going down well.

Giving up on the notion, knowing that time was up, instead he hurried across the room, gesturing with pointed fingers to get everyone into place. Near the door, he bent and picked up the solid wooden bucket that still contained a couple of inches of tepid water. Standing beside the door, he pressed his back against the wall.

The door was unlocked noisily and then opened, revealing the usual tableau: two servants, one with a bucket of water to exchange, the other with a platter of bread and a large bowl of broth to share, and an array of armed men in the corridor behind them.

Halfdan swung. The water pail struck the servant bringing its replacement in the face with a crunch, sending him flying back into the passage. Before Halfdan could follow up, though, a second attack occurred. He'd not seen Bjorn stoop and pick up the only other missile in the room, and so shock tore through him as the slop bucket whirred past his head, spilling piss and shit in its wake, and slammed into the soldiers outside.

Recovering, and trying not to breathe in the stench that now filled the doorway, Halfdan leapt.

Ulfr was already on the other servant, bread from the platter now wheeling through the air, broth falling to add to the unpleasant slick across the straw-covered floor. Halfdan barrelled past them, stepping over the man he'd hit with the bucket and throwing himself at the soldiers. He had a vague sensation of the others following, but he concentrated on taking down men as fast and efficiently as possible, grabbing the first man's sword arm so that he could not bring the weapon to bear while he slammed his forehead into the man's face. He felt his scalp cut by the edge of his opponent's helmet, but at least there was no nose guard on this one. While he sustained a cut, the damage he inflicted upon the soldier's face was terrible.

He moved on to a second man and Ulfr was beside him now, both of them laying into Acerenza's men. Behind, he could hear the strange combination of Bjorn bellowing the name of Thor as he battered a man into unconsciousness, and Fulk chanting something in what Halfdan recognised as Latin, though he understood none of it. The jarl's world became a mass of armour, weapons, arms and heads; pulling, punching, heaving, stamping. He felt blows landing on him time and again, each threatening a terrible ache in the coming days, yet none of them cutting into his flesh. As guards fell, so the prisoners swept up the discarded weapons.

Suddenly, he could see only one guard between him and the rectangle of sunlight that marked the exit to the courtyard. He and Ulfr hit the man together, driving him back against the wall and ripping the breath from him, and then, with a feeling of triumphant exultation, they were in the courtyard, spilling out of the door.

The first arrow carved a painful hot line across his bicep before clattering into the wall next to the door. The second thudded into Ulfr's shoulder, spinning him and sending him to the ground. Halfdan skittered to a halt on the gravel surface of the courtyard. A squad of soldiers stood facing them, shields locked in a line, swords or spears out ready. On the walls behind them, half a dozen archers stood with bows trained on the escapees, two of them already reloading, drawing arrows from quivers and nocking them ready for a second shot.

It was over; Halfdan knew that instantly. Even if they managed to break the shield wall, which would cost lives, the archers would kill them where they stood, and all this before they could even hope to reach the gate that led out to the city, which was resolutely shut and held by more men.

Bjorn came out behind him now, howling curses and growling like the bear for which he was named. He, too, skidded to a stop, the hopelessness of the situation filtering even through Bjorn's brain. In moments, the others emerged at a run, halting sharply at the sight of certain death awaiting them. The Wolves and their diminished Norman allies stood in silence, all jubilant hope draining from them as they eyed the lines of men.

'So,' an officer said, stepping out into the open, 'the lord's noted cousin has thrown in his lot with the godless heathens. I doubt milord Acerenza will extend the offer of a peaceful retirement a second time.'

Halfdan winced. He had no idea what a life in a Christian monastery might have been like, but compared with the edge of a blade to the neck it was hard to imagine it being worse. Their failed attempt had likely cost Fulk and his men that option. Acerenza would feel quite justified now in consigning them all to the executioner, which would neatly solve his problem of witnesses.

'Back, all of you. Back in the room, and be grateful I don't have you all cut down where you stand. There will be no more deliveries of food. You will not need them now anyway, I fear.'

At gestures from the armed soldiers, Halfdan and the others returned despondently to the darkened doorway and shuffled past the bruised and injured soldiers they had recently overcome, enduring a few revenge punches and kicks as they passed. They filed their way across the grimy, ordure-coated floor of the doorway, into the chamber that had been their home for days now, and looked like being the last one they would ever have.

As the door was slammed shut behind them, Halfdan sighed. 'Go on.'

'I need not tell you how foolish that was,' Gunnhild hissed. 'You already know. At least I still have your sword.'

He nodded dismally. He never learned, it seemed. He'd told himself again and again to trust this woman, who had never yet steered him wrong, had promised himself never to repeat the mistakes of Miklagarðr. Yet the frustration of being trapped and helpless had driven him to doing just that. Now, all he could do was trust to luck and to Gunnhild's judgement. Would the gods feel inclined to help?

'It's a shame we won't get another food visitation,' Fulk said at length.

Halfdan frowned at the strange statement. 'Yes,' was all he could think of to reply.

'No,' the Norman said. 'What I mean is that they wouldn't expect the same thing twice in a row.'

'That is because doing so would display a degree of foolishness I would hope you had all grown out of,' Gunnhild said, her tone that of a disapproving teacher. 'Learn from your mistakes.'

They lapsed into a strange silence again – Gunnhild concentrating on dealing with Ulfr's arrow wound as best she could – and remained that way as the faint glow of day faded around the doorframe. Only darkness remained, in which they sat, quiet and dejected. Time wore on, with the sense of hopelessness returning to fill the dark with shadows of foreboding. It seemed unlikely that their incarceration would last beyond the next day and night. The lord of Acerenza would need that time to make the arrangements, if the executions were to include a fire at the stake and horses pulling a man apart. Doubtless there would also be an audience. Such executions were ever the stuff of gruesome social spectacle.

The day after that they would all die, even the Normans who had originally been offered an alternative. Of that there seemed little doubt. There was no way out.

Halfdan's eyes slid to where he knew Ulfr to be sitting. The cut on his arm was little more than a scratch, but Ulfr's wound was far worse and could easily kill a man, either from the arrow puncturing his lung, or slow rot. The former had not happened and Ulfr had grunted angrily and waved away the concerns of the others, but Halfdan had also seen the tears in the corners of the man's eyes and heard the hiss of discomfort as he sank to his backside on the floor. Gunnhild had somehow managed to pull out the arrow intact, head and all, drawing small yelps of pain from her patient, and had then bound the wound. Without the usual remedies to hand, she had fed Ulfr something Halfdan had not seen, but from the way the man's eyes, gleaming in the last of the light, began to dance as he chuckled to himself, Halfdan suspected she had given him just a little of the magical compound she so coveted.

It came as a surprise to all when they heard footsteps out in the corridor. They all flinched and, though they could not see it in the darkness, Halfdan knew they were all looking at one another. They were to have no more meals, and the slop bucket had not been returned, so it was unlikely this was one of their regular visitors. There seemed no other possibility, then, than this being it. Acerenza was sending for them to lead them to their deaths.

Even in the dark, the occupants of the room rose and prepared. There would be a fight. When death was the order of the day, why worry about surviving long enough to be beheaded?

There was a clunk and a rattle. The door opened slowly and Halfdan took in the scene in the corridor. Three soldiers blocked the way down the passage, shields up and spears out, ready for anything this time. A torch had been placed in a sconce just a little way down the passageway, and lit the group from the rear. The surprise, though, was the figure standing in front of the soldiers.

A monk in his hooded robe, carrying the nailed god's Holy Book in one hand and a dribbly candle in a small pewter holder in the other. The monk looked up, the hood slipping back a little. He was clean-shaven and looked surprisingly young. He took a few steps forward, gingerly, into the room. The three spear-wielding soldiers came closer, approaching the door, keeping an eye on the prisoners, presumably for the monk's protection.

The monk cleared his throat and spoke in the Norman tongue with an odd, undefinable accent.

'On the orders of Bishop Herluin, and with the agreement of the lord of Acerenza, I am here to seek absolution for each of you. Those who accept Christ into their heart unreservedly and with the whole of their spirit are to be handed to the headsman on the morrow. His Grace has extended the forgiveness of the Church even to the giant, who profaned the sacrament, and even to the witch, for the Lord is a forgiving god, and Christ will accept even the farthest-straying lamb into his flock.'

Ulfr, panting at the effort of stretching, snarled. 'I have given all I will give to you, priest.'

'I beg you to reconsider,' the monk said in an odd tone, and turned to Gunnhild. 'As the greatest sinner of this disreputable gathering, it would set an important precedent if you were to accept absolution. Others would perhaps follow.'

The monk crossed to Gunnhild, who had dropped to a crouch once more. Without a word, he sank to his own haunches opposite her and took a deep breath.

'I have studied the tales of the old North,' he said. 'Surely you can see that your Odin is merely a reflection of Christ on the cross, sacrificing for the good of the world?'

Gunnhild gave a weird smile, made eerie by the candlelight.

'On the contrary, since your Christ came later than the Allfather, you must see that Jesus did nothing but copy Odin's sacrifice. Did he gain the wisdom that Odin claimed, though, I wonder?'

Halfdan stared, brow furrowed at this strange exchange. As he watched, concentrating on them, listening to a series of small verbal lunges and parries, he suddenly realised that something else entirely was happening. Even as they spoke, the monk was making marks in the dirt of the floor with his fingertip, the candle balanced on the bible casting its light up and shrouding that weirdly clandestine activity in deep shadow.

What was the man up to? Who was he to be so engaging with Gunnhild? Halfdan's head crept round to look once more upon the men in the doorway. They could see nothing, were oblivious, the monk with his back to them, the scribbling invisible.

'If I accept your absolution, I turn my back on Freyja. I have done so once and shall never do so again. I am her devoted servant now, my life given to the path of the völva.'

'But you will burn for your reticence.'

'Then I will burn bright, mark this,' she replied. As she spoke, she drew something on the floor with a sense of finality, and then stood, subtly wiping out anything they had drawn with her foot. The monk juggled his bible and candle back into two hands and then climbed to his feet once more. He turned to the others.

'Is this the decision of all here? The giant and the witch are determined to die in an abominable fashion in order to cling to their own demons in defiance of the light of the Lord?'

There was a series of grumbles and curses around the room, and the monk turned with a sigh. For just a moment, a single heartbeat, he paused, facing Halfdan, looking directly at him, eyes meeting eyes. The monk winked, then turned and strode from the room.

Halfdan stared, baffled, as the man left, the door was closed and locked once more and the footsteps receded as the monk and his escort retreated down the corridor.

Then realisation dawned on him, and a grin broke out across his face.

He laughed. He laughed like an idiot.

Of course he'd not known the man. He'd only seen his face, shrouded in the shadow of his hood. And he'd never seen Leif the Teeth without a beard before!

He only stopped laughing because Fulk was shaking him. 'What is it, Halfdan? What have you seen?'

Halfdan turned to look at Gunnhild, who had a knowing smile of her own now. *That* was what the weird exchange had been about. Leif had argued theology with Gunnhild, all the while passing information to her in the dirt of the floor, unseen by the guards in the door. And whatever Gunnhild now knew, it was making her smile a genuine smile.

He turned back to Fulk.

'That monk was a signal. With him, everything is about to change, my friend. The pack is reunited. The wolves are circling, now, and only your Christ can save the magpie.'

And he laughed again.

Chapter 19

The door clunked open.

'Odin's ball-sack,' grumbled Bjorn, blinking at the bright light invading the gloom of their prison.

It had been a tense night and morning. Wherever Leif had come from, and however he'd managed to assume the guise of a monk, he'd given a convincing enough performance that when he left, with a sigh of regret that he had failed to 'bring the heathen into his flock', their captors had taken further offence at their prisoners' crimes. The response had been short and brutal. The guards had come into the cell to land a few solid punches and kicks upon their charges. All in the torso, of course, so that nothing showed when they were brought out for execution. Halfdan and the others had simply taken the punishment. They had seen far worse in their time, each and every one. The guards never touched Gunnhild, though, and seemingly not out of respect of her sex, for they were lavish with their curses and insults in her direction. She just seemed to avoid their attention in that weird Seiðr way of hers.

Gunnhild had been particularly uninformative about her conversation with Leif. Halfdan had waited until the guards had retreated from their door once more, and as soon as he felt they were safe to talk, had scurried over to the völva and asked her what they'd discussed.

That they would not reach the headsman tomorrow was the main thrust of the conversation. Leif had largely been asking who Fulk and the Normans were and whether they could be trusted. Of what was to come, he had said only that they had been in the city for days now, that an execution platform and a stake and timbers had been prepared in the market square. Apparently the populace was abuzz with the news. Pagans and Greeks and a Norman traitor who had attempted to bring the city down were to be killed. Leif had said nothing of the specific plans, apparently, but had warned them to be prepared for anything, and ready to move at a moment's notice.

'How can the three of them break us out of a fortified city?' Halfdan had mused, scratching his beard.

'He says they are not alone. They have friends. Other than that, just be ready.'

So they would be.

Now the cell door was creaking open, the light afforded by the corridor outside crashing blindingly into their world of darkness. Guards lined the corridor, shields up, weapons out, more of them than they had seen on any previous visit, leaving only sufficient space for the captives to pass along the way one at a time. The officer barked at them to come out, and so they did just that, assuming a new order of travel this time. Previously, prepared to rely upon the natural social order of the region, they had been led by Fulk and his man, Gunnhild safely in the centre and the Wolves bringing up the rear.

Now, things were different. Whatever was to happen today, the Wolves were at the heart of it, and so it was now Halfdan who marched out first into that sunlight, Bjorn at his back, ready for anything, eyes darting back and forth, taking in everything. Behind him came Gunnhild, for Halfdan would not contemplate a day like this without her close to hand. Then came Fulk and Marc, with Farlof, Ulfr and Sveinn bringing up the rear. Eight figures now, of the force that had marched north through Italy.

As they reached the courtyard of the castle, they were shuffled around, at the officer's commands. Using the butt-ends of spears, the guards moved them into a column two abreast. The order was not greatly changed, with the exception that

Gunnhild, now the most reviled and distrusted of them all, was brought out front alone, to lead the way – the witch who would be the focus of public bile. Halfdan could imagine what was coming. If this had been planned to be as much public spectacle as demonstration of law, and the city's populace had their blood up, the people would probably be lining the streets with stones, rotten food and worse, to throw at the condemned pagans.

As soon as they were lined up to the satisfaction of the soldiers' leader, the order was given for them to move. Each of their thirty-two guards was heavily armoured in chain and leather, a helm with nose guard and a teardrop-shaped shield in the colours of Acerenza; spear in hand and sword at belt. Every man was clearly chosen for his size and status as a grizzled veteran. They were unlikely to be quickly overcome.

The lord of Acerenza was taking no chances with his prisoners today. As the double-file line of the condemned waited, the soldiers divided into four units of eight men. Two units took the lead, and two the rear, marching their charges toward the gate out into the city. As they approached, the guards on the gate pulled it open, while their comrades atop the walls jeered and cast insults down at the prisoners. It felt faintly ironic to have their prison of so long opened, to see the streets of the city laid before them once more, but to know that they were, if anything, more confined here than they had been in that dark room.

Soon they would enter that wide space in the city's heart, its market stalls replaced by a stake surrounded by faggots and brushwood to burn a witch, two horses and lengths of rope to tear Bjorn apart, and a man with a heavy blade ready to take seven heads for the lord of the city.

As the lead soldiers passed through the gate and the prisoners trudged along in their wake, Halfdan took three calming breaths. He was letting the situation and the uncertainty get to him. Gunnhild, marching along ahead of him, had her head held high and seemed as confident as she had ever been. He felt less so. It was nice to know that their comrades had returned, but even if they had found friends, Halfdan could not quite see how they could achieve what looked to be unachievable.

He turned his face up to the sky, eyes closed, content to shuffle along in step, feeling a light mist on his skin. The sky was clear, the palest of blues – like the rheumy eyes of an old man – and the temperature was moderate, but the morning dew had been heavy and a light residue of it remained in the air to remind them that the summer was coming to a close and the year marching on toward winter. The thought made Halfdan oddly homesick, remembering the snowy winters of his childhood: cracking the ice on ponds to seek the fish in the deeps, stamping into a hut in thick furs and shrugging off a mantle of white to warm by a roaring fire.

If they survived this day, he would see that they took whatever gold they could find and then began to move north once more. He had had enough of this hot, troublesome southern world. What was the point of having great, song-worthy adventures to fill the tales of skalds if you could not return home to hear them sung?

He opened his eyes. Just for a moment, he spotted two tiny black shapes high in that pale blue. He blinked and they were gone, but he would have given his oath on a stone of Odin that they had been there and were no figment of his battered imagination. The ravens of the Allfather had been watching. Something about that gave him heart, brought a more confident smile to his face, which he hurriedly pushed away. The last thing he wanted was to give their guards a hint that anything had changed. He forced his expression back into one of glum acceptance and lowered his gaze, now enjoying that slight dampness to the air.

He looked ahead as they emerged from the gate. Sure enough, the citizens of Acerenza had left their houses and lined the street, waiting, rotten food in hand to pelt these pagans and their demonic witch-queen. It seemed unlikely, however, that the crowd would be allowed to have their fun. The sixteen men leading them split once more into two units, eight of them moving to walk alongside them on their left, and the rearguard did the same, sending eight forward to protect the right. They were boxed in. Acerenza was determined there would be no trouble, no doubt spurred on by the memory of their attempted flight the previous day.

The waiting citizens sagged a little, realising they would find it difficult to cast their stinking missiles at the pagans without hitting a guard, which might have painful consequences. The entire column turned and marched across the open space, momentarily heading toward the city gate where they had first entered. Halfdan glanced that way and noted more of the citizens of Acerenza gathered in the open there, watching the spectacle, while women dallied with the soldiers at the gate.

Halfdan blinked. Just for a moment, he could have sworn one of those women was Anna. He would have liked to have studied the group better, to confirm his suspicion, but then they turned and marched toward the main street that led all the way to the market square, and he dared not crane to look over his shoulder. If that had been Anna, and she *was* accompanied by other friends, the last thing he should do was to draw attention to them.

Unable to see clearly ahead, past Gunnhild and the eight men of their escort vanguard, Halfdan was somewhat surprised when the column came to a sudden halt with a bark of irritation from the leader. As their escort shuffled, two of them stepping out ahead, the ranks thinned enough for Halfdan to crane and peer over Gunnhild's shoulder.

The road was blocked. A wagon's wheel had broken and the vehicle sat at a slant toward one corner, its contents – what appeared to be the bulk of a local farm's produce – had spilled out and filled what was left of the street. A second vehicle in similar disarray sat beyond it on its side, seemingly the result of a collision. A carter was busy arguing with two men in the street, gesticulating this way and that angrily, as the nag that had pulled the cart, freed of its traces, busily ate as much of the produce as possible while filling the street with dung. A small crowd had gathered around the mess.

The officer leading their escort, having marched forward with one of his men, began haranguing the arguing men, demanding that they clear the blockage instantly.

'Oh yeah?' snapped the carter, turning, furious. 'And who's going to pay me for my lost goods?'

'I don't care,' shouted the officer, 'just move it.'

'Fuck off,' the man replied, and the men with whom he'd been quarrelling said something that must have escalated the situation, for the carter turned puce and spun, landing a punch that sent one of the two men reeling. He tripped over fallen fruit and landed heavily on his backside in a pile of horse dung. Just as it looked as though the chaos might be contained by the guards, a young opportunist swept up a collection of fallen food from the ground on the other side of the street and made to run. A concerned citizen, caring little for the angry carter but unwilling to let such blatant crime pass, lunged and grabbed the scallywag, giving him a hefty clout around the ear. The boy kicked his captor in the shin and the man let go, crying out, only for the thief to be grabbed by two more people.

The officer, Halfdan was sure, was now regretting his assignment for the day, as a small army of angry people bore down on him. The carter was demanding that the man he'd punched be made to pay for the lost produce, because it was his vehicle that had emerged at pace from a side alley and caused the accident, while that man was adamant that the carter be arrested for assaulting an innocent citizen. At the same time, a small crowd was calling for the officer to deal with the larcenous boy, while the thief was busy kicking them. Around them all, the crowd in the street surged with noise, enjoying this spectacle at least as much as they would have the executions.

The officer began to argue with the people, but it was clear that he was fighting the first properly losing battle of his career.

He was being bombarded with demands and Halfdan fought down a chuckle as the man actually drew his sword and began threatening the citizens, as he extricated himself from what was beginning to look more and more like an angry mob. Certainly, the man's chances of getting through the street with his column of prisoners without calling out half the city garrison and spending an hour arresting people and moving broken vehicles and spillages, were next to none.

With a frustrated and angry tone, the officer ordered the column back the way they'd come. It would have been too much trouble to rearrange the order of the prisoners and so now they were in reverse – Ulfr leading them with Sveinn, while Gunnhild brought up the rear. The soldiers simply turned around, remaining in place, and the officer hurried past them all, joining the vanguard, which had formerly been their rear-guard.

In moments they were back in that open space before the gate. This time, Halfdan paid attention to the crowd. The chaos in the main street could not be an accident. While it seemed so perfectly normal, its timing was too fortuitous to be truly innocent. He'd not recognised anyone involved, but that it had nothing to do with Leif's plan seemed too hard to believe. Now, as his eyes played across the scene by the gate, his suspicions deepened. While he only recognised Anna among those men and women, she seemed to know the other woman who was similarly fawning over one of the guards – a dark-haired woman in a colourful dress. And there was something about the men there. They didn't stand out in any obvious way, and yet had that strange energy of a hunter eyeing the deer and taking the final breath before the shot.

Moments later they were turning into one of the other streets, one that Halfdan remembered vaguely from their various escapades in the city. This one was considerably narrower than the main street to the market, running more or less parallel to it, but not lined with waiting crowds.

In fact, the inhabitants they could see appeared to be the usual smattering of city life. A drunk or a beggar, it was hard to tell which, sat leaning against a house wall. Two women stood outside a doorway, talking. A little further along, a row of houses was having its roof re-tiled, the entire frontage covered with timber scaffolding, workers laughing and traipsing along the vertiginous planks. It was all so ordinary.

As they moved into the street past the beggar, who did not even twitch, their escort reorganised themselves once more. Thanks to the scaffolding, the alley was only wide enough for two abreast. The guards pulled out to fore and aft in groups of sixteen, alert now, since they were no longer marching alongside the prisoners. Their swords and spears were out, waiting to jab at anyone who tried to step out from the line.

Halfdan could feel it now. Something was imminent. Even without warning, he could sense the change in the air. Gunnhild showed no sign of noticing it, which was more telling than anything, since all of them were feeling it, that strange prickling of the skin when the tension mounted. She was playing it deliberately calm.

Halfdan half expected the beggar to look up and wink as they passed and felt slightly deflated when all the man did was hiccup and dribble onto his knees. His eyes locked on the two women. He'd seen Anna and someone who had to be a friend of hers at the gate. Perhaps there were more? But he didn't recognise either of them, and once again he felt the excitement fall away as the pair threw a look of disgust his way, confirming their true nature as citizens of Acerenza.

The workmen, then? Those half-dozen men ferrying tiles up three levels of scaffolding and resetting them upon the roofs above? Once again, he could not see a face he knew. They simply worked on.

The move came very suddenly and very unexpectedly. One moment the workmen were laughing and busy, labourers about their business. The next there were twice as many of them, spread across the scaffolding and the roofs of three houses, and their focus had shifted.

The guards below knew of nothing wrong until it was too late. Four of the men had picked up buckets from their eyries and upended them into the street. Halfdan saw the two ahead hit home, the buckets' black contents spilling across the sixteen soldiers leading them, and while he did not have the leisure to turn back and look, he was sure the same had happened to their rearguard. Even as the dark liquid hit, spattering and coating them, new figures had emerged from windows onto the scaffolding, carrying burning torches.

The officer at the fore was yelling suddenly, orders spilling from his mouth in desperation, but another voice cut over his and Halfdan looked up to see Ketil leaning out over the street, looking down at the soldiers. His face was strange, deformed, but it was definitely Ketil.

'Lay down your weapons,' demanded the Icelander.

The officer continued to issue commands, but his men were paying significantly more attention to their attackers, for they had come to the same realisation as Halfdan. There was a new smell in the street, and it was unmistakable – the acrid, tarry scent of pitch. Those buckets had been filled with it. This fact had connected in the minds of the soldiers with the burning torches being wielded on the scaffolding. If even one of those fell, they would go up in flames in moments.

A number of swords and shields clattered to the cobbles as men looked around. The soldiers were looking for any way to make a break for it, but they were in a narrow enough street, with few enough doors, that there were no realistic opportunities. Their only chance was to do as they were told.

'I served in the Varangian Guard in Constantinople,' Ketil told them from the scaffold. 'I saw Greek fire at work. It burns even on water. It can't be put out. It sticks like shit and burns through the flesh to the very bone. Even as you crisp it will continue to eat you. Pitch is not quite as bad, but it's similar enough that I'm sure you can imagine it will make this a very bad day for you if you don't comply. *Drop. Your. Weapons.*'

Everyone did just that, fear rippling through the soldiers. Their officer was the last to let his sword fall.

'You'll never get out of the city,' he called.

'I think you're wrong. We have the Loki-born back now. With Leif's mind and Halfdan's luck, nothing will hold us.'

The Rus appeared, looking over the edge of the scaffolding.

'The door,' he said, looking at Halfdan and pointing directly below him. Halfdan followed the gesture to see that a door had opened into one of the houses covered in scaffolding. Even as he began to move, Gunnhild had produced his sword from somewhere and handed it to him. Feeling complete once more, blade in hand, Halfdan ushered the others in through the door as the pitch-coated soldiers watched helplessly.

It came as something of a surprise when Ketil gave a snort and tossed a burning torch. The vanguard burst into flame in an instant, burning droplets splashing from those who'd been struck by the torch only to ignite the others nearby. A cacophony of screams arose in an instant, the alley enveloped in a golden inferno as flesh melted and crisped among the agonised soldiers. Halfdan shuddered at so many memories of fire.

'What in God's name?' came an incredulous call from above, in Leif's unmistakable voice.

'Fuck 'em,' Ketil replied, and in a heartbeat a second torch had ignited the rearguard even as they tried to run. More torches followed and even a flaming arrow, which caught one man trying to make a break for it ahead of the rest.

Halfdan looked back down the street. They were out of sight of both fortress and city gate. The two women had disappeared, presumably fleeing when the trouble began, and the drunk had yet to wake up. Ketil and Leif had done it. They had escaped, at least into the city.

With just a last look and a wave of nausea at the sight of the human infernos around the street, the sound of screaming and spitting and hissing meat, Halfdan ducked into the door in the wake of the others, shutting it behind him.

'This way,' someone ahead called in Greek, a development that took him by surprise as much as anything today. They were herded through doorways and rooms by men in drab and uninteresting clothes, but whose skin bore the mute evidence of a lifetime of war. As they moved, men were pounding down a staircase to join them, having left the scaffolding above. Ketil appeared, followed by an irate Rus who was calling him a monster, which clearly did not bother the Icelander one iota. Behind them came others, including a man with a bow over his shoulder and a quiver at his side.

Halfdan marvelled. It appeared that Ketil had brought a small army with him.

Within heartbeats, they were out of another house and into another alley parallel to the one they had left, but closer to the city walls and even narrower, barely wide enough for two men to walk abreast. As they moved, Ketil shoved his way to the front and gestured to Halfdan. 'Come on. We only have a short time before the city responds.'

With that, Ketil was moving, deliberately using only a half-stride to allow the others to keep pace, heading back toward the city gate.

'How...?' Halfdan began, but Ketil shook his head.

'Now isn't the time. Wait 'til we're safe.'

'How will we get out?'

'It's taken care of.'

Mere moments later, they were at the end of that alley, where it met the city walls. Ketil quickly glanced left, confirming that no danger awaited them there, and then turned right and ran along the walls in the direction of the gate.

'We'll be in full view of the fortress when we get into the open,' Halfdan panted as they ran, desperate men behind them.

'This was never going to be a secret,' Ketil answered. 'We're relying on surprise and speed.'

Keeping pace with Ketil was easy when he reined in his speed and the adrenaline lent by the sudden freedom spurred them on. They approached the main gate before Halfdan had time to worry about what came next. Even as they ran, Halfdan saw their escape being made good. The two women he had seen by the gate earlier suddenly broke off their casual conversation and stepped in close to the guards, knives lancing out from some hidden place and punching into the men's necks, spraying blood and felling them in an instant. There were other soldiers there too, four of them, but even as they reacted, they were being mobbed by the citizens gathered there, who had also produced hidden blades.

The alarm went up at the fortress, the men on those walls shouting and pointing, and it did not take long for a bell to begin its urgent tolling. But it was all so unexpected, such a surprise, that it would take time for the garrison to react. Indeed, they had not even managed to open the fortress doors by the time the fugitives were in the gatehouse in the city walls.

Anna gave him a fierce grin as she and the unknown woman lifted one end of the heavy bar, one of the men nearby taking the other end and freeing the inner gate so that others could pull it open.

The first layer that stood between them and freedom was hauled back.

'You kill without remorse now?' Gunnhild murmured to Anna as they met.

'I learned many things from you,' Anna replied archly, waving her on.

'Run fast,' was Ketil's advice as they hurtled into the gateway. Ahead, two of the men had already run the gauntlet of the gatehouse and had begun to open the outer gate. Stones were beginning to pound down between them from the murder holes above, just as they had in that dreadful trap when Halfdan had first arrived at Acerenza, but they were fewer and more sporadic. The men on the ramparts above had been taken by surprise, and few had managed to get to the waiting baskets of rocks.

Still, as Halfdan hurtled through the dark passageway with his arms crossed above his head, sword still in hand, protecting his skull from missiles, one of the men he didn't know was struck in the face, his visage mashed by the heavy rock as he fell forward to the ground, shaking and screaming.

Halfdan had rarely felt relief on the scale he experienced as he emerged onto the sloping road outside the walls of Acerenza. It was not over yet, though. Cries told him plainly that others had fallen to the rocks in the gate tunnel. Ketil pulled ahead now, jamming two fingers into his mouth and issuing a piercing whistle. To Halfdan's further amazement, another small group of men a little way down the slope emerged, leading a number of horses.

'We'll have to double up,' Ketil told him. 'We only have so many horses.'

Halfdan gave a half-mad, disbelieving laugh. Next to him, another man with the swarthy skintone of a Greek gave a similar laugh and then fell with a scream, an arrow sprouting from his neck. As he ran, Halfdan turned to look back. Three or four figures had appeared atop the gate, nocking and loosing arrows. But they would be lucky to hit anyone, for the escapees were clear now, running into the wilderness outside the city, making for that gathering of horses.

As he reached them, Halfdan grasped a set of reins, pulled himself up into the saddle and looked back up the slope. Gunnhild, Ulfr, Leif, Anna, Bjorn and Farlof were with them, and he could see Marc helping a dazed Fulk down the slope among the last of them. Others, too, but most important to Halfdan, his friends had made it.

As they all mounted, most of the horses weighed down by two riders, Halfdan smiled at Bjorn, who had a face like thunder and was complaining to Leif that he'd seen thirty men die and hadn't even had the chance to punch one of them.

Ketil turned and waved, and the fugitives began to ride, as fast as they dared with such weight on each beast. As they reached the lower slopes, following Ketil's lead, Halfdan turned to look back up at the city. He had absolutely no doubt someone was coming after them, but it would take time to produce and saddle sufficient horses to chase them down, and every heartbeat was giving the fugitives more of a lead, carrying them further from trouble and increasing their chances of survival.

Before he knew it, they were skittering with some care down a slope within the enfolding safety of a small woodland, and entering a long, shallow defile that would run with icy waters in the winter, but was now just dry and rocky. On they rode, taking turns here and there at Ketil's whim, until finally the Icelander held up a hand and slowed his mount.

A small collection of huts sat in a clearing among the trees, a narrow trail leading in from their escape route, and out again at the far side. The huge stacks of tree trunks scattered around the place confirmed its nature as a logging camp.

Handing his reins to one of the others, Ketil stamped life into his feet as he looked up at Halfdan. The jarl shivered at the sight of his old friend. In all the panic and activity, he'd not yet had a good look at the man's face, but now he saw it clear. Ketil had suffered the most appalling injury, one side of his face ruined, one eye socket hollow and gruesome. It was unpleasant to look at, but Halfdan made himself do it. More than once he had cursed Ketil for abandoning them, but it appeared not all had gone well for him either. The Loki-serpent on his arm itched and for an odd moment, he felt the presence of Odin – the Allfather, the grey wanderer with his one eye, the other piercing, shrewd.

He shivered again, but this time with the presence of power.

'How did you find us, Ketil, and who are all these people?'

The man grinned. 'I'll tell you in a bit, when we're settled and I have lookouts set. I don't think they'll find us here, but I want to be sure. This place is safe. The woodsmen... let's just say they have no use for their camp anymore.'

Halfdan let out an explosive breath. His doubts evaporated. Ketil was back. The wolf pack was whole again. 'We have much to catch up on, but I think we might want to do it fast.'

'Oh?'

'There's a man in that city with a king's ransom in gold, and now that we're free and the secret is out, he can't stay in Acerenza. Atenulf and his gold will be on the move within the day.'

Chapter 20

'Who are all these people?' Halfdan murmured, glancing out of the window at the activity in the logging camp. He took a small pull of wine from the cup before him. He kept having to give Ketil strange sidelong looks, because locking him in a gaze, eye to empty socket, was entirely unnerving.

'I have eight solid Varangians who remain from a unit of fifty Maniakes gave me on the march east. They're Christians, but they're good men in a fight. They're veterans of Sicily, Italy and service in Miklagarðr, and they have good northern ice in their blood. They were a bit battered after the fight at Thessalonika, but they're just about healed and strong again now.'

'Thessalonika?'

Ketil nodded and drank some wine of his own. 'Maniakes marched his army east toward the capital, and the emperor sent an army westward to meet him. We'd beaten every Byzantine force we met until we came to this place called Thessalonika in Greekland. We met the imperial army there and I tell you this, Halfdan, but the Allfather will be proud of us. We were winning. We had won, I reckon, but Maniakes was wounded somewhere in the days before, and in the middle of the battle he fell from his horse and was killed. Our army went to pieces and ran.'

Halfdan nodded. Somehow, he'd not believed that Maniakes would bring down the emperor. In fact, he was surprised and impressed they'd got that far. 'And Thessalonika is where you...?' He wagged a finger at Ketil's face.

'Pretty, isn't it?' the Icelander grinned, darkly. The effect was terrifying, and Halfdan shuddered as the muscles pulled at the scarred flesh around the empty eye, distorting it. 'I had to give an eye for wisdom, just like the Allfather, but at least *I* didn't have to hang on a tree.'

'So you, Leif and Anna managed to get away from the battle to safety, along with these eight Varangians.'

'Yes. The emperor's men were hunting down the survivors and by the time we managed to get somewhere safe, we'd picked up another nineteen regulars from Maniakes's infantry who'd fled the field. They've been with us ever since Thessalonika and I think any loyalty they had to the empire is long gone. They think they're wolves of the North now. They're even trying to learn the northern tongue and growing beards in imitation of their comrades. It's weird. But I've come to trust them.'

Halfdan nodded. The Wolves may be a pack once more, but what a weird pack they were. The friends who had always led were together again, but now they had Greeks, Varangians and even Normans among them. Along with Fulk and Marc, they would number thirty-eight. He frowned. That didn't account for everyone he'd seen as they settled into the logging camp.

His gaze returned to the window, to where Anna and the dark-haired woman that had been with her at the gate seemed to be having an argument.

'Tell me about the others.'

'We managed to get to the coast and secure passage to Bari, but we ended up off-course and sailing into a place called Barletta, which had just been taken off the empire by Normans. It was there we picked up our first clue about you, and the cost of that was helping a collection of Greek fugitives get out of the city. That was easy enough, and most of them went straight to Bari with their nailed-god priest, but three of them decided they would come with us.'

He took another sip of his drink. 'Cassandra – she's the black-haired wench who will not take no for an answer – and

Anna did not get on well at first, then the next thing I know they're close as sisters, like they've known each other all their lives. I think perhaps they are too alike to sit comfortably side by side. But Anna's herb-learning has been more than useful since the war,' he admitted, reaching up to touch his ruined face. 'And Cassandra? Well, for a woman, and a Greek one at that, she's not frightened to bear a blade, I can tell you. Cassandra came with us, and her uncle, a blacksmith, too. The other one is Florian. He's a hunter who's wanted by the Byzantine authorities and felt he might find life easier with us.'

'A blacksmith?' They turned to see Gunnhild in the doorway. She moved so subtly he wondered how long she'd been standing there.

'A master, from what I understand.'

She nodded, smiled, and slipped away without further explanation.

Halfdan thought back over their last moment of conversation before the interruption. That was it: the archer, the woman and the man with massive arms he'd seen just now. That seemed about right. Forty-one, and thirty-eight of them men. Bearing in mind that no jarl would ask the women to row, that was just about the crew he'd need for the *Sea Wolf*, if they ever got it back.

'So how did you find us?'

Ketil grinned again and his eyesocket drooped with the muscle movements. 'I knew you'd be looking for fame and riches, so we asked about gold. Sure enough, it was Cassandra who told us about Atenulf the Beneventan and his stolen ransom. It seemed certain that you would be searching for them, so all we had to do was find the gold and we'd find you. We started at Melfi and moved south until we heard that a small group of Varangians had been captured at Acerenza. That could only be you. Three days in the city, and Leif and Florian came up with the idea of how we could get you out. Together, they're an inventive pair.'

'Quite a hirð you've gathered, Ketil.'

The Icelander snorted. 'I've led them as best I could, but one thing I've learned this past month is that I'm no jarl.'

Halfdan nodded. Ketil had changed in their time apart. Not just that disfigurement on his face, and the missing eye, but something deeper, more profound. With some surprise, Halfdan realised that the arrogance that had been such a part of Ketil it largely went unnoticed seemed to have gone. In its place was a calmness, a respect, a considered approach. Perhaps, just like the Allfather, Ketil *had* given his eye for wisdom. He smiled. 'And I've learned that without you and Leif, and Anna, the pack is not complete. I suspect Gunnhild's been trying to show me that from the beginning.'

Ketil reached out and clacked his cup against Halfdan's. '*Skál*,' he grinned.

'Skál.'

'So,' Ketil said after a swig, leaning back in the chair. 'Here we are. I'm back with my jarl. I should give you an oath.'

'Unnecessary. We are Wolves of Odin. Nothing has changed.'

Everything had changed, but only for the better, it seemed.

Halfdan hadn't needed to be so gracious, and the Icelander knew it.

'For now, we are safe,' he said. 'I have six men on watch, covering every feasible approach, but I doubt whether the garrison of Acerenza even knows this place exists. I don't think they'll find us here, but if they do, we'll have plenty of warning. The question is what do we do next? Did you find the gold?'

Halfdan nodded, toying with his wine cup. 'It is out of reach right now. I told you Atenulf was in the city with the treasure. He's on the run and he has prize that half the powers in Italy would like to take. He can't enter the coastal territories of the Italian lords, as it's their money he's running with, and he can't rely on the empire, for it's their money too, in a way, until they get their katepan back. And he can't go north, because this Iron Arm man is also after him. He managed to take refuge in Acerenza by bribing the lord there to give him shelter, but now that *we're* free, news of Atenulf being in the city is out in the world, and so he can stay there no longer.'

'This Acerenza lord might just kill him and take the gold.'

'No,' Halfdan shook his head. 'If he did, he would have to answer to Iron Arm when he was discovered, and I get the impression that would not be a good thing. If he were wise, he would give back the share he took to Atenulf, *then* kill him and hand the gold over to Iron Arm. But from what I've seen of Acerenza, that's unlikely. He's too greedy. He'll want to keep his gold. But that means he needs Atenulf caught, so that any suspicion moves away from Acerenza.'

'So he has to let Atenulf go.'

'Exactly. But he also needs the man to be caught, just by someone else.'

'Odin, but this is as complicated as a day in Miklagarðr.'

'And it gets more complicated than that,' Halfdan said. 'Thinking it through, the only real solution for them is that Atenulf has to leave with his gold, heading south. He will have to leave Italy to survive, but he cannot rely on the western ports under Beneventan or Salernian control. And the Byzantine ports, in theory, will be closed to him.'

He stood and crossed to the door, waving. A moment later, Fulk strode in and took a seat at the table with them, pouring himself a drink. 'What?'

'If a man wanted to leave Italy and he couldn't go north, or leave through a Byzantine port or one of the Italian lords' cities, how would he do it?'

Fulk gave an odd smile. 'Atenulf. Yes, I've been thinking on that. There are a few smaller ports, down in the far tip of the peninsula, that are nominally under Byzantine control but are more or less independent, with no Greek garrison. If a man wanted to slip away from Italy unnoticed, that would be the most obvious place.'

Ketil grinned. 'So Atenulf will run for these ports and Acerenza will send out messages and get him caught on the way.'

'Not messages, I think,' Fulk said, 'but he will spread a rumour far and fast that Atenulf and the gold have been spotted south of Acerenza on the road to Reggio. That way every minor lord in the south will be looking for him, and he'll never reach the coast. He'll be caught, most of the gold recovered, Iron Arm will be happy, and no one will look to Acerenza for the missing share. All very neat. But the thief won't even get far enough for the southern lords to catch him. We'll get him the moment he's out of sight of Acerenza's walls.'

Ketil, who was clearly as wary of Fulk as the Norman was of him, at least nodded his agreement on this. The two were hungry. Truly Odin's wolves.

Halfdan had been thinking, though, while the two men had been speaking. He'd only met the two lords in the city that one time, during their sentencing, but the jarl fancied himself a good judge of character and he'd quickly formed a solid opinion of both men. Acerenza was greedy but cautious, allowing his peers to lead him at times, as the priest had done during that meeting. That was why Halfdan had calculated the man's plan as he had.

But he had also studied Atenulf as the man had stood nearby. Atenulf was no ally of Acerenza's, lying somewhere between being a partner-in-crime and a prisoner, and he had known it. He had also seen the danger of Halfdan and Fulk surviving, and what that might mean, and had lobbied for their deaths from the outset. Also, whatever deal he had struck with Acerenza, he had managed to keep personal control over the gold in the city, and had his horses and men ready to move at a moment's notice, as they had discovered the day they were caught. That all suggested that Atenulf was a lot more clever than Acerenza gave him credit for and distrusted the Norman intensely.

He cleared his throat as Fulk and Ketil mused over ways they could intercept the thief.

'He won't go for this Reggio place, or any of those safe ports in the south you mentioned.'

'What?' Fulk frowned. 'Why?'

'Because Atenulf is no fool. He will be a step or more ahead of Acerenza. If we, who are new to this land, and have no direct ties to any of this, can see what Acerenza has planned, then be sure the thief knows it just as well. Atenulf must be aware that he will be in danger the moment he leaves the walls; that Acerenza can only keep suspicion away by selling him out.'

'So where does that leave us?' Fulk grumbled.

'Atenulf has to leave, but he cannot simply walk into Acerenza's trap. This is what I would do if I were the thief.' Halfdan leaned forward and started to draw a crude map on the table in the spilled drinks. 'I would go along with Acerenza. I would make it clear that I would take the road to Reggio and that I would embark there and leave Italy. To be certain that Acerenza believed me, I would feign fear of what lay ahead and demand that Acerenza either provide an escort or send out men to be sure the way is clear, which Acerenza will refuse, of course. But it will look as though Atenulf is planning to use that route and has enough faith in Acerenza to ask for aid.'

He drew a line in liquid on the rough wood, leading from Acerenza down to Reggio.

'Yes?' Ketil urged.

'Atenulf will leave as expected,' Halfdan continued. 'I doubt he will be much further than just out of sight of the city when he changes his plan. He will have to be as far away from Reggio and the Reggio road as he can be, in order to avoid the threat of local lords looking for him.'

He now drew a new line, coming out at a tangent from the first not far from Acerenza at the start. This one then turned and ran parallel to the first.

'He will move closer to the coast still held by the Byzantines, where Acerenza's influence will be weakest. That means he will have to embark at one of the ports in the south-east.'

'But they are controlled by the Byzantines,' Ketil said, scrubbing his scalp. 'I saw as much with my own eyes. The main port, where he'd be able to load wagons full of gold and a small armed force, would be Taranto, where I left with Maniakes. Bari is still the centre of imperial power in Italy, but Taranto also has a garrison.'

Halfdan gave a little smile. 'And so no one would think of looking for him leaving there. Don't forget Atenulf has already managed to bribe a Norman lord into sheltering him. You know the Byzantines, after our time in the city. Do you think there's a Byzantine official anywhere in the world who is not for sale for the right price?'

Ketil leaned back, lifting his cup and taking a swig again. 'A Byzantine would sell his own mother for the right price.' He looked across at Fulk, who was frowning, and shrugged. 'Even honour has a price in the empire. Halfdan is right. All he would have to do is wave a bag of coins at the harbourmaster of Taranto and the whole city would look the other way while he loads his gold.'

Fulk still looked unconvinced. 'This is all conjecture. There is no fact or proof in anything you say. It is all constructed carefully on your impressions of two men.'

'Have I steered you wrong before?'

'You got us caught in Acerenza,' the Norman said.

'No. *You* got us caught in Acerenza. Gunnhild warned you that entering the city was dangerous, but you had faith in your faithless cousin and went anyway.'

'You led us in a failed escape.'

'We had little choice but to try, though I should have trusted in Gunnhild and waited for Ketil here to arrive. And we were only caught because *your* man betrayed us. No, I have been right, and if I wavered here and there, it was because I did not listen to Gunnhild sufficiently.'

Ketil tapped the table. 'You have known Halfdan for weeks. I have known him for years. He has the wisdom of Odin and the cunning of Loki. By the time you or I have made a plan, Loki-born here will have talked circles around that plan and tied it in knots. If Halfdan says this is what Atenulf will do, believe me, that is what Atenulf will do.'

'Where, then,' Fulk said, still looking unconvinced, 'do we make our move?'

'It has to be some way south. We want to be far from Acerenza and his influence. We want to make sure all eyes are on the road to Reggio when we take them. Somewhere to the south, but before he reaches Taranto.'

'*If*,' Fulk said, stressing the uncertainty, 'he makes for Taranto, then there is an obvious place.' He leaned forward and dipped a finger in the spilled drink and then used the liquid to daub an area of the wood near the far end of the two routes. 'This region is plagued with mountains and valleys. If he wants to travel with wagons at any speed, and still make for Taranto, he will have to take the road through the flatter lands near Matera.' He changed the line of Halfdan's route slightly, dragging it east, around his dappled highlands. 'He cannot reasonably take a caravan of heavy wagons through the passes to the west, and to the east of Matera, on the way to the coast, is Castellum Unitum, which is one of the strongest imperial fortresses in the region. He wouldn't be safe coming within sight of that. So from Matera he would have to follow the wide valley down to the coast, and then head along it to Taranto. *That* is where we hit him,' he said with more certainty. '*If* your theory is true. And you know why there, don't you, Halfdan of Gotland?'

The jarl peered at the new route between the roughly drawn mountains and the splodge of the Byzantine fortress. His eyes narrowed as he estimated the distances involved, and then a slow smile spread across his face.

'Ginosa.'

'Quite so,' Fulk agreed.

'What is Ginosa?' Ketil asked, chewing his lip, confused by this development.

'Ginosa was Fulk's city. When we first left you on the beach, we went to Ginosa to free Fulk from a Byzantine siege. We've been with him ever since. *We* know Ginosa quite well – and Fulk knows it *very* well. If Atenulf and his men have to pass by Ginosa there will be no better place to take him.'

'Is this our plan, then?' Ketil asked.

Halfdan looked to Fulk, who clearly still had doubts, but who nodded anyway, then back to Ketil. 'This is our plan. The problem we face is one of equipment. Many of us lost weapons and armour and all our goods in Acerenza. If we are to take on Atenulf, regardless of when and where, we will need to re-arm and armour ourselves. And we will need more horses. We really need one each, plus spares as pack animals. And I for one have no silver. All our goods were taken in Acerenza.'

Ketil shrugged. 'We have a few spare weapons and a small fund of gold Leif and I managed to acquire in Dyrrachium. Horses are easy enough to come by, so long as you don't mind paying above the odds for them.'

Halfdan turned to Fulk and pointed at the map on the table. 'If we follow this route, ahead of Atenulf, where will we first find Byzantine territory?'

The Norman peered at the table, scratching his head. 'The borders shift all the time now, but here,' he tapped the map, 'is Montepeloso. That was taken by a Norman force only a year or so ago. Incidentally, it was Atenulf who led the forces and captured the katepan there. Just south of it, Matera is still in Byzantine hands, so it is somewhere between the two places where we will find Byzantine control begins.'

Halfdan pursed his lips. 'All right. We use whatever gold and silver we have to buy horses sufficient for the whole hirð. There are bound to be farms in the area where such a trade can be done without going into the city. Then we move, making sure to stay ahead of Atenulf. As soon as we find a small enough Byzantine patrol or garrison, we take it down. That way we should be able to get the weapons and armour we need. Very well,' he said, leaning back. 'I have another idea.'

They had spent the night at the logging camp, with the watch changing several times to allow plenty of rest. The next morning, the blacksmith, being unknown to anyone in the city and having the accent of an Italian, entered Acerenza and spent several hours in the city. Upon his return, he reported that the guard were on high alert and that the house where Atenulf had been staying was preparing for departure. Fourteen wagons had lined up outside and armed men with horses had gathered. Atenulf was still in Acerenza, but would move within the day.

Armed with this information, the Wolves had broken camp and moved as quickly as they could through the woodlands, led by the hunter, who had spent time scouting the area while they'd planned Halfdan's rescue. They had found the road south from the city – Acerenza now just a grey blur on a hilltop in the distance – and had followed it until it met a larger thoroughfare, running east to west. There they had crossed a ditch filled with stunted trees and undergrowth and found a place on the high ground on the far side, sheltered among more trees, which offered an excellent view of the junction. The majority of the Wolves continued on up the slope for a quarter of a mile until they were out of sight of the city and both roads, while Halfdan, Fulk, Ketil and Gunnhild remained hidden among the trees.

Four hours they waited there, taking turns to watch the road, until finally Gunnhild called them over and the four of them stood, tense, under the trees. They watched a cloud of dust approaching along the road from Acerenza, and Halfdan found himself twitching, rubbing his hands, waiting to see if his appraisal of the situation would be borne out. He felt sure. Gunnhild had agreed with him, and even Ketil had accepted it as fact. That Fulk remained uncertain had begun to gnaw at Halfdan's confidence. What if he *was* wrong? What if Atenulf made straight for Reggio? Then there would be little chance of managing to take him on once he was out of the reach of Acerenza, but before any other lord found him. He rubbed the

Loki serpents on his arm. Was the mark itching or was he just imagining it, forcing an itch with the desperate need to be right?

The junction, the hunter Florian had explained, would be the decider. To the west the route would connect with a major road that would lead south-west, to the very tip of the peninsula and the safe port of Reggio, the route everyone would expect Atenulf to take. To the east, the road passed close to what was still Byzantine territory, and would connect with the route that ran south through Matera and eventually to Taranto.

The four of them watched, silent and alert. The cloud resolved as it approached, into the shapes of a number of armoured horsemen followed by covered wagons, each with its own mounted escort. A man in the colours of Benevento was just visible in the group, surrounded by soldiers and close to the wagons. The caravan slowed as it approached the junction, and Halfdan's level of tension reached a new high.

He fretted. He watched.

The lead riders pulled out onto the road, the first of the wagons following, turning as they emerged…

…to the west.

Halfdan felt his plans crashing down around him. He had been so sure. Why had he? He could feel the irritation and frustration emanating from Fulk beside him as wagon after wagon turned, and the caravan made for the west, heading for the route that would take them close to the coastal domains and toward distant Reggio.

As the last wagon turned and its rearguard followed on, Halfdan sagged.

'Plans,' he chewed angrily, slapping himself in the forehead. 'I made plans. I had it all set out. Atenulf cannot be so stupid as to blunder into Acerenza's trap. I was *sure* he was shrewder than that.'

Fulk took a deep breath. 'We need to change the plan. We need to work out where we can meet them sufficiently far from here to avoid trouble with Acerenza, yet before they fall prey to any lord who knows they're coming.'

'Patience,' Gunnhild said, her voice little more than a whisper.

'What?'

'Watch.'

They gazed off into the distance, toward the city. It took only minutes. Half a dozen riders, dressed in drab and casual clothes for the road, apparently unarmed and unarmoured, reached the junction. They peered off after the cloud of dust to the west and then scattered, riding across country to the south of the caravan, skirting Atenulf's convoy, just out of sight, and riding off to plant the seeds, to spread the tidings that the thief and his gold were heading that way, just as Halfdan had anticipated. Acerenza had done his part. He had taken the gold, freed Atenulf, and his riders were now setting the trap so that some southern lord could gain the glory of capturing the rogue prince of Benevento.

'I think we will find it difficult to spring our own trap before the Normans spring theirs,' Halfdan sighed. 'I was right about Acerenza. I cannot believe I was so wrong about Atenulf. I had him marked as cleverer by far than his host.'

'Patience,' Gunnhild said again, earning her frowns from the other three. She simply continued to watch. As the minutes passed, the cloud of dust that marked the column of wagons and its armoured escort faded further and further into the distance until it was barely visible, the riders sent from Acerenza lost to the horizon, gone ahead to set the trap. The junction was peaceful once more, quiet, the dust settled.

'I don't understand why we wait,' Fulk muttered irritably.

'Nor I,' Halfdan admitted, 'but when Gunnhild tells you to do something, you do it, whether she has seen something walking with the goddess, or is just using her own wit.'

And so, they continue to wait, in silence. Almost an hour had passed when finally, as Halfdan and Fulk had begun a whispered argument about whether they should be leaving or not, Gunnhild shushed them, pointing out from their hidden spot beneath the branches. Scurrying forward with the Norman, Halfdan looked in the direction she was pointing, toward the city, and his eyes widened.

Wagons and horsemen were approaching. They were moving slowly, *very* slowly, which did mean that it would take them some time to get clear of the city, but it also meant that they raised very little dust, and certainly not the telltale cloud that had announced to all and sundry that the last caravan was there.

He boggled as this second column approached the junction. Five wagons. Just five. And an escort of around a dozen men, each wearing a drab riding cloak, but each with a shield slung on his back and a sword at his belt.

'I don't believe it,' Fulk hissed.

'Atenulf,' Halfdan said, a smile creasing his face. He turned to Gunnhild. 'How did you know? The goddess?'

She gave him a withering look. 'I used my eyes and the thing that sits behind them. The first caravan was a decoy. Why else would they be bearing the colours of Benevento? Only a fool would advertise himself so, and as you noted, Atenulf is no fool. But the clearest indication was that there were only nine wagons in that caravan, and we know from the smith's report that fourteen had gathered in the city.'

Ketil laughed. 'He *is* clever. Now Acerenza's men will be concentrating on that road, setting a useless trap, while Atenulf can slip away with a much smaller and less conspicuous group. He has few men, though. We could take him before he gets much further.'

Halfdan shook his head. 'Not so. The wagons are covered. They will be filled with gold, and you can see as much from the way they sag, low between the wheels, pressing on the axles. But I suspect at least four men occupy each wagon. We may number forty-one now, but they could have almost as many, including men hidden in the wagons, and while we are poorly equipped, they will be Atenulf's best, armed for war. An attack now would be far from certain of success. See how the wagons glint with steel and not gold?'

As the wagons turned, catching the sunlight, they could see distinct flashes and glimmers of silver within the shadowed interiors, a suggestion of armoured men inside.

Fulk straightened. 'It is as you said, *Gotlander*. And so we shall do precisely as we planned. The new caravan moves slow to prevent notice, but soon they will be far from Acerenza and they will move faster. We need to cross these hills and get ahead of them, and we need to find horses. Then we ride south.'

Halfdan nodded and rolled his shoulders. Finally, they were free, the Wolves were back together, a king's ransom was rolling toward Ginosa, and they had a plan.

The gold of Atenulf awaited.

Part Six

ᚹᛞᚱᚠᛗᛋ ᛠᚠ ᛠᛞᛁᛏ

Iron and Gold

Chapter 21

'Act natural. You've had a career preparing for that,' Ketil said, speaking out of the corner of his mouth as they climbed the slope. His gaze slid occasionally to the woodlands below, and then back to their destination.

Behind him came the eight Varangians he had served with since the day Maniakes had given him the unit, and behind them fourteen of the nineteen Byzantine infantry who had escaped the field at Thessalonika. The eight Northmen, largely Rus and Svears, were kitted in chain shirts with swords or axes as was their preference. They wore once again the colourful tunics and scarves that had been their choice during service in the imperial guard, and which they had since worn only periodically, when safety allowed. The infantry were once more in their uniform, not worn since the day they crossed the sea back to Italy. The uniforms were crumpled and in poor condition now, but only someone highly observant would notice, and only someone truly bored would care. The five infantrymen who no longer had serviceable uniforms had been left behind with the others. The result was that the twenty-two men climbing the slope – led by the tallest man in Apulia, with a fierce-looking missing eye – would appear at first glance, and even at second, to be a regular unit of Byzantine troops, not a strange sight at all in imperial-controlled south-east Apulia.

Reunited, they had crossed the hill from which they'd observed Atenulf's clever escape, moving at speed to get ahead of the slow and carefully moving wagon train of the thief and his gold. When they rejoined the same road some distance south and east, they had sent Florian, the man most at home in the wilds, back to check on Atenulf. He returned to report that they were perhaps three hours ahead of the wagons. Over the day, that changed as the Wolves managed to make significant gains, having now acquired sufficient horses for all, between a local village and a helpful farmer. They were not the best of horses, but one per man made a difference, even if they were nags.

By the end of the day, they had covered twice the distance of Atenulf's caravan, a fact confirmed by Florian on a second scouting mission. They were half a day ahead, which was comfortable, although a full day would be better. That night they had camped on a hilltop from which they could look back at the small town of Montepeloso, the site of Atenulf's victory and the capture of the katepan that had been the catalyst for this adventure. Somewhere back past that, the thief was camped with his wagons.

The second day they had capitalised on their speed, gaining further. By the time the sun was sliding toward the hills in the west, they presumed they would now be a full day ahead of the thief, and that Atenulf would be camped somewhere close to where the Wolves had spent the previous night.

It was as the golden light began to cast long shadows that they found their first sign of Byzantine control. Ahead, on a hill surrounded by woodland, stood a watchtower, and even from a distance they could see the imperial banners flying. Leif had felt a little uncomfortable at the notion of attacking an outpost of Byzantine soldiers for no other reason than acquiring arms and armour, which showed just how long he had been away from the North. Ketil had told him to grow a pair of balls, in a flat tone, while Bjorn had begun a lively debate about whether a Byzantine would look better headless or with no arms.

The plan was simple enough. The watchtower was designed to send out signals or messages in case of Norman aggression from the north, which would then be passed to the garrison in Matera. If they did not want to bring down upon them the whole force of that city, they needed to crush the tower without a message being sent.

As they entered the woodlands, Halfdan and the others had separated from Ketil's unit and melted away into the woods. Anna, Cassandra and the blacksmith were left to watch over a sizeable corral of horses while Halfdan and the others slipped up the slope between the trees, unseen by the occupants of the watchtower.

While they maintained their stealthy approach, however, Ketil and his men took another tack entirely. Ostensibly Byzantine, they marched up the road directly toward the install-ation.

Now, as they crested the slope and approached the watchtower, he took everything in. The place consisted of a circular palisade wall with fighting platforms at the highest point of the hill. Inside were four buildings, the roofs of which he could see over the edge of the palisade. The snickering of horses suggested more than one beast present inside. The heart of the place, though, was a timber tower, two storeys high, with an iron brazier on a tall stem, filled with brushwood, at its top. The logic of setting a fire atop a wooden structure escaped Ketil, but the fact remained that it was there. A single flame touched to that brazier and the blaze would alert the garrison of Matera.

'Remember,' he said to the others, 'that you are the garrison of a fort from up near Gravina. Just loiter, mingle and spread out around the compound. Don't move until I give the signal.'

There was a low rumble of affirmatives behind and Ketil walked on, satisfied. He had a plan. It felt pretty strange to strategise in such detail, in that he was a man largely given to extemporised action.

'Hold,' came a voice from the platform above the gate. 'Identify yourselves.'

'Tired and hungry,' replied Ketil in north-accented Greek.

'Aren't we all. Who are you?'

'Garrison from up north, past Gravina. We've been relieved and are on our way to Matera, but the sunset caught us by surprise. We thought we had a few more hours yet.'

'You don't expect us to put you up?' came the reply. 'We only have barracks for our own.'

'Just let us camp down inside the palisade. We're far too close to the mercenary bastards up in Montepeloso for comfort.'

'That we are,' agreed the man. There was a moment of debate and a message sent to some officer, and in minutes the gate was opening. Ketil led the men inside and as they passed through the palisade, his one eye roving over everything, he tried to keep his posture as relaxed and normal as possible. He turned to the others. 'Find yourselves some space for the night,' he said, the men falling out with sighs of relief, which sounded a little forced and theatrical to Ketil.

There were maybe a score of men here, two dozen at the most. Two of the four huts were clearly barracks, the third a stable and the latter a smithy from the look of it, with the water butts outside, the heavy chimney and all the soot. A stack of kindling lay by the palisade on the far side from the gate and Ketil spotted a number of barrels of water around, and buckets close by, ready to deal with any conflagration that spread and got out of hand. Three horses, he reckoned, from the size of the stable. Two men stood on top of the tower and torches burned there, partially for light in the coming evening, but also to touch to the brazier in case of trouble. There was a lot to overcome – and quickly – before the signal went out.

As Ketil's men spread out, gradually occupying the entire compound, the officer of the installation emerged from the doorway of the tower, hands clasped importantly behind his back. He was pasty pale, with a neat black beard and a silver diadem holding back his hair, his uniform over-rich and ostentatious. Ketil decided at first sight that the man would be no loss to the world. As that thought passed through, he put on a tense smile and strode over to him.

'I would take it kindly,' the officer said in an imperious tone, 'if your men kept to themselves and tried to stay at the periphery.'

Ketil nodded. 'Thank you for the hospitality. We've had a long and tiring walk, always looking over our shoulders. Which reminds me, can we head up there? I could swear I felt someone following us these last few hours, and there should still be enough light to check the area.'

'If you are being followed, my men will see it.'

'Still, for my own peace of mind,' Ketil persisted. He would have loved to have pulled up the self-important prick on his claim, for his men could not be that observant. They hadn't noticed that the unit now within their defences had lost several members and all the horses they should have spotted on the road to the north.

The officer looked irritated at his word being called into question. He huffed and without actually answering swept a hand toward the darkened doorway, an unspoken invitation. Ketil nodded his thanks and stepped in, ducking his head as he moved inside. The officer followed him.

'You lost your eye in the troubles up north?'

'Iron Arm's archers,' Ketil replied. 'Arrow nearly did for me.'

The man replied with just an impressed silence. Ketil looked around what was clearly the man's office or headquarters – just a chair, a table, two maps and a cupboard. In the corner, a staircase climbed to the next level. With the officer leading, they crossed to the stairs and ascended. The second level was given over to a large table and half a dozen seats. The remnants of a meal lay on the table, making the Icelander's mouth water. They climbed on, past the mess hall and emerged into the temperate late evening air. Ketil looked around as they took the last step. This was not going to be easy. There were two torches, but they were on opposite corners of the tower, as were the two men. Taking both out before the signal could be sent would be hard.

That, of course, was where plans fell down. You were guaranteed that something would go wrong at some point, and then you were back to acting on instinct. He would have to do as much now. Leading the way, he crossed to the northern corner where a guard stood in the golden light of the torch, staring out into the countryside, looking but probably seeing little. Such was the case with men expected to watch for hours on end. Before long they defocused and you could walk an elephant past them without drawing attention.

'Where would you be?' Ketil murmured to himself, putting a hand over his eyes in a somewhat theatrical move. In truth, his eye had swivelled down, looking for any sign of Halfdan and the others at the edge of the woods that stood some twenty feet back from the palisade. He could see nothing. Hopefully they were there and well hidden, not still some way down the slope, struggling with the climb.

'I can see nothing,' the officer said, peering into the distance, standing to Ketil's left, the guard to his right.

'Look. Out there, past the woods,' the Icelander said, pointing.

The officer leaned forward, squinting, hand going up to cover his eyes.

'Now,' bellowed Ketil. His left hand, which had sneaked down behind the man while he looked out, suddenly gripping the officer's sword belt and heaving upward. The man had the chance to utter no more than a surprised 'Urk' as he was pitched up and over the tower's lip, falling two storeys to the hard ground.

'What the—?' began the guard on his other side, but Ketil had already turned, tearing his sax from his belt. The blade slammed into the man's neck, punching through the cartilage, and he tore it to the side with some effort, ripping a jagged line that sprayed warm blood as the man toppled.

Ketil turned again. The other guard was considerably more alert. The moment things had begun to happen, he had leapt for the torch nearby and was now gripping it, raising it as he stepped toward that beacon in the iron brazier. Ketil felt anger rising. He would never reach the man in time.

The guard took another step forward, stretching, ready to push the burning brand into the combustible beacon when he gave a yell. Ketil was running now, but the man was done for already. An arrow stuck out of his back as he lurched and staggered, still gripping the torch, his other hand reaching for the weapon that had impaled him. Before Ketil could reach him, the man took a wrong step in his agony and pitched over the edge, falling with a cry.

Ketil hurried to the parapet, the elation at success falling away as he realised the man with the torch had fallen into the pile of dry cordwood below. Already flames were starting to lick up around him. The Icelander waved to his men, who were busy putting down the garrison, and a couple looked up. He pointed at the stack of wood, and the men burst into fresh activity, grabbing buckets, dipping them in the barrel and hurling them at the growing fire. Ketil hissed irritably. They might contain it. They might not. There was nothing more he could do right now.

As he moved back around the tower, his roving eye caught the rest of the Wolves pouring from the trees now, running for the palisade, and he could see Florian with his bow, lowering it after his shot.

'Arsehole,' Ketil shouted down at the hunter.

The man probably thought he'd done well, stopping the guard lighting the beacon. But the shot had been poorly executed. Ketil was a better shot and he knew it. Had it been him with the bow, he'd have killed the man outright, and the torch would have fallen harmlessly to the tower floor. Ketil felt an odd hollowness, then. How long had it been since he'd held a bow? Not since Miklagarðr, at least. He tried not to think on whether he would ever be able to achieve his legendary good aim again with one of his eyes gone.

Grabbing the torch from the other side, he dropped it to the heavy wooden platform and stamped on it a few times, rolling it around with his foot until it fizzled out and his boot felt uncomfortably warm. At least the flames up here had been extinguished and there was little chance of the beacon being lit. Taking a breath, he hurried over to the edge and looked down. Half a dozen of his men were now pouring bucket after bucket down on the pile of wood and the fire seemed to be almost out. Indeed, as he looked about, it seemed his men had gained control of the compound, few of the enemy living.

A loud splintering sound rent the golden evening, and his head snapped around in time to see the stable door open and a Byzantine emerge on a horse. Ketil's men were taken by surprise and ran to intercept, but the man was already moving, picking up speed. A second rider appeared now, behind him. If they got out and away, they would be in Matera in no time, turning out the garrison, making life hard for the Wolves as they moved south.

He had acted before his mind had actually registered what he was doing, and in that heart-stopping moment, Ketil once more acknowledged that perhaps there was room in the world for a little planning.

He dropped through the air, having hurled himself from the parapet, angling out as much as down, arcing over the drop. Thor and Odin were watching over him this day. He could so easily have hit the ground and broken a number of bones.

Instead, he hit the second rider hard, landing on his shoulders. How it hurt the man, the Icelander could hardly imagine, for it was agonising for Ketil, the air slammed out of his chest, every muscle bruised and strained. As he recovered, as swiftly as he could, free hand grappling for a grip on the rider, sax still in hand, the man similarly began to recover, lurching this way and that in an attempt to shake off Ketil as he hurtled toward the gate in the palisade.

His eye came up over the man's shoulder and he saw the lead rider fall. As the horse passed through the gate, Gunnhild struck from the side, the pointed butt of her staff rammed into his ribs, pulverising his middle, ripping the life from him. The horse barrelled on, with the dying rider on its back, until Halfdan appeared from somewhere and ran at it, grabbing the reins and pulling himself up, pushing the dying soldier from his saddle and then taking his place, reining in the horse and turning it, riding it slowly back toward the compound.

Ketil struggled. He managed to get his sax down to the man's thigh and stabbed deep and hard, his other arm coming up and around the man's neck, anchoring himself in place even as the rider thrashed and jerked, trying to throw him off. The man screamed at the leg wound, but continued trying to dislodge his unwanted passenger.

Ketil's heart froze for just a moment as he once again managed to look over the man's shoulder only to see Leif leap in the way of the charging horse, throwing axe up by the side of his head.

'Oh, shiiii—'

The axe jerked forward, hurled with a deft flick of the wrist. Ketil threw himself clear, rolling with care so as not to impale himself on his own sax. As he tumbled and came up once more, rising to his feet, he turned to see the horse in a heap, Leif's weapon embedded in its head between the eyes. The rider had been thrown clear and was now lying nearby as two men hacked him to pieces with their blades.

He turned, blinking his remaining eye. Leif was wandering over to the horse, where he pulled out his axe with some difficulty.

'We could have used that horse,' Ketil said accusingly.

'You're welcome,' Leif replied, eyebrow arched.

'You could have gone for the rider.'

'Then I might have hit you. I'm starting to wonder whether that would be such a bad thing.'

Ketil gave him a glare, but Leif just snorted and went off in search of someone else to maim. Heaving a sigh of relief, the

Icelander wandered back through the carnage, cleaning his sax and taking in the last stages of the fight as he did so. He smiled to see Bjorn and Ulfr together. They each had hold of one arm of a surviving garrison soldier, arguing over who got to kill him while their prey panicked and struggled. Ulfr must have said something insulting to the big albino, lost beneath their victim's screams, for Bjorn took a step forward and poked the shipwright in the shoulder, where his arrow wound was only a few days old, still bound and healing. Ulfr yelped and let go, cursing as Bjorn whooped in triumph and slung the panicked soldier over his shoulder, walking off to find somewhere to have some fun.

Farlof was walking among the bodies of the fallen, plunging his sax into them whenever he found one not yet dead. Ketil waved to him. 'Make sure not to damage any armour.' Farlof nodded back. Good man, Farlof, for one of Halfdan's new recruits. A proper Northman. A real Wolf of Odin.

He entered the tower again, contemplated the room for a while, wondering whether there was anything worth having there. Deciding not, he climbed to the next floor. He spent a happy ten minutes or so there picking over the remains of dinner, better food by far than any he'd had in weeks. Finally, he located a jug of bitter wine and swiped it, climbing to the tower top. The sun was now little more than a low twinkle on the hill and it took only minutes, as he drank a little of the wine, for that golden orb to sink completely and evening to settle across the world. It was still quite warm and he relaxed, leaning on the parapet and looking south, across the main part of the compound with the buildings, out toward their destination and this place called Ginosa where they would make their stand against Atenulf.

He heard footsteps, but didn't bother moving. There was no one here he felt he needed to guard against. He mentally amended that as Fulk de Courvaudon reached the parapet and leaned on it beside him.

He couldn't say what it was that made him twitch. He was self-aware enough to recognise that it might be tinged with jealousy. Ketil had abandoned his jarl and gone off on an idiot quest to put a giant on a throne and had come thoroughly unstuck as a result. And while he, Leif and Anna had been off in the east chasing smoke, this Norman had become Halfdan's ally, almost a second in command. Though Ketil knew that Gunnhild came above everyone in the pecking order of Halfdan's hirð, if there was a second for the jarl, a right-hand man, Ketil was confident that it should be him. He had been the one with the ship and the crew at the start of all this, after all. And that the Norman lord seemed to have taken that place in his absence irked him.

Then there was the fact that every enemy they had met since landing back in Italy was one of these so-called Normans, from the mouthy fuckers in the taverns of Barletta to the treacherous lord of Acerenza. That Halfdan could put his trust in such a man beggared belief. An unhelpful part of Ketil's mind reminded him that he was as ready as any Northman to go back on his word if the decision carried sufficient reward. He brushed it away. That was the old Ketil.

'Have you given thought to what you will do?' Courvaudon asked as he looked down.

'What?'

'When you have your share of the thief's gold?'

'I shall have my prick gilded,' Ketil grunted. He felt no compunction to play nicely.

The Norman gave a strange snort-chuckle. 'I am trying to persuade Halfdan that the gold can be of more use than as mere treasure.'

'Sounds stupid to me.'

The man chuckled. 'That seems to be what most of you think. But hear me out.'

Ketil turned his one-eyed, shudder-inducing glare on Courvaudon. 'What?'

'William de Hauteville, who they call Iron Arm, rules in Melfi, commanding the council of our lords.'

'Not *my* lords.'

'Granted, but Iron Arm has only been in Italy six years and he has gone from a mercenary captain in service of the Byzantines to being a lord with a domain that covers a huge amount of this peninsula. We men of the North are not easy to bind into service. We like our freedoms, yet Iron Arm has risen to being our lord through sheer strength and wit.'

'Very well, so your lord is a powerful one. So what?'

'It is said that the gold Atenulf stole could rebuild a nation's coffers. That would be a healthy sum even split between the forty or so of us. But if, instead of dividing the gold, we delivered it to Iron Arm, and explained that the missing portion is at Acerenza, the possibilities are endless.'

'I don't follow you.'

'Iron Arm has let it be known that he will bestow lands and titles on those who might bring him this stolen gold.'

'I don't want a title. And this land is dry and too warm.'

Courvaudon sighed. 'You're all thinking too small. The Byzantines are done in this land. Within the decade they will be little more than a memory. The lords of Salerno and Benevento are being forced to make terms with Iron Arm. He is stronger than they. *We* are stronger than they. Within our lifetime, Icelander, Hauteville and his allies will take this whole peninsula, at least as far as Rome. Imagine the possibilities. Just a share in that gold against the chance of becoming a real power in the world. The riches to be had by being a lord of this land make a share in the gold pale into insignificance.'

Ketil rounded on the man. 'You are not listening to me. I do not want to be a lord of this parched, featureless land. I do not want to bend my knee to your Iron Arse...'

'Iron Arm.'

'...even if it means that he places a crown on my head. You Normans have been away from our homeland for too long. The ice in your veins has melted. I want enough gold to buy good drink, good food, a pliable woman for a night or two and a good ship to sail the whale road. I was born to travel and to raid. Had I never met Halfdan I would still be doing that, ravaging the Finn coast. I will live fast and live loud, and I will gather about me friends and adventure and there will be stories told about me and my travels long after I am dead. Ketil of Stöð, who stole the skull cups of the Pecheneg giant. Ketil of Stöð, who defeated Greek fire with an arrow. Ketil of Stöð who escaped the clutches of the Byzantine emperor with his own gold. *That* is what life is about, Norman. Not castles and lands and crowns. Life is for living. It is not a preparation for something else.'

Courvaudon sighed. 'I had a feeling you might see it that way. I understand. Really, I do. Gold in itself is a reward, and seeing Atenulf robbed of it will be a bonus. I had to try. But we shall still be rich men and I shall stand by Halfdan through it all. I bound myself with an oath on the Good Book.'

Goody, thought Ketil grumpily, as the man turned and wandered away in the growing darkness. Down below, Anna and Cassandra were leading in a roped line of horses while Gunnhild was in deep conversation with the smith among them, gesticulating at the smithy in the compound and pointing to her staff.

Alone again, Ketil swigged the wine until the jug was dry and then threw it down at Bjorn, who was busy dancing some sort of jig and laughing at Leif while waving a severed leg. The Albino, almost brained with the thing, looked up and cursed all Icelanders.

'Making friends again?'

He turned to see Halfdan walking toward him. The jarl took the same place the Norman had occupied so recently. 'I am of two minds,' Halfdan murmured. 'We have taken stock of our gains and we are now well supplied with weapons and armour, and we even have food for a few days.'

'Good. It was a success.'

'The question is whether to camp here or to move on and camp elsewhere. It is becoming increasingly dark, so travelling on holds difficulties, but staying here we risk random Byzantine patrols coming across us.'

Ketil simply nodded.

'What do you think?' the jarl asked.

Ketil glanced sidelong at Halfdan. Maybe he *was* still the second, after all. He shrugged. 'Better to stay here. If the roads are dangerous for us in the dark, then they are for Byzantines, too. Unlikely they'll come during the night.'

Halfdan nodded. 'And Gunnhild has work for the smith while he has the facilities. She wants to stay long enough for him to work something for her. But we leave at first light and put some miles between us and this place before anyone from Matera comes up to check on it.'

'Agreed.'

Halfdan smiled and looked down. 'A funny-looking crew we've put together these days, old friend, but it works. The Wolves run in a pack again.'

Ketil's eye fell upon the Norman below, sitting with his own. *Not only wolves*, he thought, rather ungraciously. *Wolverines, too.*

Chapter 22

'I have not ridden this far in such conditions just to leave Ginosa alone,' Fulk de Courvaudon snapped, tearing his eyes from the flapping Byzantine banners on the city's towers.

Halfdan took a slow breath. He was starting to feel the anger boiling up now.

'We thought we could set a trap here for Atenulf, because we knew the place and could use it well. Now we know it has a new Byzantine garrison, working from Ginosa is impossible. Just staying in the area invites disaster, let alone changing our plan and marching on the place.'

'We don't know how many there are in there,' Fulk argued. 'They could be few. *I want that town.*'

'No,' Leif interjected from nearby. 'I don't think there's any doubt that they outnumber us.'

Bjorn snorted. 'I don't give *Surtr*'s sweaty flaming ballsack how many there are, we can take them.'

Halfdan shot his friend an irritated look. This was no time for Bjorn's particular brand of violent, blind enthusiasm. 'No, you big oaf, we can't.' He turned back to Fulk. 'If we took Ginosa from its new garrison – which you know is not easy, for a few months ago it was *you* holding onto that rock – it would cost us enough men that we would then face dangerous odds when we met Atenulf. We cannot afford to waste men here that we will need later. Ginosa was a nice idea, but we have to change our plan.'

'Besides,' Ketil added, leaning closer, 'we cannot even guarantee that Atenulf will bother with Ginosa. He's avoided built-up places ever since Acerenza.'

'He will need to know more about the situation on the coast,' Fulk insisted. 'Passing close to Ginosa he will have to realise that he would learn that in the city.'

'You only wish to take Ginosa,' Gunnhild put in, 'because it was yours and you lost it. It angers you that the Byzantines hold it now. You want Ginosa back, as well as Atenulf's gold. You cannot have both. We do not have the force to take both. Listen to your jarl.'

'My *jarl*?' There was something in Fulk's tone that was almost a sneer, but Halfdan let it pass without comment. Fulk was a jarl of his own people, after all. He had given his oath not to betray Halfdan, but that did not make him one of the hirð.

'We are running out of time while you two argue,' Leif said in exasperation. 'By now, Atenulf might only be half a day behind us and until Florian returns, we don't know. If he really pressed hard for the coast, he could be even closer than that.'

'The fact remains that Ginosa is our proposed base,' the Norman said. 'I have heard you, Halfdan, more than once argue the importance of not leaving an enemy behind you. The men controlling Ginosa are the emperor's men. They would kill me, as an enemy of the empire, they would kill you and yours for having left service in the Varangian Guard and become mercenaries in Apulia, and they would kill every last soldier we have with us for their part in Maniakes's revolt.'

There was a murmur of agreement from among the Byzantine infantry now, for the argument had become loud enough to be heard across the grassy sward, even over the gentle patter of autumn rain that had been falling almost non-stop for the past two days.

'I am not denying that they are our enemies and a danger to us, Courvaudon. In a better time, I would gladly help remove them from the city and put you back on your throne, but this is not a better time. Ginosa may or may not be Atenulf's next target on his way to the coast, but whatever the case, if we base ourselves around Ginosa we run the risk of starting our own war here. And if we attack the place, we will lose too many men to be comfortable about dealing with the thief.'

'Then we wait for nightfall and we take them by stealth,' the Norman's bannerman, Marc, suggested. 'We can be in the city and killing before they realise we are enemies. We could even try Ketil's ruse from the outpost.'

'We do not have *time*,' Halfdan said with strained patience. 'Atenulf is at most a day behind us, and possibly much closer. Odin, but you Christians are pig-headed.'

Fulk's eyes narrowed dangerously. 'I am your friend, Halfdan, and your ally, but neither of those things is a given. Test me and see how far I will go before I break.'

Bjorn stepped closer now. 'There are three of you, little Norman. Might want to rethink your threats.'

'Gah,' Halfdan snapped in frustration, turning and stamping away through the squelching grass. Behind him, he could hear Bjorn and Fulk engaged in the slinging of insults, and he stopped a short distance away, rolling his eyes skywards and sagging. Why could the man not see sense?

'I do not like the Norman,' came a familiar voice by his shoulder. Halfdan turned to see Ketil standing just a pace away.

'I have had that impression ever since Acerenza.'

'I do not trust Normans. They are like us, but with no honour.'

Halfdan let a small snorted laugh loose before he could stop it. 'Sorry. Honour, my friend, is a very rich-looking garment. You put it on when you want to look impressive, but when there's real work to do you have to take it off to stop it getting dirty.'

Ketil laughed now. 'I have always thought as much, but I had you figured for higher things.'

'I am a Northman. I wear my coat of honour when it suits me, just as Loki would.'

'We need to find a new ambush site while we have time. Somewhere away from Ginosa.'

'I know, but I have to persuade Fulk that Ginosa is too costly first, and he will not listen.'

'Maybe we can just stick a sword up Fulk's tight arse and walk away. Three Normans aren't going to change our odds much.'

Halfdan chuckled. 'There was someone standing here with me a moment ago accusing the Normans of having no honour. He looked a lot like you.'

'Fuck off, my jarl.' The Icelander snorted. 'We have to do *something*.'

'I know. But I gave my word, and for now, I'm still wearing that coat.'

'Let me help you out of it.'

The two men lapsed into silence once more, in the background the gentle hiss and patter of rain overlaid with the muted arguments of Bjorn and Fulk. Any time now they would start pushing one another, and Bjorn might just pull an axe to make a point.

Then he heard the other noise. For a moment he'd not noticed it, for it blended so seamlessly with the drumming of the rain, but now he could hear the hooves of a horse coming closer. He tapped Ketil on the shoulder and turned, running across to where the others were standing and arguing. The debate petered out into nothing as everyone turned to see Florian, the hunter from Barletta, pelting in their direction across the open grassland, his horse sweating and exhausted.

Fulk and Bjorn had hold of each other's shirts now, but both let go and turned.

'Problem,' bellowed Florian as he closed on the small gathering.

'What is it?' Halfdan said, stepping out in front as the rider slowed his horse, and slid from the back, breathing hard. The Gotlander had slipped automatically into the role of leader once more, and Fulk had stepped back, letting it happen.

'Atenulf is not coming for Ginosa.'

A series of curses, some eye-wateringly biological, arose from the bedraggled party. Halfdan winced and rubbed water from his scalp. 'Explain.'

'They passed the hills to the north just as we did, a little over half a day behind us, but where we turned left and took the coast road that ran down past Ginosa to the sea, the thief's caravan has turned right.'

'God in Heaven, could he be making for Reggio after all?' Leif grumbled.

'No,' Fulk shook his head. 'Every Norman lord from Acerenza to the Sicilian Strait will be looking for him by now. He would be suicidal to do so. Halfdan was right that he would come to Taranto. He's just taking a different route.'

'But *why*?' Marc said with an exasperated sigh.

'We rode hard,' Halfdan said. 'We had our supplies and rode hard to stay ahead. We got here and found out that the Byzantines had reoccupied Ginosa with a solid garrison. We never stopped in any village on the way here, but I would wager good silver that if we had, they could have warned us of the new garrison.'

'You think Atenulf has learned that Ginosa is held against him now?' Fulk mused.

'It is more than possible, and would explain why he takes a wide route to circle around the place.'

Fulk nodded and deflated a little. 'Ginosa becomes irrelevant.'

'If Atenulf avoids it, then so do we.' Halfdan rubbed his head again and then flicked the rainwater away. 'I have only passing memories of this area. We came north to Ginosa and then went straight from there up toward Acerenza. You,' he added, pointing at Fulk. 'You were lord here. You must know the region.'

'Adequately so, yes.'

Halfdan moved across to where half a dozen trees stood in a knot, the ground beneath them dusty and as-yet dry. He used his foot to kick the stones and detritus out of the way, smoothing the dirt. 'Show us.'

Fulk scouted around, found a small stick, and then crouched and began to draw. He marked a rough triangle, then extended two of the lines beyond their angles. He pointed to the top one. 'The road from Acerenza.' And the one on the right. 'The road to Taranto.' He now put a mark halfway along the diagonal between the roads. 'Here is Ginosa. We came from this road, along here, and it continues on down to the coast and then away to Taranto. Atenulf is going the long way round to avoid Ginosa. It will take at least an extra half day, maybe even a day, but he will avoid anything larger than a village until he reaches the port.'

Halfdan squatted and peered at the map. 'We have to catch him before he disappears along the coast road. Then he will be getting close to Taranto and there will be imperial patrols. If he is following these roads, is there somewhere that lends itself to an ambush? A large wood or something?'

Fulk sucked his teeth as he shook his head. 'It's all open farmland. Nothing like that. Except...'

The Norman frowned and then brandished his stick once more. Leaning down, he drew a new line that crossed the coast road and meandered in a northerly direction not far from Ginosa. 'This is the Lato River. It comes from the hills up near Laterza and passes through a long ravine before coming out across the fields down to the coast. The only bridge anywhere useful is on the main coast road. Atenulf will have to cross it.'

Halfdan drummed his fingers on his wrist. 'I have seen the rivers around here. They are streams at best most of the year. More often they are just dust. Will he have to use the bridge? It has been raining for two days, but not enough to swell a river.'

'Whether there is much water in it or not, it is a river, with banks and a stony bed, reeds and the like. A man or a horse might walk across it, but a heavily laden wagon?'

Halfdan grinned. 'You're right. So we know that he is not coming along the Ginosa road, but when he reaches the coast he cannot turn west, for the Norman lords there are looking for him. He will have to turn east for Taranto and to do so he must cross that bridge.'

'Exactly.'

'And we can easily reach the bridge before him?'

'It will take us half a day to get there. It will take him at least twice that. And if we move faster, we could gain even more time.'

Halfdan rose to his feet. There was a feeling of positivity around him once more. The arguments had gone and were forgotten. Now there was just a new plan and the expectation of violence and reward.

A few moments later, the tidings and the new plan passed on among the others, the entire group was mounted once more and turning, beginning the ride onwards along the road, past forgotten Ginosa and toward the coast. As they rode, Fulk pulled level with Halfdan.

'The Lato bridge is not long, but it will allow us to cut their caravan in half.'

Halfdan just nodded, and the Norman continued. 'Atenulf and his best men will be riding out front. You and your men wait on the east side, out of sight, and once the vanguard has crossed you can fall on them. I will take the Byzantine infantry and seal them off from behind. The infantry should be adequate for securing the wagons and any resistance from the rearguard.'

Halfdan pursed his lips, counting through the numbers in his head. By his reckoning, Fulk's division of men would give them roughly equal forces both in front and behind the column, but Halfdan's would be the more brutal of the two, which would well match the higher quality warriors Atenulf would undoubtedly have out in the vanguard. It sounded like a reasonable plan.

For the rest of the day they rode at a steady, mile-eating pace along the road to the coast, often able to see the ribbon of white and the ever-shifting choppy surface of the sea beyond.

Once they were down from the higher ground, though, and moving through seemingly endless fields of flat, giving earth, they lost sight of their destination until finally they emerged at a junction with the coast road and, ahead, through sporadic and scattered undergrowth, they could once more see the sea. Here, at Fulk's directions, they turned east and made their way along that better-used thoroughfare until finally the Norman pointed ahead, indicating a line of green vegetation that cut across the fields, rising above them. A wide timber bridge, broad enough to allow two carts to pass simultaneously, rose and crossed an unseen channel among the greenery.

'This is it.'

Knowing they had plenty of time before Atenulf and his caravan could even hope to close on the bridge, they spent a couple of hours familiarising themselves with the site. It was, Halfdan was happy to admit, as good a spot for an ambush as he had ever seen. Trees and undergrowth rose from both banks and would give adequate concealment for nearly a score of infantry under Fulk's command on the western side. On the eastern side, a farm with several outbuildings only forty paces from the bridge would offer plentiful space to hide Halfdan and his warriors. Best of all, though the river was nothing compared to the icy, fast-flowing torrents the Northmen were used to in their homeland, it was at least far from flat, dry and easy to cross. A shrub-and-tree-filled bank dropped more than the height of a man to a channel some thirty feet wide, in the bottom of which sat stagnant, weed-filled pools left over from the last deluge, which would only disappear when the winter rains came and filled the channel once more. A horse would cross it without too much difficulty, but even a rider would think twice about the wisdom of doing so, and only a desperate infantryman would try. A wagon would stand no chance. They *had* to use the bridge, and with appropriate cover, Halfdan and Fulk and their men should be able to trap them on both sides of the river.

A short discussion led to the universal conclusion that there was no real hope of Atenulf and his wagons reaching the bridge before the next day, and if he travelled only by daylight, it would likely be afternoon at least before they arrived. Consequently, they made camp for the night in two groups: Fulk and the infantry, along with Marc, off the road some way to the west; Halfdan and the others behind the farm buildings. Fulk would set a watch for the night, keeping an eye out should Atenulf suddenly appear from the west, and Halfdan would do the same in case of roving Byzantine patrols from the east. Content that all was well, Halfdan decided it was time to deal with the locals. Taking Cassandra with him, as someone who could speak the local tongue, he approached the farm, where the owners cowered inside, wary of the armoured force encamped on their land.

At his insistent rapping on the door, the farmer finally pulled it open, wide-eyed and pale. With Cassandra translating, he tried an easy smile.

'We are not raiders and we have no interest in your farm or your family.'

This did not seem to put the farmer greatly at ease.

'An enemy is coming and we will defeat him at the bridge. All we want is to take cover behind your buildings and stay out of his sight. For that, I offer you this.'

With that he lifted a flat palm, holding a number of gold and silver coins out. Even before Cassandra had finished translating, Halfdan knew he had the man, for the eyes wide with fear had become sharp and hungry now. He trotted out a string of local syllables, which Cassandra translated as his ready compliance, and the matter was settled. Halfdan was content that the farmer was not going to do anything stupid to endanger the ambush.

As he returned to the camp, he passed two figures standing in a field near one of the barns. Realising who they were and what they were doing, Halfdan waved the women on back to the camp, and leaned against a fence post, watching the pair. Florian the hunter was explaining the finer aspects of his bow, holding it like a delicate lover as he gestured to it and manoeuvred it in his hand. Ketil was watching him with a level of impatience that made Halfdan grin.

Finally, as the pair fell silent, Florian drew an arrow from his quiver and nocked it. He lifted the bow, stretched, sighted, breathed out, sighted again, steadied and loosed. The arrow whipped from the bow through the evening air and buried itself in one of the uprights of the barn, clearly his intended target. The hunter relaxed, rolled his head, stretching out his neck, and turned to Ketil. He grunted angrily as the man all but yanked the bow from his hand and reached down for an arrow. Halfdan smiled. Florian was good, but in Georgia he had seen his Icelander friend put arrows into targets almost too small to see, at incredible distances, and even from moving platforms and in strong winds. Ketil was no novice.

Which was why he was surprised, and even a little dismayed, when Ketil's arrow thumped into the turf a couple of feet short of the barn. Ketil released a blistering series of curses and stomped over to the arrow, pulling it from the ground and examining it as though it might uncoil and strike him. Halfdan realised suddenly that the damage done to Ketil's face, the loss of an eye, had changed his vision entirely. Ketil had been the best archer Halfdan had ever seen, but now he couldn't even hit the side of a barn. Literally. And while that disappointed Halfdan, he could not even imagine how it felt for his friend. It would be worse, probably, than having lost the eye in the first place.

He stood silent, watching, as Florian tried to tell Ketil something in a low voice, some piece of advice that had the Icelander snapping angrily back at him. The Byzantine, stony-faced, reached out a hand to take his bow, but Ketil instead stooped, snatched up three arrows from the quiver in a handful. In quick succession he released the three arrows. Halfdan, in some analytical corner of his mind, noted with appreciation

336

that the three shots were progressively better, but would have admitted, when pressed, that even he could have managed that, or perhaps better. The first arrow fell short even of the previous shot, the second struck the barn where it met the ground, and the third thudded into the timber a good four feet from the intended target.

Halfdan could not hear what Florian said, but he could tell it was in a conciliatory tone. Any sympathy fell from Ketil like water from rock, however, and the big man stomped away angrily into the night, casting the bow to the ground as he went. Halfdan watched Florian retrieve the arrows, find a quiet corner, and start work on repairing them with the kit he had at his belt. He wondered whether to go after Ketil, but in the end decided against it. The two men had only recently been reconciled, and the Icelander was different in many ways to the man who had left. Halfdan was still learning who this new Ketil was, and intruding on a moment of personal loss might damage what closeness they could still claim.

For a moment, he contemplated striking up a conversation with the hunter, but decided against that, too, and stalked off back toward the main camp. The first thing he noticed was that Gunnhild and Bjorn were missing – their absence was always obvious. Gunnhild had been spending a lot of time with the smith, but he was present, so she was not with him now. The völva carried such a presence that the entire clearing seemed somehow incomplete without her. And Bjorn? Well, Bjorn was such a larger-than-life character that the lack of his booming voice making outrageous boasts or telling appalling jokes was an instant giveaway.

He spent a few moments looking around, and finally spotted a twinkling light somewhere off in a field beyond the farm. Such a thing was unlikely enough that it seemed clear it must be the work of Gunnhild, and so Halfdan passed through the camp, nodding at anyone who spoke to him, and then strode off across the fields. He was some distance from the camp, and closing on the site, when Bjorn stepped out of a patch of undergrowth, scaring the wits out of Halfdan, who'd been entirely unaware of the albino's presence. Bjorn was not a man given to easy concealment, and as Halfdan tried to slow his pounding heart and recover, the big man grinned.

'Too dangerous for a woman out here alone. Even a woman who could eat a bear and pick the claws out of her teeth.'

The jarl smiled. Bjorn teased her repeatedly, but had become extremely protective of Gunnhild throughout their time in the south.

Halfdan turned. The völva had been dancing her dance and singing her song, as was clear from the fact that even now she was shrinking back down into her own body as the melody trailed away into the patter of leaves in rain and the rustling breeze. A strange hiss came from the torch jammed into the ground illuminating the scene, as the raindrops turned to steam in the fire. He noted with interest that the staff she twirled now had an ornate iron extension shaped in old ways, a tangled dragon in the shaft, a wicked point at the end. The reason for all her time with the smith was finally apparent. To be a true völva, she had to have a völva's staff. It seemed she had finally acquired just such a thing. It was a thing of beauty, of Seiðr and of death.

A shiver passed through him as Gunnhild rose, unfolding, and looked directly at him.

'What did you see?' he breathed.

She strolled across the ground toward him, dropping her beads and silver and the rest back into her pouch.

'Something is amiss,' she said, walking past him, as though that should clarify all. He turned and hurried after her. She was not particularly tall, yet seemed to have a massive stride when she was full of purpose. Even Bjorn was almost jogging to keep up.

'What?'

She stopped and turned, fixing him with an irritated look. The two men had taken two further steps before they reacted and stomped back over to her.

'If I knew what, do you think I would just say '*Something*'? I am no Byzantine soothsayer. No. All I can see is a mess. The tapestry is… I cannot tell.'

'Speak to me,' Halfdan urged.

'The threads of our lives are about to become knotted. Yours. Mine. Ketil and Bjorn. The Normans and the Byzantines. Even the prince-thief Atenulf. The tapestry of the Norns is no longer straight and clear. There are knots in the threads.' She turned, reached out and grabbed Halfdan by the cheeks, cradling his face. 'Be prepared for the unknown. Something is about to happen, and I do not think even the Norns know what it is.'

And with that she let go and stalked off in the direction of the camp. Halfdan shared a look with Bjorn that for just a moment he thought was erudite and serious, until the man let rip a fart that split the night and sagged with contentment.

'Ah, she's just worrying about nothing. She's a woman. Let me tell you about a whore I once knew who thought she was growing an extra tit…'

Halfdan rolled his eyes as Bjorn began his unlikely tale. But as they walked, he could not shake the memory of that image. A knot.

Even the Norns were unsure.

Chapter 23

'Half a mile, no more,' Florian said, sliding from his horse as he rounded the corner of the barn behind which Halfdan and several of the others waited.

The jarl nodded, turning to his men. He waved a signal and from two other spots across the farm, not visible from the bridge, hands waved back in response. They were ready, and Fulk and his Norman-and-Byzantine force would be ready on the far side of the river, warned by the hunter as he rode past. All was set.

There was no grand plan. They would move when Fulk sent the signal, for he would be the one who could see when the caravan was halfway across the bridge, the column neatly bisected by the river. He would wait until they were at their most vulnerable and then give the call. He and his force would then flood out from the undergrowth and the trees and cut the enemy off from fleeing the way they had come. At that signal, Halfdan and his men would charge from the barns and head off the vanguard, preventing escape that way, and between the two forces they would trap the enemy, kill them all and take the gold.

Only two things had been made clear. Firstly, it was the gold that mattered. Any of Atenulf's men who managed to get away would be an irritation, but it was the wagons and their prize that counted, for all of them. That was a general agreement. That being said, every one of them was aware of the danger of leaving an enemy behind you, and so, despite the gold being the thing, they were all equally determined to let no one escape.

Secondly, Halfdan had made it known that Atenulf was his. No one else was to kill the thief-prince. Bjorn had snorted, in that *We shall see what happens* way of his, and so Halfdan had been very clear with the big man. If he took Atenulf down, he would be Bjorn *Halfdan*-torn from then on. He'd given plenty of reasons, all spurious, for the naked truth was that he wanted Atenulf. He was the jarl of the Wolves, and Atenulf was the jarl of his own crew. It was how things should be, and if songs were to be sung around bright northern fires in the days of his dotage, he wanted the skalds to be singing of Halfdan, slayer of the thief-prince, not of Bjorn. Selfish, but respectably so.

The world seemed to be holding its breath. The only noise across the whole farm was the occasional quiet cough or the clonk of an axe haft on a shield, followed by a hissed curse. Birds wheeled above, their cawing a constant companion. The gentle rain that seemed to be a permanent fixture now pattered against the buildings and the parched ground, dampening what sound there was.

Men kissed the Mjǫllnir pendants around their necks, praying that Odin would grant them victory today – or if not, then a clean, glorious and heroic death about which others would sing and tell tales, which would see them sitting with their ancestors in Valhöll, waiting for that last great struggle. Halfdan could see the small knot of women, standing in the shadows near the edge of the olive grove: Gunnhild, with Anna and Cassandra, sheltering behind the ancient, gnarled trunks.

He was struck suddenly, and worryingly, by the similarity between the three women and an image he'd seen graven on a stone in Visby: the three Norns, weavers of the fate of men, laying out the path of a man's life at his birth. The three women beside the olive tree might be shorter than Halfdan, and younger than most of the Wolves, but one glance at them now carried a suggestion of power, stature and wisdom far beyond the normal ken. He shivered and looked away. Such an image could only be Seiðr – the work of gods, or elves, or other sorcerers, good or bad.

He was still trying to shake off the image of the three women as giantesses when he heard it. The distant rumble of wheeled vehicles on hard-packed dirt and the myriad thuds of many hooves. The treasure caravan of the Beneventan prince was coming. Indeed, the real need for any signal from Fulk was made moot as the noises changed. The hoofbeats became hollow, woody thumps instead of muted thuds as they moved from the packed dirt of the road to the damp timbers of the bridge. He tried to count the horses, but lost track. A creak made him turn, to see that Florian was now close by once more, bow out, arrow nocked and string drawn halfway back, ready. Behind him waited Ketil, Bjorn, Ulfr and Leif, the core of the Wolves.

He turned, ready to run. They had opted to effect the ambush on foot rather than on horse, despite their enemy being mounted, for no matter how far they had now ridden, all the Northmen were far more comfortable relying on two feet than on four hooves. Besides, a man was a small target, but when he was attached to a horse, that target became far larger. Fulk would be on foot for much the same reason, the bulk of his force being infantry.

'Attack,' came a bellowed call in the distance, followed by the roar of many voices raised in belligerent fury.

Halfdan frowned. What was the man doing? He had been listening and so far he'd heard only horses on timber. There were five wagons, so there should have been the telltale groans and creaks of at least two of them on the bridge before the attack began. Still, the signal had been given, the game begun, and there was nothing for it now but to join the fray.

Waving to the others, Halfdan ran.

As he rounded the corner of the barn, he took in the scene. Six men on horses, armoured in chain shirts with long sleeves, solid steel helmets with strong nose guards and legs padded with thick trousers. Teardrop-shaped shields were on their arms and spears in hand. They were the vanguard, and he could see

Atenulf clear as day, sitting atop the bench of the front wagon, armoured but without helmet or shield, riding in comfort. The wagons, though, were only just now reaching the bridge as the ambush began. Fulk had attacked too early and failed to cut them off in the middle. Now Halfdan and his men faced the heavy vanguard, while Fulk would have to deal with most of the remaining force, the fool.

Even as they ran, men began to pour out of the wagons, drawing swords and yelling in alarm. Two of the riders from the vanguard put their heels to their mounts and broke into a run, spears levelled ready to impale, charging at the running warriors. The lead man was aiming for Halfdan as the front runner in the ambush, but before he could cover half the distance, an arrow thudded into the horse's neck. The beast stumbled, screeching, and then fell, ploughing through the damp mud as it slid to a thrashing halt. The man on its back stood no chance, anchored as he was by the stirrups. Though he attempted to get free, as the animal fell, crashing onto its side, the rider's leg was hopelessly crushed beneath the horse's weight, and he screamed, pinned, and then issued a series of agonised howls as the animal thrashed in pain, smashing what was left of its rider in the process.

The other horse was still coming for them, but even as Halfdan tried to decide how to deal with it, Ketil was suddenly powering past him, his long legs eating the distance as he growled menacingly. The Icelander ran straight at the charging horse but at the last moment swerved aside, swinging his axe. The weight of the blade, added to the combined speed of Ketil and the horse, was enough for a killing blow. The axe cut the man's leg just above the knee, carving deep enough to smash the femur, and the weight of the armoured man and the force of gravity did the rest. As Ketil ran free and made for another of the riders who had not yet charged, the stricken horseman simply leaned further and further to his right as the weight pulled him down, nothing but a little muscle and sinew left holding his limb together. Finally, the leg tore apart, the lower half flopping around in the stirrup until it fell away as the screaming rider toppled out of sight on the other side.

The other four riders hefted their spears. Halfdan could see it coming. As he and the others ran in Ketil's wake, swerving around the two fallen horses, the four mercenaries pulled back their arms and cast their weapons, hands immediately going to their belts to draw their swords. Ketil was lucky indeed, for a spear passed by his head with just inches to spare, thudding into the damp ground behind him. Halfdan managed to get his shield in the way in time, but felt the impact all the way up his arm and into his shoulder, momentarily numbing the limb. As he knocked away the missile, gripping and ungripping his hand to get some feeling back in the arm, he took just a moment to look back. Farlof was cursing, the chain at his shoulder torn by the spear that had caught him a glancing blow, and Florian was down, halfway through nocking his second arrow, a spear pinning him to the ground as a long tendril of bloody drool ran from his mouth. They had lost their archer, but at least the time for such things was past. This was a battle of blades now.

Halfdan looked at the remaining four riders. They were lined up, ready to defend their master and his wagons, still feeling superior as heavily armoured, mounted warriors facing a rabble on foot. Behind them, maybe half a dozen more men had lined up across the bridge, sealing off access from this side. The bulk of Atenulf's force had moved to the rear, where the ground was more open and the wagons more at risk. Had that been Fulk's plan? To draw most of the enemy in his direction?

Halfdan could see Atenulf on his wagon bench, still seated, but now shouting orders to his men, sword out and gesturing this way and that. Halfdan needed to get to him, but couldn't see an easy way. He could probably bypass the four horsemen, who were in the open on this side of the bridge, but then he would find himself face to face with that line of six men, and he would simply have to batter his way through them to get to the thief-prince.

Opting for at least skirting the riders, he began to pull out to the side, veering left, heading toward the river bank. A series of curses at his back suggested that Bjorn, at least, was with him. The others engaged the riders. Ketil hit them first, ahead of the rest as he was. He took a number of sword blows on his shield as he busily hacked away at the horse to his right with his axe, chopping its leg and shoulder into meat and then leaping sharply out of the way as the beast fell, crying in agony. Leif was there a moment later, despite his short legs. Once again, it struck Halfdan how far Leif had come from the loquacious scholar they had met in Kiev to the ruthless killer he was now. The little Rus turned aside two blows with his shield as he stabbed again and again into the rider's leg with his sax. And so it went with the riders. Men were hammering, slashing, stabbing, battering, screaming and cursing. Blood and ordure filled the air. Halfdan heard a scream tailing off into a curse in the old northern tongue and knew he had lost one of his men, but he had no time to worry who, for he was now past the riders and pounding toward the six men on the bridge.

He was not alone. Bjorn and Farlof were with him, as he knew now, for they pulled out level with him, puffing and snarling, weapons and shields hefted. Halfdan grinned viciously. The Wolves were together once more and they were more dangerous than ever. Ketil and Leif were busy tearing into those riders, with the Varangians providing steel-edged assistance, and here was their jarl, racing into the heart of it all, with two of their best at his shoulders. Bjorn had ever been his right arm, but it was good to realise that Farlof, only an acquaintance now for a matter of months, had become as close a member of the pack as any, running at his jarl's side as they made for the great enemy at the centre of the caravan.

The six men hefted their shields, held before them and covering much of their bodies – the rest coated with chain and steel helmet, swords ready to stab and swing. If Halfdan got entangled with all of that, Atenulf would have time to rally more men to his defence, or to turn and race back among the bulk of his soldiers. He had to get to the thief without engaging the men in between, yet they blocked the bridge. He did not have the height or momentum to go over them, and the drop into the river made it impossible to go around them. He contemplated attempting to go under them, through their legs as Leif had done back in Miklagarðr, but then there was every chance of him sliding to a halt, tangled in their limbs and unable to push through, which would leave him prone and in danger. He sighed as he ran. If he couldn't go under, over or around, then there was only one option. He would have to go *through*.

'Bjorn, take the right three, Farlof the left,' Halfdan said in a gasp of breath as he ran. The two men grunted their understanding.

He hoped they were up to it and found that he believed they were. Bjorn was at his best with several men to fight, and Farlof had proven himself more than capable over the months. Halfdan steadied his breath, pulled his sword in and held it vertical behind his shield, which he lifted flat in front of him, covering everywhere from his nose down to his groin, the somewhat battered boards providing what defence they could. The shield was a little larger than he was used to, one of those taken from the Byzantine outpost to the north, and it still displayed Greek images on it. Sometime soon he would have to ask Leif to paint the wolves on it once more.

As they ran at the waiting mercenaries, Halfdan, at the last moment, lowered his face, pressing his forehead against the flat of his blade, which in turn rested against the inside of his shield.

They hit the six-man wall of armour. With a roar, Bjorn and Farlof struck out with axes, chopping and hammering, cursing and growling. Halfdan did not rush to engage, though. Instead, he kept his arms in tight behind his shield, putting all his weight and momentum into the charge. He hit the centre of the line hard and just kept running. He felt the moment of resistance as he ploughed into the men, felt several blows batter against his shield, one lucky one crashing across the chain shirt over his shoulders with a blooming pain that suggested future bruising and a lot of slow recovery. Still, it was not debilitating for now, and adrenaline was dulling any pain.

With that, he was through the line and racing for the lead wagon, Farlof and Bjorn keeping the half-dozen men busy. He felt the weaving of the Norns unfolding before him and, drawn by some unidentified sense, turned for a moment and glanced back from the bridge. Gunnhild, Cassandra and Anna stood in the open now, a trio of strong women, watching the fight, far from the fray and yet somehow, inexplicably involved. The Norns, the weaving…

The knot.

He looked up. Atenulf had been wrong-footed. He had sent the vast majority of his men to the rear to face Fulk's concerted attack on the wagons and trusted to six riders and six infantry to hold the bridge in front. Unfortunately, he had not accounted for the ferocity of the Wolves' attack, for already the riders were down and fighting their last and, even at three-to-one odds, the mercenaries on the bridge were fighting for their lives against Bjorn and Farlof, and more of the Northmen were now on their way to help.

Atenulf was alone on the wagon seat. Even the driver who had been seated beside him had dropped from the vehicle and gone to cower somewhere. The thief had apparently not noticed the failure of the wall of men protecting him, for as Halfdan ran, shield coming out to the side, sword opening up once more, the Beneventan prince was facing the other way, bellowing something at his men in the unintelligible Italian language. As he spun back, he saw for the first time a grimacing, blond-haired, armoured killer running at him.

Atenulf's eyes bulged as he pulled himself round and brandished his own sword, ripping a dagger from his belt with his other hand. Halfdan reached the wagon and leapt. His foot touched the timber tongue that stretched from the wagon between the two nags pulling the vehicle and he pushed down, using it as a springboard. He reached the seat mid-jump, the thief-prince hissing curses as he tried to bring his sword to bear. But he was not fast enough. Halfdan hit the man and the two of them tumbled back from the seat into the covered wagon interior. Atenulf bellowed something, furious, and, unable to use his long broadsword in such a space, stabbed out with his dagger, trying to get Halfdan somewhere he could cause a vital wound. The jarl felt the blows thumping into his chain shirt again and again. Torso, arms, back – each blow unable to penetrate the chain, and yet each one taking its toll in bruising and dull pain, each one carrying the risk of broken bones. Equally, until they separated, there was insufficient space for Halfdan to use his own sword. All he could do was slam his shield against Atenulf again and again, attempting to drive the breath from him.

He was winning and he knew it. Despite Atenulf's desperate stabs with the dagger, which Halfdan felt as dull pains here and there, it was only a matter of time until his repeated battering with the shield took its toll and the thief lost control of the dagger or passed out. It came as something of a surprise, then, when the man suddenly bucked, using a reserve of strength Halfdan had not anticipated, throwing him off him long enough to struggle away and turn, panting.

Halfdan gave him no chance to turn the respite into full recovery. Rolling, he leapt once more, this time his shield taking a hit from the thief-prince's sword. He stabbed and felt his blade strike chain, the numbing shock travelling into his wrist, but the blow further troubled Atenulf, who let out an 'Urk!' noise as he rocked back on his knees, unable to stand fully in the covered wagon.

Before Atenulf could come around for another swing, Halfdan dived again, landing on the thief and pushing him back down so that his knees bent awkwardly. Atenulf let out another squawk of pain and thrashed with his blades, trying to stab Halfdan any way he could. Unable to do much in the press, Halfdan saw the only opening and took it. Bunching his muscles, he jerked his shield upward a few inches – all he could manage, but it was enough. The rawhide edging slammed up into Atenulf's chin, cracking his teeth together hard. He yelped in pain and in that moment of distress, his dagger and sword fell away.

The Wolves' jarl took advantage of the moment, slamming the shield now to the left, where it smashed into his opponent's sword arm with the audible crack of a broken bone. Before the dagger could come around for a blow, Halfdan struck again, driven by desperation and the desire to kill. His short, straight blade slammed up where his shield had so recently struck, the tip ripping into Atenulf's throat, up through his mouth and deep into his brain until it reached the inside of his skull with a clunk. Just to be sure, Halfdan, with some difficulty, gave the sword a half-twist, mincing the innards of the thief-prince's head.

Atenulf began to shake wildly, his weapons falling away from madly flailing arms; Halfdan, sweating and shaking from his exertions, reared back to avoid them. For the first time, he looked back past the body, and all they had done became worthwhile. The wagon was filled with wooden boxes, each fitted with iron hinges and clasps, each roughly two feet long and a foot wide and deep. Just to be sure, he scurried over to the nearest, leaving the shaking corpse, and brought the pommel of his sword down hard on the clasp, bursting the box open. He lifted the lid.

Gold shone with that lustre that even grey cloud and drizzle cannot dull. The whole box was filled with coins of gold, minted with the image of Constantine Monomachos, Emperor of Byzantium. His watering eyes took in the coins for only a moment before he shut the lid once more and then looked around, counting the number of wooden boxes. There had to be more than twenty of them in this wagon alone. This was a fortune to match, or even to exceed, the one Harðráði had purloined in the great city. It was, truly, a king's ransom.

Halfdan realised suddenly that he'd been crouching there, dreamily, for some time, his eyes locked on the boxes of gold. The reality of the situation insisted itself once more as the sounds of fighting reached him from outside. Grabbing up his sword and shield, he rose to a stoop and shuffled out of the covered wagon. From the bench seat, he could see the Wolves putting down the last men on their side of the bridge.

Then something odd struck him. There was no sound of jubilation, no cheering as the noise of battle faded. His men had seemed to be looking at him, but now he realised that was not the case. They were looking *past* him. He turned, but the covered wagon obscured whatever they were looking at and so he staggered forward, the adrenaline of combat and the euphoria of victory keeping the aches and pains at bay, and dropped from the wagon to the timbers of the bridge, turning and looking back.

Fulk and his companions had climbed onto the next wagon, the Norman lord with his sword high, Marc before him.

'Stand down, Odin's men,' Fulk bellowed.

Halfdan's brow creased. He looked past the Norman. They had won. The Byzantine infantry might be slightly fewer than they had been, but they had taken all of Atenulf's men. Not one of the mercenaries was still upright as the infantry clambered around the wagons, securing them and putting down any remaining teamsters. It was over.

But it also *wasn't*.

'What are you doing?' he demanded.

Fulk turned, noticing him for the first time. 'Sorry, Halfdan, but alliances can only go so far. I can't let you have the gold.'

'You swore on your god's book,' Halfdan hissed.

'And I shall atone for that in due course. But now there is something more important. This gold is worth a great deal, Halfdan, but it is worth more as patronage. Iron Arm will make me a rich and powerful lord for this, and any man who comes with me can also ride that wagon of wealth. Do not be short-sighted, Northman. Even a wagon full of those coins is worth less than the goodwill of the most powerful man in Italy.'

Halfdan shook his head. 'Every man here gets their share. That was the deal. What you do with yours is your own business, but we have need of ours.'

'Then I am afraid I shall have to take it. Last chance, Halfdan... walk away while you can.'

'Norman, there are two of you. You're hopelessly outnumbered.'

'Think again.'

And then the jarl realised that the Byzantine soldiers were lining up, facing the Wolves, while one particularly large soldier stepped forward to join Marc in protecting the lord. This had been Fulk's plan since they had reached the bridge, at the least. That was why he'd sprung the trap too early. He had the Byzantines on his side. He must have bought their loyalty on the journey with the promise of a grand future here, for they could never go home. And he'd attacked while the wagons were still on his side of the river so that he had control of them while Halfdan and the Wolves took out the most dangerous of the enemies in the vanguard, including Atenulf himself. It was well played. A masterstroke of betrayal. Even as he realised what had happened, Halfdan knew that now Fulk's force outnumbered his. Only by a little, but it might be enough.

'Courvaudon, we're not going to let you walk away with the gold.'

'Then you'll have to fight us for it.'

Halfdan looked around. His men were some way back. Bjorn and the others had overcome Atenulf's riders and the other defenders while he dealt with their master, but had come no further, and now they stood, stony-faced, staring at the man who had betrayed them. Even as Halfdan focused on them, he saw every pair of eyes turn to him, a question there. He answered them with a roar, turning, sword up, running for the Normans.

As he ran, he realised the danger he was in. He was considerably ahead of the others and would have several long moments fighting the Normans before anyone came to his aid, but he could not afford to wait. He knew how crews worked, and he knew how mercenaries worked, and he knew how the Byzantine mind worked. If they could overcome the three leaders, the resolve of the other Byzantines would crumble, for without Fulk to mediate with Iron Arm, they were powerless. He had to kill Fulk before the soldiers rushed forward to surround him, which meant he had to face Fulk, Marc and the Byzantine alone.

Still, he had no choice.

Gritting his teeth, he repeated his earlier attack, running at the wagon on which the three men stood and leaping, using the wooden pole-tongue to vault up onto the bench seat where they awaited him. Unlike Atenulf, however, these men were more than prepared for him, and the two remaining soldiers they had saved from the siege at Ginosa so long ago had stepped in front of their master to protect him.

Halfdan swung. Keeping his shield up to save him from Marc's sword, he lashed out against the Byzantine, who was already wounded, sporting a bloody line down his side. If he could take him down, it would drop the odds by a third. His sword struck the man and in that moment Odin was with him, and Loki was watching, for though the strike was wild and not enough to truly wound, the Byzantine had lurched back to avoid the blade and his foot had caught the edge of the bench and slipped. In a heartbeat, the wounded man disappeared from the wagon with a shriek, crashing painfully to the bridge on his wounded arm, which caused him to howl all the more, and roll around, clutching the damaged limb.

Halfdan had no time to savour the victory, though. His shield had taken Marc's initial swing, but the man was on him now with a vengeance. Halfdan had seen Marc fight often over the past months, and he was hard and dangerous. As the jarl turned, trying to bring his own sword to bear, Marc was hammering blow after blow, and Halfdan could feel the shield disintegrating under the concerted attack, his arm becoming numb. Worse still, Fulk had leapt forward now, his own shield up, his own sword swinging.

Halfdan felt himself losing under the barrage of the Normans' attack. The Byzantines were running forward to preserve their new benefactor, and – a quick glance over his shoulder confirmed – Bjorn, Leif, Ulfr and the others were all pounding across the bridge, rushing to help take down the traitors before their Byzantine turncoats could leap to their defence. It was going to be close. Too close for comfort, especially since there was every chance that Halfdan would be dead before the decisive blow was struck.

He was in the fight of his life now, using both sword and shield to block the Normans' attacks, unable to find an opportunity in the flurry of strikes to fight back. He was being pushed back, almost to the edge of the wagon, where he would fall. He was losing, and there was nothing he could do, no way to find a moment to fight.

Marc gave a sudden gasp and Halfdan, who was desperately trying to hold him off, felt the hammering that had been pushing him back lessen. He risked a look over the top of his shield and blinked at the sight of the arrow sticking out of the Norman's eye. Marc was slowly toppling backward, his face transfixed by the shaft that had killed him. Fulk, aware that he was now alone, took a step back, trying to buy time for the Byzantines to reach him. Halfdan felt the fight flow back his way now and as he trod forward, bearing down on the Norman, he glanced back to see Ketil lowering Florian's bow, a horribly smug smile on his face. Halfdan was going to be made to pay for that little move later, he was sure.

He turned. For now, there was a traitor to kill.

He took a step forward and shivered. He could feel the Seiðr in the very air around him, crackling across the boards of the wagon, prickling his skin. He could feel the eyes of everyone on him, especially the three women standing back across the river – friends and companions, and yet ancient giantesses who wove the fates of men at birth and who tended the world tree. He could feel it, the stuff of legend, the duels of the ancients. Halfdan was the centre of all attention, as was Fulk de Courvaudon.

The Norman took a step, hefting his sword and shield. Halfdan – feeling the gods with him, feeling no pain, no fear, only certainty – cast away the damaged shield and jumped. Fulk saw him coming and swept his sword down hard, but Halfdan was quick, leapt inside the blow and hit the Norman hard, barging him, knocking him back. Fulk twisted in panic and pain; he fell, Halfdan toppling with him, dropping from the side of the wagon.

Fulk hit the timber deck of the bridge with a heavy thud, all the breath knocked out of him as Halfdan landed on top, slightly winded but saved by the cushioning of the Norman beneath him. The jarl looked up, wreathed in Seiðr. Every eye was upon him and Fulk, including those of the three women, who had come closer and were now standing not far from the bank. There was not a sound. All those present had stopped, watching the duel, intent on it and each knowing it would be over before they could intervene. No birds cawed in the sky now, no shield clonked, no chain shirt shushed, no sword struck sword. The only sound was the gentle hiss of the falling rain and the laboured breathing of the two men.

Fulk bared his teeth, blood on the gums around them where he had bitten his tongue in the fall.

'Fuck you, Northman,' he snarled, and a hand appeared from somewhere holding a small dagger. The blade came up sharply, nothing there to prevent it, and slammed into Halfdan. The gods held their breath. The blow had been aimed for his throat, but at the very last moment, the two men had shifted very slightly, and the blade struck Halfdan's chain shirt, right at the collar. The Norman pressed hard, trying to push home the knife, for if he could shift it even half an inch it would skid off the metal links and plough into Halfdan's throat, killing him swiftly.

Then Fulk gasped.

His hand faltered and the pressure on Halfdan's neck eased as the Norman's eye swivelled down. Halfdan's short sword had sheathed itself in his opponent's nethers even as he struggled with the dagger, the short, razor-sharp sword stabbing up beneath his own chain shirt and into his groin. Blood washed out of the Norman's pelvis, flooding down into the boards of the bridge, severed arteries spraying it in hot gushes, draining the Norman of his life at massive speed.

Fulk stared up at his killer and Halfdan watched the man die, surprised at how the Norman's flesh visibly paled as the blood drained from him in torrents. By the time he yanked his blade free and sagged back on his knees, Fulk had gone the colour of a winter morning in the northern mountains, a colour no man could survive.

'See you in hell, Loki-born,' Fulk gasped with his last whisper.

Halfdan shook his head. 'Not me. I shall be in Valhöll, you vicious, treacherous bastard.'

With that he rose to his feet, Norman blood dripping from his blade. He turned. Gunnhild was nodding. As he spun further, Ketil still had that smug grin, Leif and Ulfr looked on with pride, and Bjorn was displaying that disgruntled look he always reserved for when someone cheated him out of a good fight. The Wolves had triumphed. The gold of Atenulf was theirs.

Another turn, and he saw the Byzantine soldiers staring in horror. They had wagered on the wrong contestant this time and they knew it. They had been Halfdan's men, with a place in the world, and had given that place up for the glory promised by Fulk. But now Fulk was gone, and they had severed their ties with Halfdan. They had nothing but the memory of their betrayal and the disfavour of the one man who could have been their lord. As sons of the rebel army, they could not even run home to Byzantium. They had nothing and nowhere to go.

Halfdan looked at the men who had betrayed him, then turned to Bjorn and the others.

'Kill them. Kill them all.'

Epilogue

William de Hautville stood at the narrow window, looking out longingly over his domain. Not a longing to be *in* it, or even conquering lands to extend it, per se, but a longing to be anywhere else but here, in this moment. He reached up and rubbed his temples with his forefingers, something his mother had taught him as a child to soothe a headache. The headaches had once come regularly, as his father banged on again and again about their old northern roots, and how their ancestors had been the first to cross the grey seas in their dragon boats and to bring terror to the poor monks of Britannia.

But it was not his father, long dead, may his soul rest in God's grace, who currently filled the air with the constant hiss of noise. Today it was his sister.

He winced at one of her particularly inventive and biological turns of phrase – one that would have had her confessor fingering his rosary in panic and sending her for a well-deserved beating – and once again wondered at his family. They were the strongest of the strong among the Norman lords. Of the sons of Tancred de Hautville, most were powerful knights and renowned lords, many of them down here in Apulia, far from their homeland. Their father had instilled the iron of their ancestors in their soul, for while he may have prayed to the Lord, the son of God and the blessed Mother, he never surrendered the tales of where they had come from, of the cold lands of rock and ice that had forged a people who had changed the world. And they had gone forth into that world like Vikings of old, taking up arms with one side or another until their success had allowed them to carve out their own niche in this southern land.

He, of all of them, was the most successful, the most feared, the most victorious. Warriors who had spent all their lives fighting, who had never flinched in battle, counted him the better man. Iron Arm, they called him, and well they might, for he had used his iron arm and the iron sword clenched in it to wrest a huge swathe of land from its former owners. He was afraid of no one, and, short of the Pope himself in his hallowed halls, no one was *un*-afraid of him. No man, anyway.

And that was why it was particularly infuriating to find that while he could make Byzantines, Apulians, Italians, Venetians and even his own Norman countrymen cower with fear, even his strongest voice had little effect on Beatrix. Indeed, he was considering starting a rumour in the castle that her nickname at home was *Iron Mouth* in the hope that it stuck.

'If the climate does not agree with you,' he said in a voice strained with patience, 'then *go home!*'

'Oh, you would love nothing more, wouldn't you, *sweet William?*'

The most powerful Norman lord in the entire Mediterranean spun on his sister. 'I told you before that if you call me that again, I will have you bound and gagged and shipped back to your husband like a merchant's linen bale.'

She glared at him, narrow-eyed. 'You would never dare, and he is not my husband, as you know.' Before he had any hope of replying she began to fill the room with a fresh torrent of verbal abuse that heaped curses upon the name of her brother, her father and various powerful lords of Normandy. Unable to penetrate this latest slew of ill-placed slander, he turned back to the window with a sigh.

Yes. Iron Mouth. He would start the rumour before dinner tonight and see how many tongues it reached by the third course. As he mulled this pleasing thought, he became aware of noises outside, beyond the normal daily hum of life in Melfi, and found himself managing to fade Beatrix's diatribe into the background as he focused on the source. A small caravan seemed to have reached the outer gate of the castle and was sitting in the city street beyond, attracting all sorts of attention, while a number of heavily armoured men with no colours on show argued with the gate guards.

Intrigued, he tried his best to hear what was being said across the courtyard, but Beatrix's voice was just too shrill and insistent. In the end, he closed the drapes of the window behind him, helping seal him off from the room and mute the noise. The fact that the monologue didn't stop suggested that his sister was so intent on her harangue that she hadn't even noticed he was no longer present.

The din reduced somewhat, he found now that he could make out a lot of what was being said. A captain had been summoned to the gate and was arguing with a blond-haired man who looked the very epitome of the warriors William's father would have lauded as their great, cold ancestors. Better still, behind the blond leader stood the tallest man William had ever seen, dressed all in black and with some horrible facial wound discernible even from here, alongside a white mountain of a man.

The captain was denying them entry.

Fascinated, William watched as the big white giant moved to thump the captain in his own castle, surrounded by guards. Only a sharp word from the blond set him back in his place. The captain told them to take their stinking wagons away. The blond replied that it was important they see the lord of this place. The captain politely, and rather coldly, informed them that they were more likely to grow a second arsehole while they waited. Iron Arm grinned. Good man. He needed promoting. Still, he was far too intrigued.

Five wagons, all weighed down with heavy contents, escorted by around twenty men. No, strike that, several of them were women. Women riding horses! He blinked. What in the name of sweet Jesus was happening in a world where women rode proud as men? He tried not to think about Beatrix, though her voice was still droning on behind him.

Two more of the newcomers had left one of the wagons now and joined the leader, carrying a banner and a shield with vaguely familiar colours. He wracked his brain, trying to identify the insignia and remember to whom they belonged. As his memory furnished him with a name and, more importantly, with a location, several things fell into place. A number of thoughts struck him at once and he frowned. Yes. This was worth a look.

Leaning into the window above the courtyard, he waved. 'Ahoy, captain?'

The officer looked around and, eventually identifying the source of the voice, snapped smartly to attention. Yes, a promotion, for sure.

'Let them into the courtyard. I shall attend presently.'

The captain saluted sharply and then turned away, as William Iron Arm, Lord of Melfi, spun and fought his way back through the heavy drapes into the room.

'You have heard nothing I have said,' his sister snapped.

'Quite true, dear heart. Quite true.' He flashed her an infuriating smile and then walked straight past her and out of the room, feeling better than he had all day. It took him only moments, trotting down the stairs and into the hall below, to find Berner, who looked up in surprise at his name.

'Berner, what do we know of the Beneventan renegade and his latest movements?'

The man looked around, scratching his beard, and puffed out his lip. 'Well, we have unsubstantiated but very tempting rumours that place him recently at Acerenza with one of your minor vassals. There was some altercation there including Devil worship and an actual witch-hunt, if accounts are to be believed.'

Something else fell into place. Iron Arm found himself picturing those women on the horses, and especially the one in the green dress with the staff. 'Go on.'

'Well, public rumour then has him on the road to Reggio, though no lord between there and Acerenza claims to have seen a hint of him.'

'And they are telling the truth. What I have offered would override their personal greed. So he was probably at Acerenza. We will have to deal with the lord later, for if this is true, then he has been disloyal. And Atenulf cannot have gone to the coast, neither east nor west, for the Italian lords rule the west, and Argyrus controls the east and is most peeved at his missing gold. So he can only have gone south, and likely south-east, given he has been watched for in the west. Tell me, Berner, is Ginosa in that region?'

'Why yes, I do believe it is, milord.'

Iron Arm found himself grinning. 'Do you remember Fulk de Courvaudon?'

The man frowned again, pursing his lips. 'I believe I do. He is a good and loyal man, though only master of a small force and a minor fief. We put him in Ginosa to hold it, on the promise of bigger things.'

'I suspect Ginosa has fallen once more, and that master Courvaudon is no more. I also suspect that Atenulf of Benevento passed through there and, if I am not mistaken, *he* is no more, too.'

'Really?'

'We have visitors playing a most audacious game, Berner, and I am in a whimsical mood. Prepare the hall for guests and send word to the kitchens to over-cater.'

Leaving with an odd smile, Iron Arm hummed a jaunty tune as he descended the stairs and entered the courtyard, crunching across the gravel toward the blond-haired warrior and his friends. The various soldiers around smartened themselves up a little and a small gathering of them moved over to supply a guard for their lord. He was further intrigued by the fact that the visitors barely moved, let alone offered any obeisance or gesture of respect.

As he closed on the gateway, the most dreadful smell wafted across him and he frowned. He had been around dead men often enough to recognise the smell, but corpses were usually in the ground and he long gone before they began to smell *this* ripe, and there had to be a few of them to raise such a cloud.

Trying not to gag, he approached the leader and stood in front of him, close enough for a blade to strike, to prove that there was no fear in him. He folded his arms.

'I am both fascinated and appalled. You appear to have arrived in my city bearing corpse-wagons and demanding to see me.'

His eyes slid to the hairy specimen holding Courvaudon's banner, then back to the blond man.

'We are carrying our dead north,' blondie said. 'It is our custom.'

'Heavens, men,' Iron Arm snorted, 'but have you never heard of the *Mos Teutonicus*? You can boil the flesh and fat off them and carry home only their bones. Perhaps put their vitals in a sealed container. If you keep carrying their untouched corpses, they're going to be liquid when you arrive wherever you're going.'

The blond man shrugged. 'We'll think on it. Are you Iron Arm?'

The audacity. William liked the man already. All the more so because he was being so blatant and showing absolutely no fear. 'I am. William de Hautville, in fact, and I am the master of Melfi and of the council of nobles. And you are not of my homeland, although you seem to have some connection; nor are you Italian or Greek. And yet you carry the banner of Courvaudon. You have a tale to tell, I am sure.'

The blond man nodded somberly. 'We aided Courvaudon in the defence of Ginosa. It has been a long fight with several sieges, in fact. I regret to tell you that the city has fallen to the

Byzantines once more. Courvaudon gave his life in the end, as did his men, but it was not enough.'

Iron Arm waved a hand negligently. 'Ginosa is a minor inconvenience. It will change again soon enough, and there are more troublesome cities closer to hand. You are mercenaries, then?'

'We signed on with Courvaudon,' the blond nodded. 'We gave plenty of blood and a number of good men, but once the lord and his corps were gone, there seemed little point in staying and being killed.'

'How very sensible of you,' Iron Arm smiled. He felt like testing this man. 'Your wagons ride low, with heavy contents. You must have many fallen.'

'Many,' blondie replied.

'May I pay my respects?' He almost laughed at the shifty way the visitors looked at one another, only their leader holding his gaze. Blondie gave a shrug. 'If you wish.'

With the man leading the way and several guards staying close, Iron Arm followed him into the gate and to the first wagon. He noted with interest the way the blond man moved, as though every muscle hurt and bruises covered all flesh, the sign of a man recently in the thick of battle. He even limped a little. As the man threw back the cover, the Lord of Melfi struggled not to throw up, but also not to laugh out loud. Three corpses lay mouldering, at least five days old by the smell, wrapped rather insufficiently in blankets. Below them, the wagon was filled with something that lay under a layer of sacking that barely concealed the shape of boxes beneath. He staggered back out of the miasma, making the sign of the cross.

'God, man, but you need to use the German rite and boil them down. You cannot travel further like that. The wagons ride so damn low, your men must have the heaviest of bones.'

The man's eyes narrowed and Iron Arm suddenly found himself re-evaluating the leader. The rest may be daft as a bag of old fruit, but blondie was clever. Iron Arm already knew the wagons carried Atenulf's gold. He'd been pretty sure before he even descended the stairs, but now he knew it for certain. A huge wealth of gold rather feebly hidden beneath a few reeking corpses. But what he now knew, which was something of a surprise, was that blondie *knew* that he knew it. The two men looked at one another for a time, both well aware of what was happening, yet neither speaking of it.

Iron Arm weighed up his options. There really was an absolute fortune in gold, enough that he'd made it widely known he wanted it and would reward handsomely for it. These men could not be unaware of that fact and yet they were not making any offer. They intended to keep it for themselves, which was so utterly outrageous and audacious that William found himself slightly envious that he was not in their place, doing this himself.

'You came to deliver the news and Courvaudon's banner?'

A nod. 'And to seek your permission to pass through your lands without trouble.'

Of course. With wagons of gold, they would want as little trouble as possible. He really was having trouble not laughing. He could have them killed, of course, and take the gold, but their death would be a waste. He could take the gold and *not* have them killed, but that would be making dangerous enemies and then keeping them alive, which was a terrible idea. Or he could let them get away with it, and he was oddly inclined to do so. The man deserved *some* reward for such brazenness, after all.

'I will not let you go until you have dealt with your dead properly. You will all contract pestilences travelling like that. I shall have all the facilities made available to you to boil down your bodies and save what organs you must. We have a slaughterhouse here, so you can do it near there without bothering too many people. And then you can rest and stay the night and dine with us. In the morning, you will pass on, heading north with my blessing. In return for a small favour, I might add.'

The blond looked to the others, who seemed sceptical. 'That will depend upon the favour. And our own must deal with the dead. It is our way.'

Again, William almost laughed. 'You have my word.' He waved to the captain. 'Have them bring their wagons in and take them to the sheds near the slaughterhouse. Have someone help them with the Mos Teutonicus. This man—' he paused. 'I'm afraid I do not know your name.'

'Halfdan.'

'Halfdan will accompany me up to the hall, with whomever he cares to bring.'

The blond spoke to one of his men, and a moment later stepped forward with the pink-eyed, white-skinned giant and the woman in the green dress, who was the very prettiest witch Iron Arm could ever imagine. He could imagine men organising a witch-hunt, but probably not with execution as their intent. Today was turning out to be a most interesting day. And perhaps the resolution of a truly insistent and tedious problem. As he climbed the stairs toward the hall, the three visitors following, the blond spoke first.

'I think you and I are on the verge of an understanding. I know what I get out of it. I have yet to know how it benefits you.'

As they emerged into the hall, Iron Arm spotted Beatrix, standing at the far side of a table being hurriedly laid by many servants, her expression cold, arms folded defiantly. When she saw he was not alone, she turned and stalked off angrily. As she left the room, Iron Arm turned to Halfdan.

'My sister, Beatrix. She is something of a law unto herself. She is matched in marriage to Armand de Mortain, but thinks to avoid matrimony. She was under the impression I could be coerced into taking her side, but she is wrong. It is a good match, and a necessary match. She might have fled all the way from home to this land to avoid her husband, but there is no corner of the world far enough. She will return, and she will marry.'

'I see,' Halfdan said, his voice betraying no opinion.

This time, William Iron Arm gave a little chuckle openly. 'I think you can see where this conversation is heading. You have something you shouldn't have, which half the world wants, and I have both the right and the ability to pluck it out of your hands. But I am engaged in a delicate situation here, in a lull between disastrous wars, and I cannot afford to take my eye off things, nor to devote men to carrying a troublesome woman home. If a certain group of strong warriors were to commit to my cause and agree to escort Beatrix back to her husband-to-be in Normandy, then I might be tempted to look the other way in the matter of stolen moneys.'

The woman in the green dress fixed him with a frown. 'You would trust your sister to strangers?'

Again, he chuckled. 'You have not met my sister. And she would not travel alone. She will have guards, servants, attendants. She will be well protected. What she needs is a group of strong and determined warriors to make sure that she actually goes home. Her marriage is worth more to my family than any Byzantine gold, and, to be frank, I would pay twice that just to get her out of Melfi right now. I think the deal I offer is more than fair. I urge you to take it. I might be inclined to take your prize for my own and try and hire enough men to do the job, but this is so much easier and appeals to my sense of humour.'

He saw the conflict in Halfdan as he considered this, and was not at all surprised when the man looked to the woman in the green dress, only turning back when she nodded.

'All right,' Halfdan smiled. 'We have a deal.'

Before Iron Arm could lean forward and shake his hand, the big, white-skinned brute stepped forward. 'Good. Now, before dinner I could do with a fight, a pint and a fuck.'

Iron Arm collapsed in mirth. Today was truly an entertaining day and he almost felt sorry for Beatrix, though not as much as he felt sorry for Halfdan and his men.

'Walk this way,' he grinned at the giant.

The big man chewed his lip for a moment before replying. 'If I walked that way, I probably wouldn't want a fuck,' he decided.

Historical Note

This book was born of three different aspects. Firstly, having dealt with the reign of the empress Zoe in Byzantium and all the troubles around Harald Harðráði in *The Bear of Byzantium*, I felt that the last days of Georgios Maniakes deserved to be recorded. Maniakes is one of the greatest 'what ifs' of Byzantine history. The empire suffered a steady decline from Constantine Monomachos onwards and, had he been replaced, perhaps history would be very different. Although Maniakes died in his attempted rebellion, I felt the need to tell the tale.

Secondly, there are the Normans. We are familiar with the Normans, in the UK at least, in the form of William the Bastard, Duke of Normandy and the invasion of 1066. But before the infamous conquest of Britain, the Normans were at work in the Mediterranean as fierce mercenaries, fighting for one side and then the other until they managed to carve out their own power-base in the south of Italy. The fact that these Normans were only a century diluted from having been fully fledged Vikings meant that the meeting of my own Scandinavian heroes and these pseudo-Vikings looked too much fun to ignore. That their language was not yet French and still held much old Norse within it also meant that communication would not have to be too much of an issue.

Finally, there came the plot hook. As so often happens, this plot grew from the smallest thing. Though the history of the Normans in eleventh-century Italy is tumultuous and thrilling, it just so happens that the very year my heroes entered the fray, very little was actually happening. The major wars that had put the Normans in such a position of power were over, and the next set of troubles had yet to begin. I spent some time reading everything I could find on my specific era, and then up popped the story of Atenulf, Prince of Benevento, who negotiated for a huge ransom in gold and then either fell foul of his peers or promptly vanished with it. What self-respecting Viking could ignore such an opportunity? I had the hook.

In *Blood Feud*, the story was solely that of Halfdan, with the rest of the Wolves as a supporting cast. When I came to *The Bear of Byzantium*, I was constrained by what Gunnhild could do in the city. She couldn't join the Varangian Guard, after all. And so, I experimented with continuing Halfdan's story, but now adding Gunnhild's tale running parallel. Having done that with, I think, a solid level of success, I had to decide whether to do something similar and explore another of the Wolves in more detail. I had been toying with the story of Ketil anyway, as he is the only one who might ever have challenged Halfdan for leadership. Knowing now that I wanted to tell the tale of Maniakes's revolt, but also the story of Atenulf and his gold, I suddenly needed two protagonists, and so Ketil moved into the foreground. Thus over three books, I have now told the story of three of the Wolves.

–

Our story begins on a beach in southern Italy. There are differing accounts of what happened there, though all of them agree that Maniakes was to be replaced and that in response he rose in revolt against the throne. The entire tale of Maniakes's revolt is given only minor treatment in all three of the Byzantine chronicles that cover the era. John Skylitzes tells us that Maniakes had been considering revolt ever since he'd first been sent to Sicily, that the move was triggered by Skleros ravaging his estates in Anatolia and raping his wife, and that he slew Pardos, sent to replace him, on the beach. Michael Attaleiates writes only that Maniakes revolted because the emperor overlooked him and they did not get on. Michael Psellus has the envoy sent to recall Maniakes slapped by the general and then slain by his troops. My brutal, and somewhat peculiar, account of the death on the beach is taken from *The Deeds of Robert Guiscard*, by William of Apulia, in which he tells us: 'This unfortunate man [Pardos] was captured by Maniakes, who inflicted various tortures upon him and then had his nose, ears and mouth stuffed with horse dung, and thus had him put horribly to death in a stable.'

The effect of the revolt on Byzantine control in Italy is clear, for the withdrawal of such a number of men for Maniakes's failed insurrection can only have left a military dearth in the peninsula. From this point their position went into a steady decline as the Normans capitalised on their advantage.

Once the Wolves have split into two groups – one led by Haldfan, the other by Ketil – our first location is Ginosa. For the record, Fulk and his men are a fictional creation. Ginosa is not. Ginosa had become a Norman stronghold by 1080, when its castle was begun, and prior to that had been a Byzantine city. My notion of it having been temporarily held by a minor Norman mercenary in 1042 is far from unrealistic given the shifting divisions and the near-constant warfare of the period. The rock-cut villages of the ravines around Ginosa are still there and were occupied into the twentieth century. The water channels and wells are still visible, though my specific geography of them is a conceit of the author, due, sadly, to the effects of Covid preventing a research visit to the site. In this scene, Gunnhild poisons the garrison with *Mandragora*, the Latin name for mandrake. Mandrake is both poisonous, emetic and hallucinogenic in the appropriate concentration, and the plant grows free and wild in southern Italy. And so, over the first part of the book, Halfdan frees Fulk from Ginosa.

Focus then shifts to the revolt of Maniakes. The sources actually tell us very little about the campaign. What is clear in all accounts is that an imperial army, led by Stephanos, met with

Maniakes's force somewhere near Thessalonika and defeated them there. According to Attaleiates, Maniakes received a mortal wound while fighting and fell from his horse. The battle, which had been going his way until then, suddenly changed, the heart going out of the rebel army. Skylitzes places the battle at Ostrovo (modern Arnissa), some forty miles west of Thessalonika, and he has Maniakes fall from his horse with no visible sign of injury until his armour is removed and a mortal wound revealed. This is the tack I took, which suggests that he was already suffering from the injury before the battle. Psellus gives us a direct description of Maniakes being hit in the battle. Of the conflicting tales, I chose Skylitzes's. And so the revolt fails, Byzantium declines, Maniakes disappears from history, and three of our Wolves flee west once more.

Back to Acerenza, then. Once more, my Norman lord of Acerenza is a fictional one. The city was conquered by the notorious Guiscard in 1041 and the walls and castle were strengthened thereafter. My descriptions of eleventh-century Acerenza are not based on the current city street-plan, which has changed several times since the days of Halfdan, but follow the rough geography of the city as it would have been in the period, with buildings and architecture that are endemic of medieval Italy.

If the punishments awaiting our heroes in Acerenza seem extreme or more fitting to the seventeenth century, they are still appropriate for the time. By the eleventh century, Catholicism in Italy (the religion followed by the Normans as well as the indigenous Italian people) had truly taken hold; paganism was relatively unheard of and therefore increasingly associated with Satan. The enemies of the Faith at the time were mainly the Muslim peoples, who had been fought back out of Sicily very recently, and a few issues of dogma with Byzantium's Orthodox church. Within a century and a half of our story, however, the pope would call for crusades in the Baltic against the pagan peoples of the region, which gives us some idea of the papal view on such matters. Less than twenty years before the Wolves met Maniakes on the beach, Bishop Burchard of Worms had written of 'wicked witches'. Charlemagne in the early ninth century had instituted a law to prevent the burning to death of women believed to be witches, which suggests that such a thing was not uncommon by even the ninth century. Indeed, the witches of Forres, in Scotland, had been burned at the stake in 968. As for Bjorn's intended fate, the eighth-century *Liber Historiae Francorum* tells us that the Merovingian queen Brunhilda was, in 613, 'tied to the feet of wild horses and torn apart limb from limb.' Execution by the sword, of course, is a common method throughout history.

When Bjorn takes his revenge upon the traitorous Norman, I have fallen somewhat into the camp of legend – the 'Blood Eagle' punishment may be a later literary invention. It is mentioned in five sources, with varying descriptions that do not always agree, between them telling of the end of three different men at different times. There is no surviving visual representation and no archaeological evidence has been found. This, of course, does not mean that the Blood Eagle is a fiction. The jury is out. I chose to use it with Bjorn as it is one of those things that can only be applied to the pagan Vikings of the Dark Ages, and so fitted my characters well. Now our heroes languish in prison at Acerenza.

Meanwhile, the journey to the coast for Ketil and friends is a fictional invention. The pirates they encounter are based upon the Narentine pirates of the Balkan islands, who had become such a problem that the Venetians campaigned against them and destroyed their power in 1000 AD. That at least some level of piracy survived and continued in the ensuing decades seems likely. Similarly, Venice at this time was yet to become the world-famous naval power of the following centuries, but she was well on the way. And even a cursory reading of the history of the Venetian Republic confirms the mercenary nature of their expansion. The exact dates on which towns and strongholds changed hands between Byzantines and Normans is not always recorded. I have therefore, for my tale, made Barletta one of their earlier conquests along the Bari coastline.

So the Wolves of Odin are reunited and with the goal of capturing Atenulf's gold. What follows on to the end of the book is my own tale. History does not relate what happened to Atenulf and his treasure. William of Apulia tells us: 'The wretched Exaugustus was led in chains to Atenulf's city, walking before the victor's horse, since his enemy wanted to emphasise the scale of his triumph.' Amatus of Montecassino, in his *History of the Normans*, tells us the prisoners were given, 'to Atenulf, their prince, so that he might question them and decide what should be done. Atenulf thought to make himself rich from these prisoners.' In his seminal work *The Normans in the South*, John Julius Norwich gives us a potted version, telling us that Atenulf was discovered to have sold the prisoner back to the Greeks and kept the ransom money. One source writes that Atenulf fell foul of the Normans for his crime, while most tell us either that Atenulf escaped to Byzantine lands with the gold, or more often tell us nothing at all. Clearly I was able to form my own opinion of the end in my tale.

There is little to tell of the finale, I feel. A betrayal was coming, and I imagine you all saw its spectre once or twice before it happened. And that has to lead me briefly to two other characters. My good friend and partner in crime, Gordon Doherty, holds charity book auctions every Wednesday to raise money for the Myeloma UK charity (sterling work), and one week auctioned a copy of *The Bear of Byzantium* before its publication. The response, and the winning (and second-place) bid, were so overwhelmingly generous that we sent out two books with a small prize bundle, including the incorporation of the winners as characters in my next book. I would like you all, then, to laud and celebrate Mark (Taff) James, who graces these pages as Fulk's competent bannerman, Marc, and Sandra Pascoe, now the Byzantine refugee Cassandra. Thank you to you both.

My final scene, taken from the new perspective of the most powerful and most famous Norman in Italian history, of course, sets the scene for the next book. Halfdan's time in Italy has been something of a catalyst and a turning point. He has evolved beyond the young and uncertain man we first met in *Blood Feud*. He has become a jarl in every sense, and now even Ketil respects that. Moreover, their time in the south is done. Their eyes (only one in Ketil's case) are drawn once more to the North and to their homelands. There are tales to come yet, but now the Wolves are once more on the rise and moving into more familiar territory.

Thank you for reading.

Simon Turney
April 2022

Glossary

Aesir – one of the two groups of Viking gods, including Thor, Odin, Loki and Tyr

Berserkr (pl. berserkir) – lit. 'bear shirts'. The berserkers of Viking fame who were overtaken by battle madness in the name of Odin

Draugr (pl. draugar) – the zombie-like restless dead, occupying graves and guarding their treasure jealously

Dromon – a Byzantine warship powered by sails or by banks of oars akin to the Roman trireme or Ottoman galley

Excubitores – an elite Byzantine regiment with an origin as imperial bodyguards, by this time part of the garrison of Constantinople

Freyja – the most powerful goddess of the Vanir, whose realm includes magic, fertility, war and the gathering of the slain to her land of Fólkvangr

Gotlander – one of the three peoples of modern Sweden, the Goths occupied the island of Gotland

Holmgang – an official, ritual form of duel between two opponents

Jarl – a noble of power (the derivation of the English 'earl') who receives fealty from all free men of a region

Karl – a free man. Neither a noble, nor a slave

Katepan – regional governor of the Byzantine empire

Loki – a trickster god, a shape-shifter, who is destined to fight alongside the giants against the other gods at the end of days

Miklagarðr – Viking name for Constantinople, the capital of the Byzantine Empire, now Istanbul

Mjǫllnir – Thor's hammer

Norns – the female entities who control the fates of both men and gods

Odin – most powerful of the Aesir, the chief god and father of Thor, who gave an eye in return for wisdom and who has twin ravens and twin wolves, and an eight-legged horse

Ragnarok – the end of the universe, including a great battle between gods, giants, monsters and the slain who have been gathered by Odin and Freyja

Rus – the descendants of the Vikings who settled Kiev and Novgorod and areas of Belarus and Ukraine, from whom the name Russian derives (Rusland)

Sax – a short sword or long knife of Germanic origin, known to the Saxons as the seax

Seiðr – a form of magic that flows around men and gods, which can be used and understood by few, the source of divination

Svear – one of the three peoples of modern Sweden, the Svears occupied the northern regions of Sweden, around Uppsala

'Tafl – a Viking board game akin to chess or go, where one player has to bring his jarl piece to the edge of the board

Theotokos [Pammakaristos] – lit. 'Mother of God'. Greek terms of Mary, mother of Jesus

Thor – son of Odin, the god of thunder, one of the most powerful of the Aesir

Thrall – a slave with no will beyond that of his master, often a captive of war

Valknut – a symbol of interlocked triangles believed to bind an object or person to Odin

Varangian – the Byzantine imperial bodyguard, formed of Northmen

Varangoi – Greek term for the Varangian Guard

Völva (pl. völvur) – a wise woman or witch or seeress with the power of prophecy and the ability to understand and manipulate Seiðr